ETERNAL EMPIRE

WESLEY WONG
COLOR FLATTING ASSISTS

SPECIAL THANKS
MARY BEAMS
ROMMEL CALDERON
LANE FUJITA
ERIN GOLDSTEIN
KAREN HILTON
TIM INGLE
ED LOPATEGUI
LEAH LY
LAUREN SPENCE
DEAN WHITE
GIANCARLO YERKES

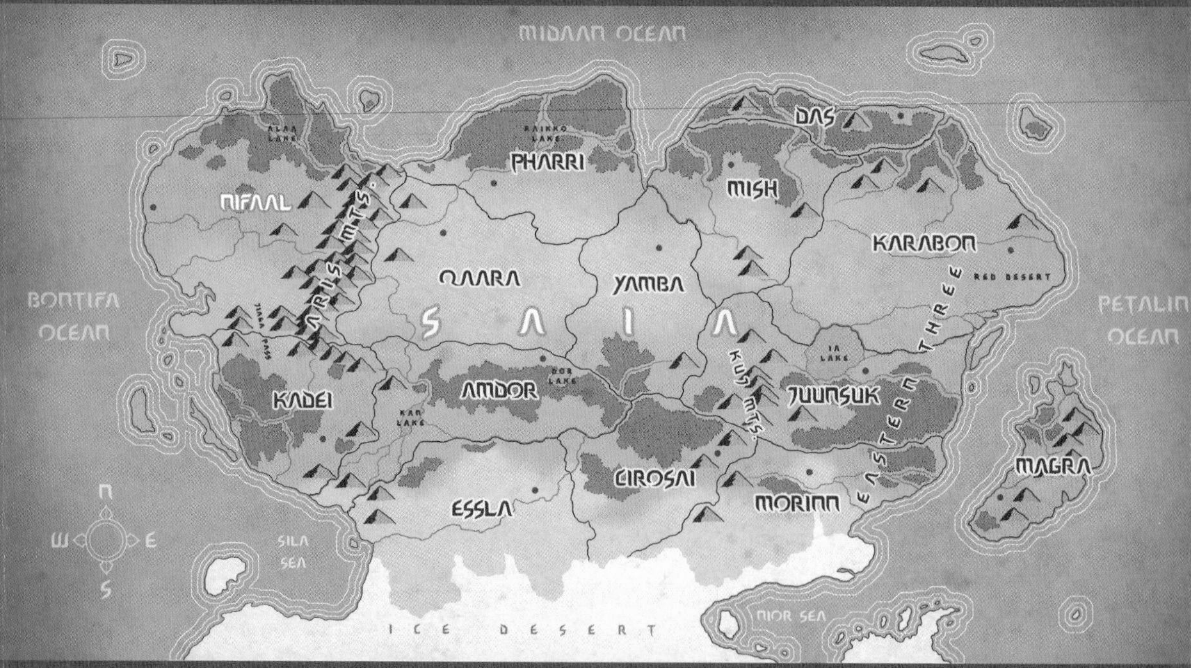
MIDAAN OCEAN
DAS
PHARRI
NIFAAL
MISH
KARABON
ARIS MTS.
QAARA
YAMBA
RED DESERT
BONTIFA OCEAN
PETALIN OCEAN
S A I A
EASTERN THREE
KUSI MTS.
AMDOR
KADEI
JUUNSUK
MAGRA
CIROSAI
ESSLA
MORINN
N
W
E
S
SILA SEA
NIOR SEA
ICE DESERT

IMAGE COMICS, INC.

ROBERT KIRKMAN Chief Operating Officer - ERIK LARSEN Chief Financial Officer - TODD MCFARLANE President - MARC SILVESTRI Chief Executive Officer JIM VALENTINO Vice President - ERIC STEPHENSON Publisher - COREY MURPHY Director of Sales - JEFF BOISON Director of Publishing Planning & Book Trade Sales - CHRIS ROSS Director of Digital Sales - JEFF STANG Director of Specialty Sales - KAT SALAZAR Director of PR & Marketing - BRANWYN BIGGLESTONE Controller - KALI DUGAN Senior Accounting Manager - SUE KORPELA Accounting & HR Manager - DREW GILL Art Director - HEATHER DOORNINK Production Director - LEIGH THOMAS Print Manager - TRICIA RAMOS Traffic Manager - BRIAH SKELLY Publicist - ALY HOFFMAN Events & Conventions Coordinator SASHA HEAD Sales & Marketing Production Designer - DAVID BROTHERS Branding Manager - MELISSA GIFFORD Content Manager - DREW FITZGERALD Publicity Assistant - VINCENT KUKUA Production Artist - ERIKA SCHNATZ Production Artist - RYAN BREWER Production Artist - SHANNA MATUSZAK Production Artist - CAREY HALL Production Artist - ESTHER KIM Direct Market Sales Representative - EMILIO BAUTISTA Digital Sales Representative - LEANNA CAUNTER Accounting Analyst - CHLOE RAMOS-PETERSON Library Market Sales Representative - MARLA EIZIK Administrative Assistant

IMAGECOMICS.COM

ETERNAL EMPIRE, VOL. 1. First printing. NOVEMBER 2017. Published by Image Comics, Inc. Office of publication: 2701 NW Vaughn St., Suite 780, Portland, OR 97210.

Printed in the USA. For information regarding the CPSIA on this printed material call: 203-595-3636 and provide reference #RICH-768297. For international rights, contact: foreignlicensing@imagecomics.com. ISBN: 978-1-5343-0340-9.

JONATHAN LUNA

STORY
SCRIPT ASSISTS
ILLUSTRATIONS
LETTERING
DESIGN

SARAH VAUGHN

STORY
SCRIPT

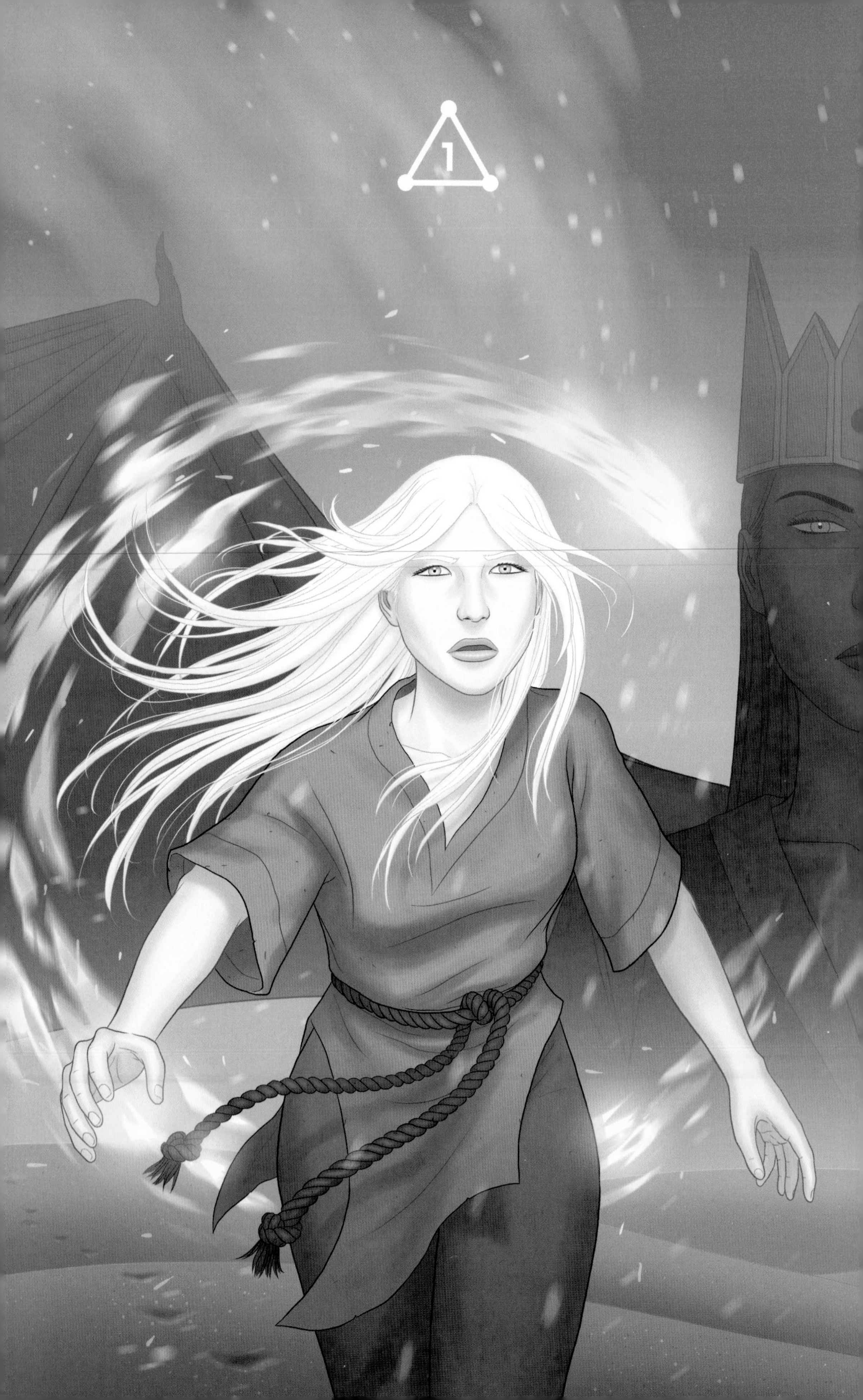
1

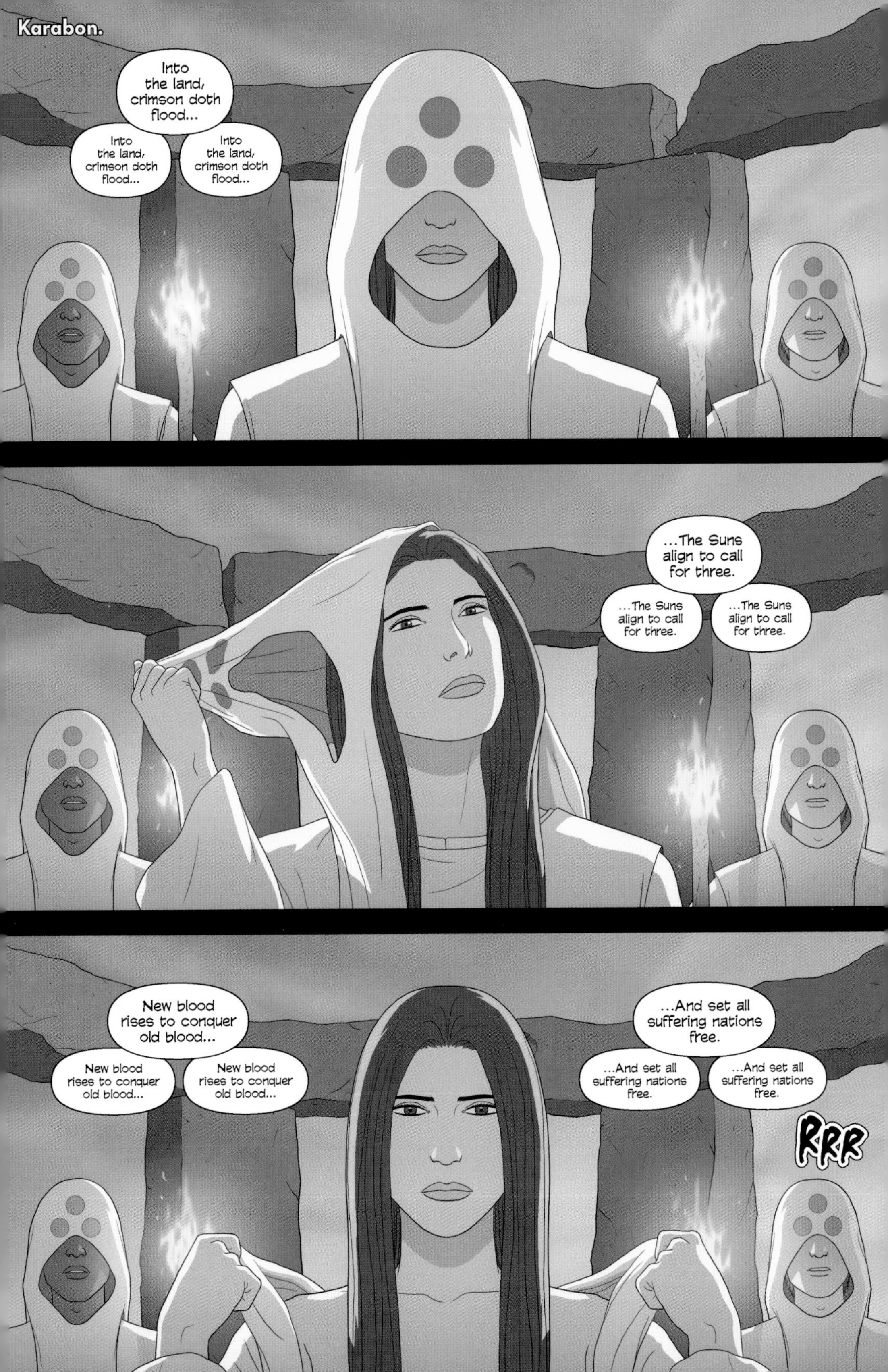
Karabon.
Into the land, crimson doth flood...
Into the land, crimson doth flood...
Into the land, crimson doth flood...
...The Suns align to call for three.
...The Suns align to call for three.
...The Suns align to call for three.
New blood rises to conquer old blood...
New blood rises to conquer old blood...
New blood rises to conquer old blood...
...And set all suffering nations free.
...And set all suffering nations free.
...And set all suffering nations free.
RRR

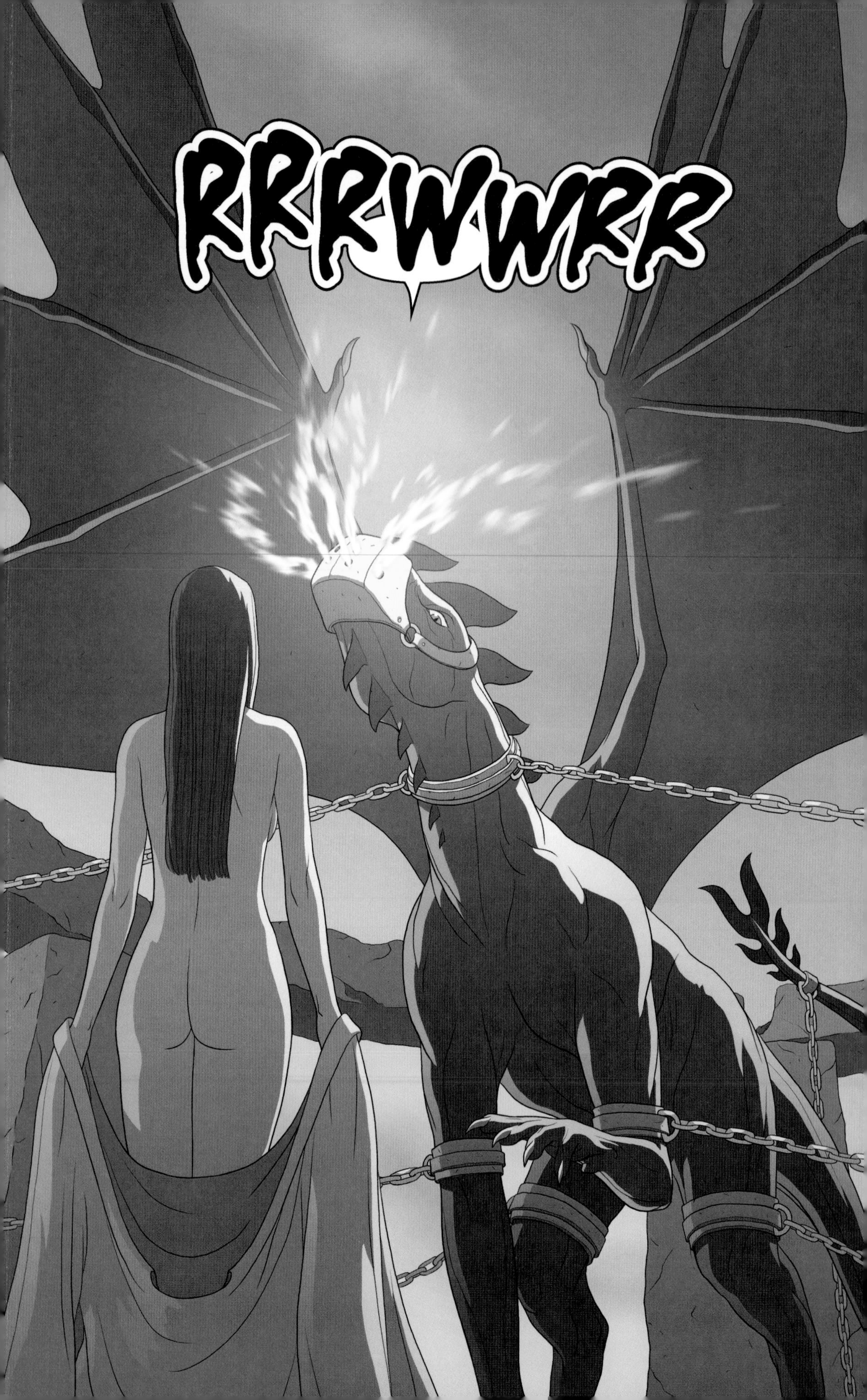
RRRWWRR

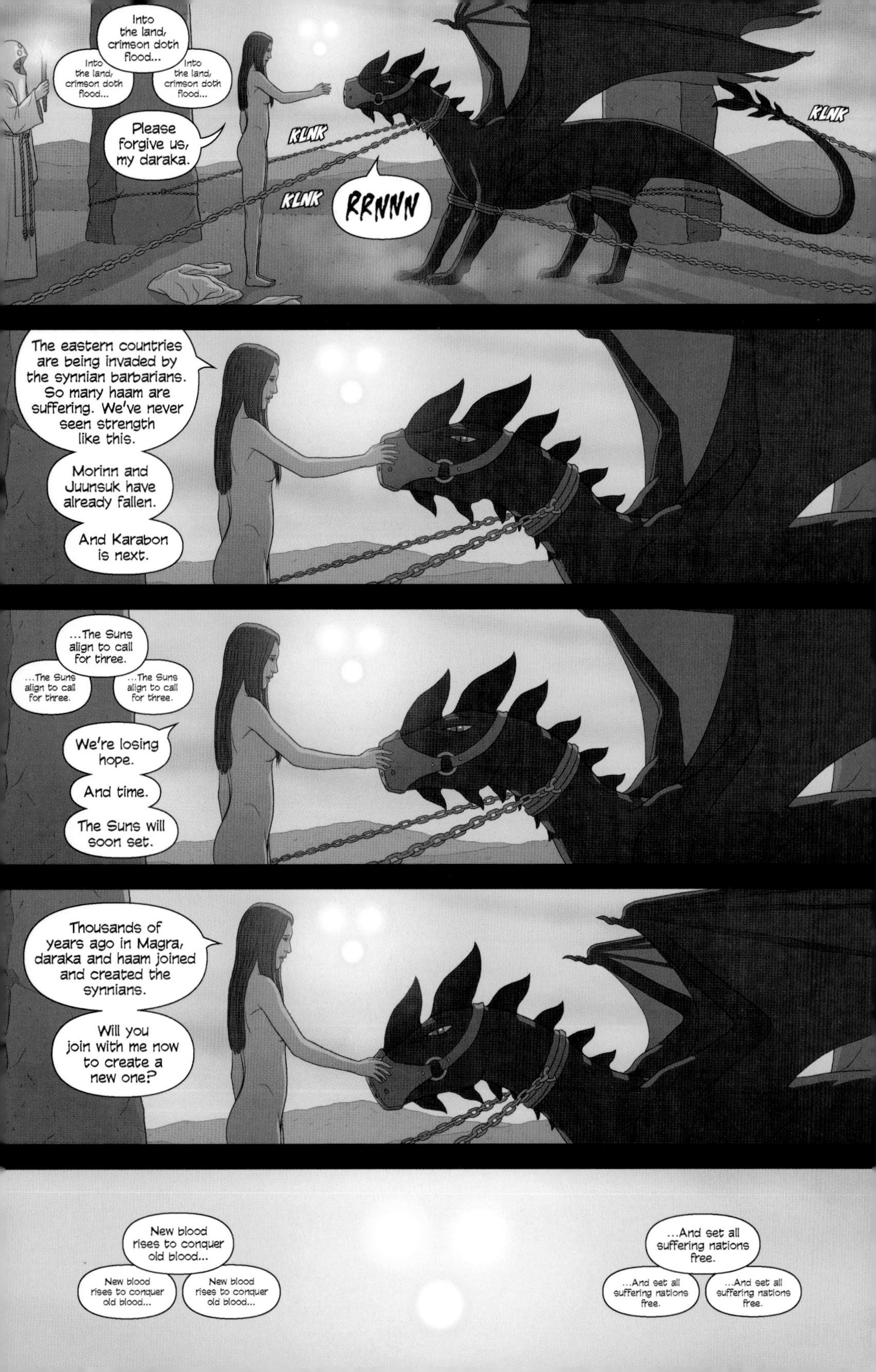

Into the land, crimson doth flood...
Into the land, crimson doth flood...
Into the land, crimson doth flood...
Please forgive us, my daraka.
KLNK
KLNK
KLNK
RRNNN
The eastern countries are being invaded by the synnian barbarians. So many haam are suffering. We've never seen strength like this.
Morinn and Juunsuk have already fallen.
And Karabon is next.
...The Suns align to call for three.
...The Suns align to call for three.
...The Suns align to call for three.
We're losing hope.
And time.
The Suns will soon set.
Thousands of years ago in Magra, daraka and haam joined and created the synnians.
Will you join with me now to create a new one?
New blood rises to conquer old blood...
New blood rises to conquer old blood...
New blood rises to conquer old blood...
...And set all suffering nations free.
...And set all suffering nations free.
...And set all suffering nations free.

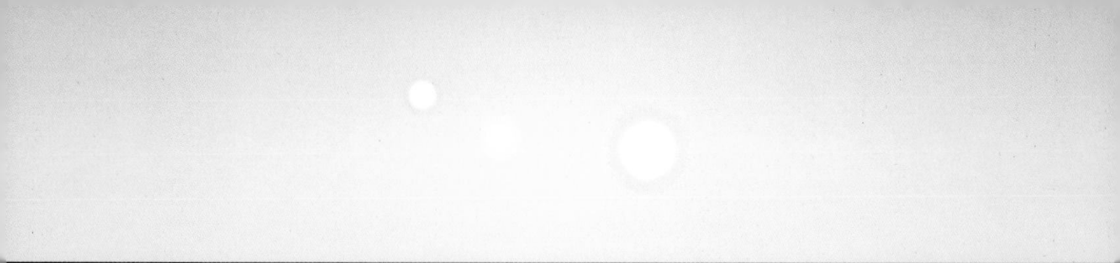

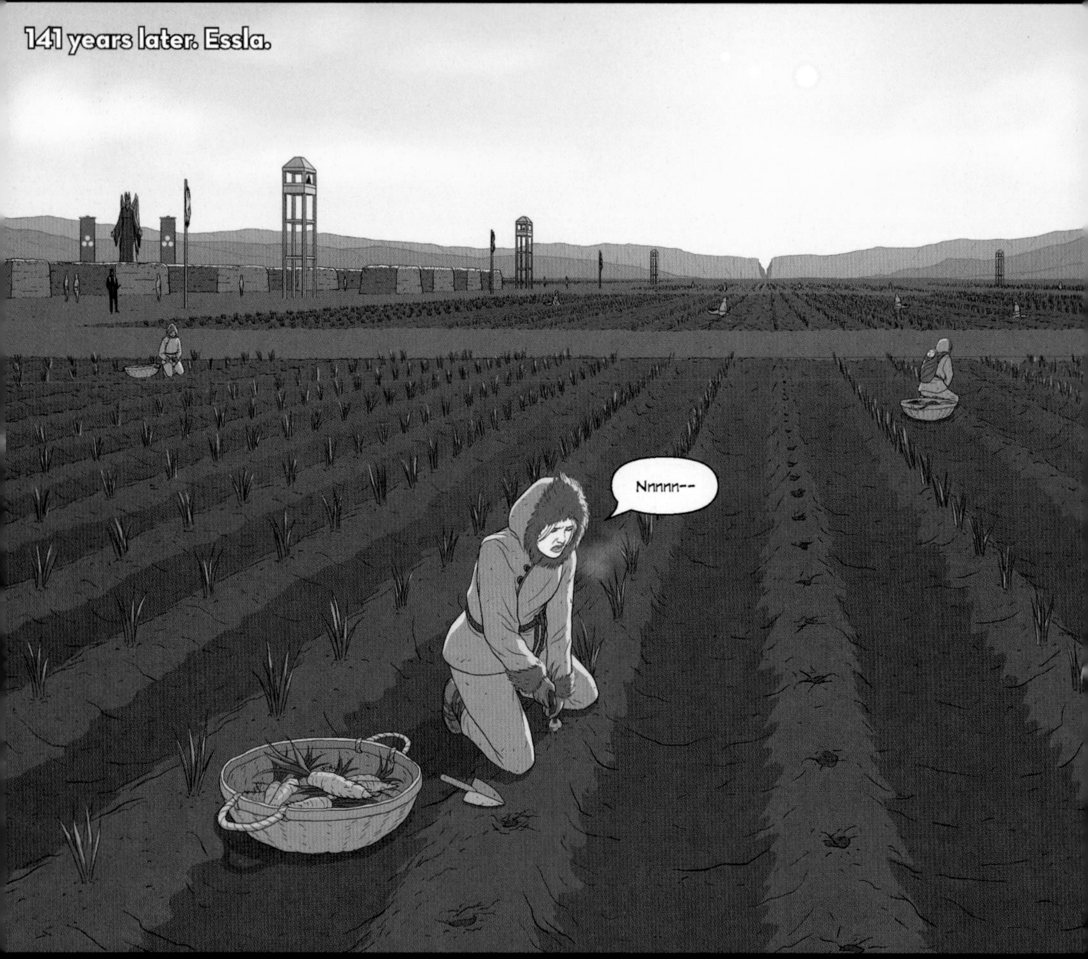
141 years later. Essla.
Nnnnn--

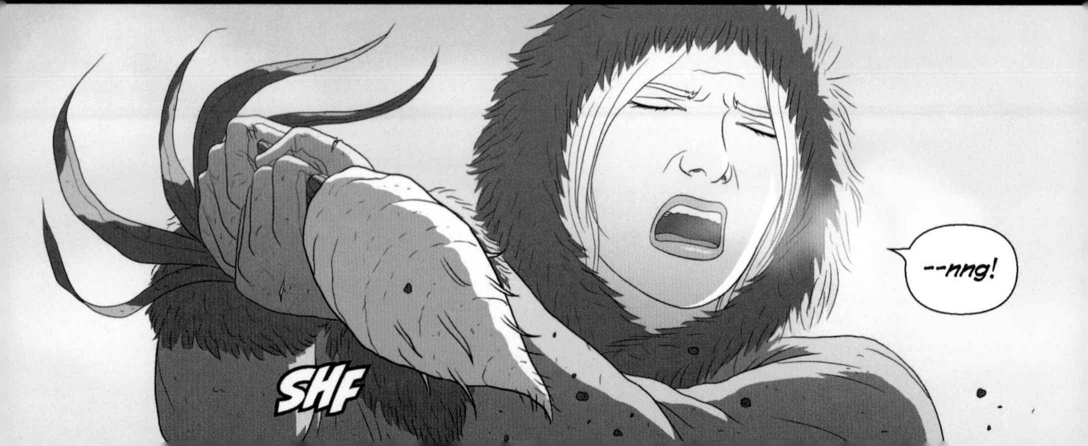
--nng!
SHF

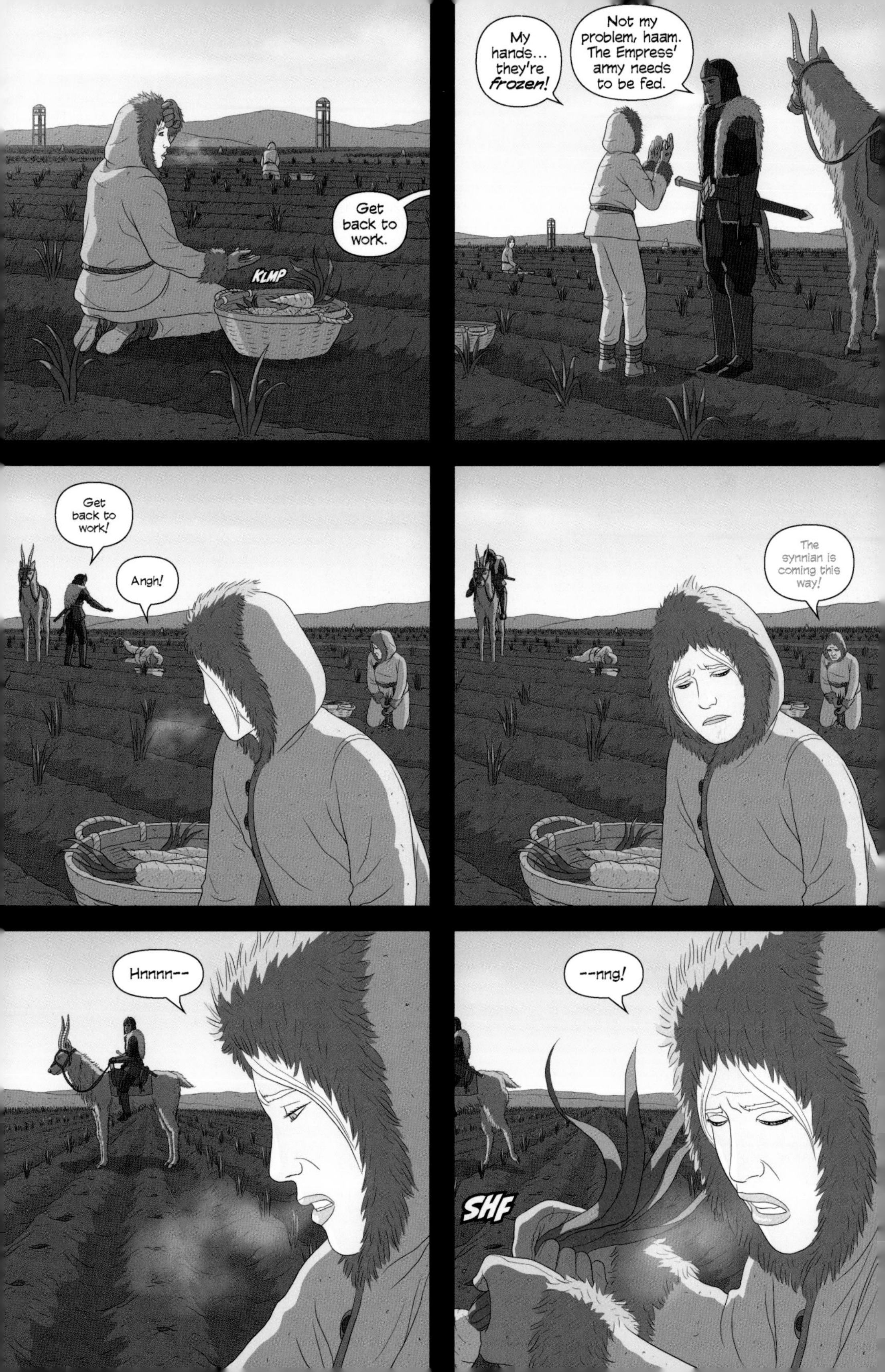

KLMP
Get back to work.
My hands... they're *frozen*!
Not my problem, haam. The Empress' army needs to be fed.
Get back to work!
Angh!
The synnian is coming this way!
Hnnnn--
--nng!
SHF

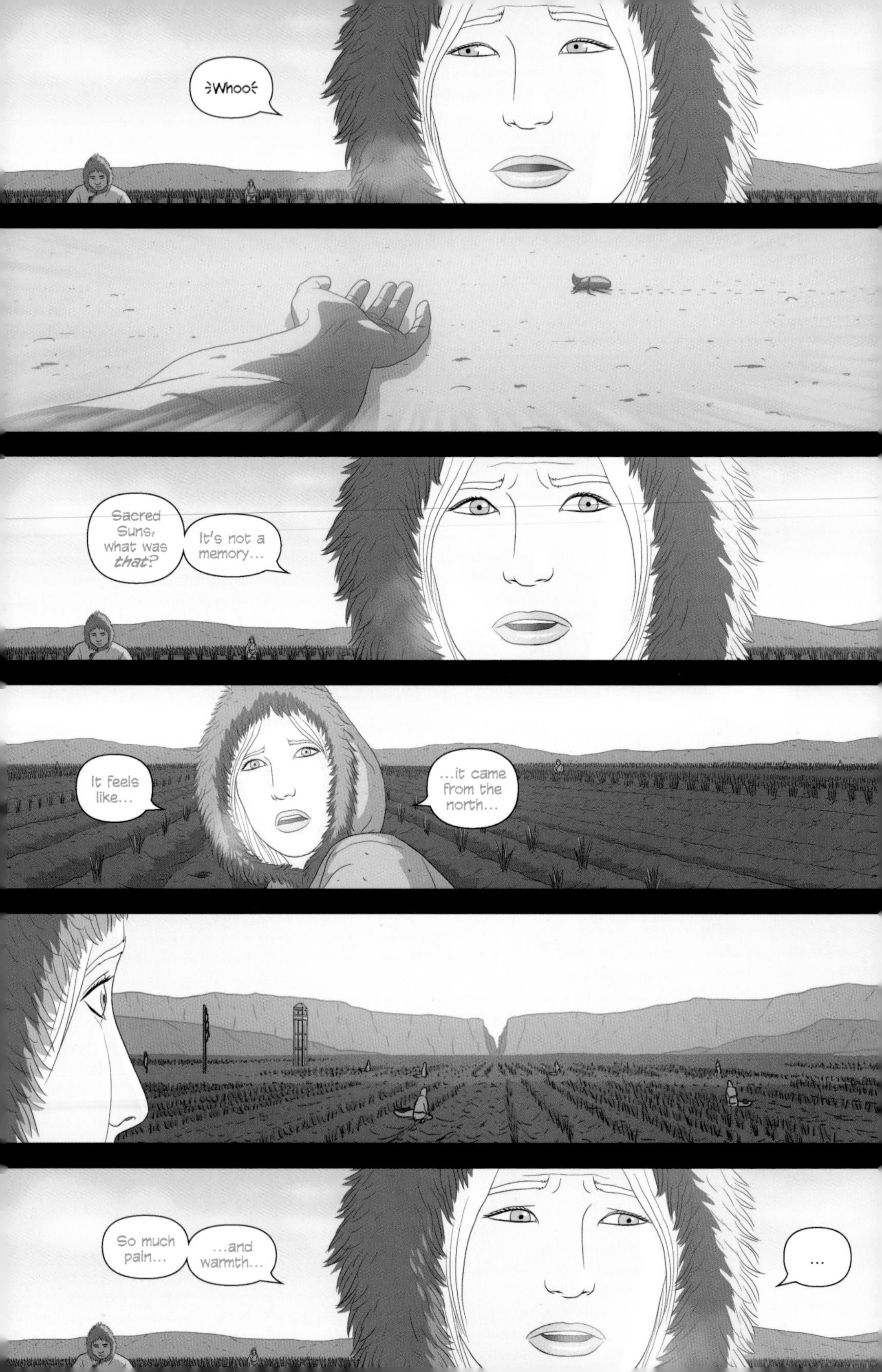
Whoo
Sacred Suns, what was *that*?
It's not a memory...
It feels like...
...it came from the north...
So much pain...
...and warmth...
...

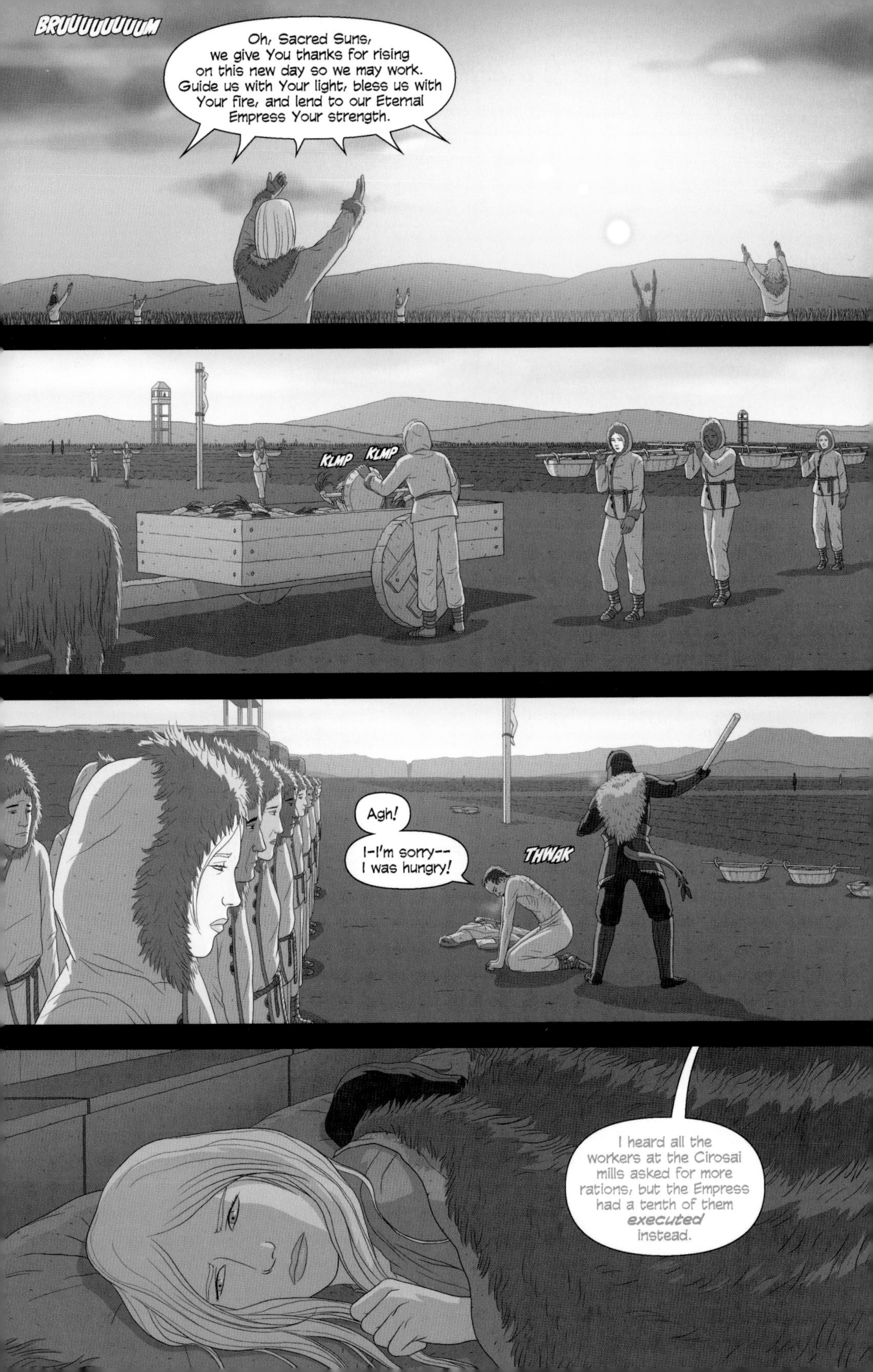
BRUUUUUUUUM
Oh, Sacred Suns, we give You thanks for rising on this new day so we may work. Guide us with Your light, bless us with Your fire, and lend to our Eternal Empress Your strength.
KLMP KLMP
Agh!
I-I'm sorry-- I was hungry!
THWAK
I heard all the workers at the Cirosai mills asked for more rations, but the Empress had a tenth of them *executed* instead.

BRUUUUUUUM

BRUUUUUUUM

BRUUUUUUUM

People of Essla!

You are gathered here for an important announcement from the Imperial Palace!

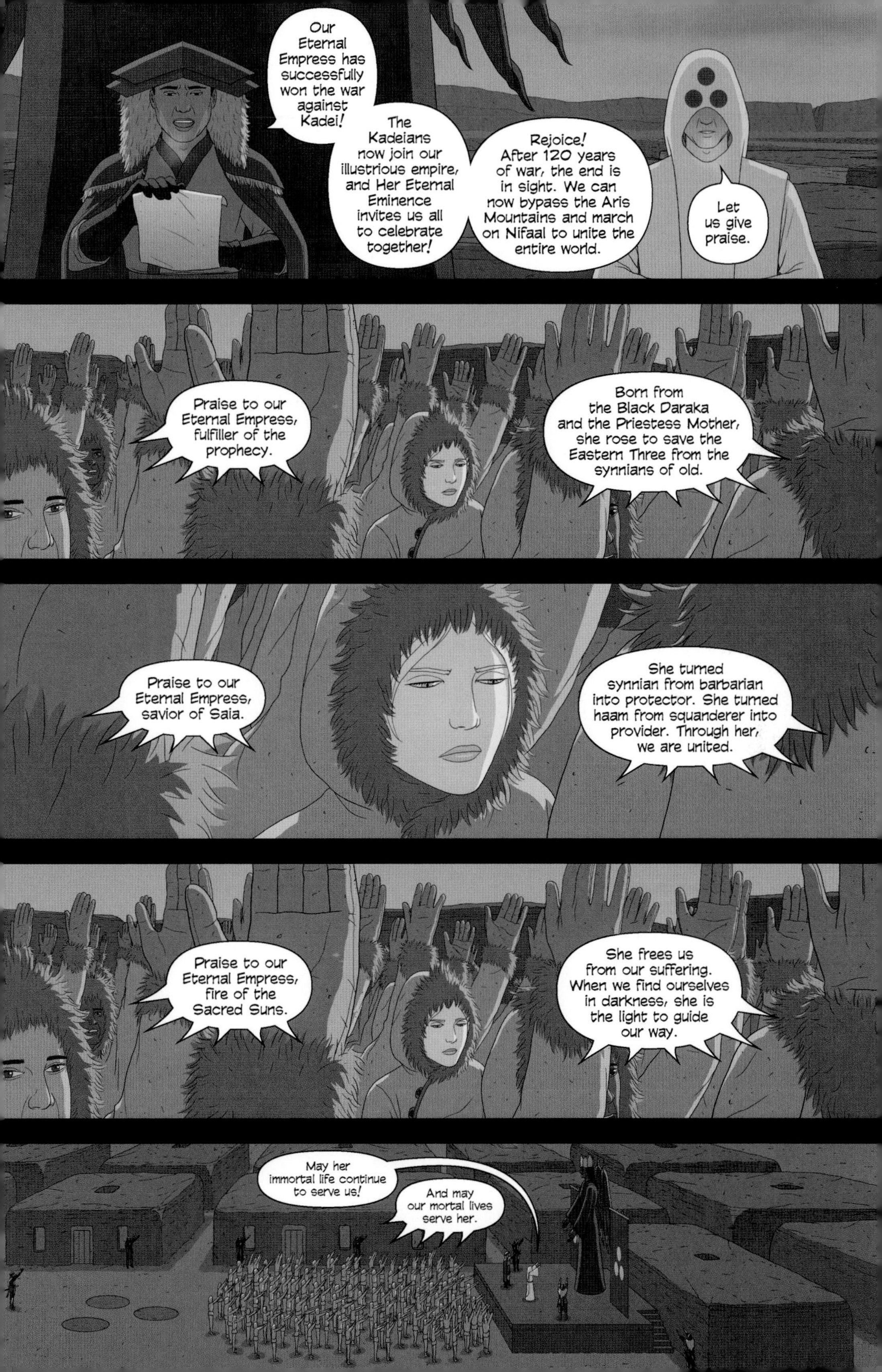
Our Eternal Empress has successfully won the war against Kadei!
The Kadeians now join our illustrious empire, and Her Eternal Eminence invites us all to celebrate together!
Rejoice! After 120 years of war, the end is in sight. We can now bypass the Aris Mountains and march on Nifaal to unite the entire world.
Let us give praise.
Praise to our Eternal Empress, fulfiller of the prophecy.
Born from the Black Daraka and the Priestess Mother, she rose to save the Eastern Three from the synnians of old.
Praise to our Eternal Empress, savior of Saia.
She turned synnian from barbarian into protector. She turned haam from squanderer into provider. Through her, we are united.
Praise to our Eternal Empress, fire of the Sacred Suns.
She frees us from our suffering. When we find ourselves in darkness, she is the light to guide our way.
May her immortal life continue to serve us!
And may our mortal lives serve her.

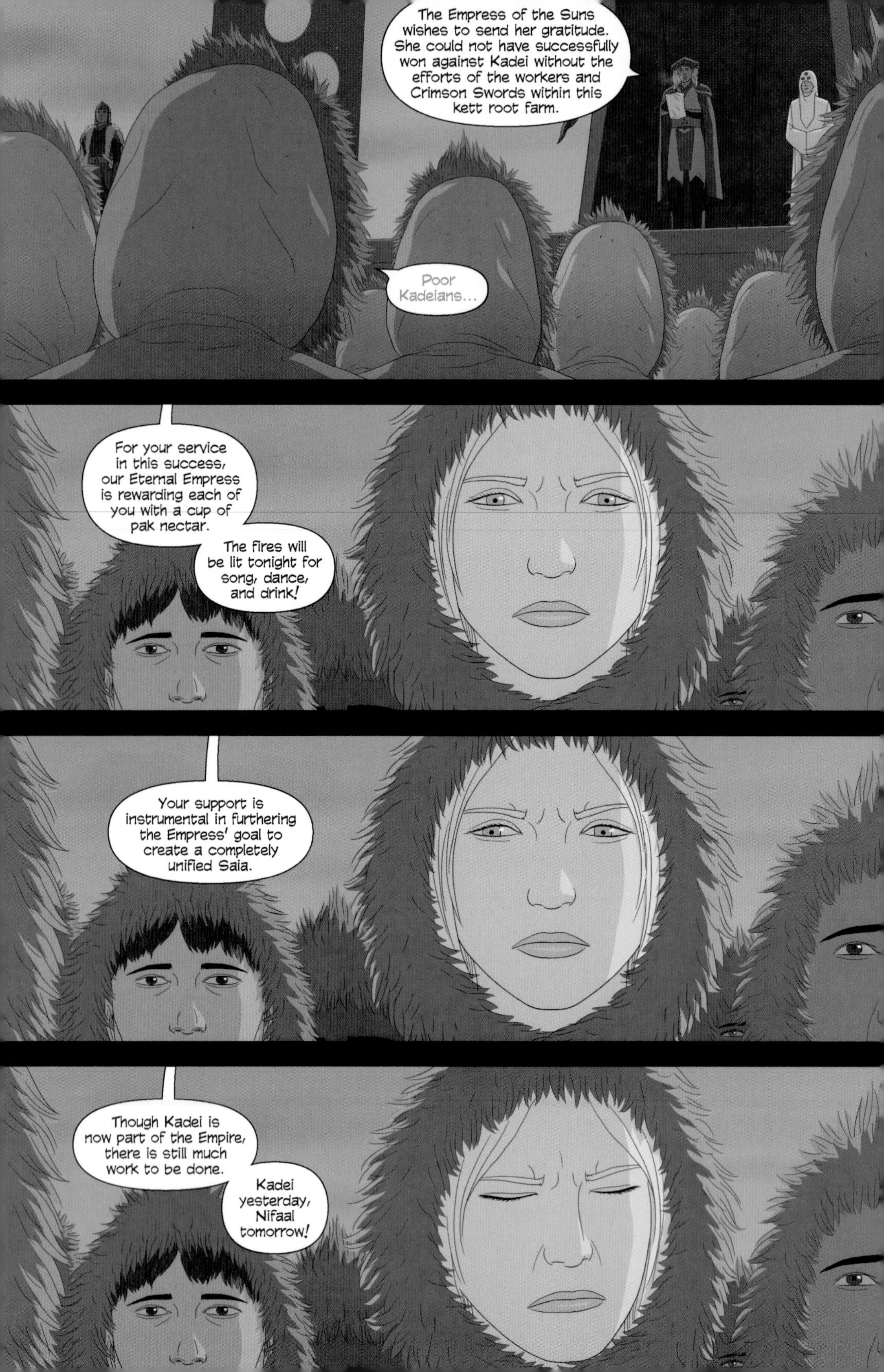

The Empress of the Suns wishes to send her gratitude. She could not have successfully won against Kadei without the efforts of the workers and Crimson Swords within this kett root farm.
Poor Kadeians...
For your service in this success, our Eternal Empress is rewarding each of you with a cup of pak nectar.
The fires will be lit tonight for song, dance, and drink!
Your support is instrumental in furthering the Empress' goal to create a completely unified Saia.
Though Kadei is now part of the Empire, there is still much work to be done.
Kadei yesterday, Nifaal tomorrow!

...

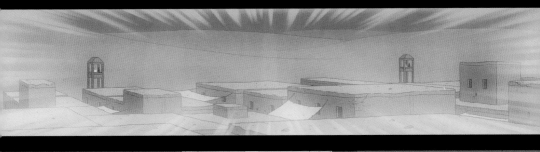

Another vision...

Get back to the ceremony, "Snow Hair."

Oh-- I'm...

I'm just catching a breath.

I've watched you-- you haven't taken **one step** toward the fires.

Liar.

Agk!

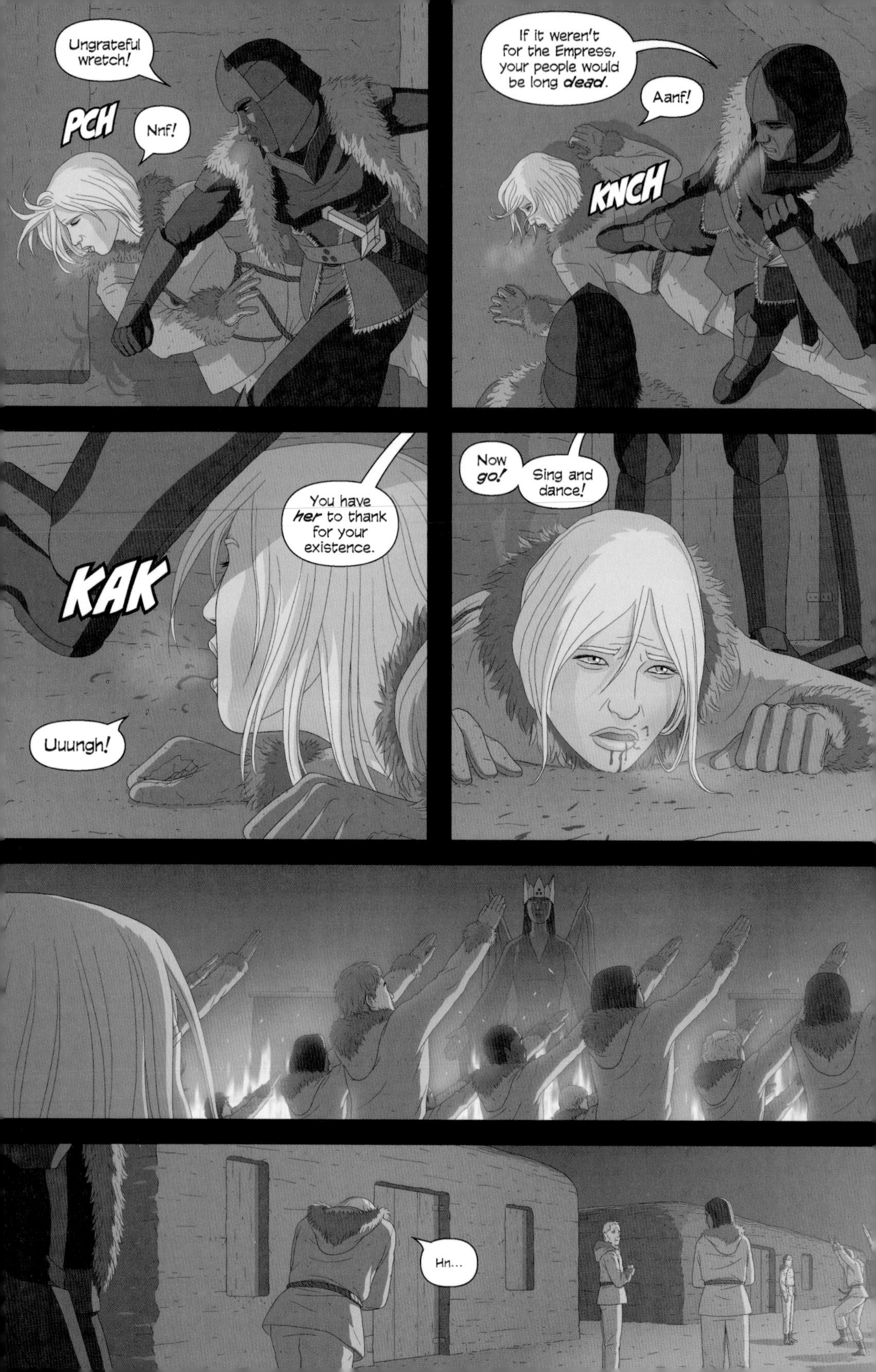
Ungrateful wretch!
PCH
Nnf!
If it weren't for the Empress, your people would be long *dead*.
Aanf!
KNCH
You have *her* to thank for your existence.
KAK
Uuungh!
Now *go!*
Sing and dance!
Hn...

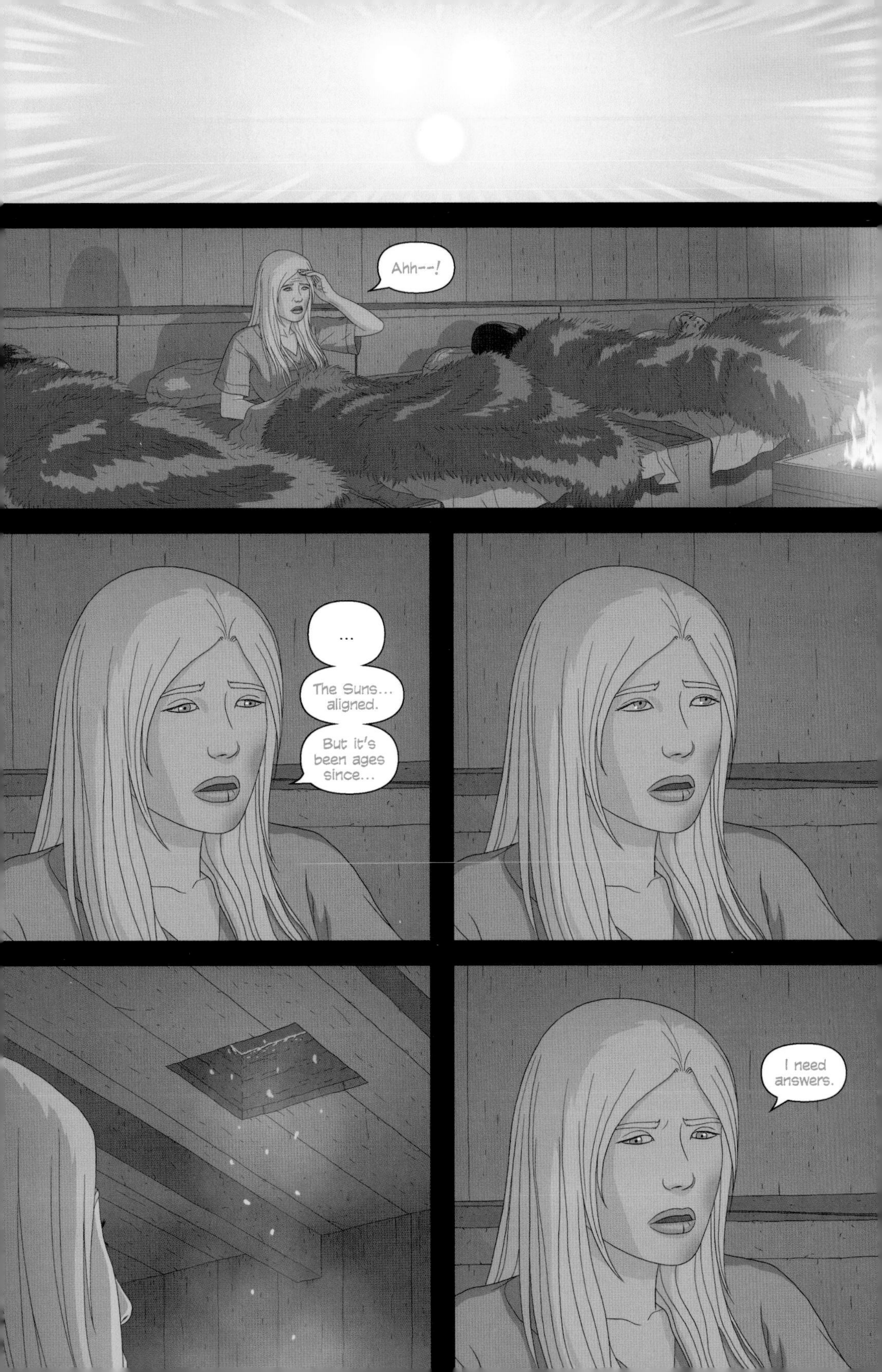
Ahh--!
...
The Suns... aligned.
But it's been ages since...
I need answers.

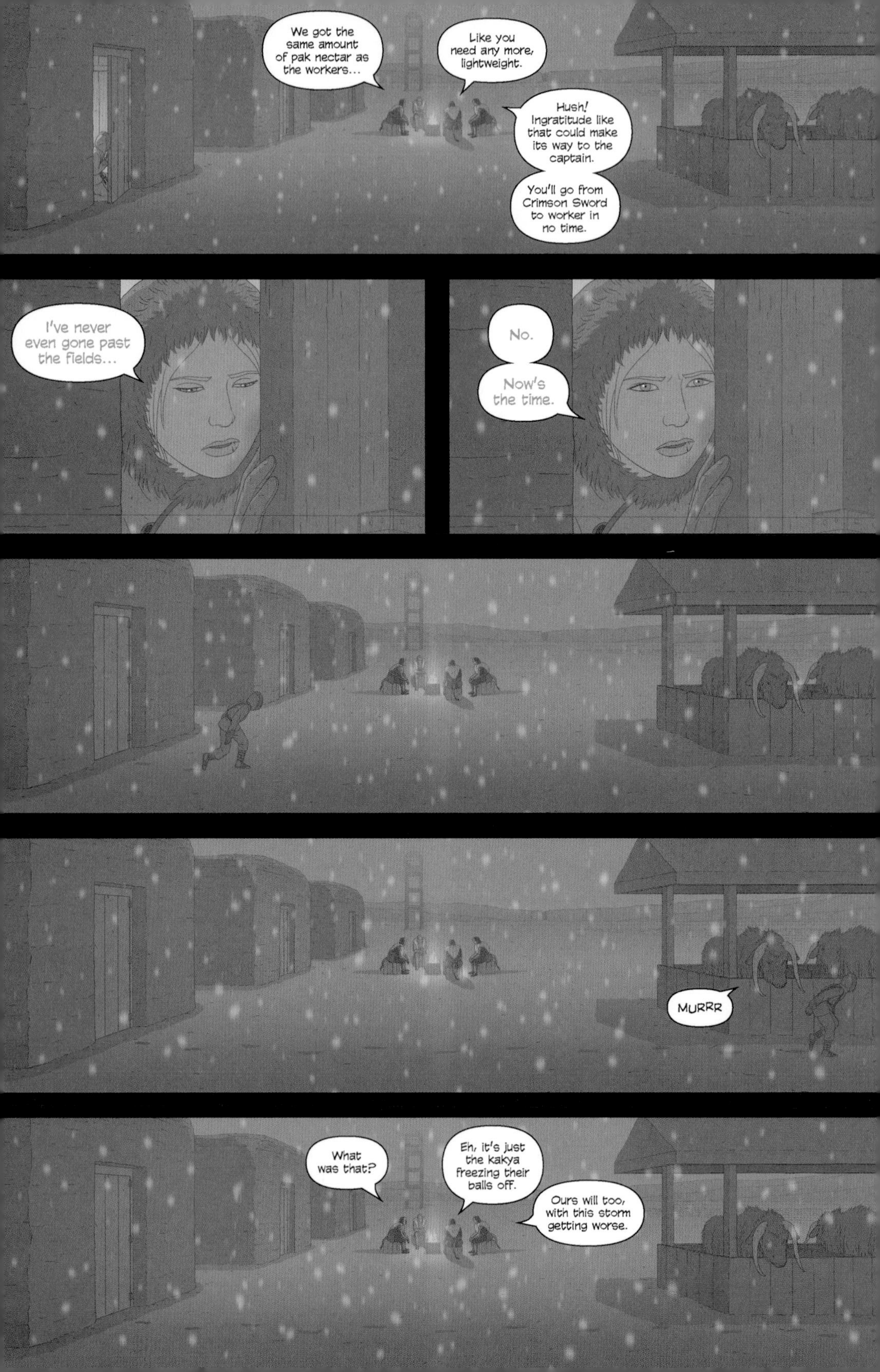

We got the same amount of pak nectar as the workers...
Like you need any more, lightweight.
Hush! Ingratitude like that could make its way to the captain.
You'll go from Crimson Sword to worker in no time.
I've never even gone past the fields...
No.
Now's the time.
MURRR
What was that?
Eh, it's just the kakya freezing their balls off.
Ours will too, with this storm getting worse.

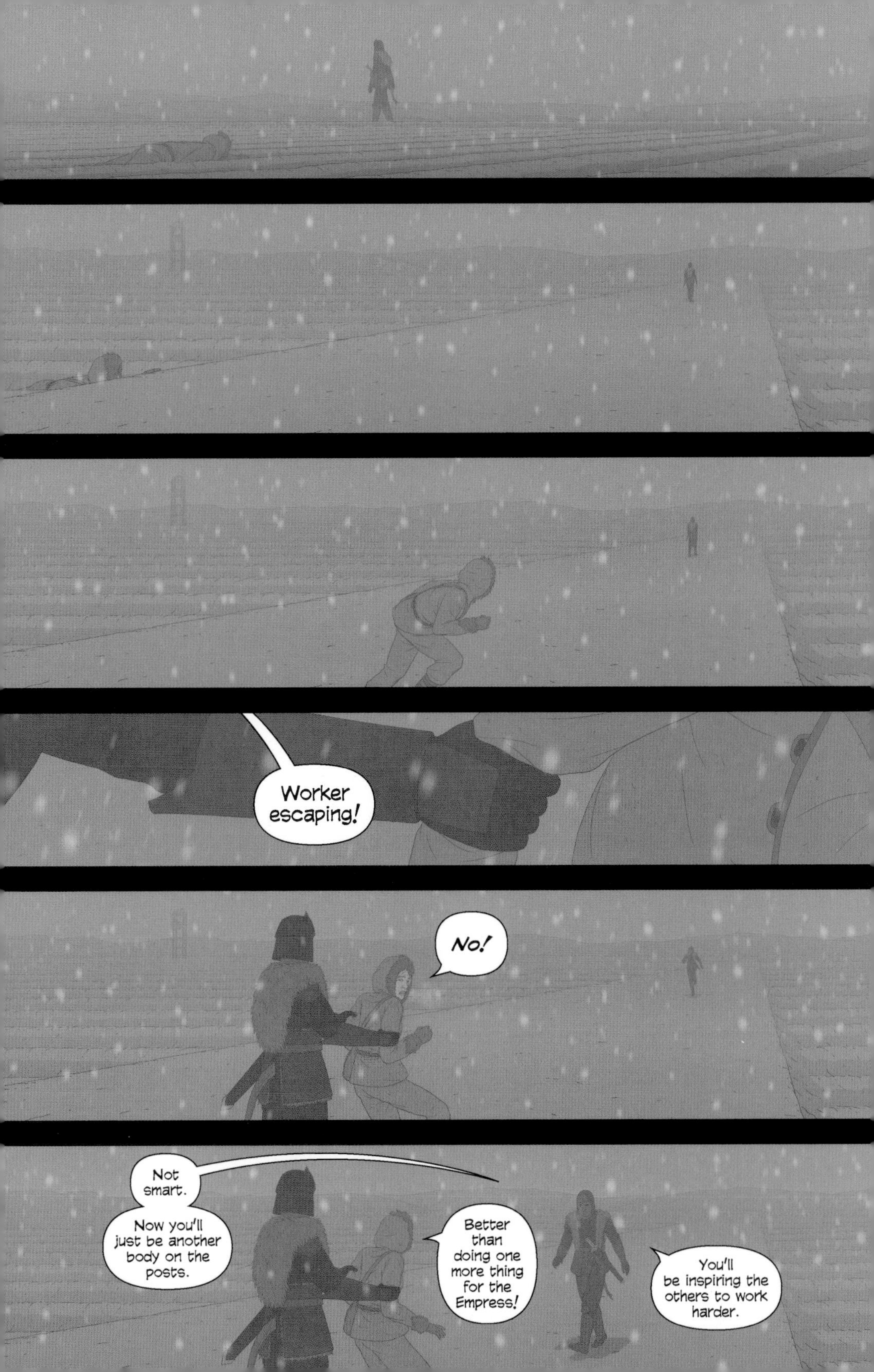

Worker escaping!
No!
Not smart.
Now you'll just be another body on the posts.
Better than doing one more thing for the Empress!
You'll be inspiring the others to work harder.

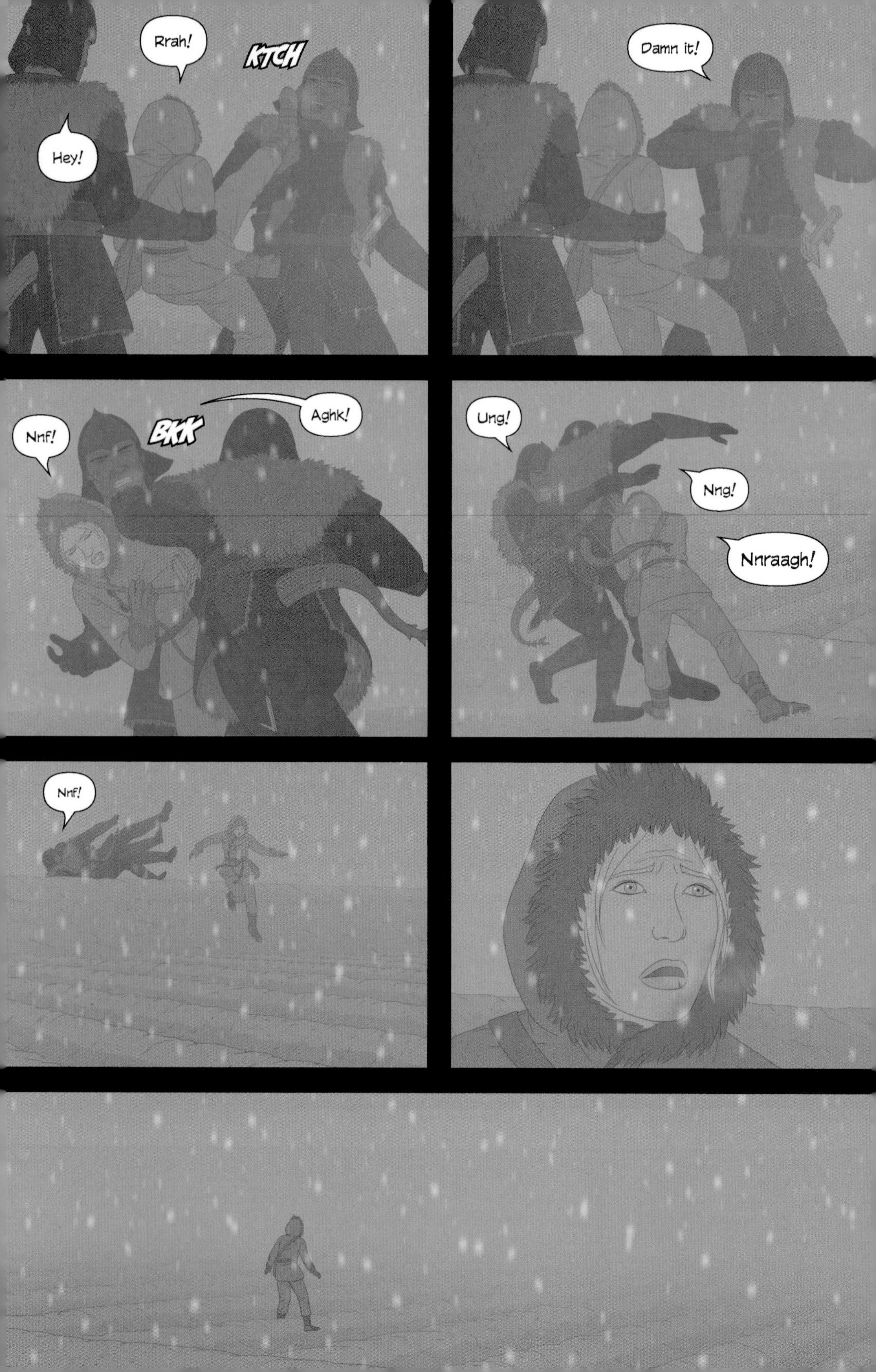
Rrah!
KTCH
Hey!
Damn it!
Nnf!
BKK
Aghk!
Ung!
Nng!
Nnraagh!
Nnf!

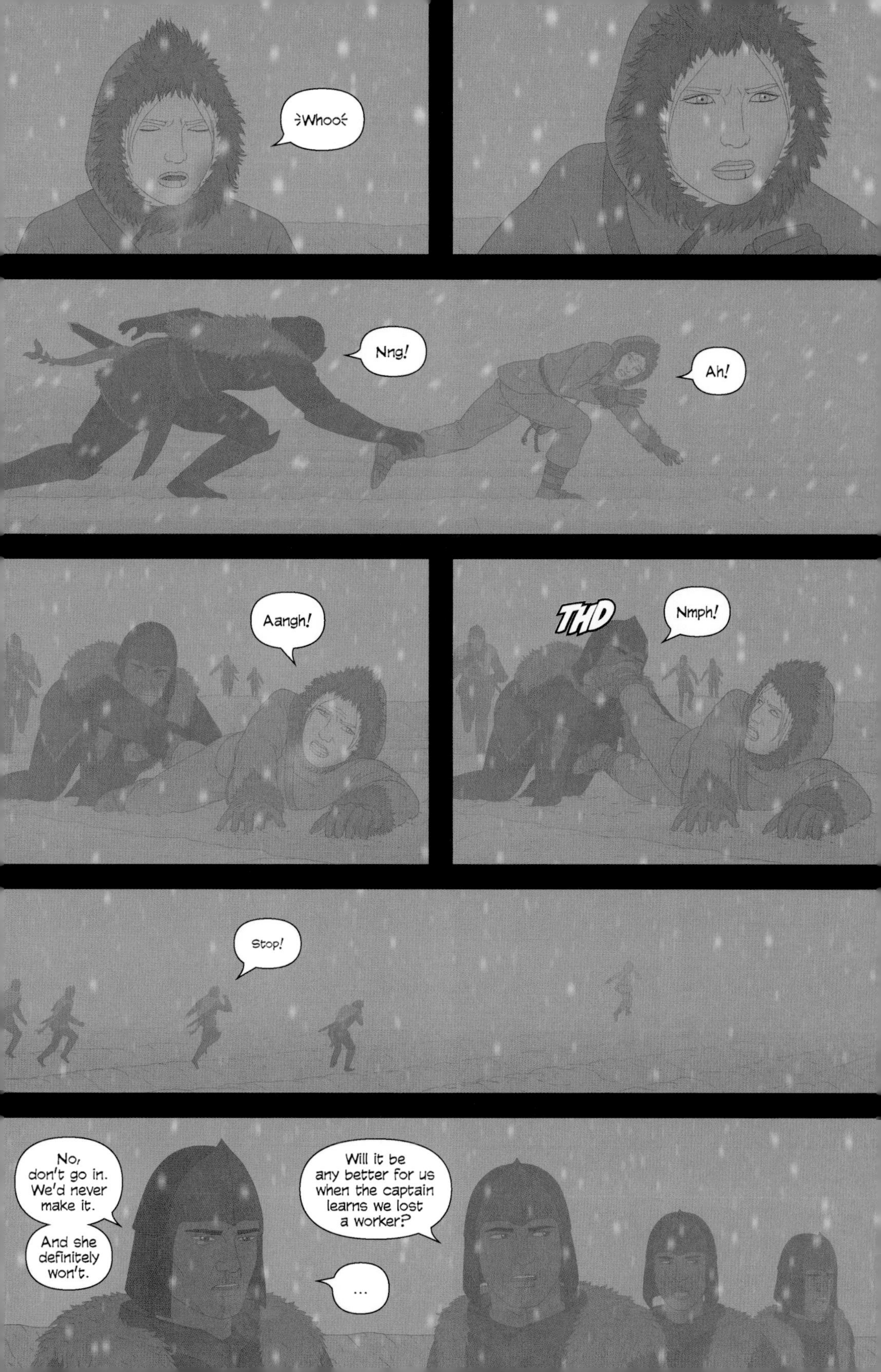
Whoo
Nng!
Ah!
Aangh!
THD
Nmph!
Stop!
No, don't go in. We'd never make it.
And she definitely won't.
Will it be any better for us when the captain learns we lost a worker?
...

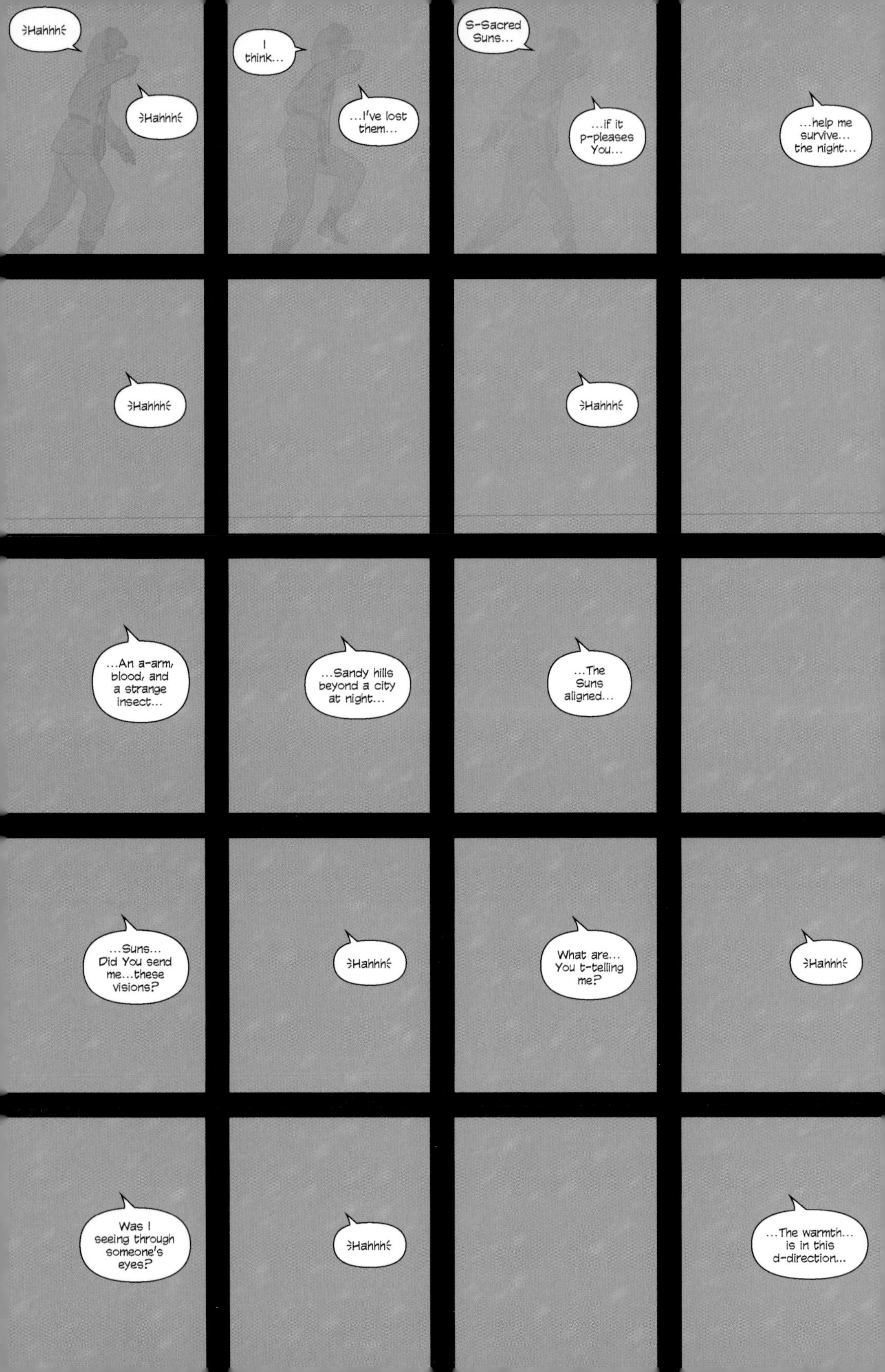

Hahhh
Hahhh
I think...
...I've lost them...
S-Sacred Suns...
...if it p-pleases You...
...help me survive... the night...
Hahhh
Hahhh
...An a-arm, blood, and a strange insect...
...Sandy hills beyond a city at night...
...The Suns aligned...
...Suns... Did You send me...these visions?
Hahhh
What are... You t-telling me?
Hahhh
Was I seeing through someone's eyes?
Hahhh
...The warmth... is in this d-direction...

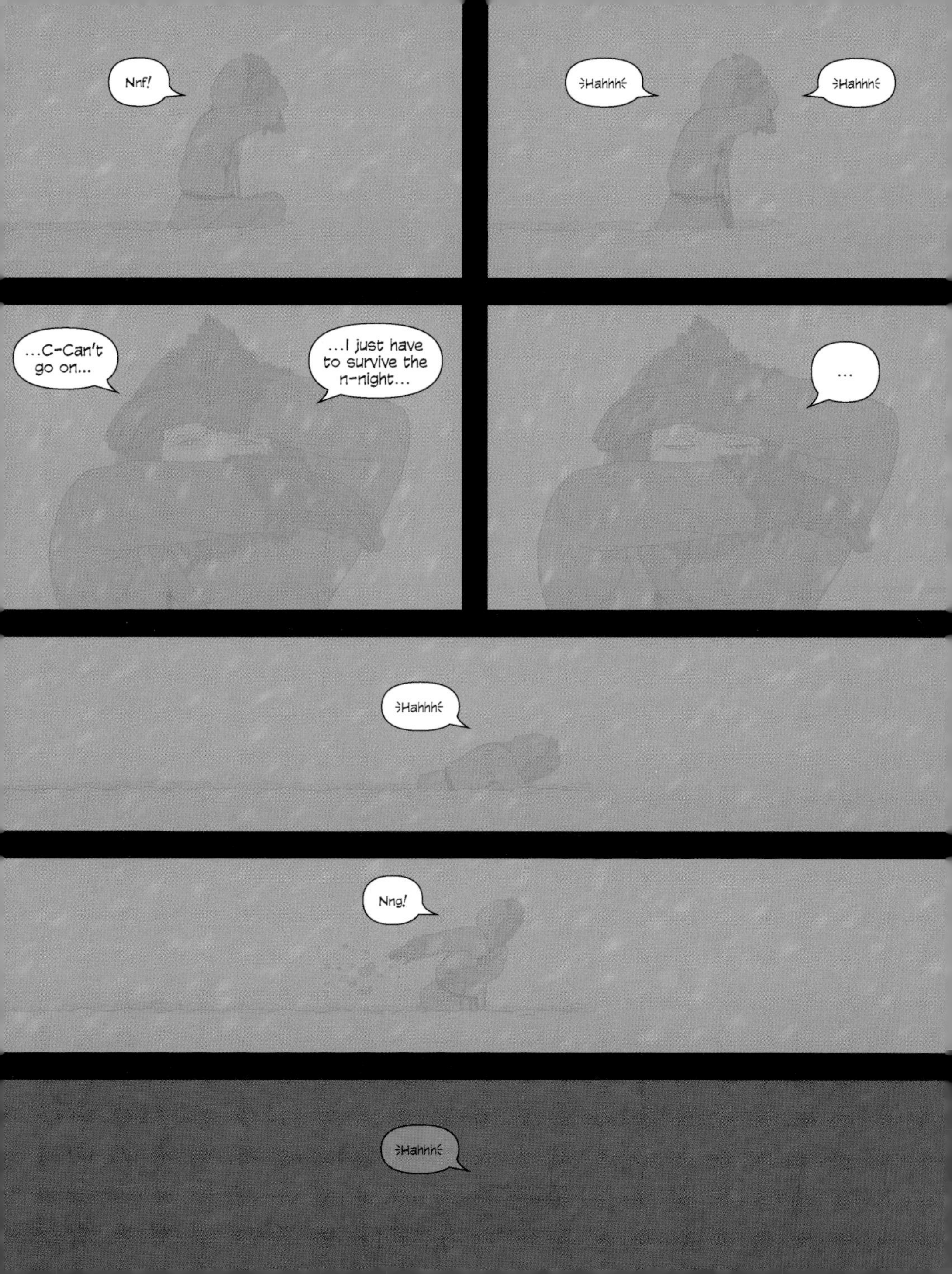
Nnf!
Hahhh
Hahhh
...C-Can't go on...
...I just have to survive the n-night...
...
Hahhh
Nng!
Hahhh

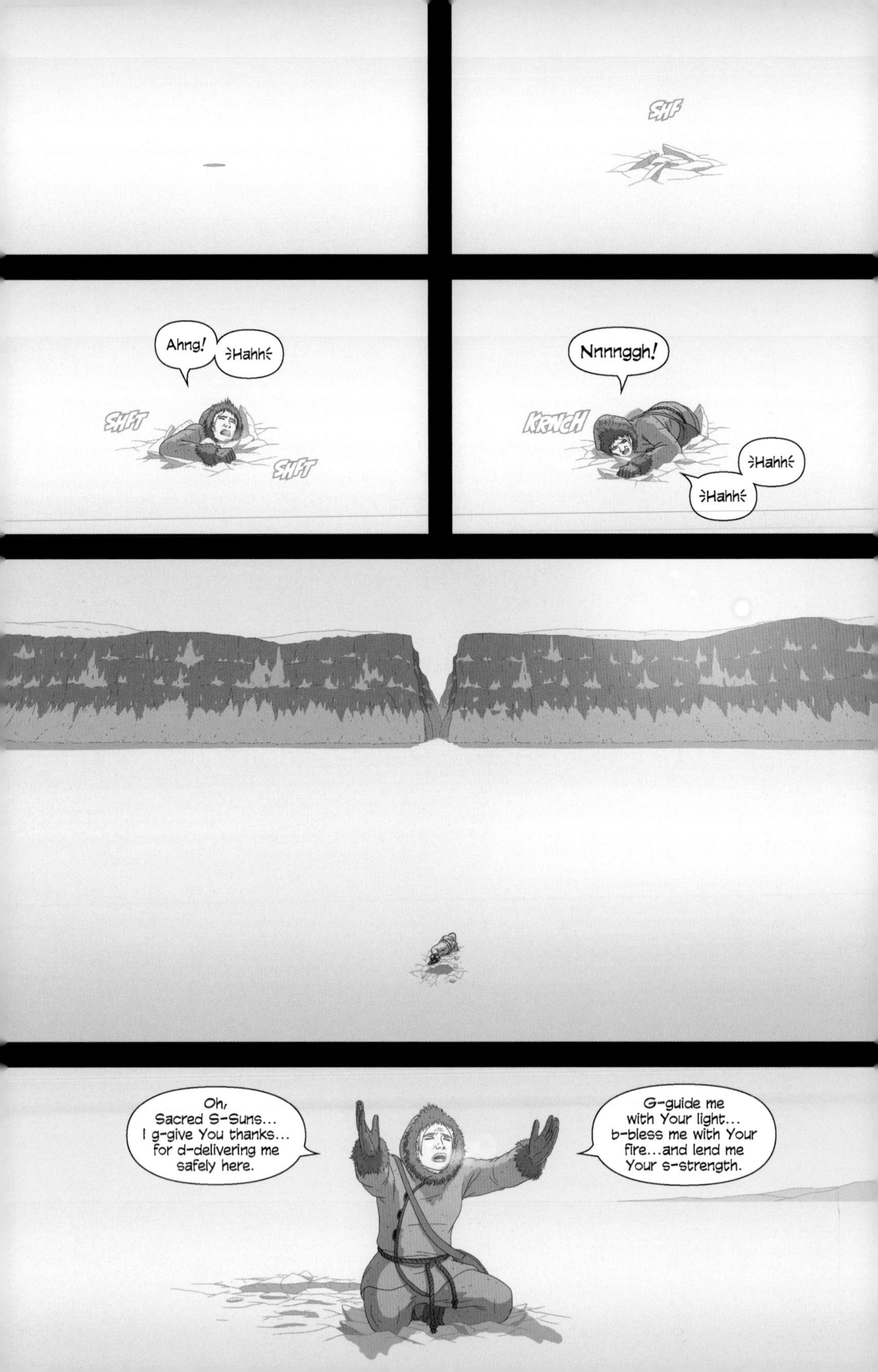
SHF
Ahng!
Hahh
SHFT
SHFT
Nnnnggh!
KRNCH
Hahh
Hahh
Oh, Sacred S-Suns... I g-give You thanks... for d-delivering me safely here.
G-guide me with Your light... b-bless me with Your fire...and lend me Your s-strength.

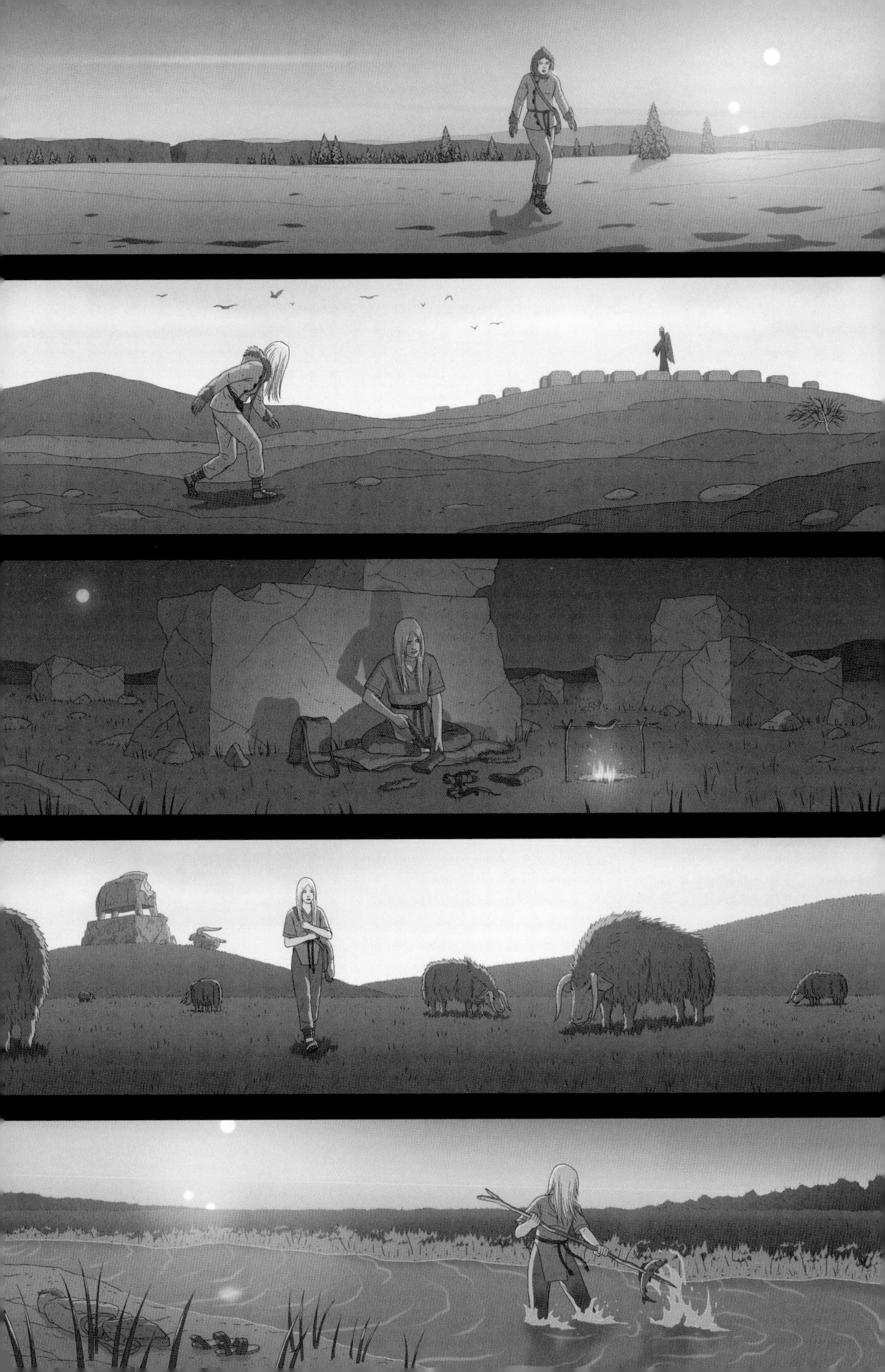

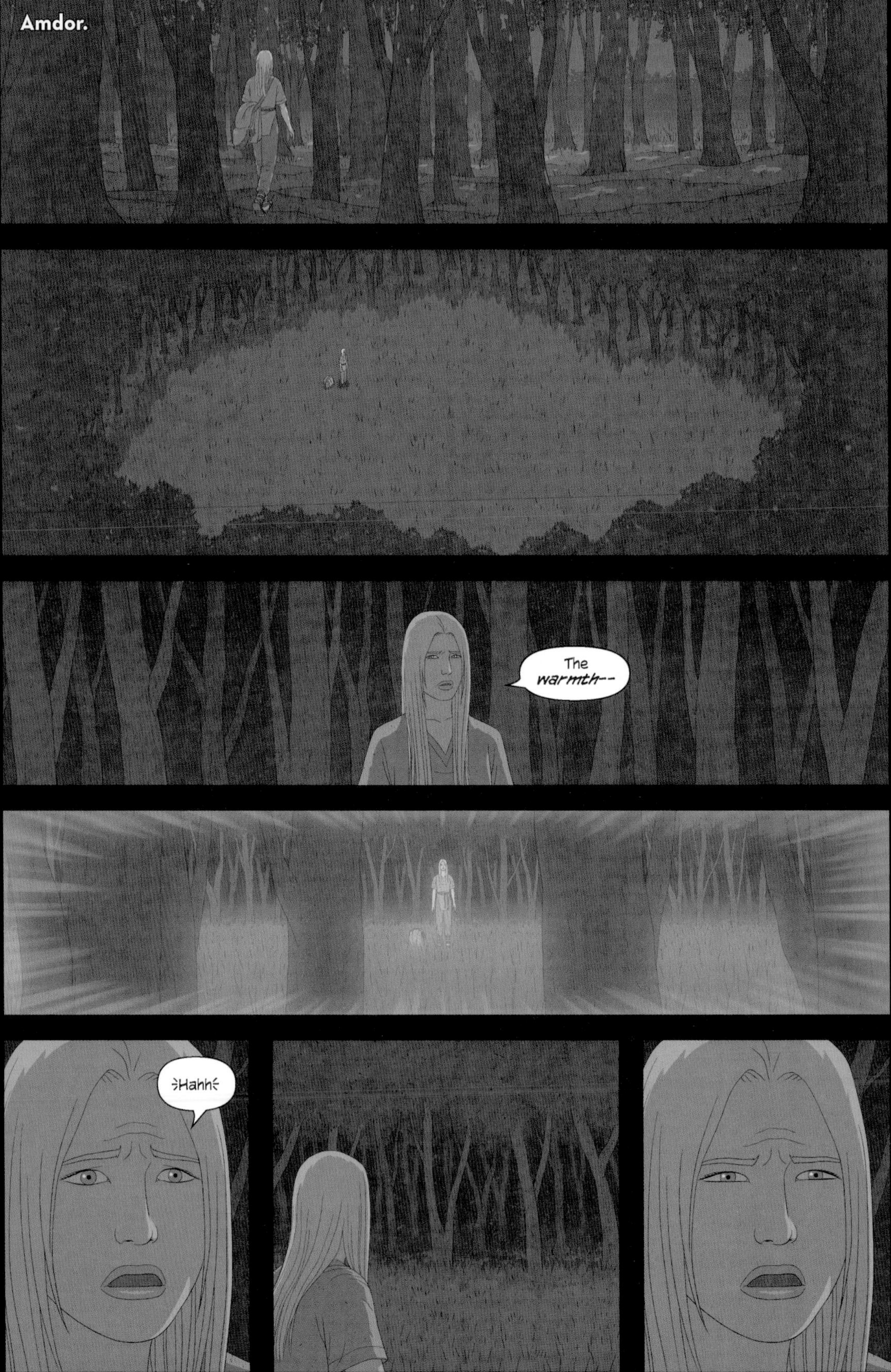
Amdor.
The warmth--
Hahh

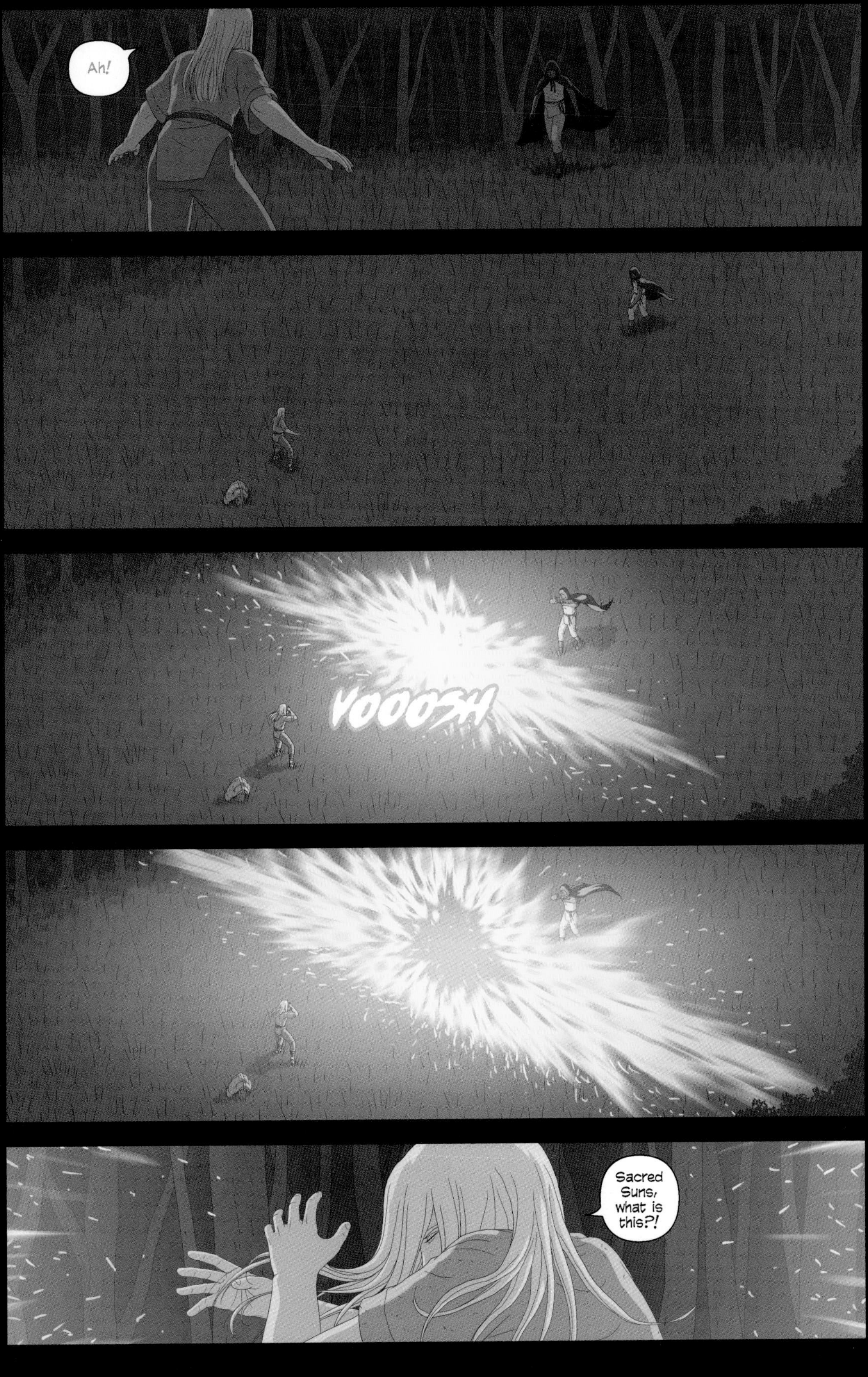
Ah!
VOOOSH
Sacred Suns, what is this?!

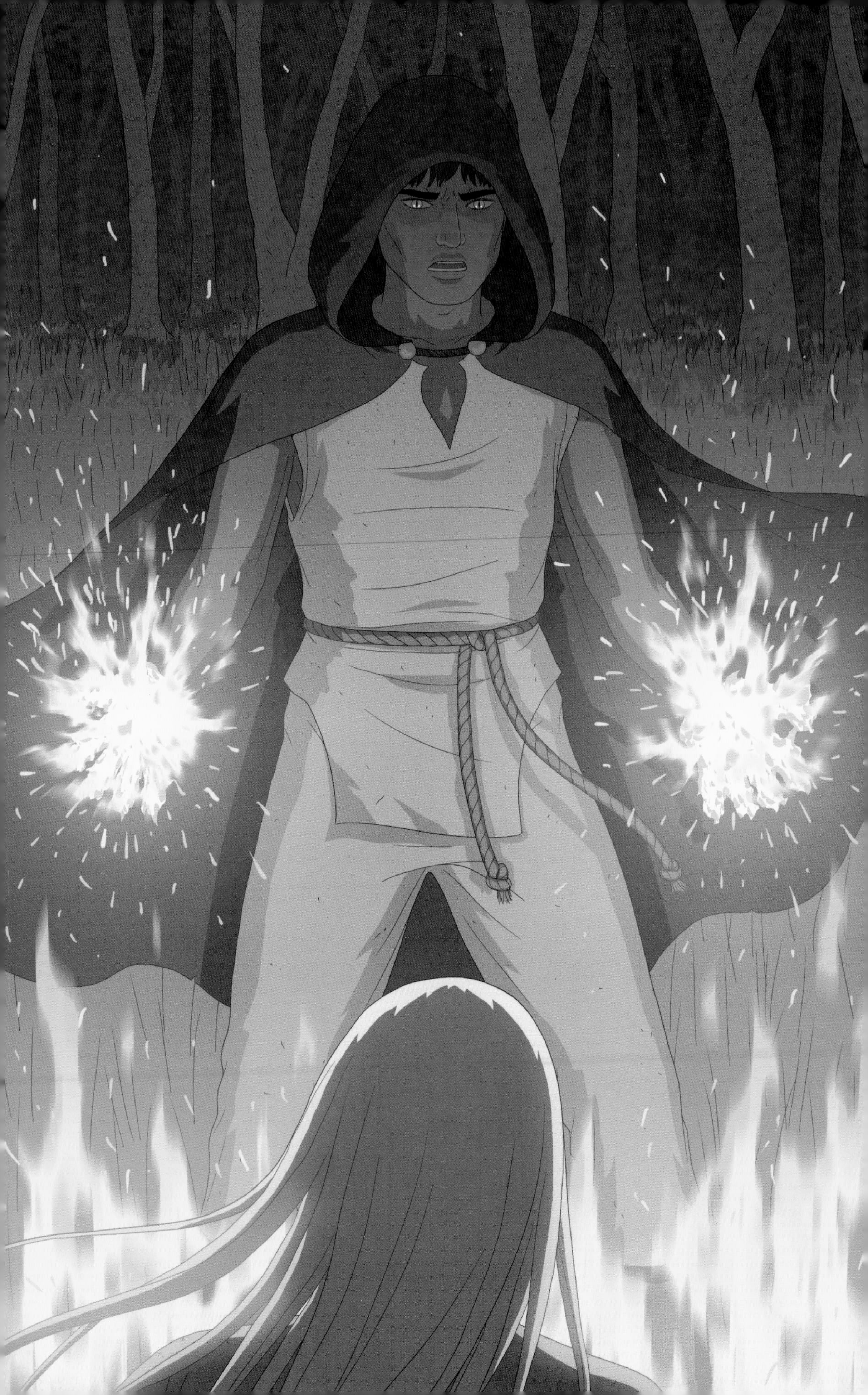

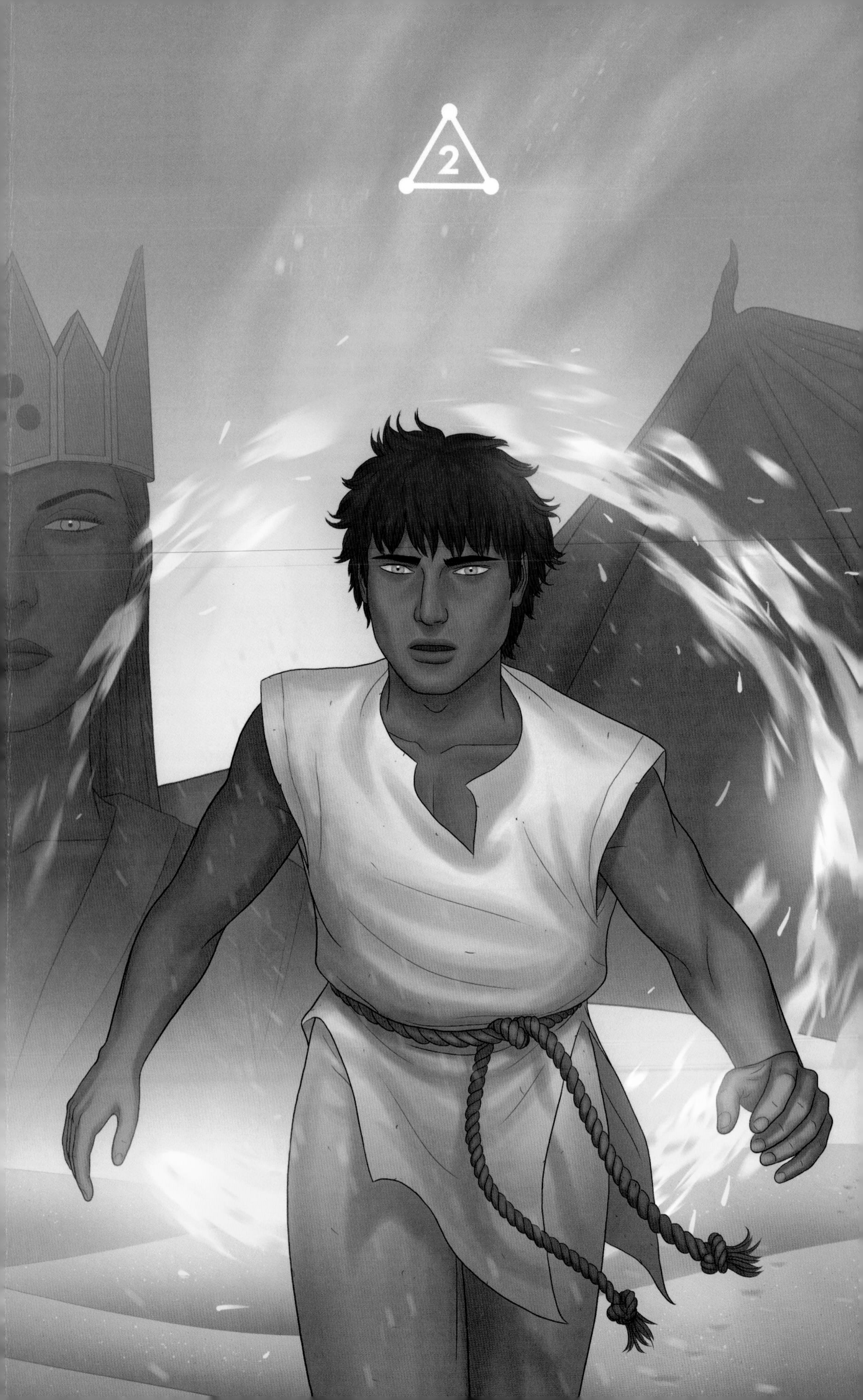
2

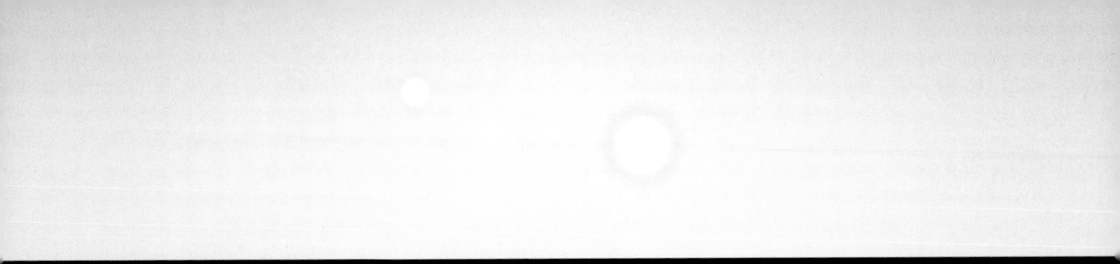

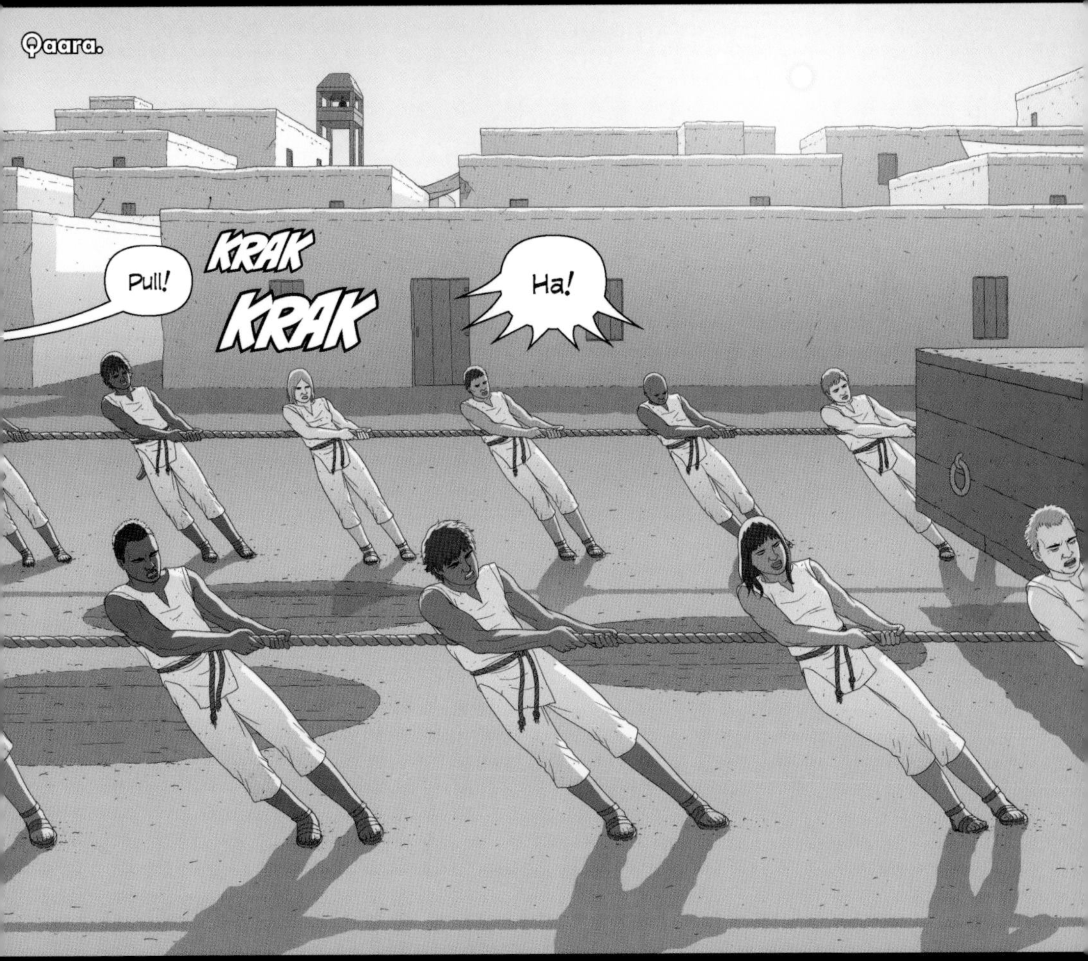
Qaara.
Pull!
KRAK
KRAK
Ha!

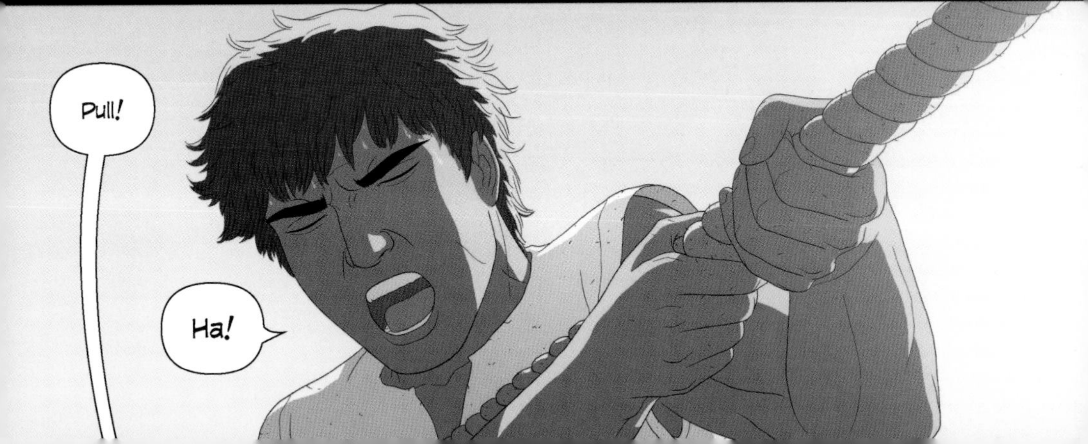
Pull!
Ha!

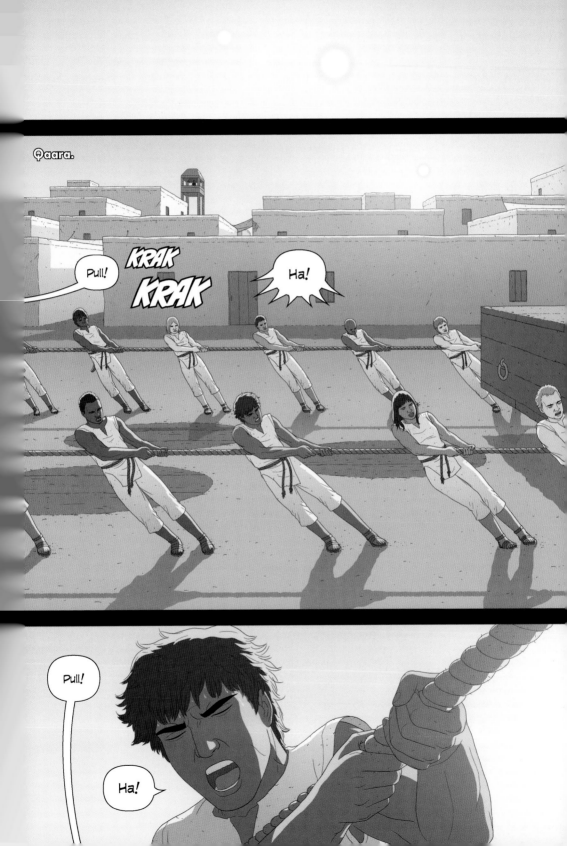

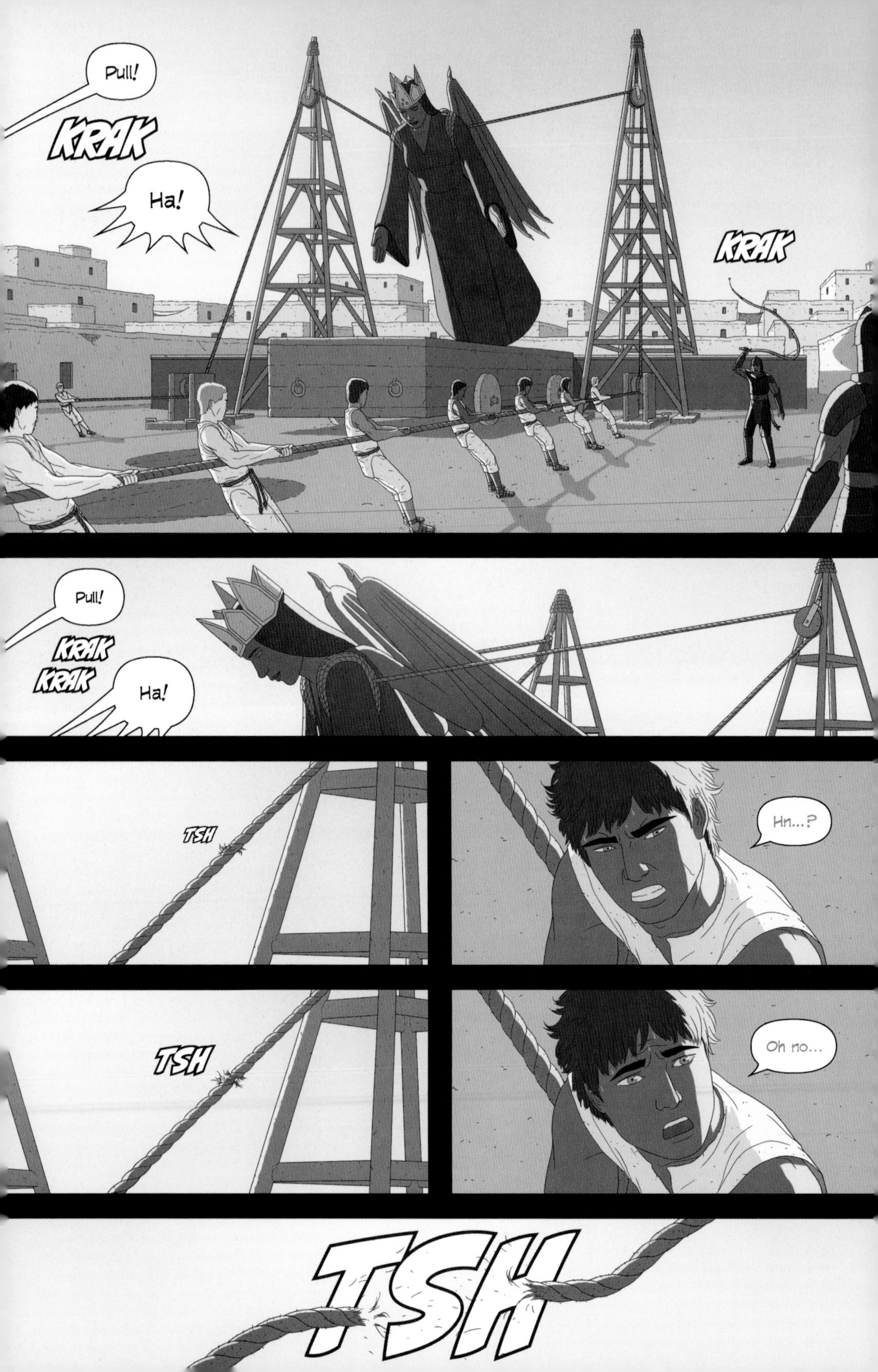
Pull!
KRAK
Ha!
KRAK
Pull!
KRAK
KRAK
Ha!
TSH
Hn...?
TSH
Oh no...
TSH

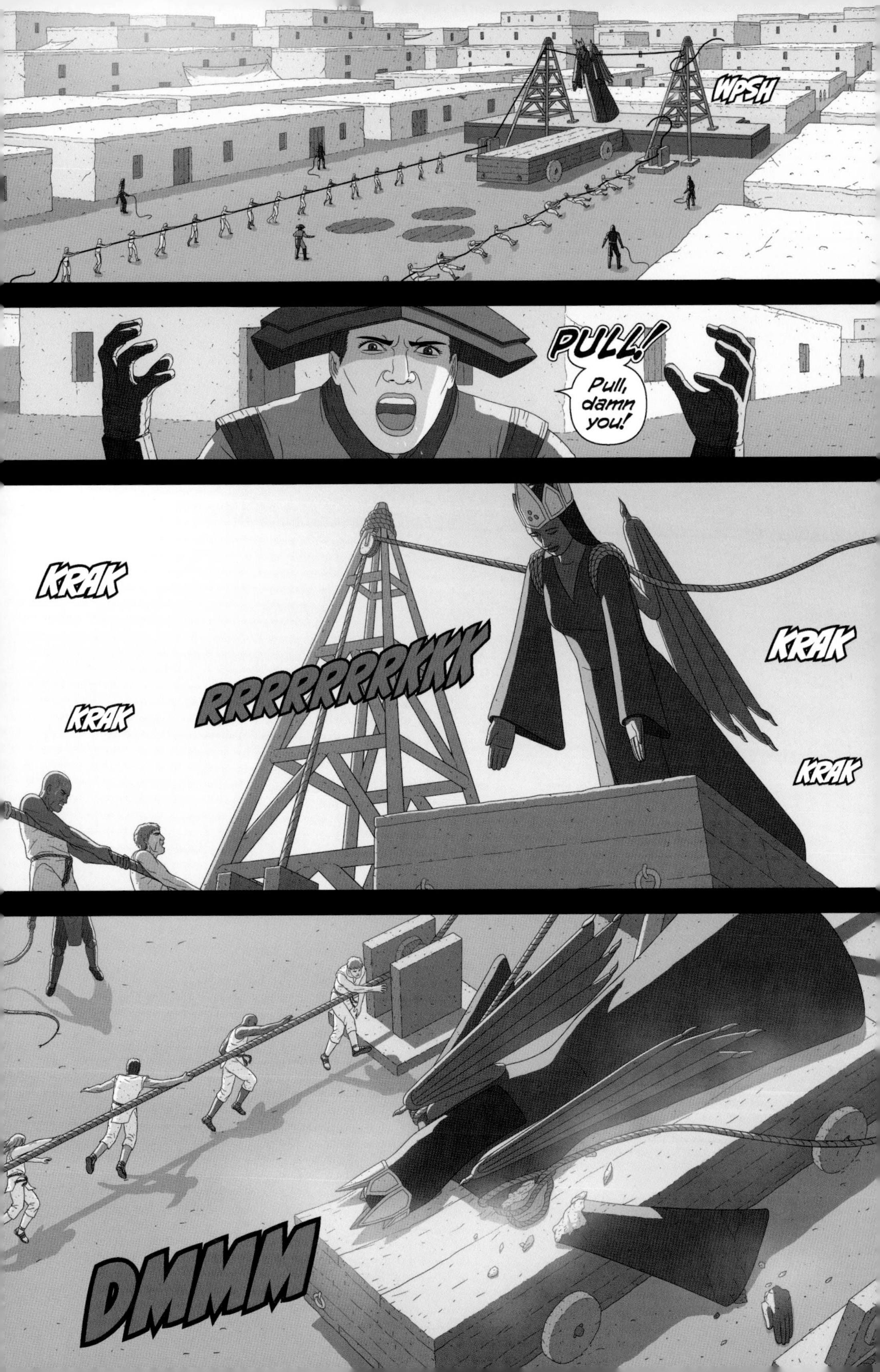
WPSH
PULL!
Pull, damn you!
KRAK
RRRRRRRKKK
KRAK
KRAK
KRAK
DMMM

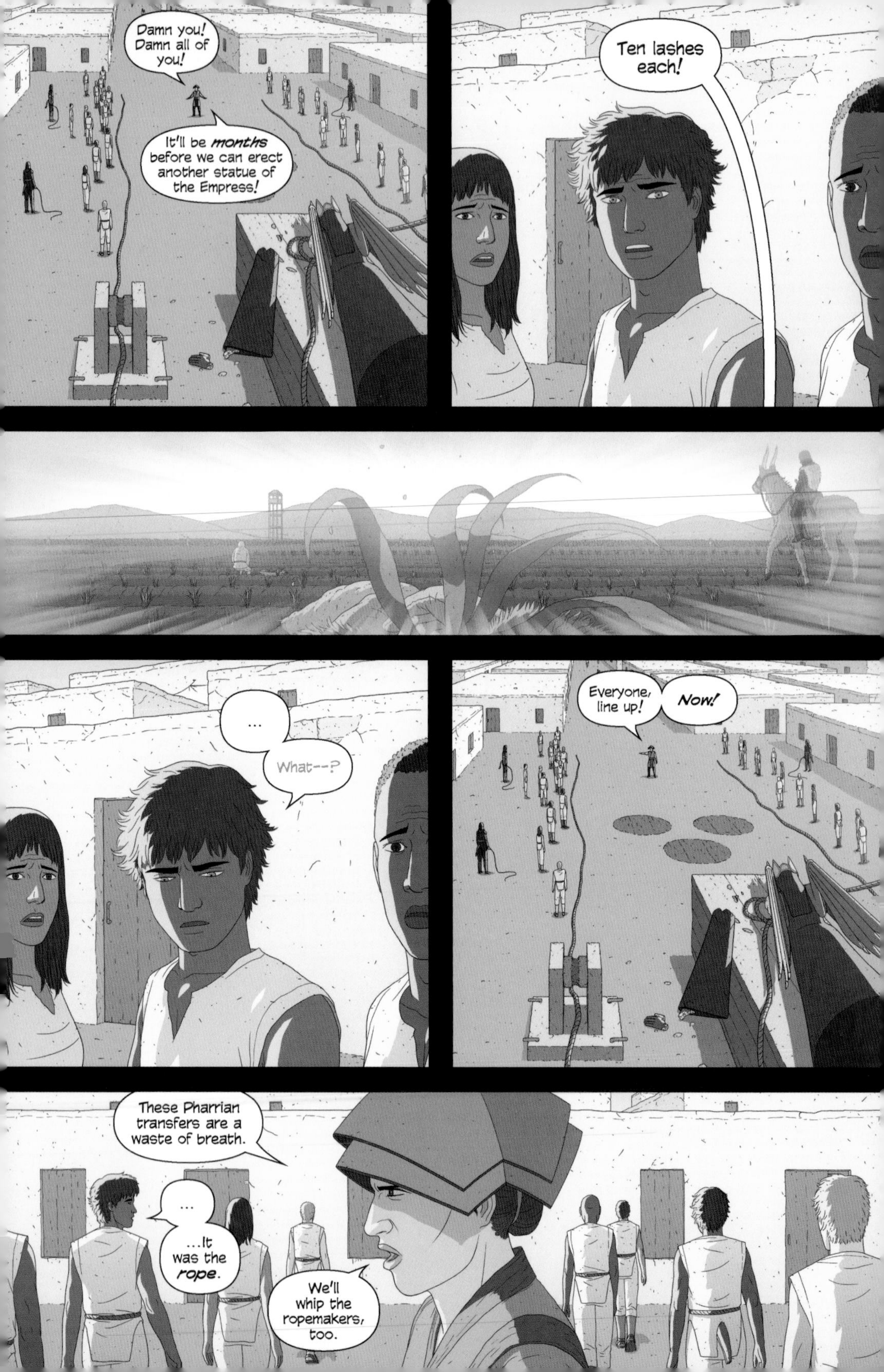
Damn you! Damn all of you!
It'll be *months* before we can erect another statue of the Empress!
Ten lashes each!
...
What--?
Everyone, line up!
Now!
These Pharrian transfers are a waste of breath.
...
...It was the *rope*.
We'll whip the ropemakers, too.

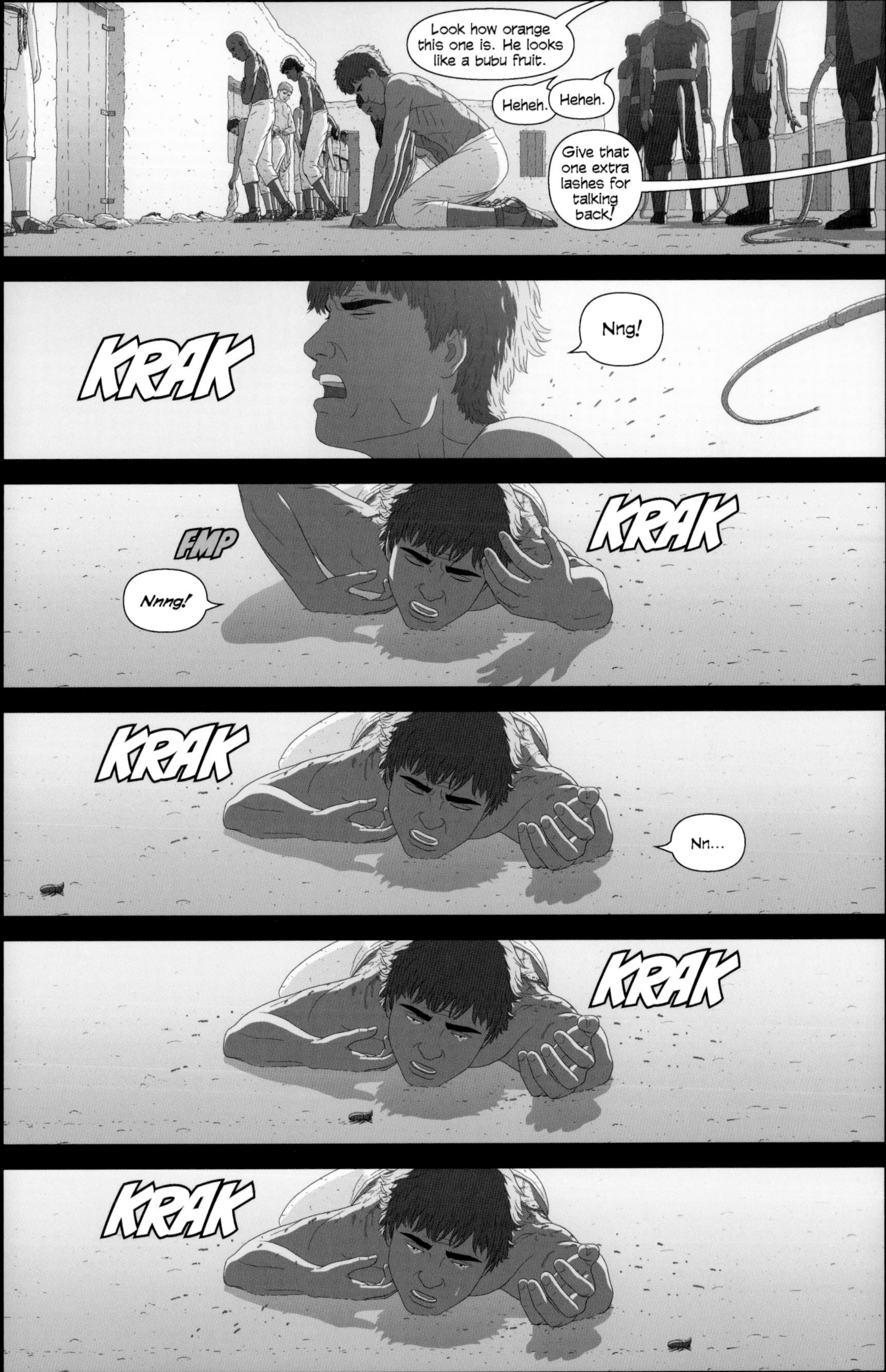
Look how orange this one is. He looks like a bubu fruit.
Heheh.
Heheh.
Give that one extra lashes for talking back!
KRAK
Nng!
FMP
Nnng!
KRAK
KRAK
Nn...
KRAK
KRAK

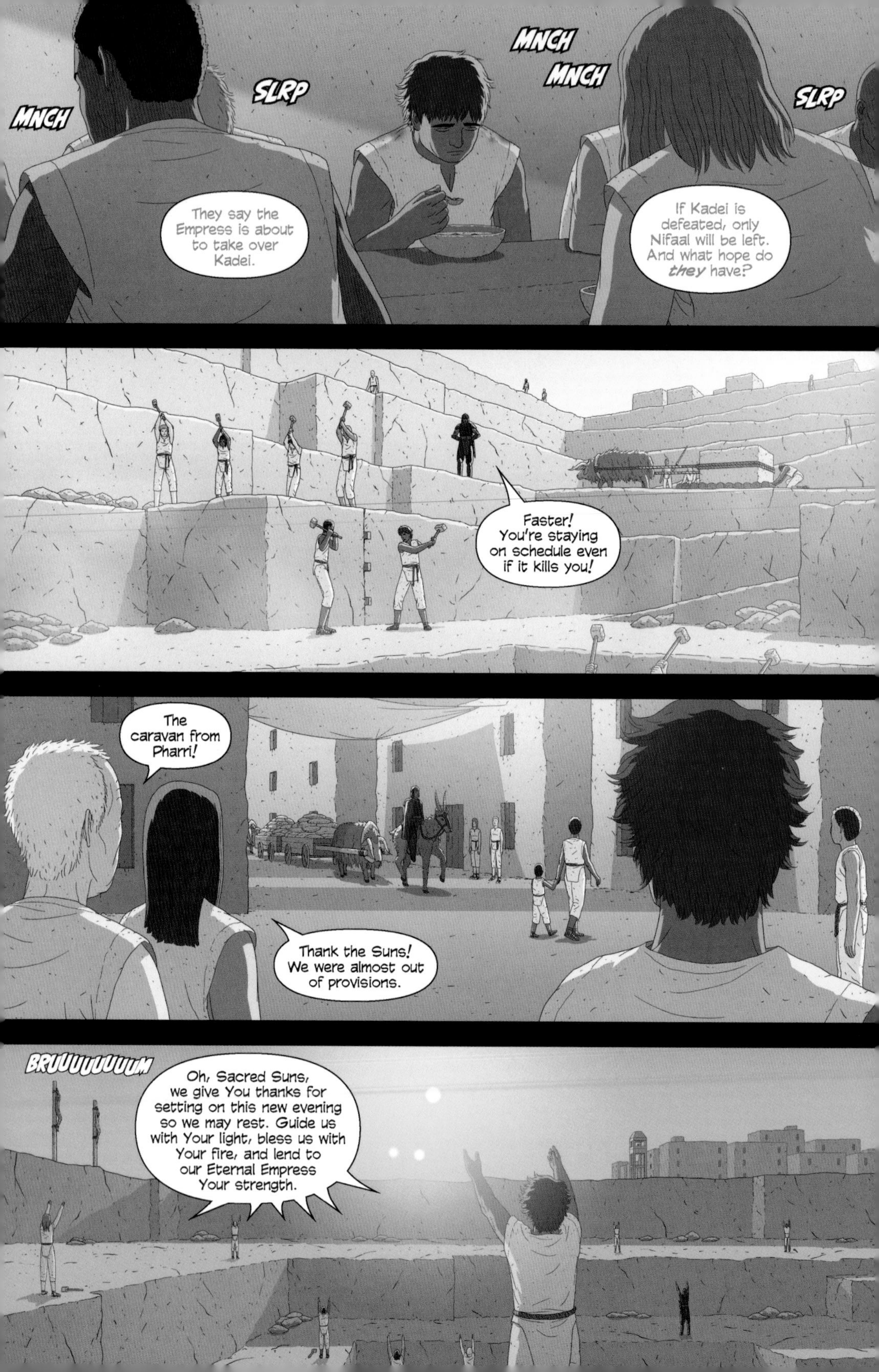
MNCH
SLRP
MNCH
MNCH
SLRP
They say the Empress is about to take over Kadei.
If Kadei is defeated, only Nifaal will be left. And what hope do *they* have?
Faster! You're staying on schedule even if it kills you!
The caravan from Pharri!
Thank the Suns! We were almost out of provisions.
BRUUUUUUUUM
Oh, Sacred Suns, we give You thanks for setting on this new evening so we may rest. Guide us with Your light, bless us with Your fire, and lend to our Eternal Empress Your strength.

BRUUUUUUUM

BRUUUUUUUM

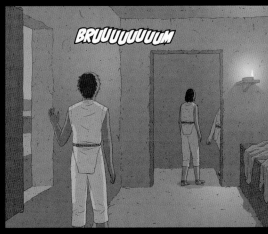

BRUUUUUUUM

Nnf!

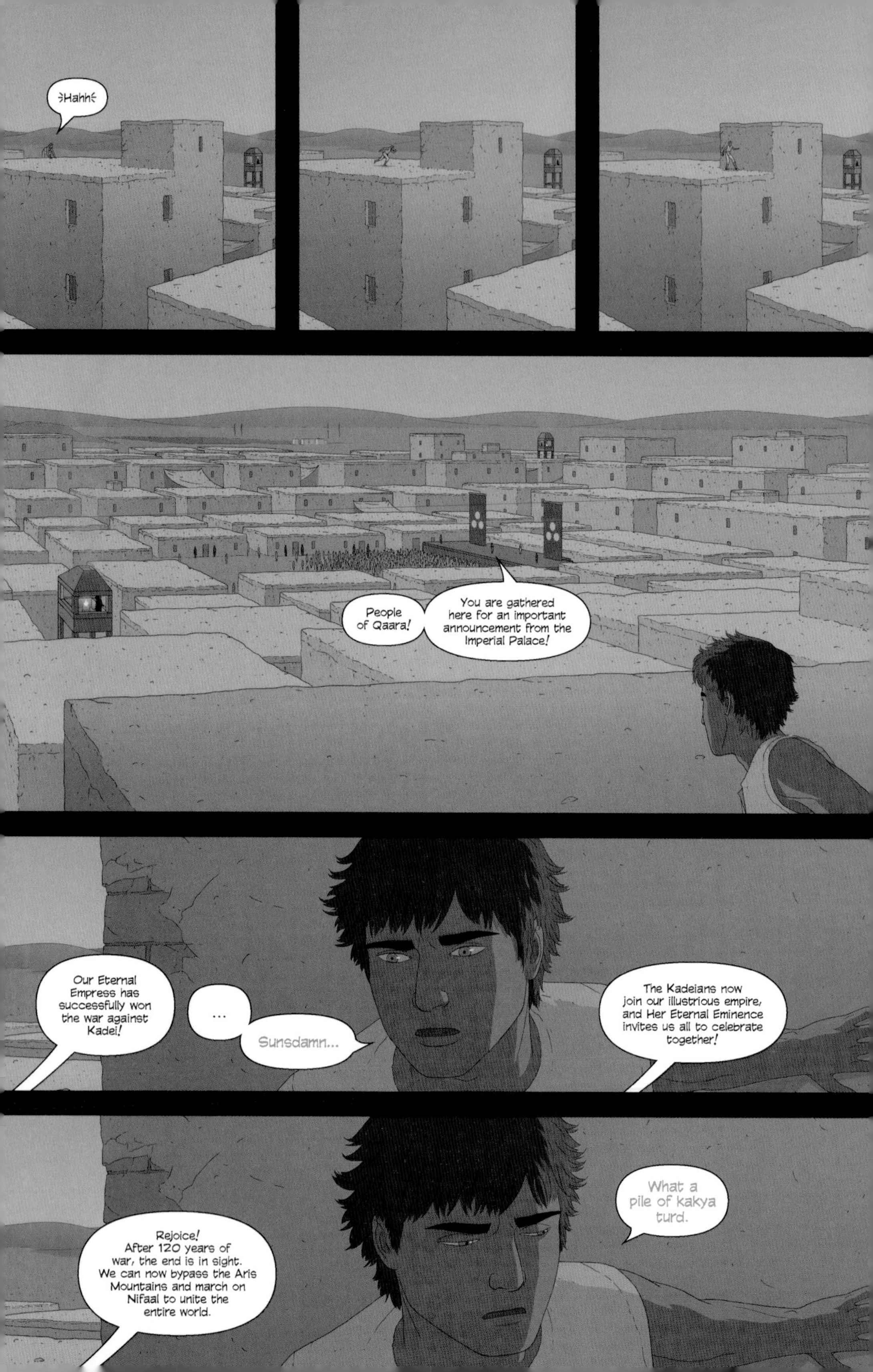
Hahh
People of Qaara!
You are gathered here for an important announcement from the Imperial Palace!
Our Eternal Empress has successfully won the war against Kadei!
...
Sunsdamn...
The Kadeians now join our illustrious empire, and Her Eternal Eminence invites us all to celebrate together!
Rejoice! After 120 years of war, the end is in sight. We can now bypass the Aris Mountains and march on Nifaal to unite the entire world.
What a pile of kakya turd.

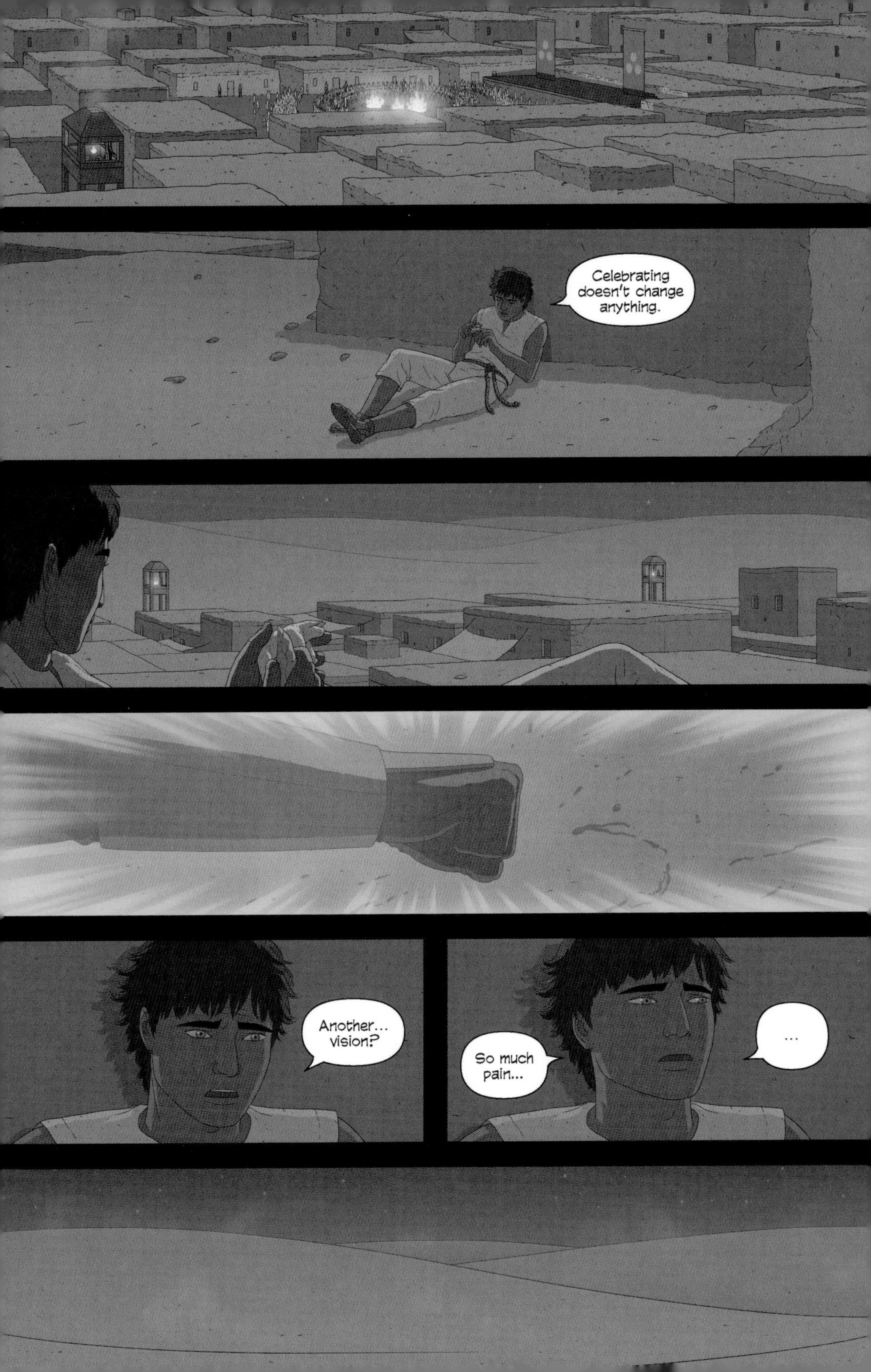
Celebrating doesn't change anything.
Another... vision?
So much pain...
...

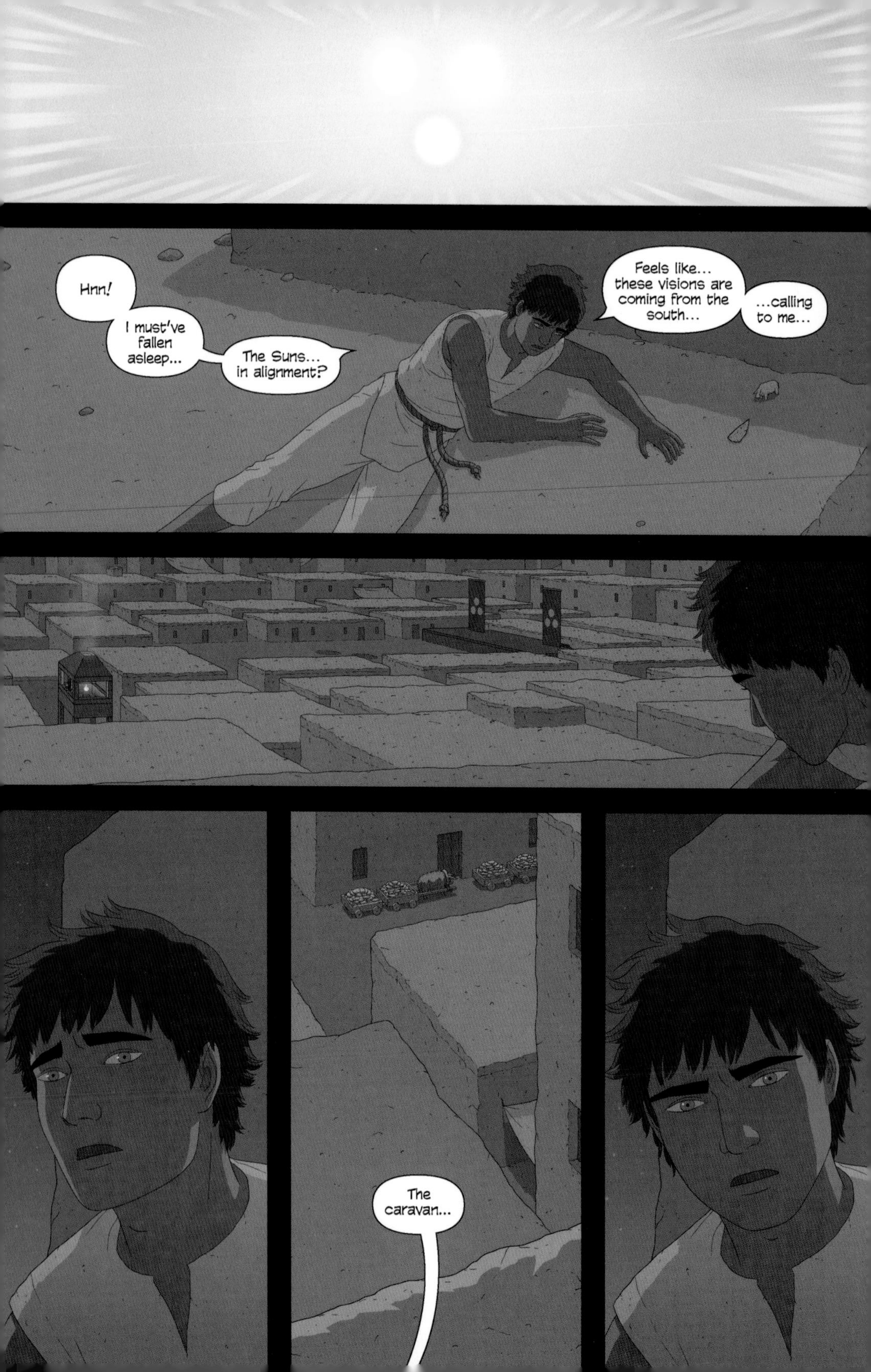
Hnn!
I must've fallen asleep...
The Suns... in alignment?
Feels like... these visions are coming from the south...
...calling to me...
The caravan...

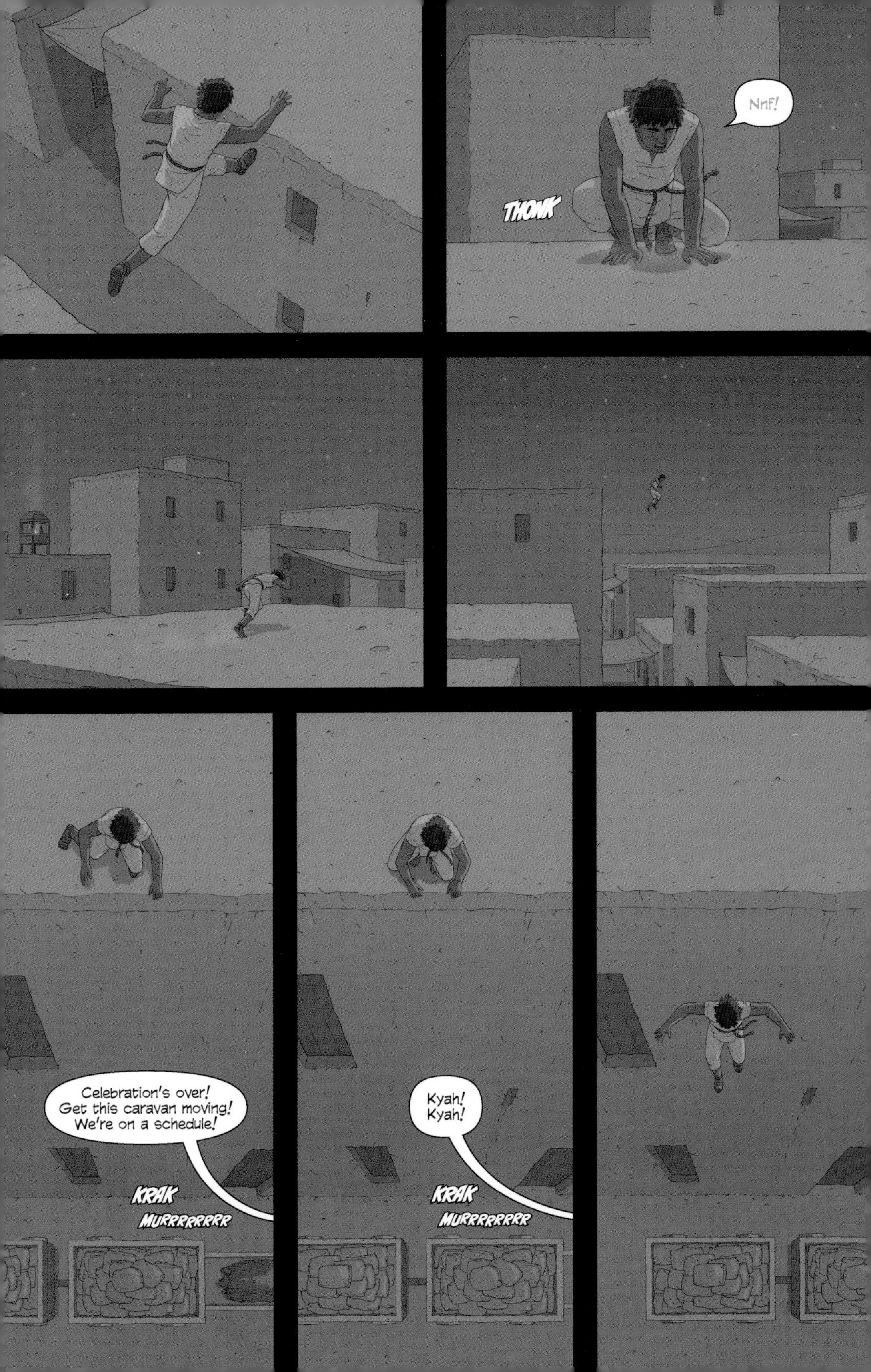
Nnf!
THONK
Celebration's over! Get this caravan moving! We're on a schedule!
KRAK
MURRRRRRR
Kyah! Kyah!
KRAK
MURRRRRRRR

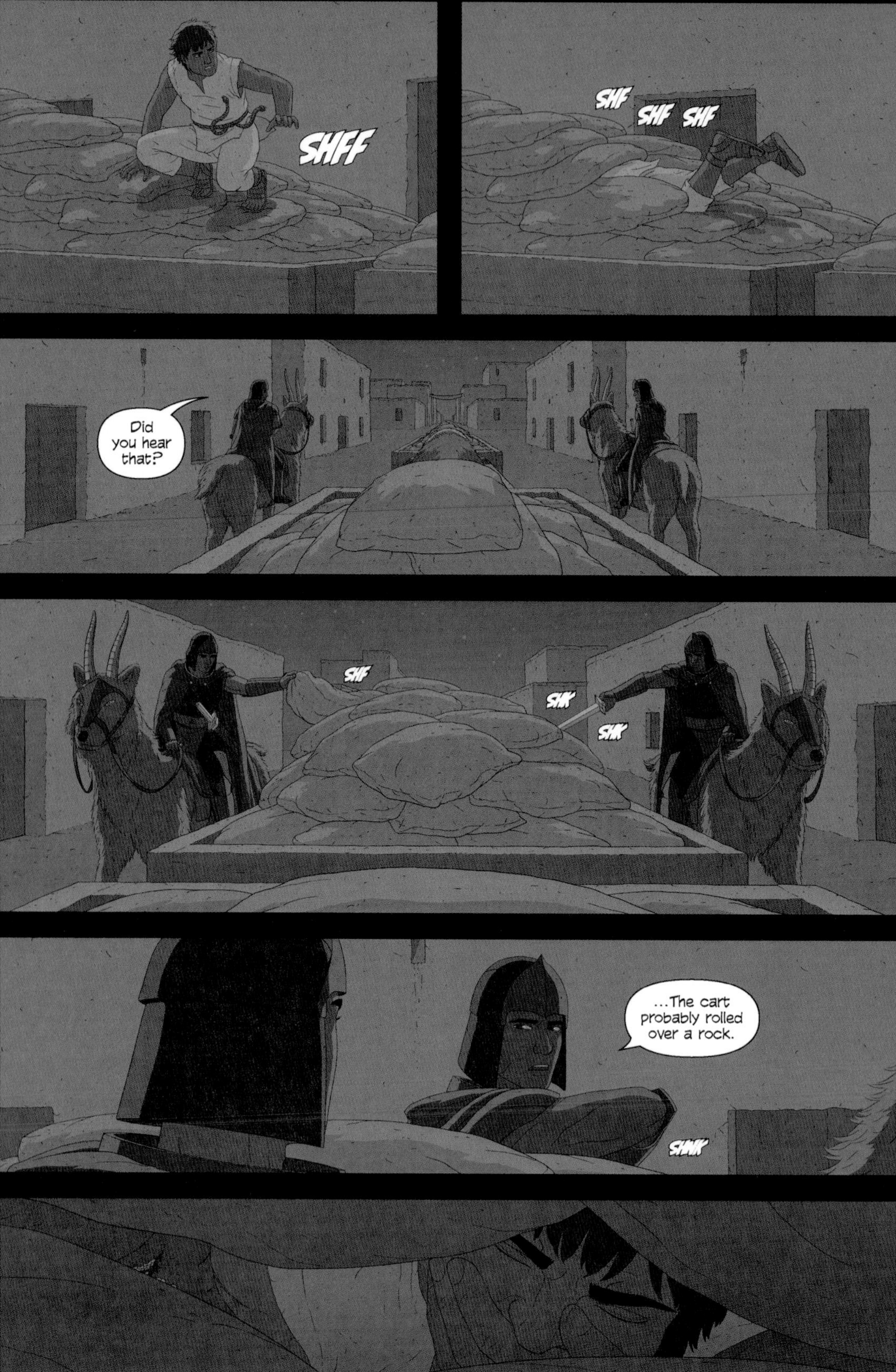
SHFF
SHF
SHF
SHF
Did you hear that?
SHF
SHK
SHK
...The cart probably rolled over a rock.
SHNK

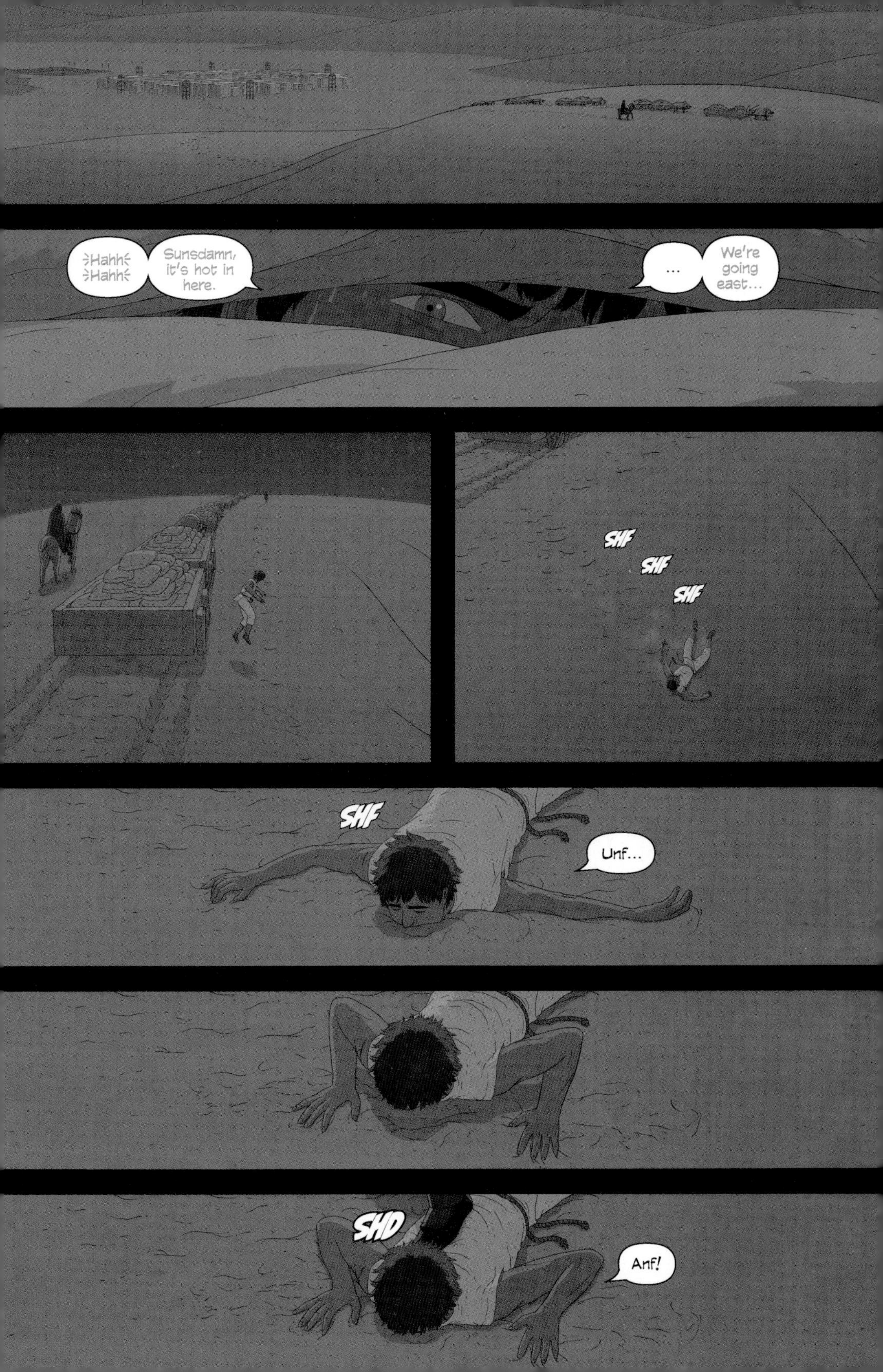

Hahh Hahh
Sunsdamn, it's hot in here.
...
We're going east...
SHF
SHF
SHF
SHF
Unf...
SHD
Anf!

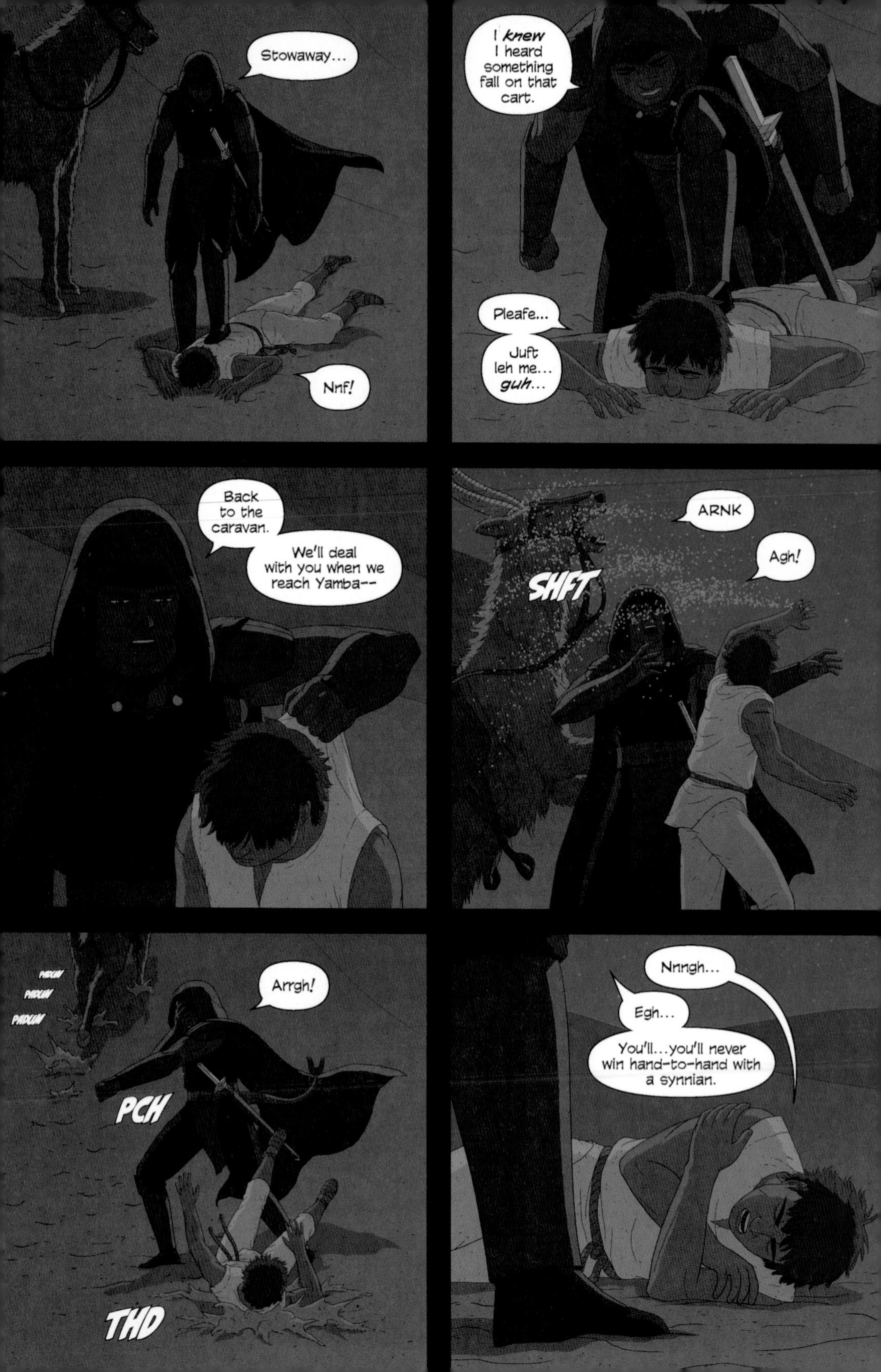

Stowaway...
Nnf!
I *knew* I heard something fall on that cart.
Pleafe...
Juft leh me... *guh*...
Back to the caravan.
We'll deal with you when we reach Yamba--
SHFT
ARNK
Agh!
PHDUM
PHDUM
PHDUM
Arrgh!
PCH
THD
Nnngh...
Egh...
You'll...you'll never win hand-to-hand with a synnian.

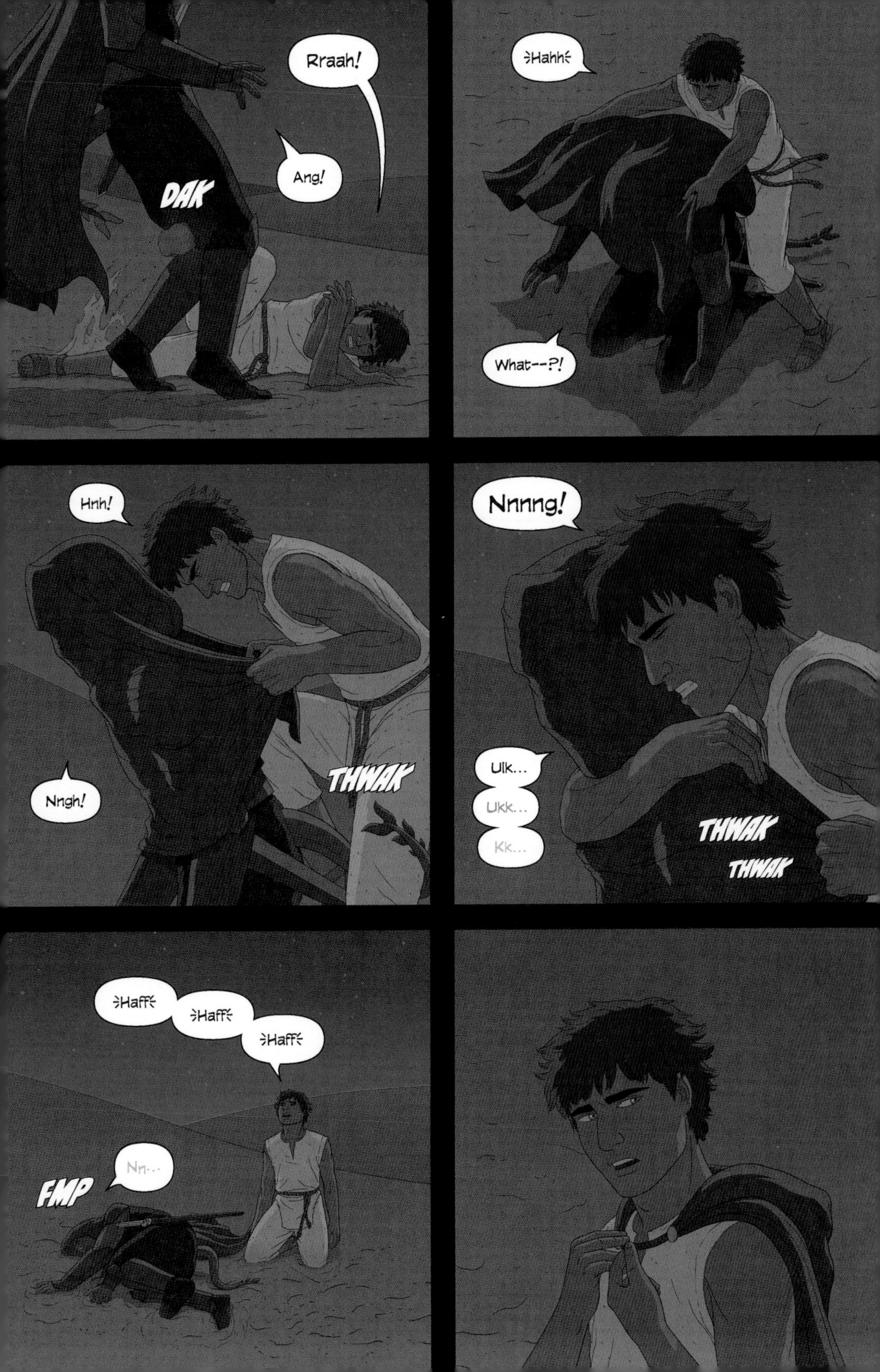
Rraah!
Ang!
DAK
Hahh
What--?!
Hnh!
Nngh!
THWAK
Nnnng!
Ulk...
Ukk...
Kk...
THWAK
THWAK
Haff
Haff
Haff
Nn...
FMP

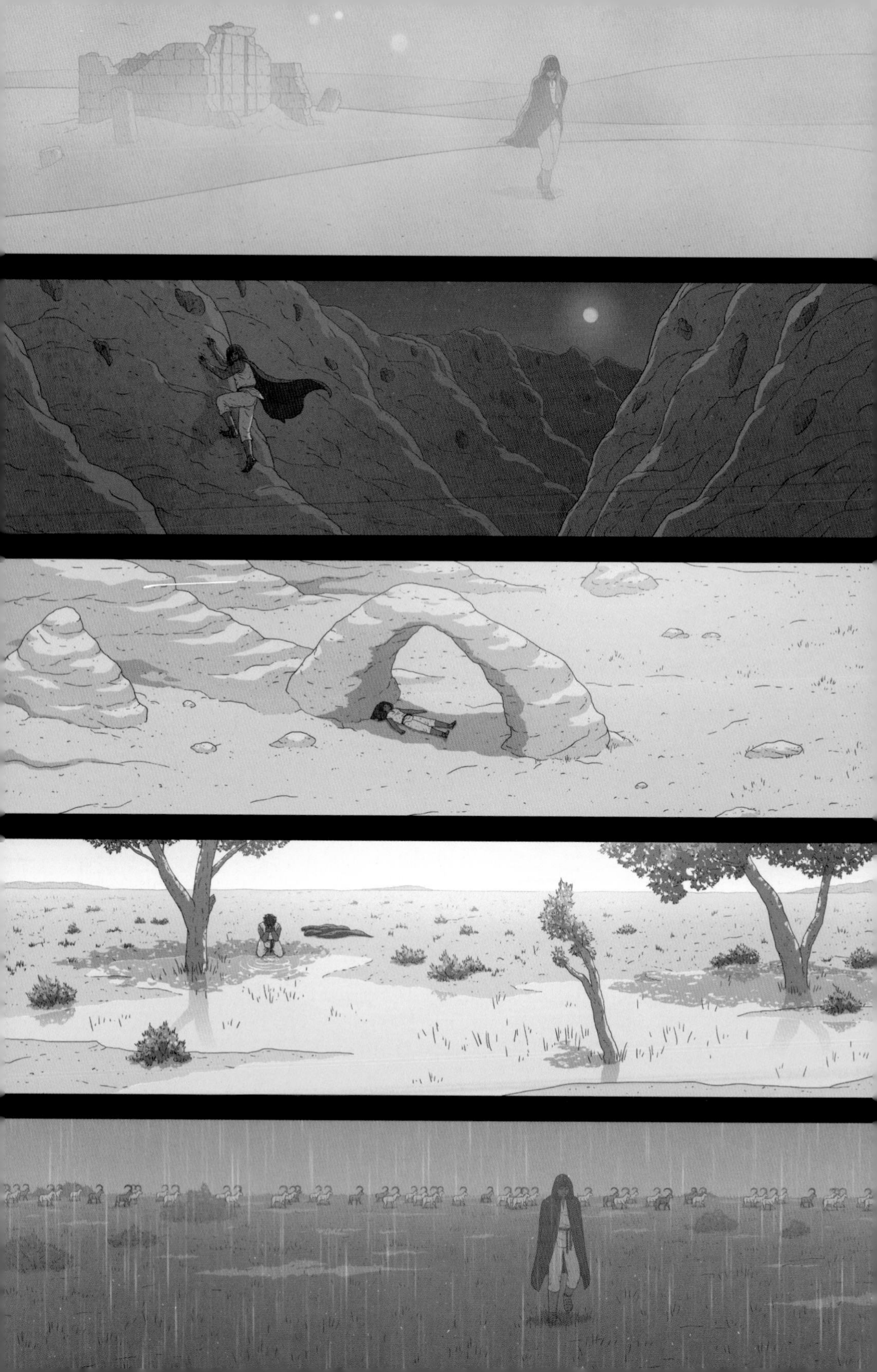

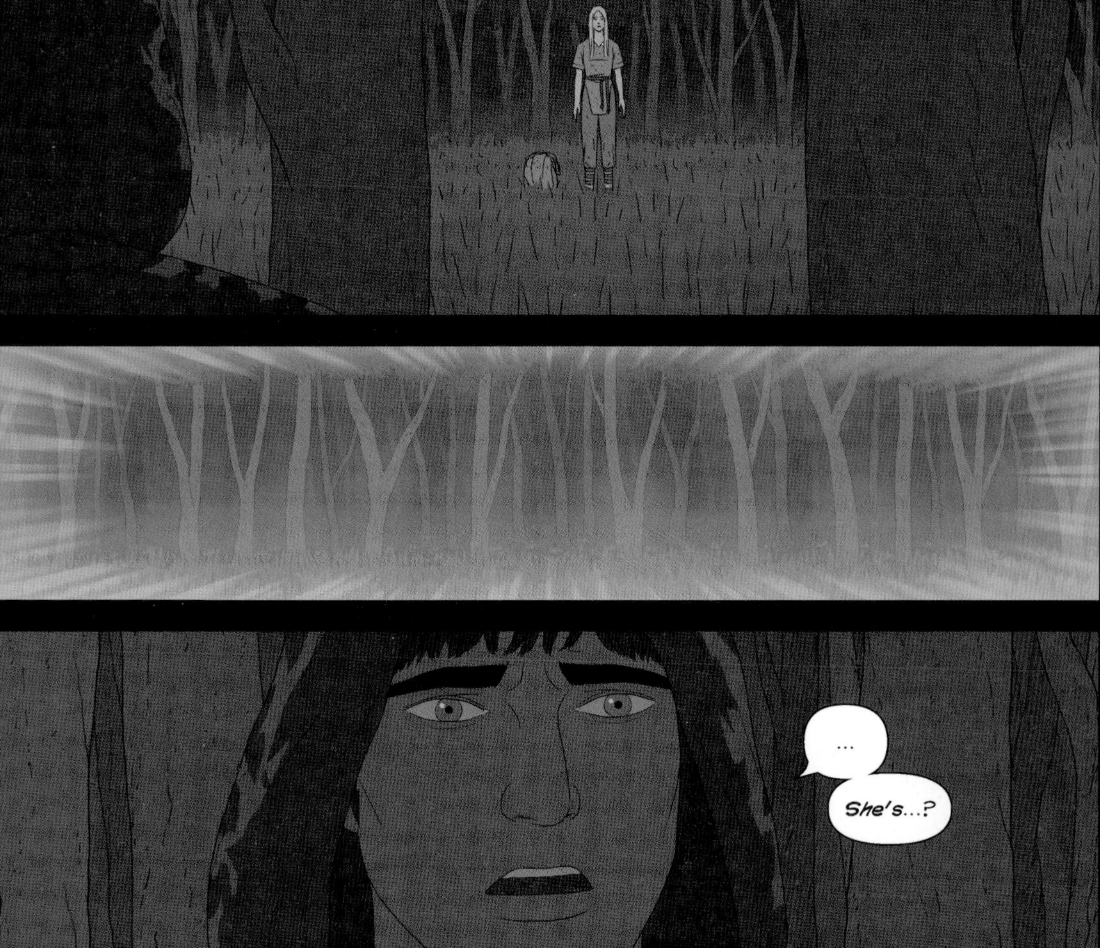
...
She's...?

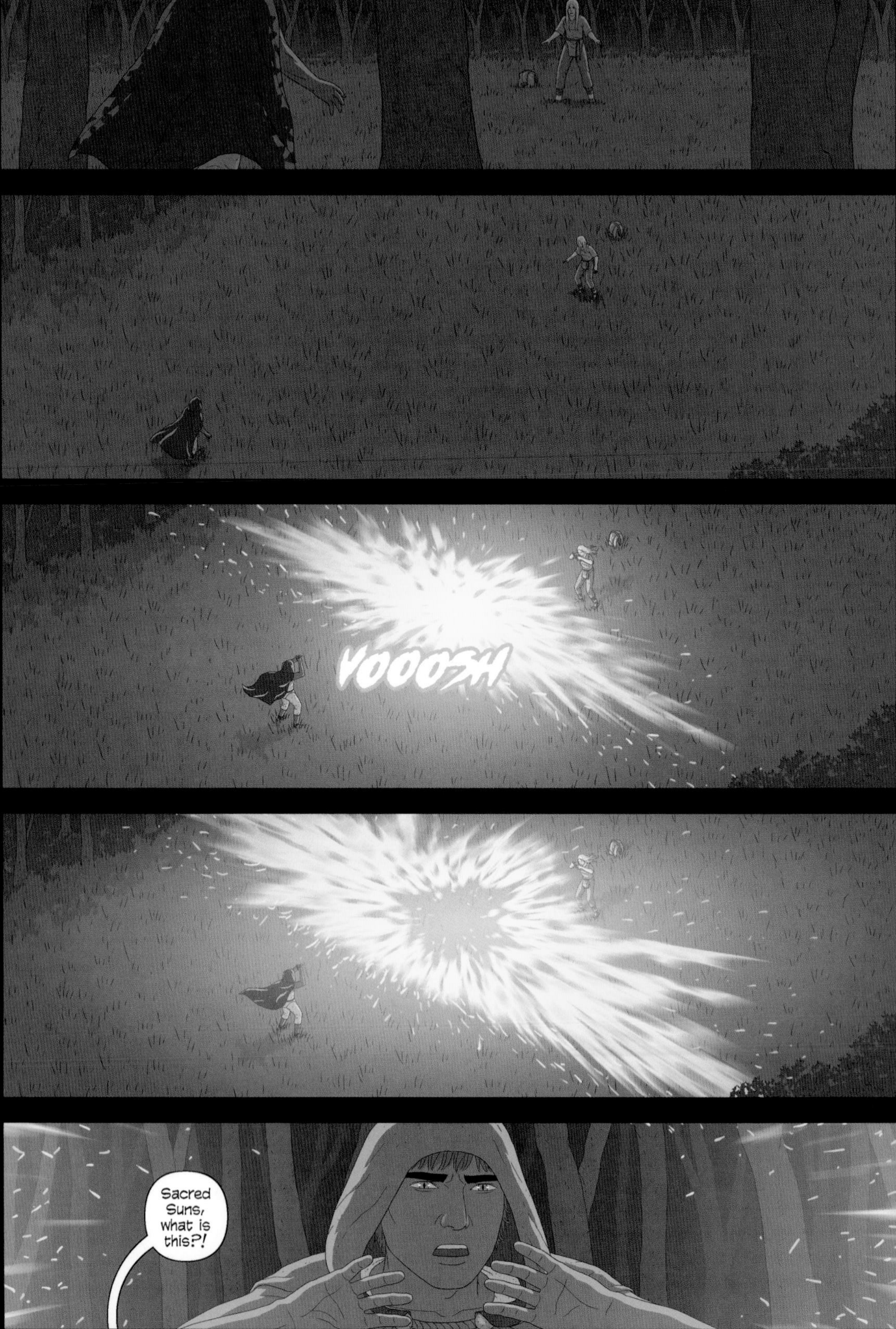
VOOOSH
Sacred Suns, what is this?!

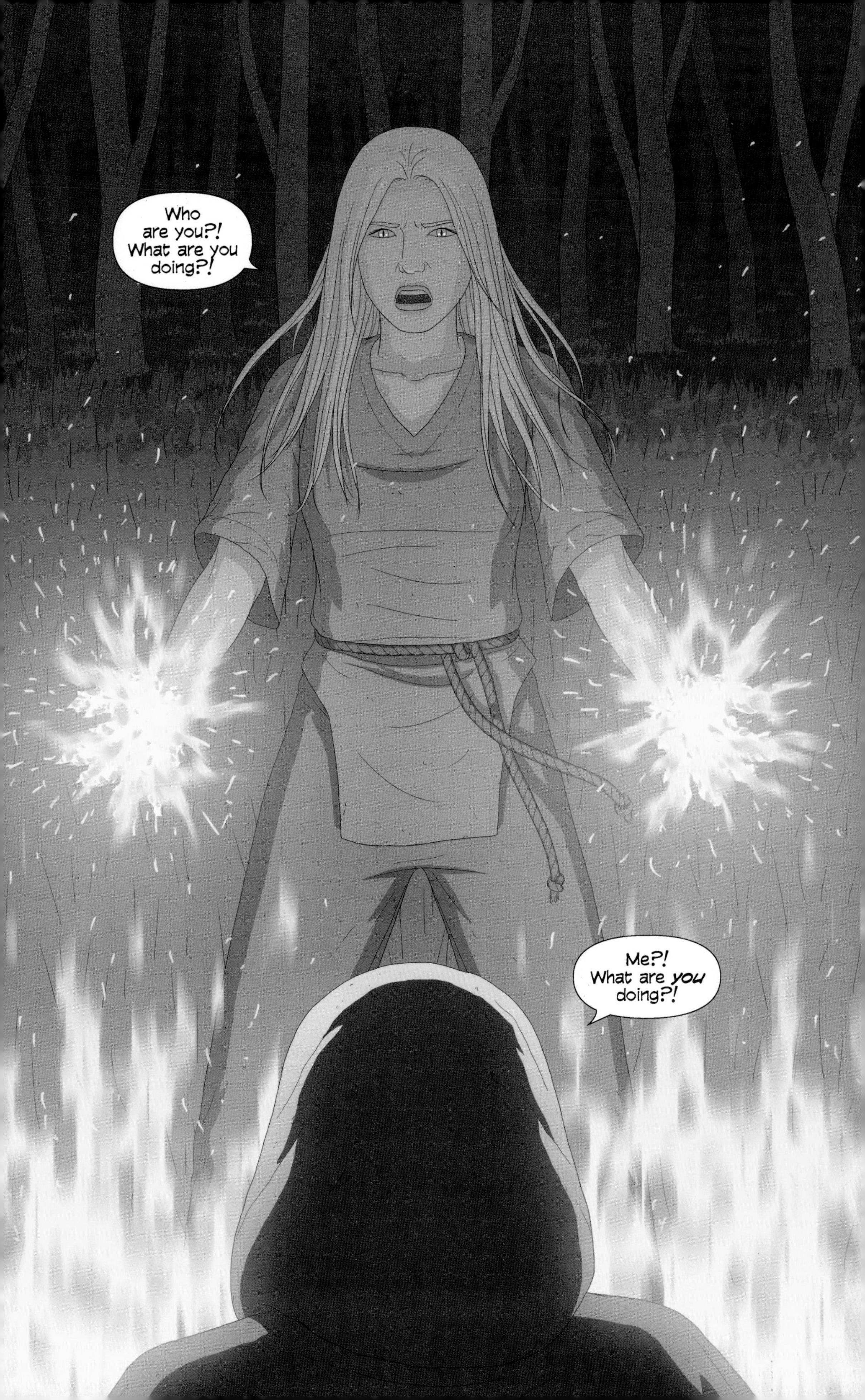
Who are you?! What are you doing?!
Me?! What are *you* doing?!

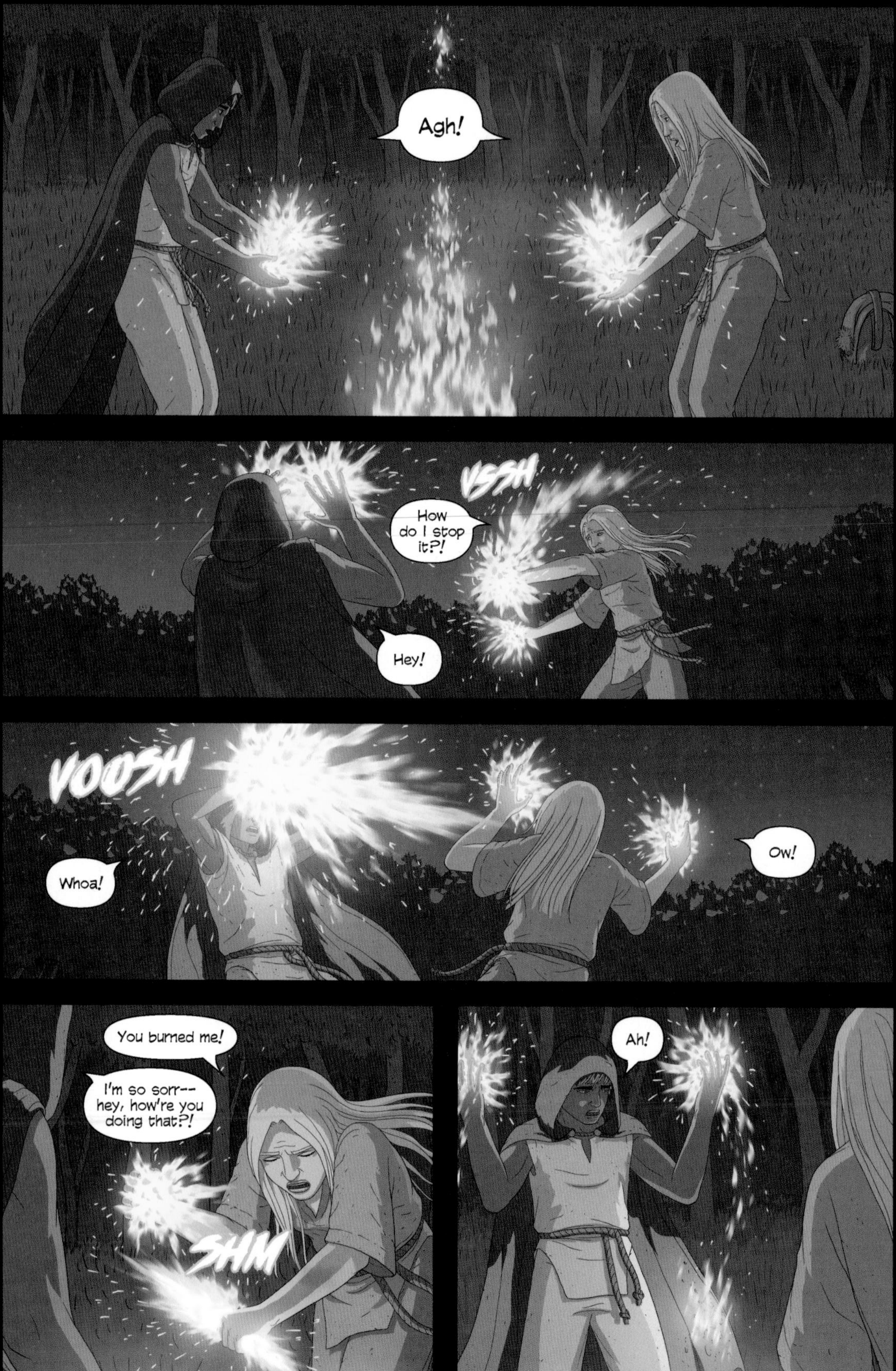
Agh!
VSSH
How do I stop it?!
Hey!
VOOSH
Whoa!
Ow!
You burned me!
I'm so sorr-- hey, how're you doing that?!
SHM
Ah!

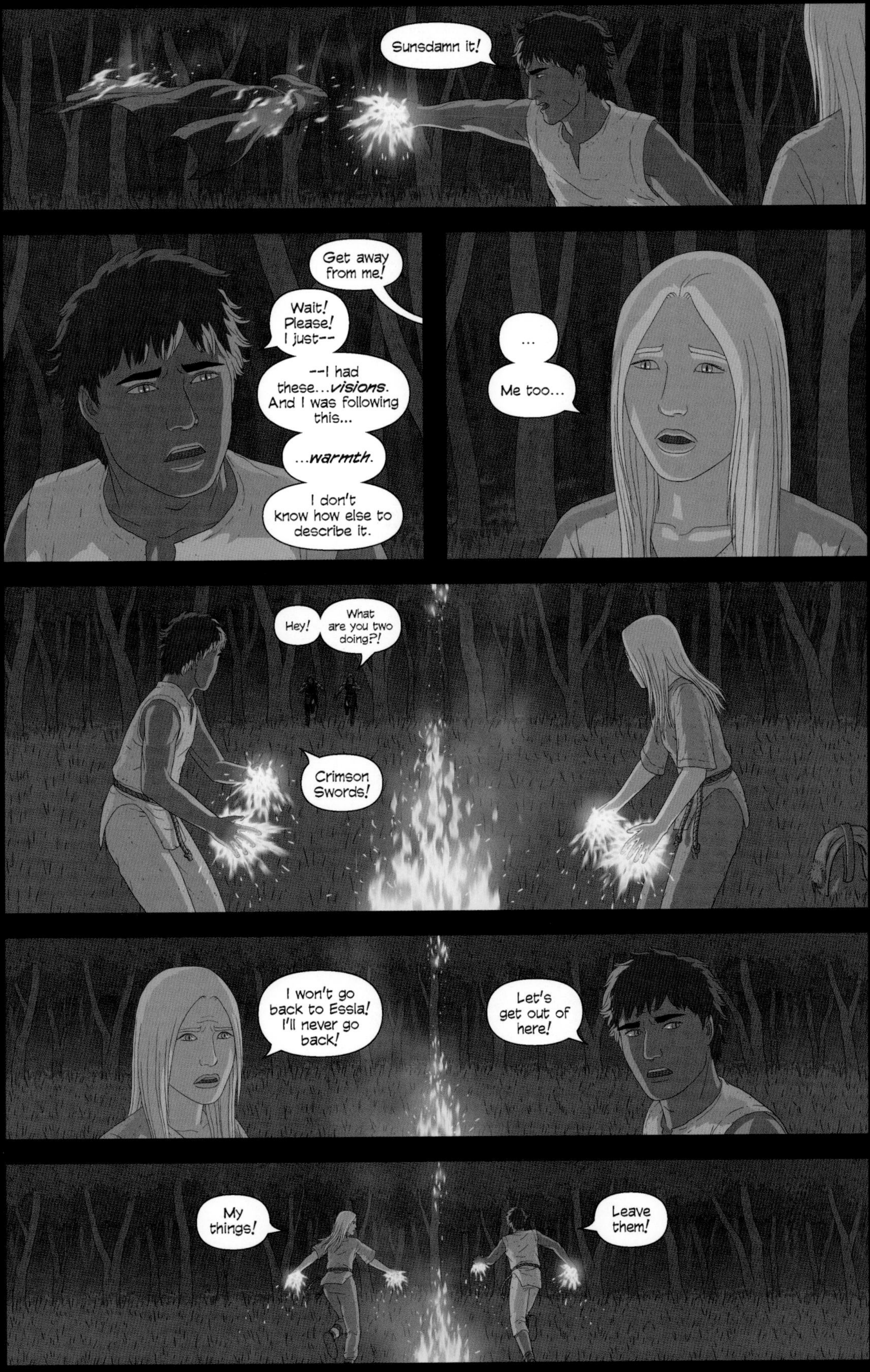
Sunsdamn it!
Get away from me!
Wait! Please! I just--
--I had these...*visions*. And I was following this...
...*warmth*.
I don't know how else to describe it.
...
Me too...
Hey!
What are you two doing?!
Crimson Swords!
I won't go back to Essia! I'll never go back!
Let's get out of here!
My things!
Leave them!

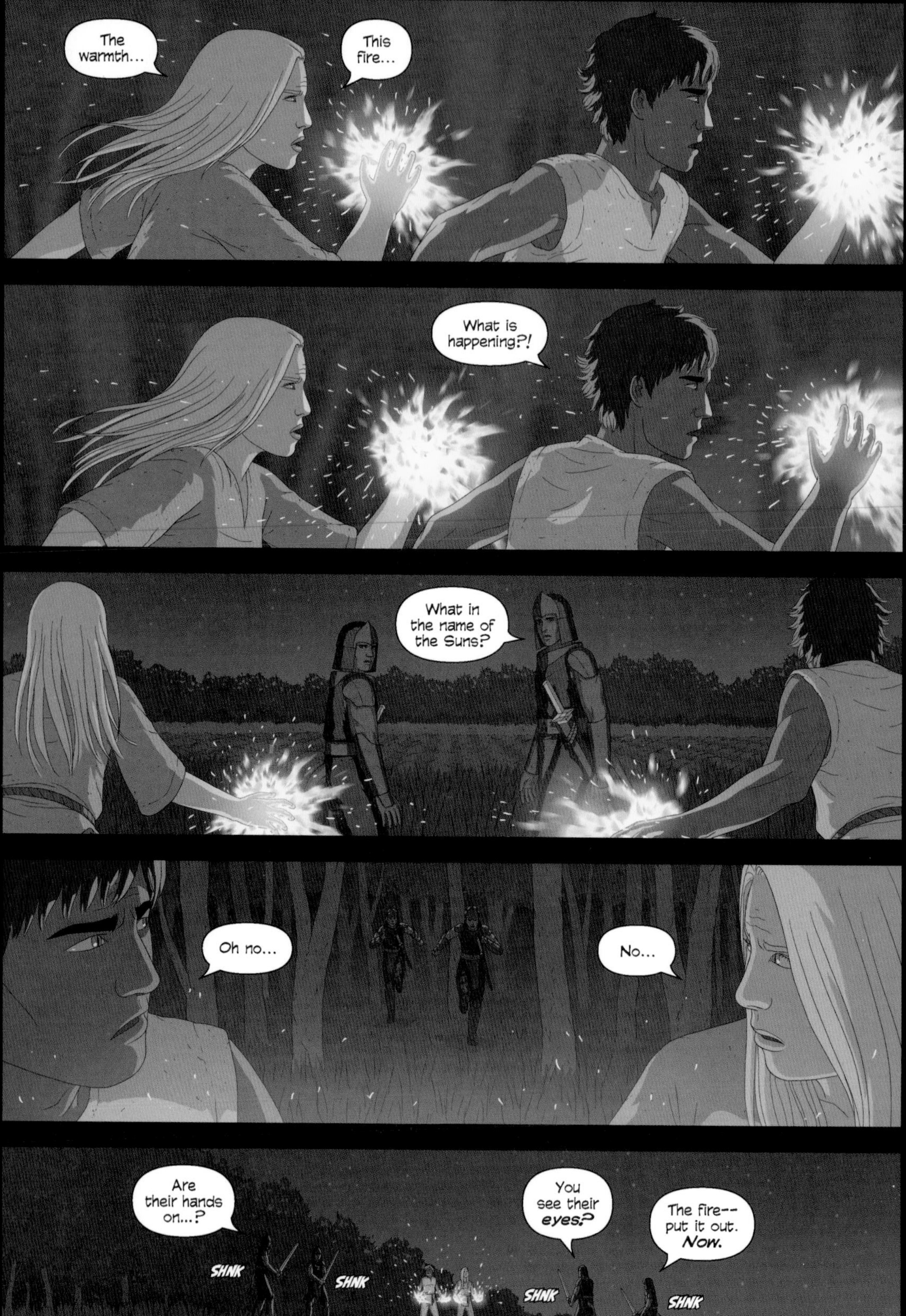
The warmth...
This fire...
What is happening?!
What in the name of the Suns?
Oh no...
No...
Are their hands on...?
SHNK
SHNK
You see their *eyes?*
SHNK
The fire-- put it out. ***Now.***
SHNK

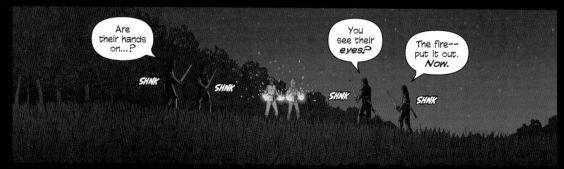

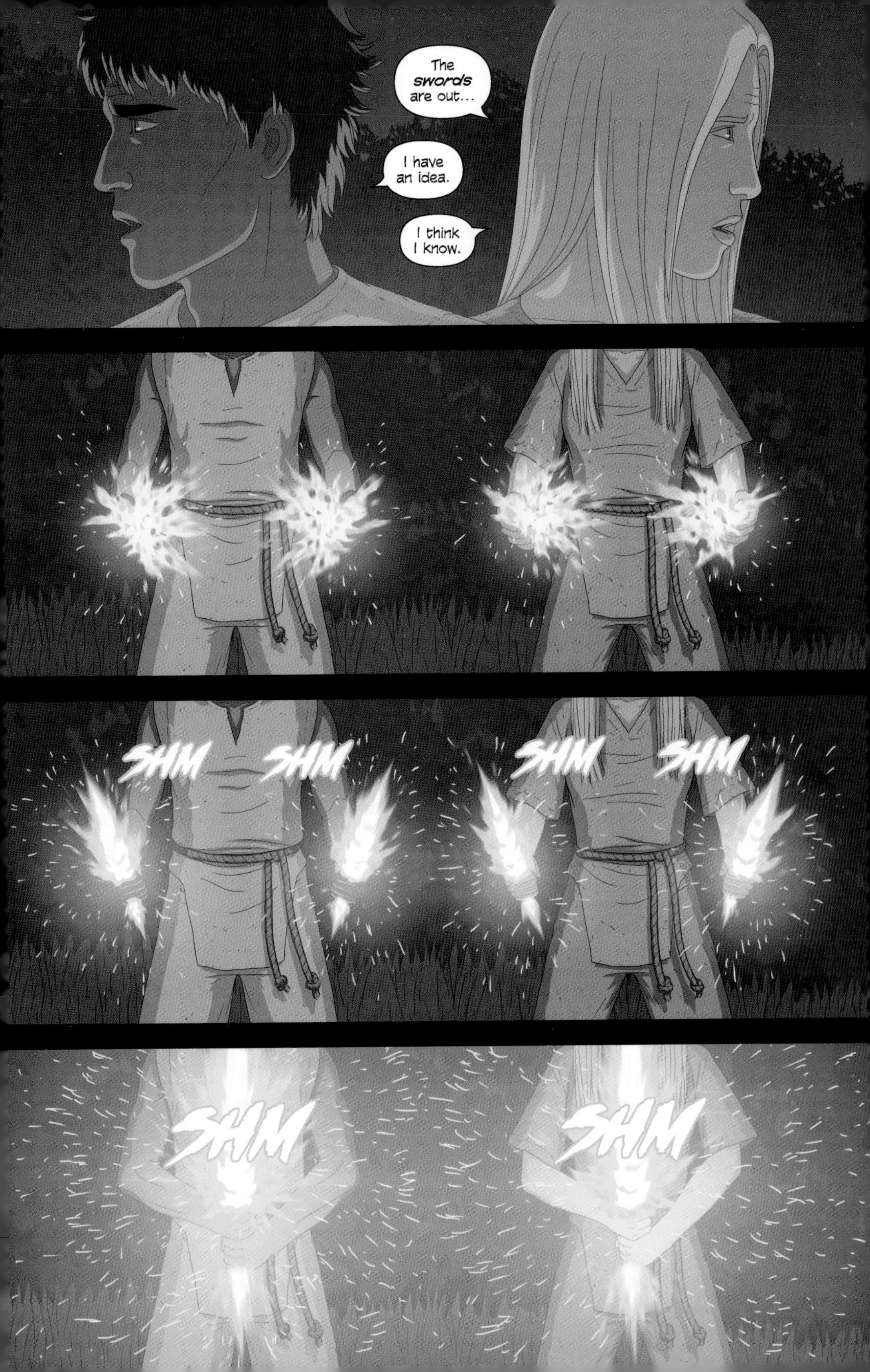
The swords are out...
I have an idea.
I think I know.
SHM
SHM
SHM
SHM
SHM
SHM

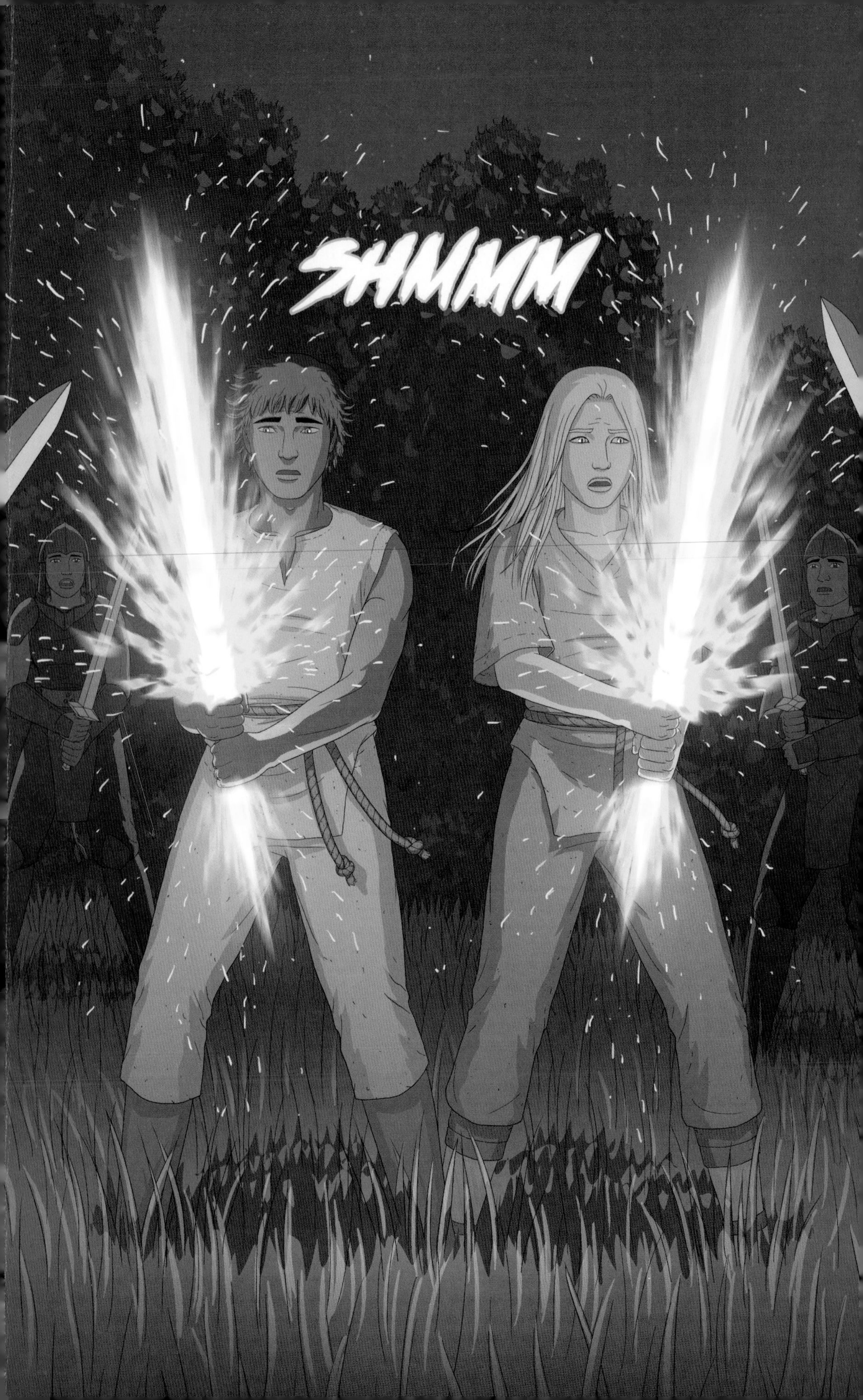
SHMMM

3

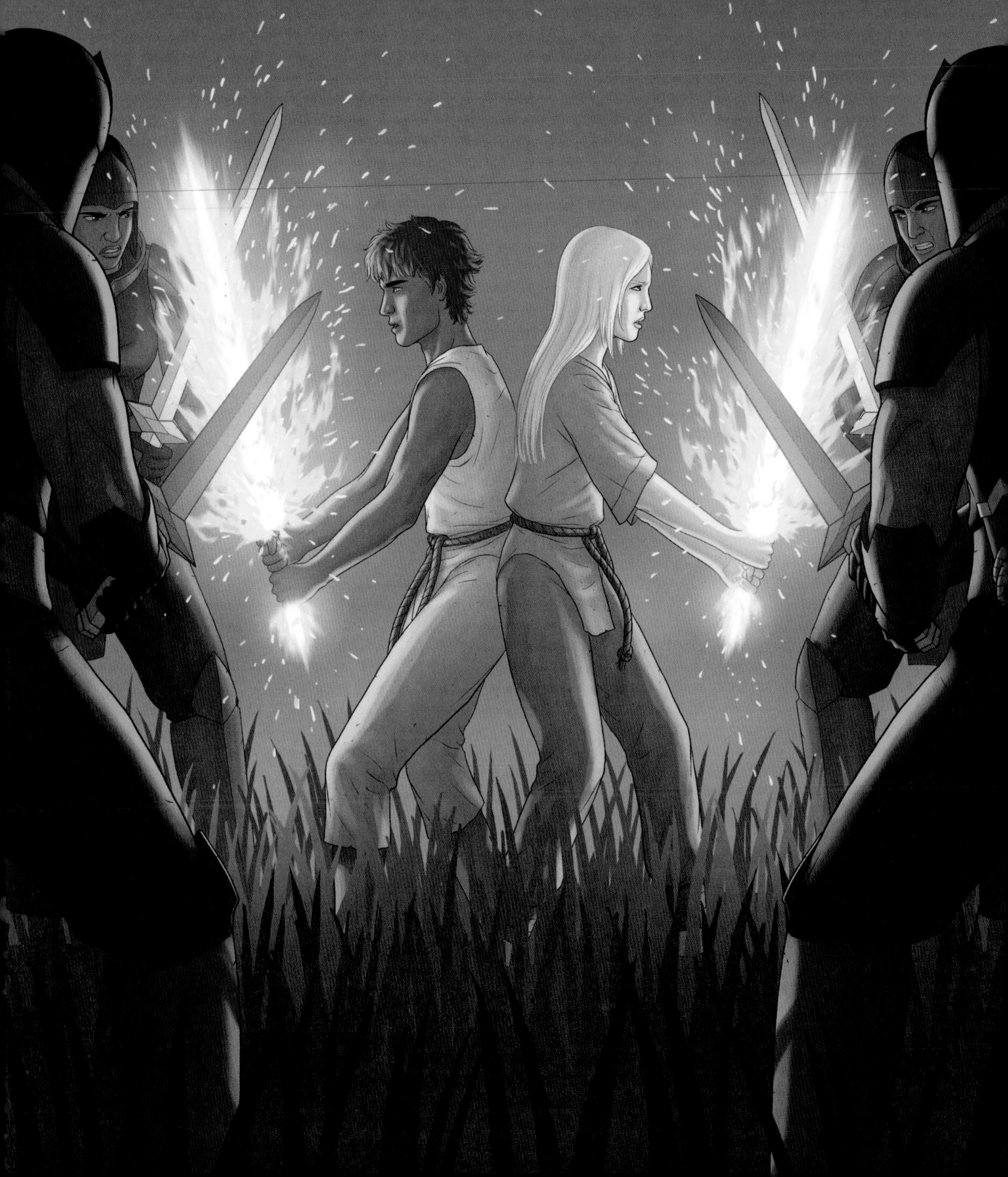

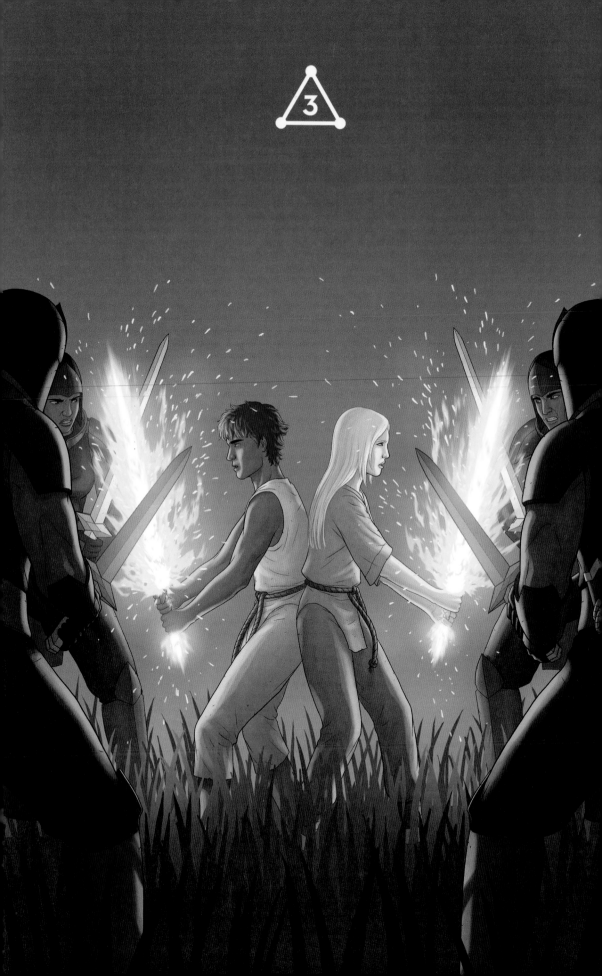

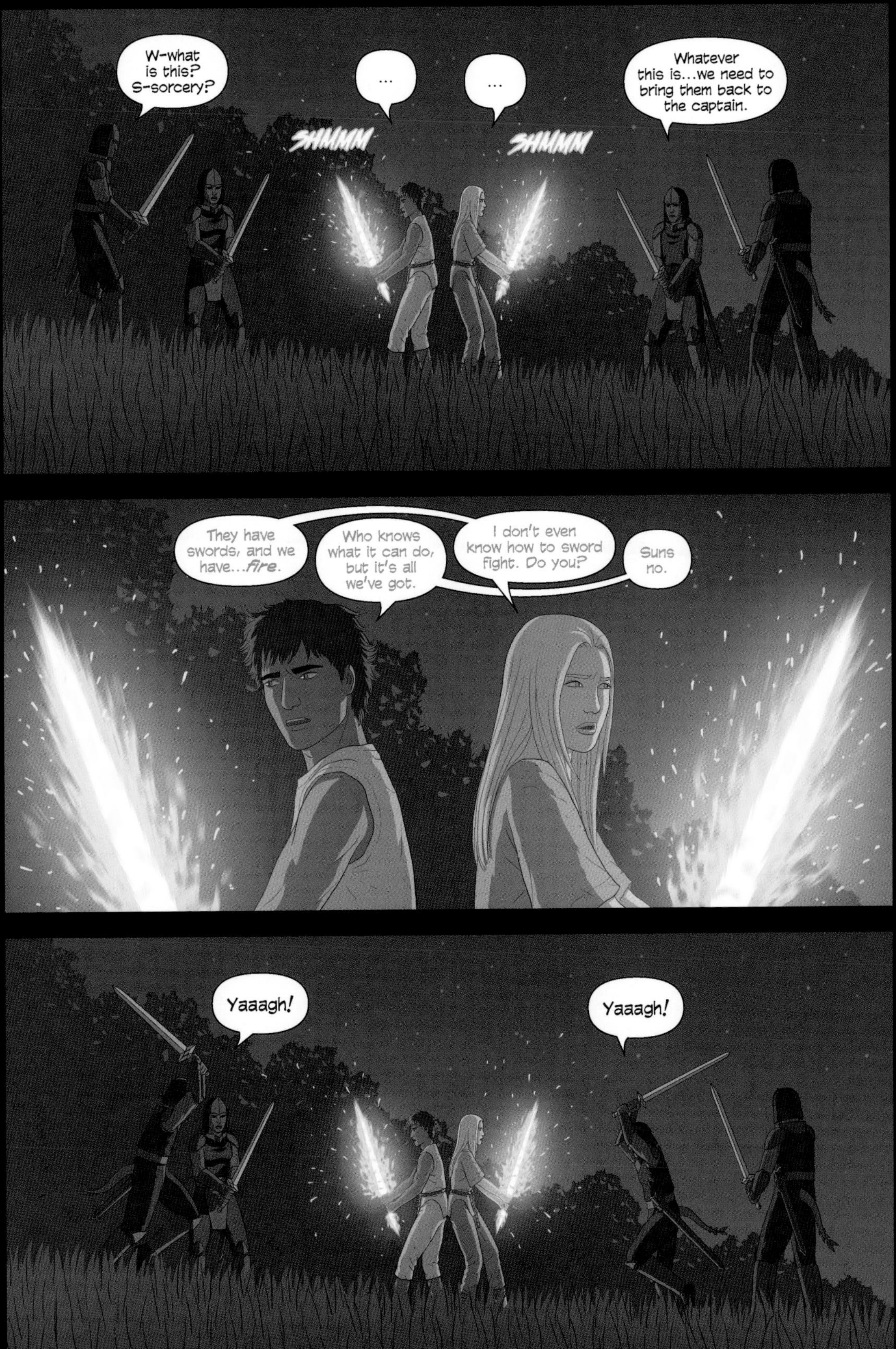
W-what is this? S-sorcery?
...
...
Whatever this is...we need to bring them back to the captain.
SHMMM
SHMMM
They have swords, and we have...*fire*.
Who knows what it can do, but it's all we've got.
I don't even know how to sword fight. Do you?
Suns no.
Yaaagh!
Yaaagh!

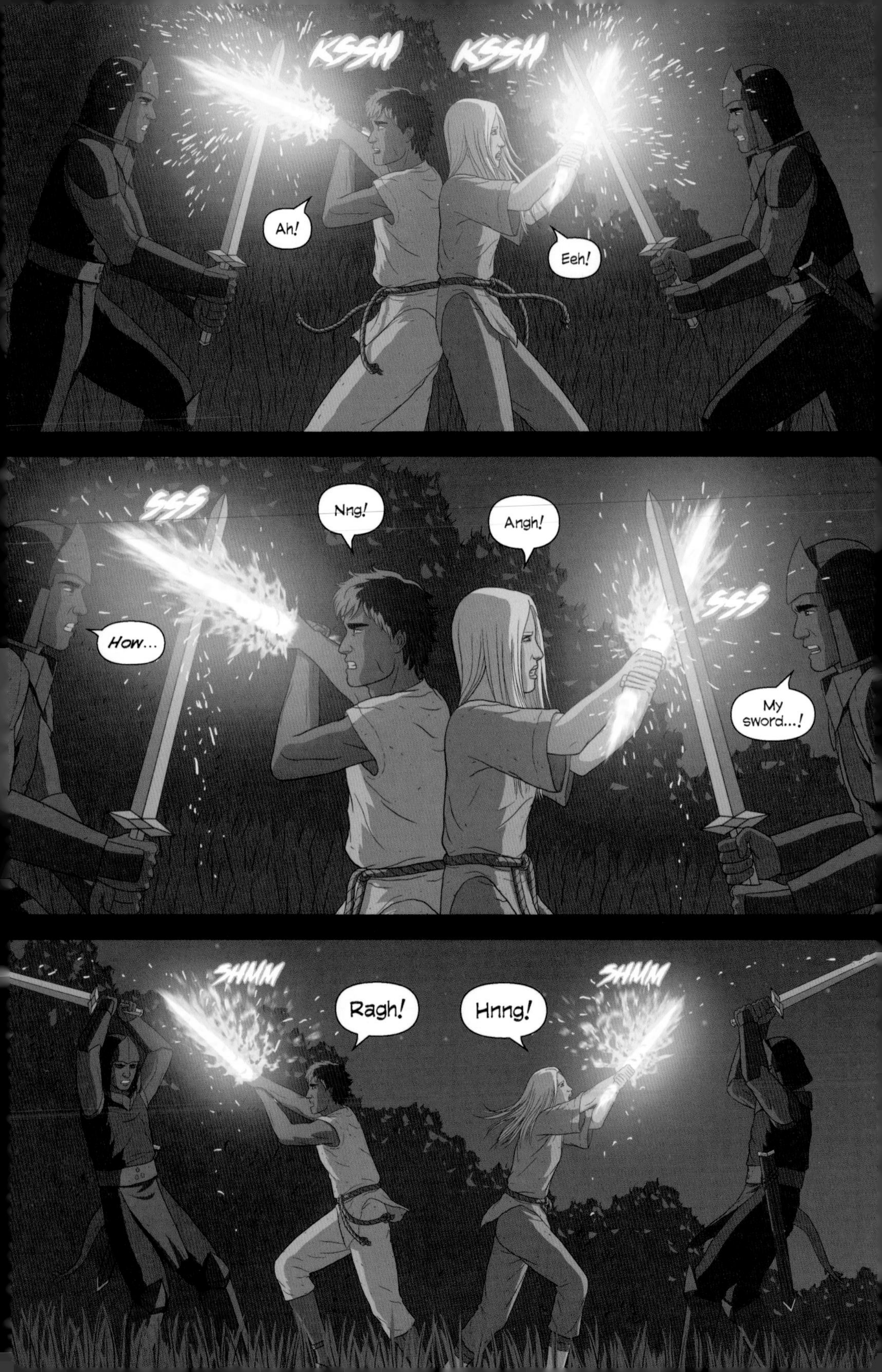
KSSH
KSSH
Ah!
Eeh!
SSS
Nng!
Angh!
How...
SSS
My sword...!
SHMM
Ragh!
Hnng!
SHMM

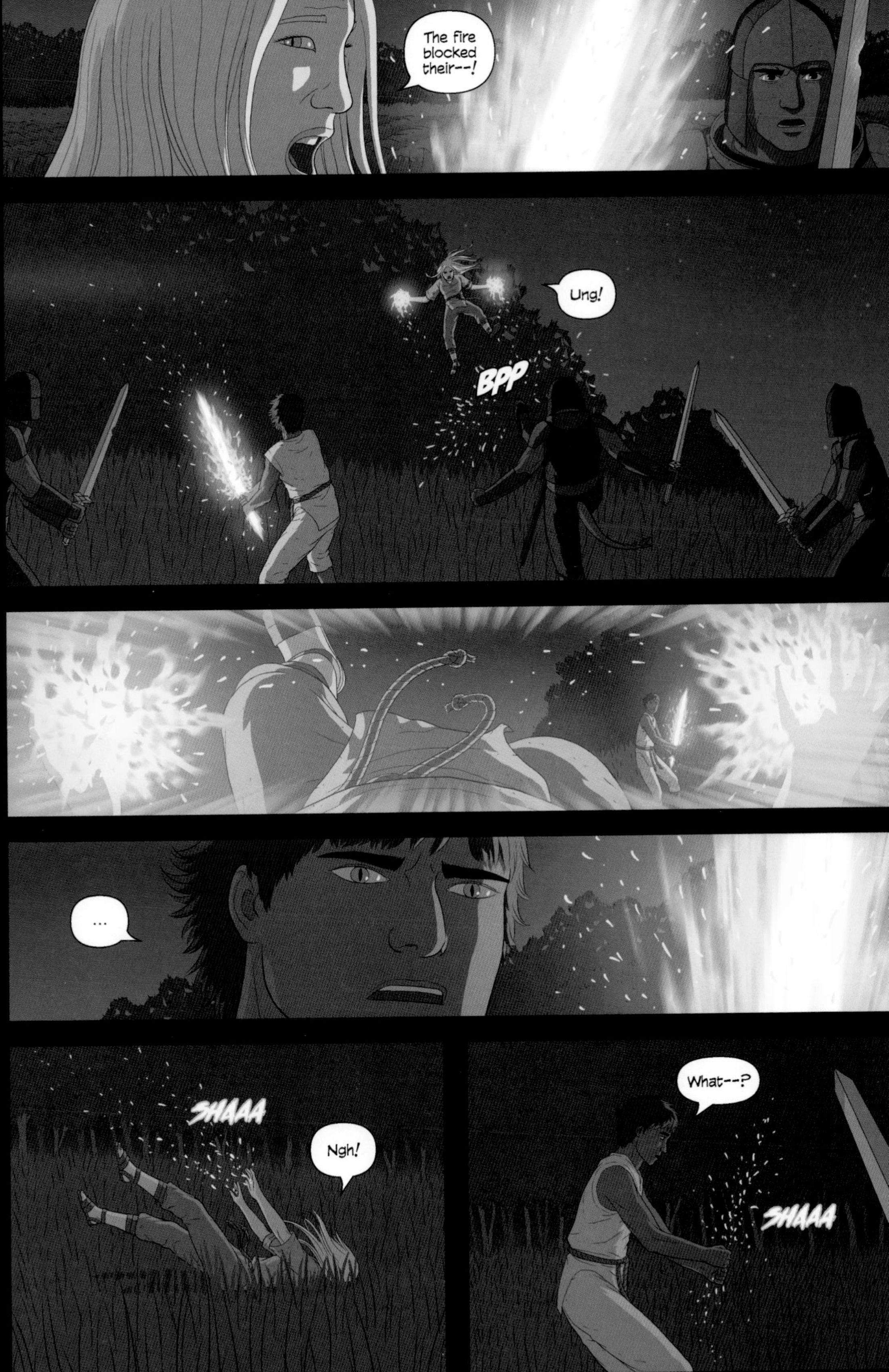
The fire blocked their--!
Ung!
BPP
...
SHAAA
Ngh!
What--?
SHAAA

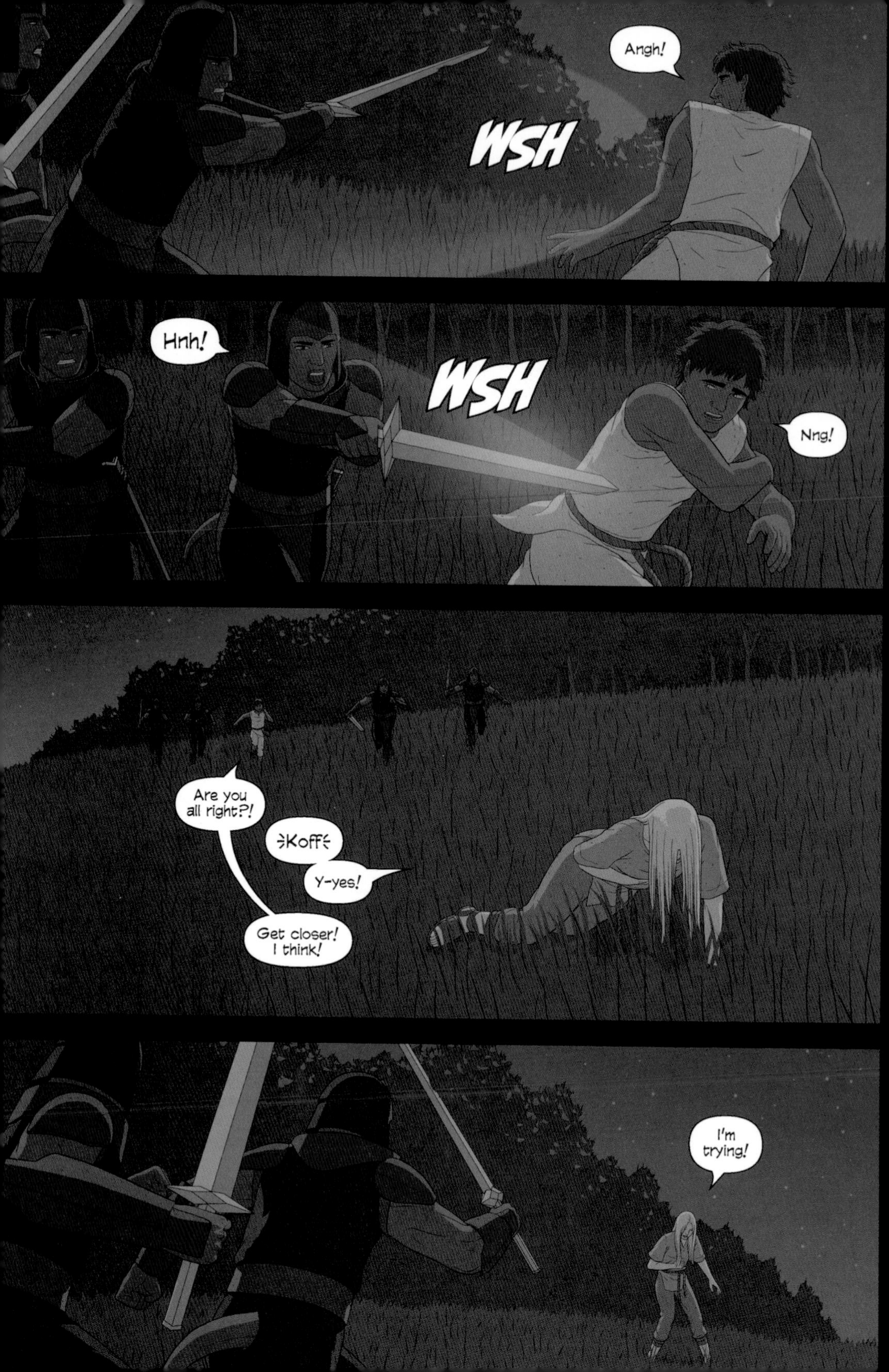
Angh!
WSH
Hnh!
WSH
Nng!
Are you all right?!
Koff
Y-yes!
Get closer! I think!
I'm trying!

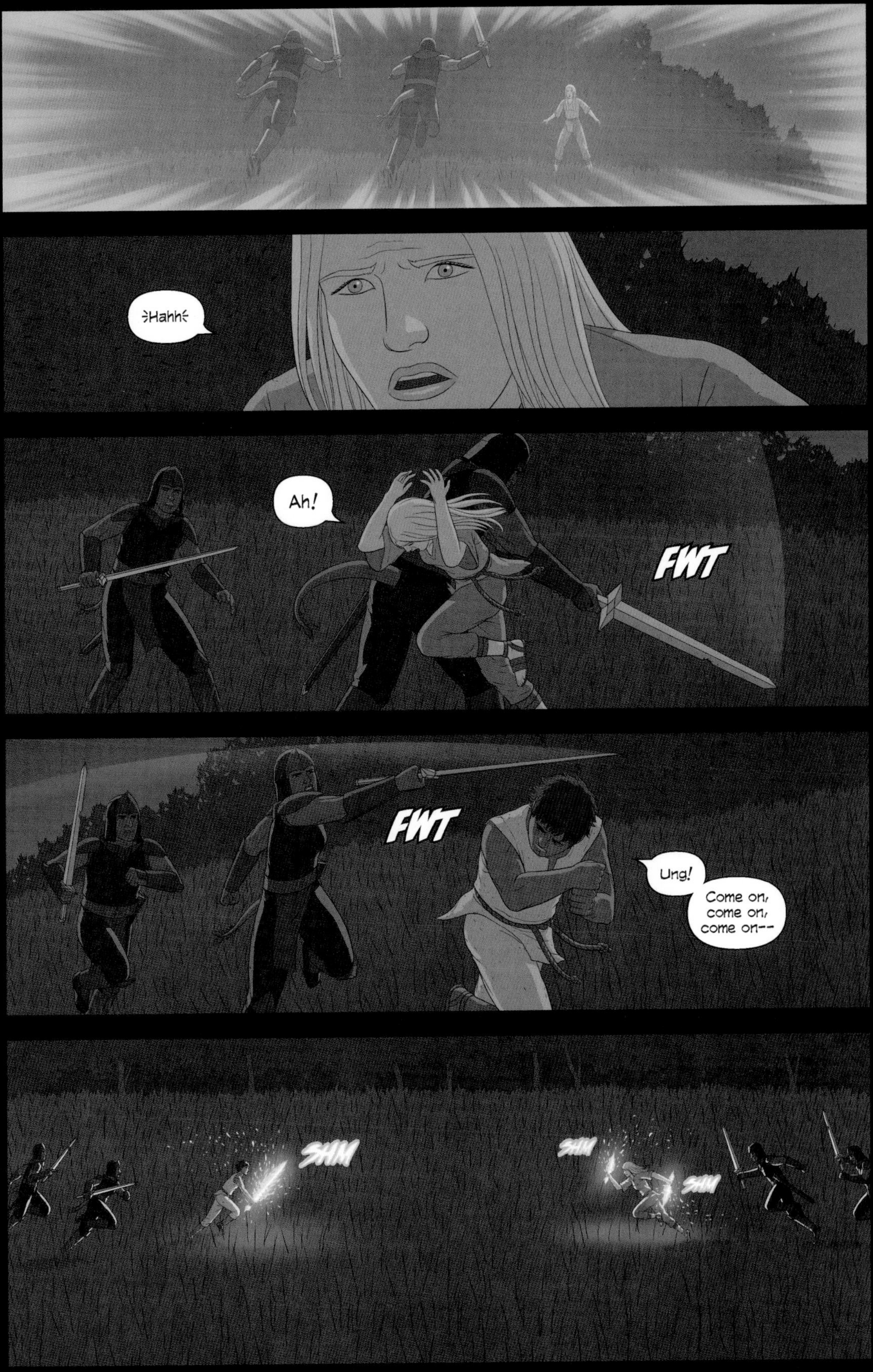

Hahh
Ah!
FWT
FWT
Ung!
Come on, come on, come on--
SHM
SHM
SHM

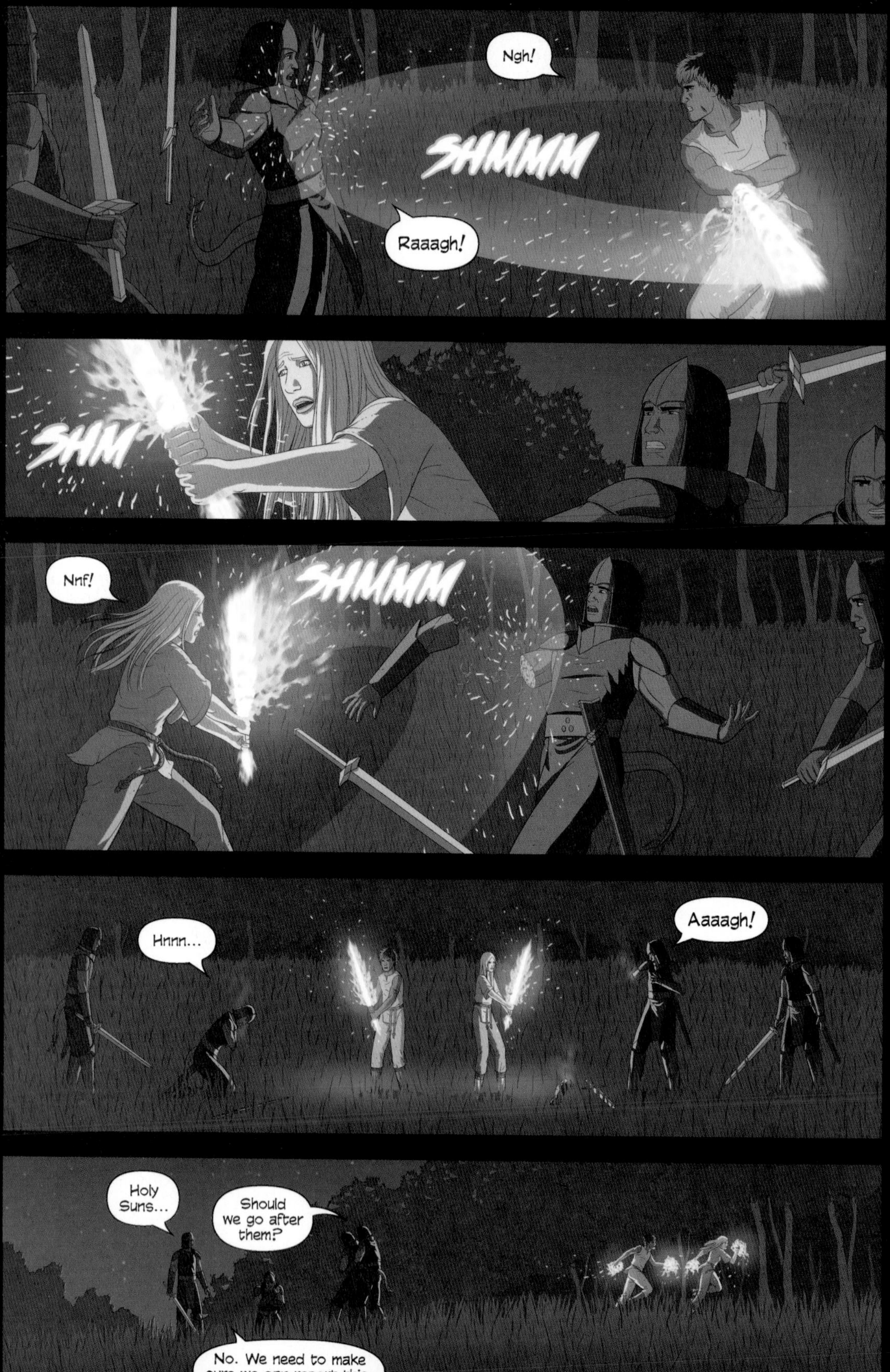
Ngh!
SHMMM
Raaagh!
SHM
Nnf!
SHMMM
Hnnn...
Aaaagh!
Holy Suns...
Should we go after them?
No. We need to make sure we can report this.

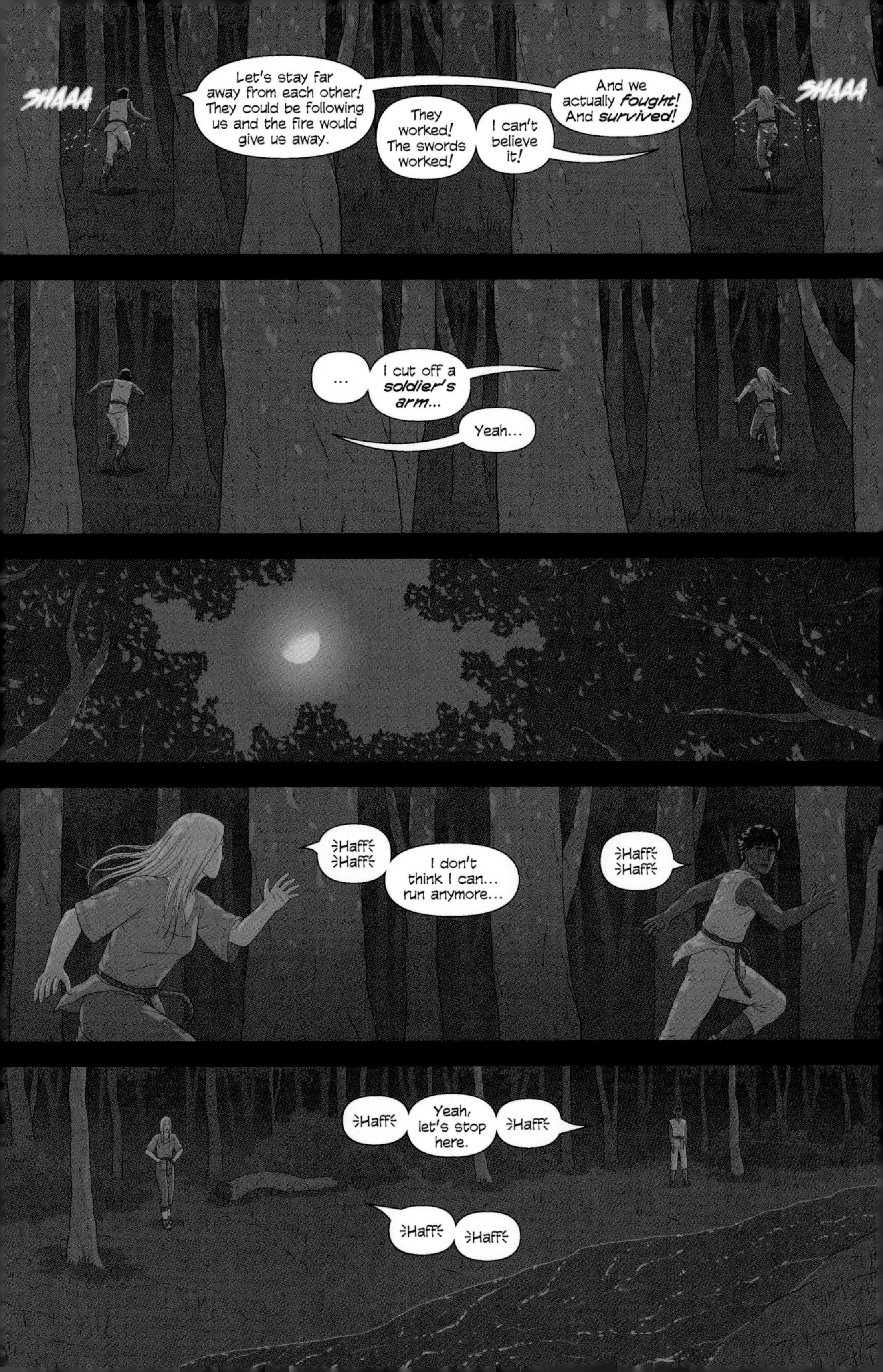
SHAAA
Let's stay far away from each other! They could be following us and the fire would give us away.
SHAAA
And we actually *fought*! And *survived*!
They worked! The swords worked!
I can't believe it!
...
I cut off a *soldier's arm*...
Yeah...
Haff Haff
I don't think I can... run anymore...
Haff Haff
Haff
Yeah, let's stop here.
Haff
Haff
Haff

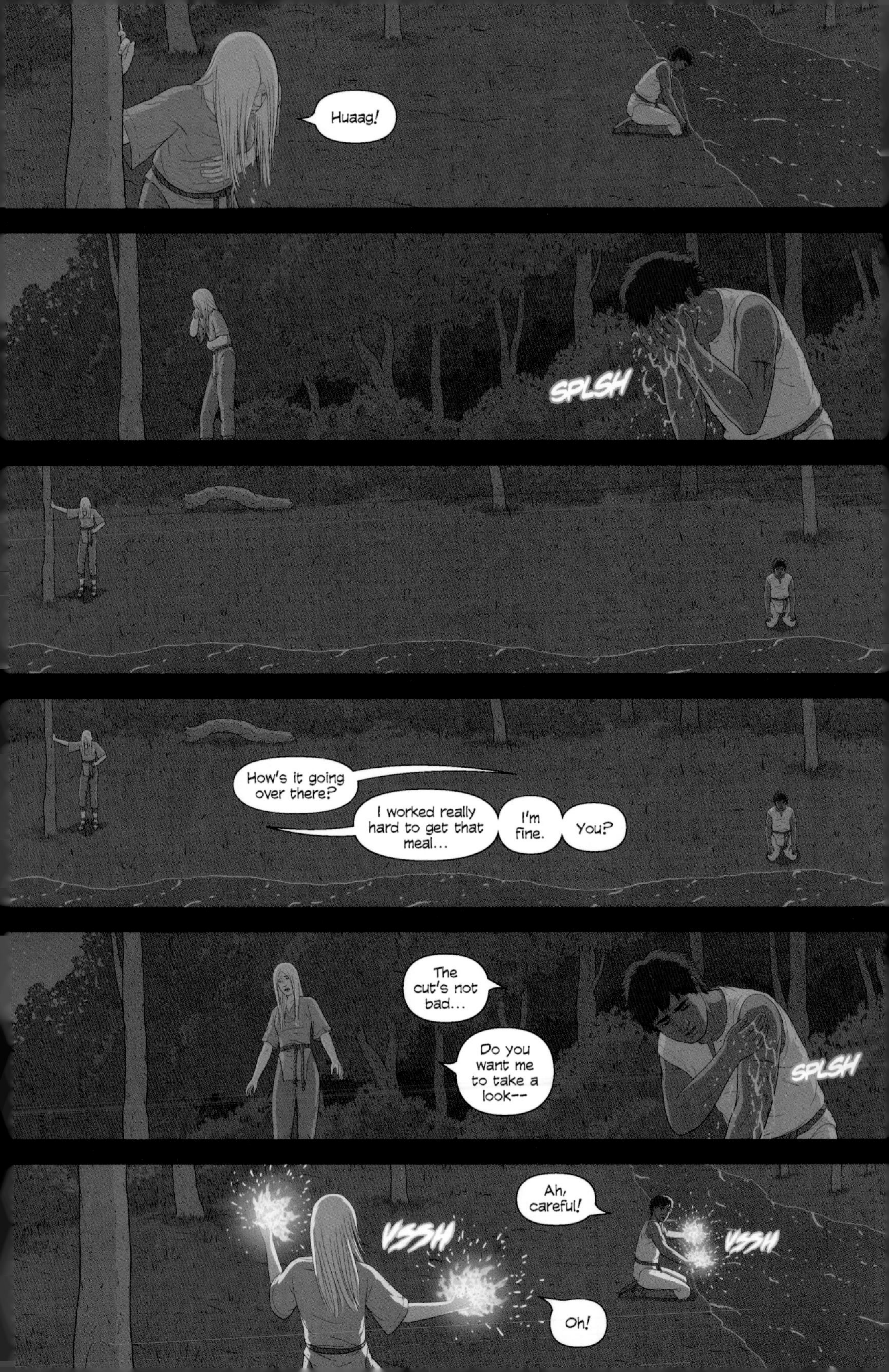
Huaag!
SPLSH
How's it going over there?
I worked really hard to get that meal...
I'm fine.
You?
The cut's not bad...
Do you want me to take a look--
SPLSH
VSSH
Ah, careful!
VSSH
Oh!

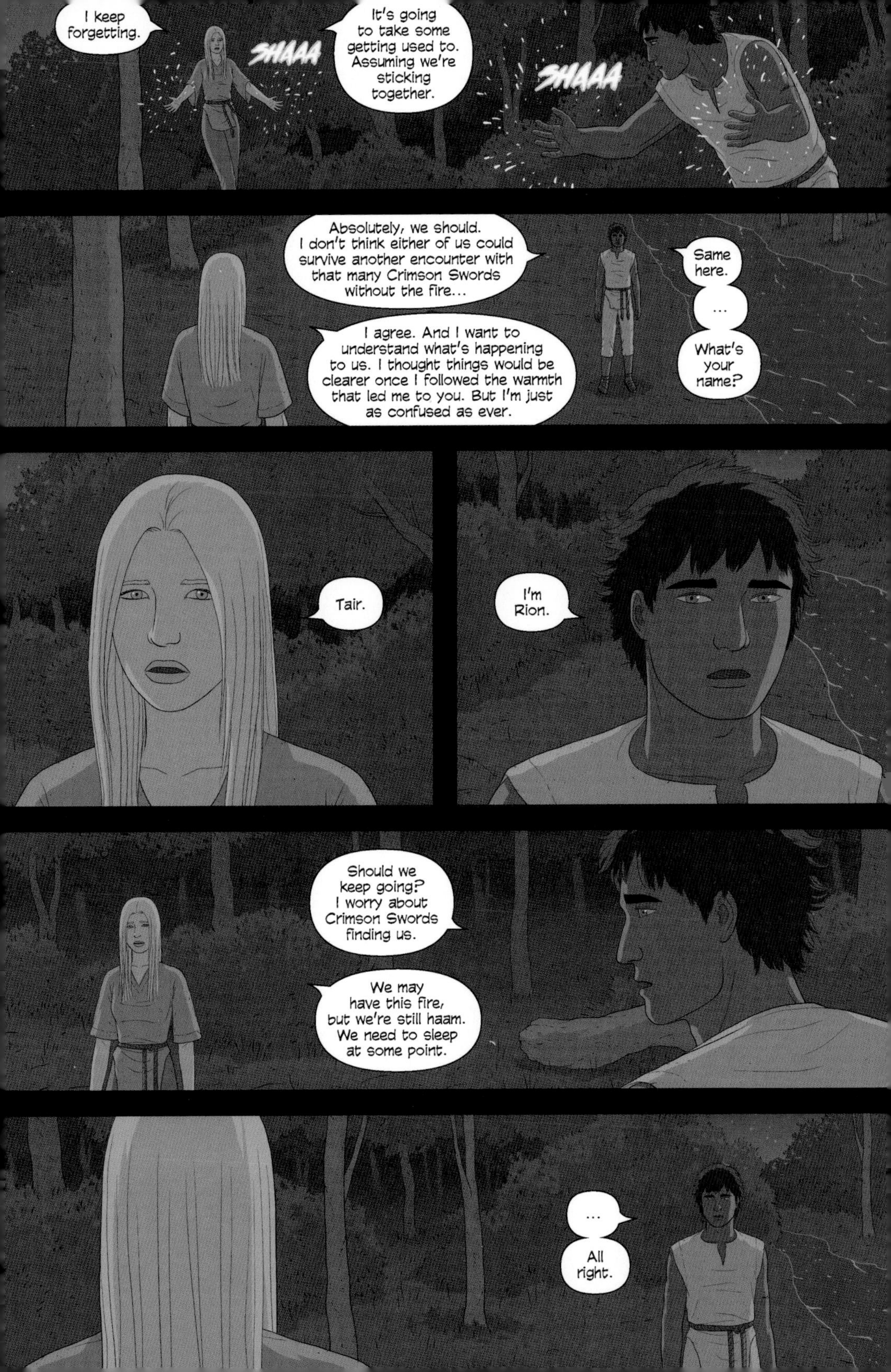

I keep forgetting.
SHAAA
It's going to take some getting used to. Assuming we're sticking together.
SHAAA
Absolutely, we should. I don't think either of us could survive another encounter with that many Crimson Swords without the fire...
I agree. And I want to understand what's happening to us. I thought things would be clearer once I followed the warmth that led me to you. But I'm just as confused as ever.
Same here.
...
What's your name?
Tair.
I'm Rion.
Should we keep going? I worry about Crimson Swords finding us.
We may have this fire, but we're still haam. We need to sleep at some point.
...
All right.

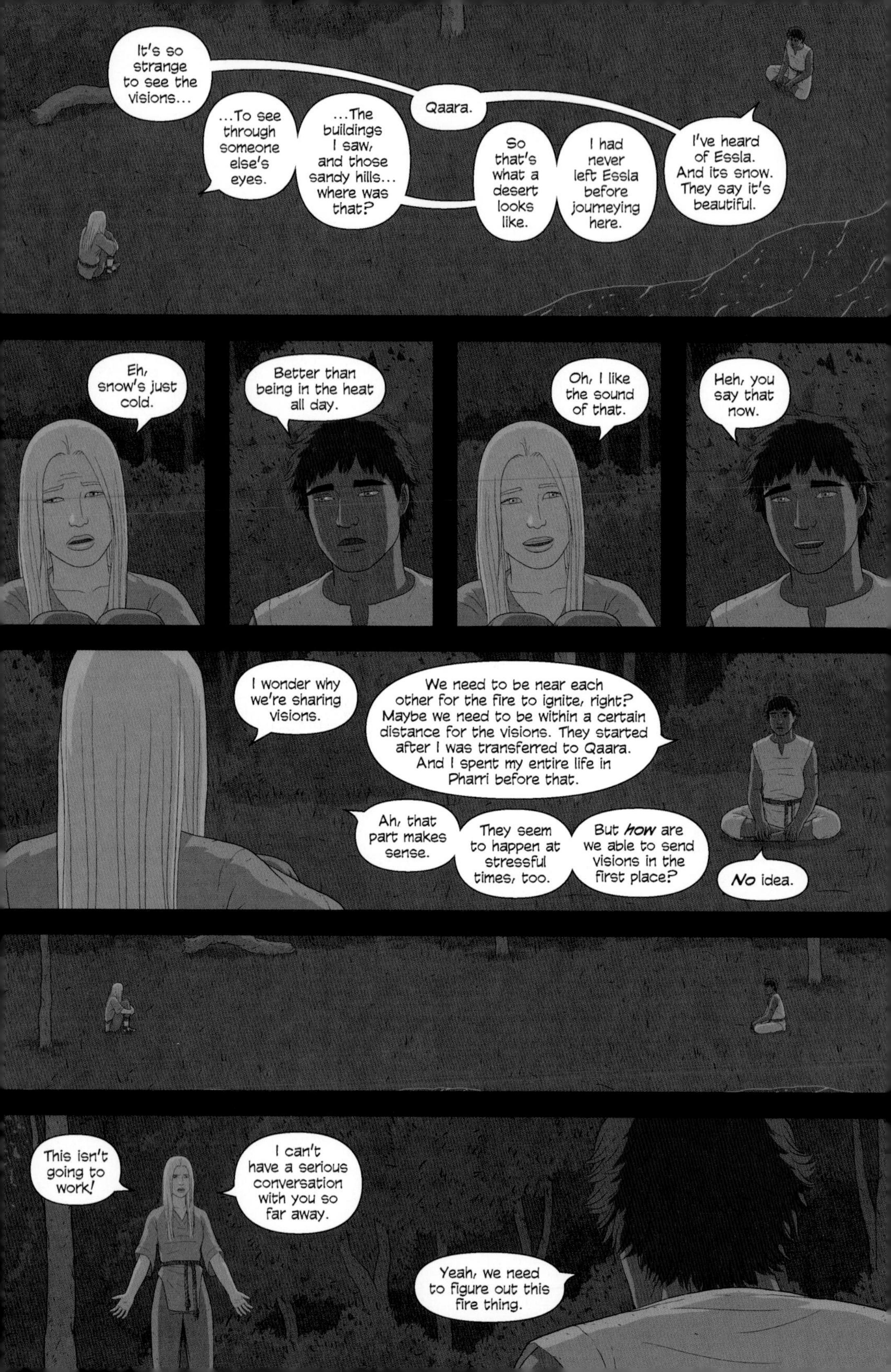
It's so strange to see the visions...
...To see through someone else's eyes.
...The buildings I saw, and those sandy hills... where was that?
So that's what a desert looks like.
Qaara.
I had never left Essla before journeying here.
I've heard of Essla. And its snow. They say it's beautiful.
Eh, snow's just cold.
Better than being in the heat all day.
Oh, I like the sound of that.
Heh, you say that now.
I wonder why we're sharing visions.
We need to be near each other for the fire to ignite, right? Maybe we need to be within a certain distance for the visions. They started after I was transferred to Qaara. And I spent my entire life in Pharri before that.
Ah, that part makes sense.
They seem to happen at stressful times, too.
But *how* are we able to send visions in the first place?
No idea.
This isn't going to work!
I can't have a serious conversation with you so far away.
Yeah, we need to figure out this fire thing.

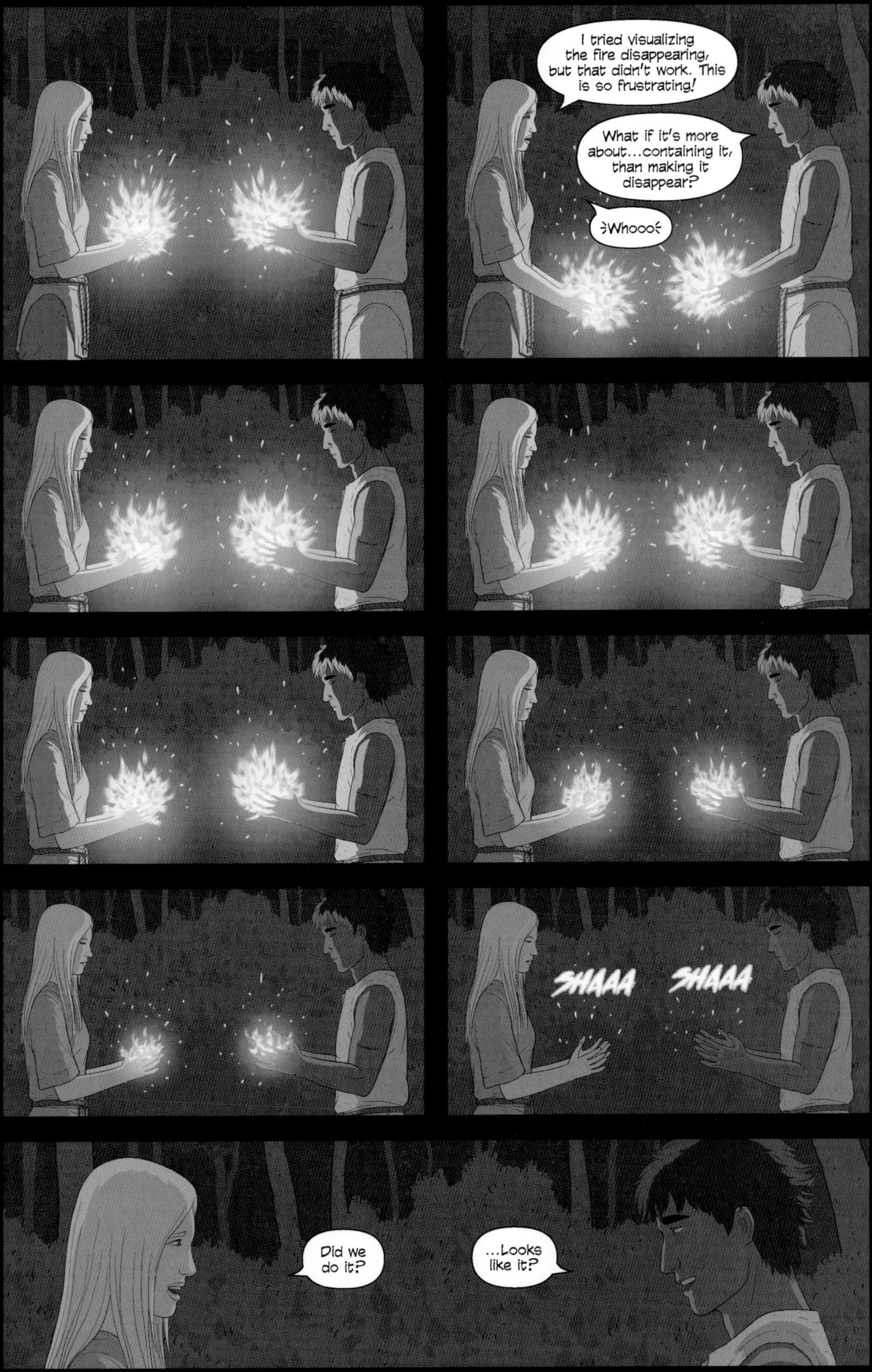
I tried visualizing the fire disappearing, but that didn't work. This is so frustrating!
What if it's more about...containing it, than making it disappear?
Whooo
SHAAA
SHAAA
Did we do it?
...Looks like it?

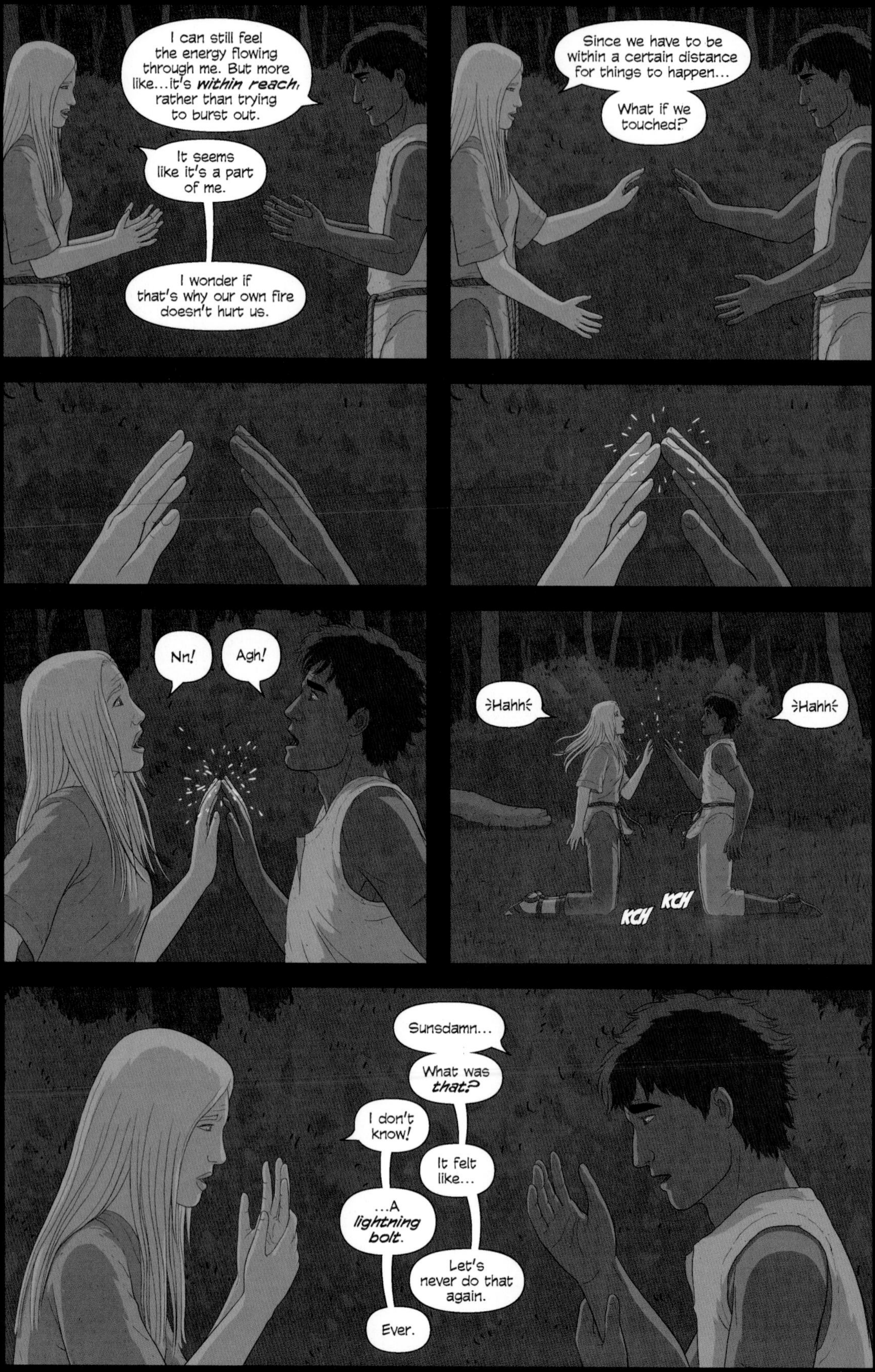

I can still feel the energy flowing through me. But more like...it's *within reach,* rather than trying to burst out.
It seems like it's a part of me.
I wonder if that's why our own fire doesn't hurt us.
Since we have to be within a certain distance for things to happen...
What if we touched?
Nn!
Agh!
Hahh
Hahh
KCH
KCH
Sunsdamn...
What was *that?*
I don't know!
It felt like...
...A *lightning bolt*.
Let's never do that again.
Ever.

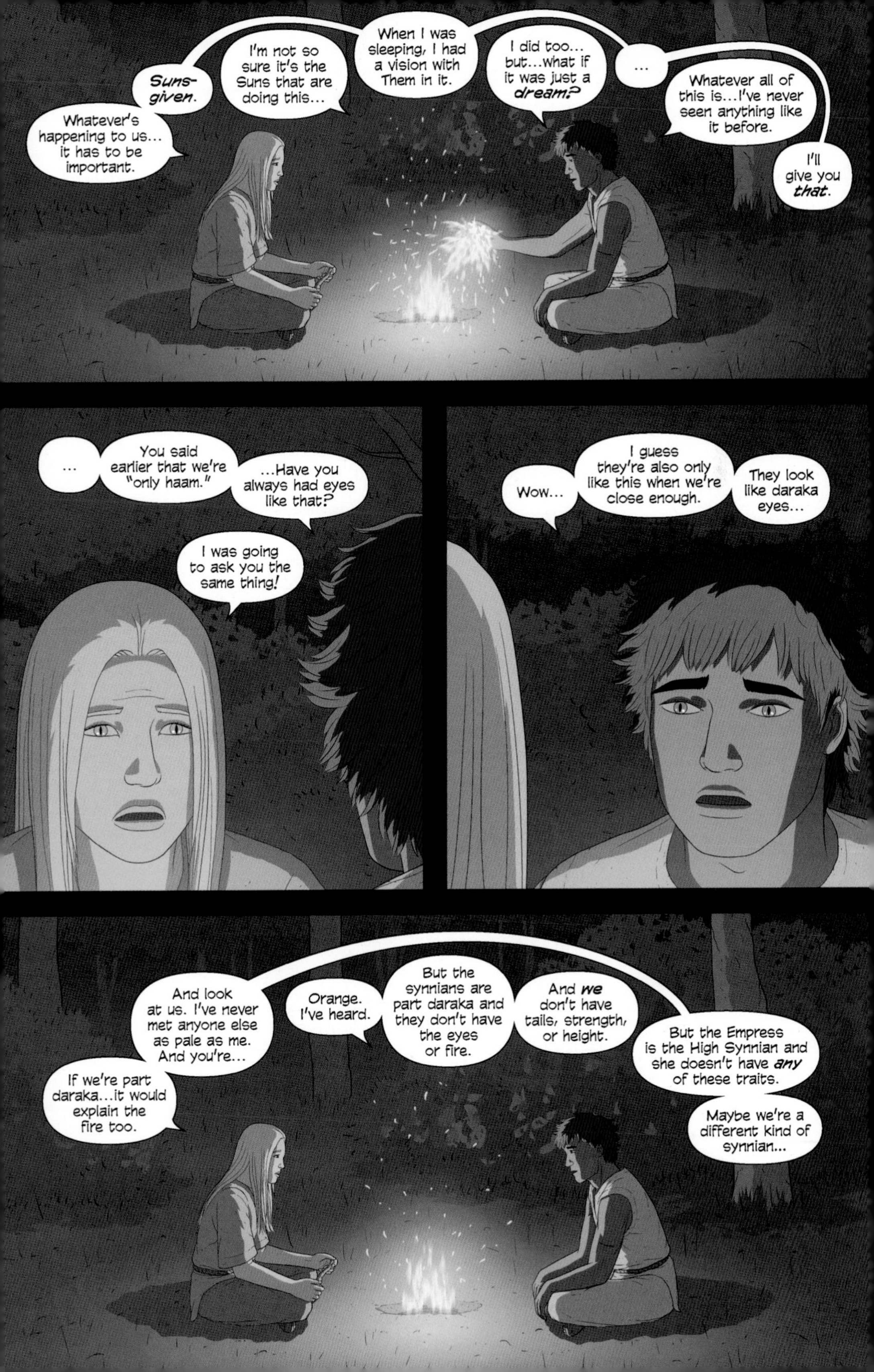
Whatever's happening to us... it has to be important.
Suns-given.
I'm not so sure it's the Suns that are doing this...
When I was sleeping, I had a vision with Them in it.
I did too... but...what if it was just a *dream?*
...
Whatever all of this is...I've never seen anything like it before.
I'll give you *that*.
...
You said earlier that we're "only haam."
...Have you always had eyes like that?
I was going to ask you the same thing!
Wow...
I guess they're also only like this when we're close enough.
They look like daraka eyes...
And look at us. I've never met anyone else as pale as me. And you're...
Orange. I've heard.
But the synnians are part daraka and they don't have the eyes or fire.
And *we* don't have tails, strength, or height.
But the Empress is the High Synnian and she doesn't have *any* of these traits.
If we're part daraka...it would explain the fire too.
Maybe we're a different kind of synnian...

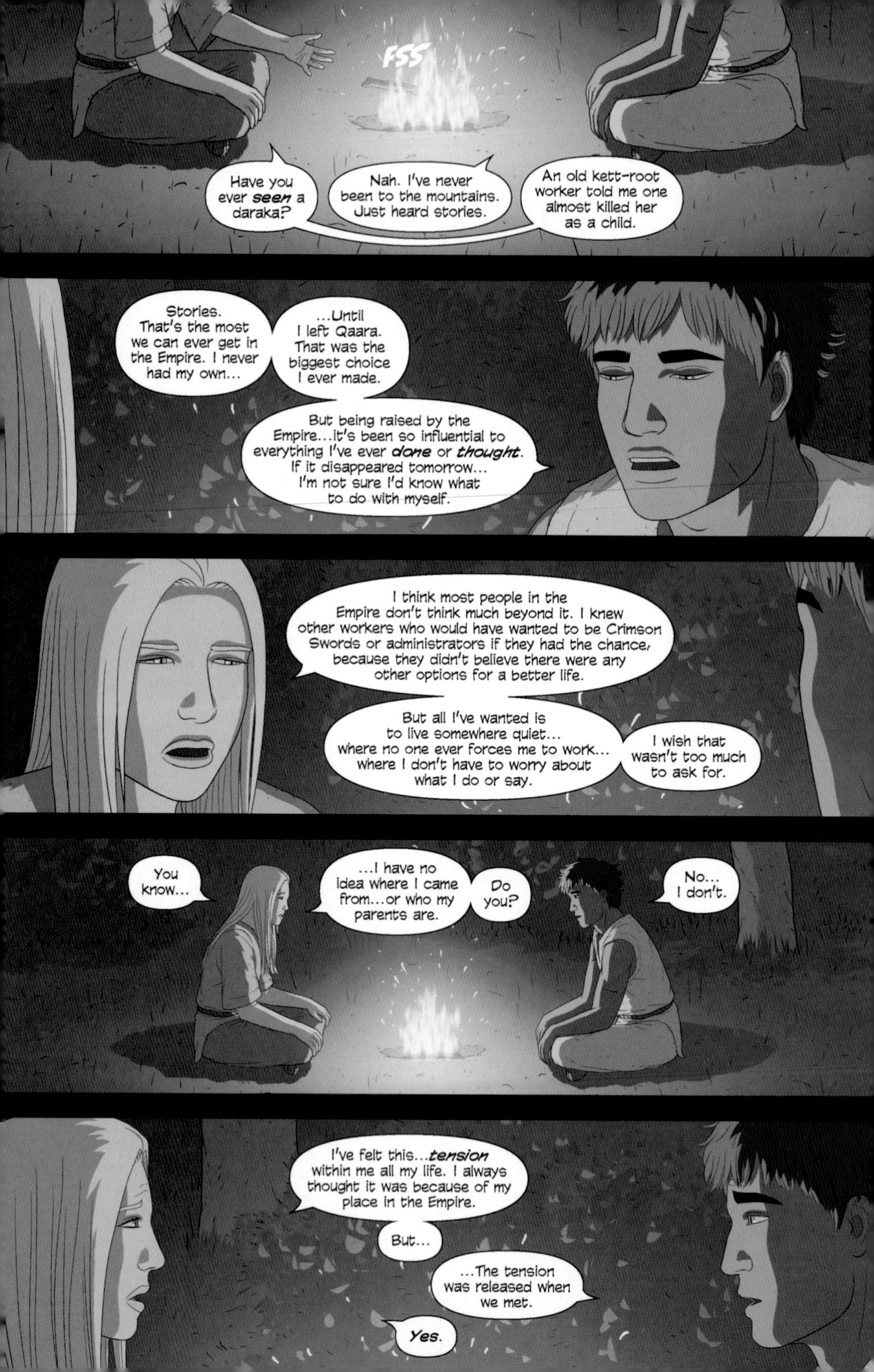
FSS
Have you ever seen a daraka?
Nah. I've never been to the mountains. Just heard stories.
An old kett-root worker told me one almost killed her as a child.
Stories. That's the most we can ever get in the Empire. I never had my own...
...Until I left Qaara. That was the biggest choice I ever made.
But being raised by the Empire...it's been so influential to everything I've ever done or thought. If it disappeared tomorrow... I'm not sure I'd know what to do with myself.
I think most people in the Empire don't think much beyond it. I knew other workers who would have wanted to be Crimson Swords or administrators if they had the chance, because they didn't believe there were any other options for a better life.
But all I've wanted is to live somewhere quiet... where no one ever forces me to work... where I don't have to worry about what I do or say.
I wish that wasn't too much to ask for.
You know...
...I have no idea where I came from...or who my parents are.
Do you?
No... I don't.
I've felt this...tension within me all my life. I always thought it was because of my place in the Empire.
But...
...The tension was released when we met.
Yes.

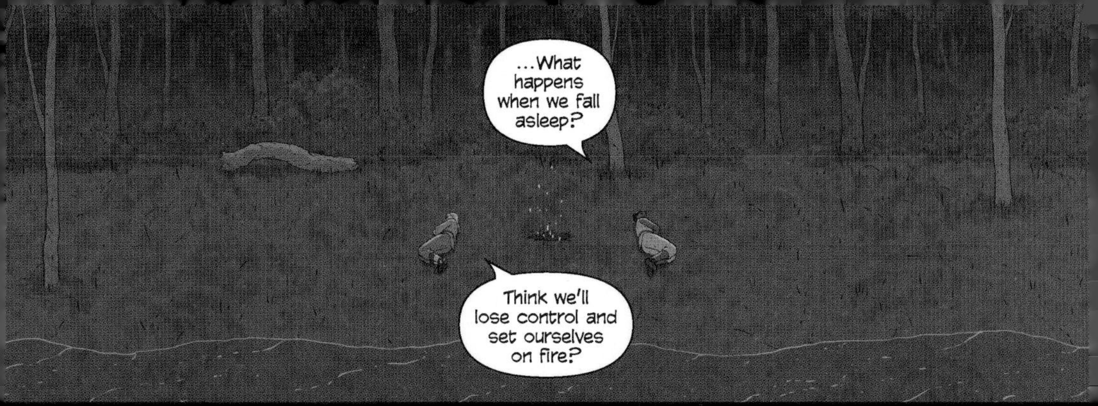
...What happens when we fall asleep?
Think we'll lose control and set ourselves on fire?

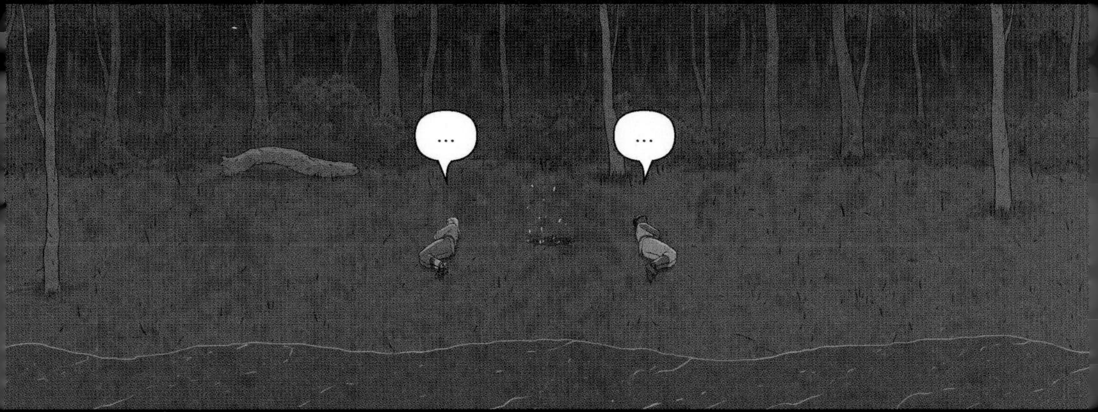
...
...

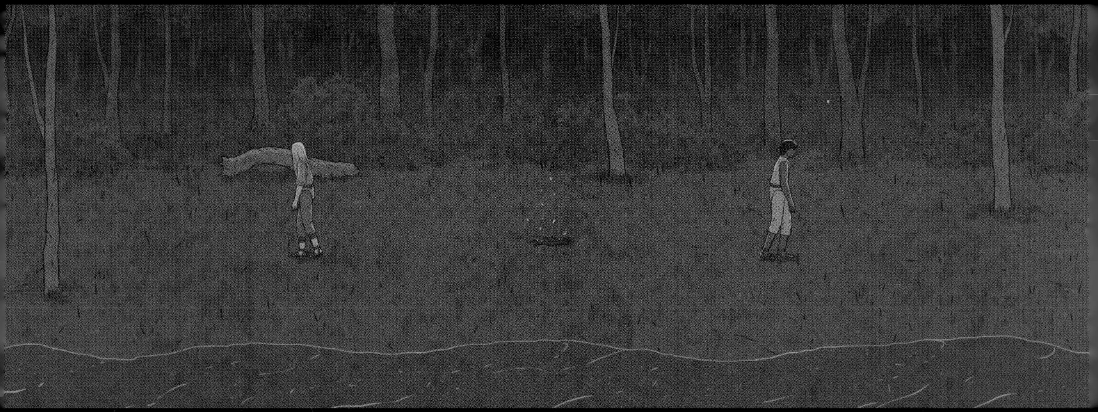

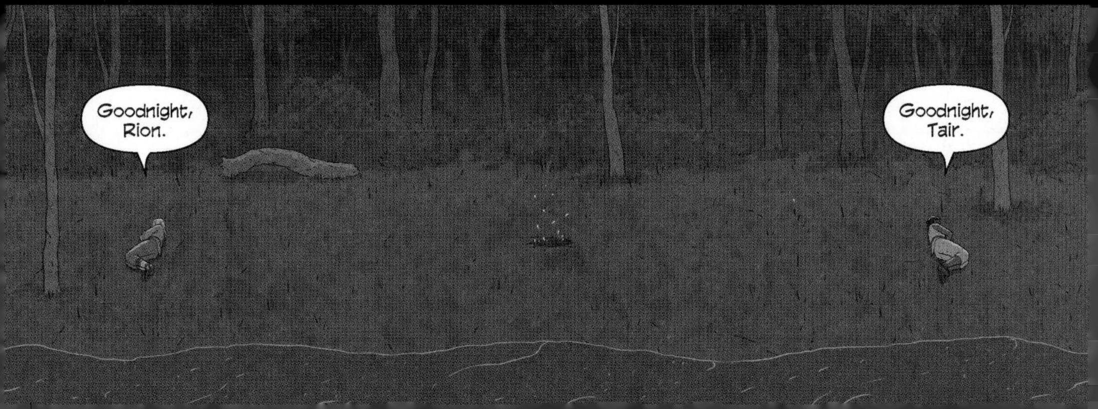
Goodnight, Rion.
Goodnight, Tair.

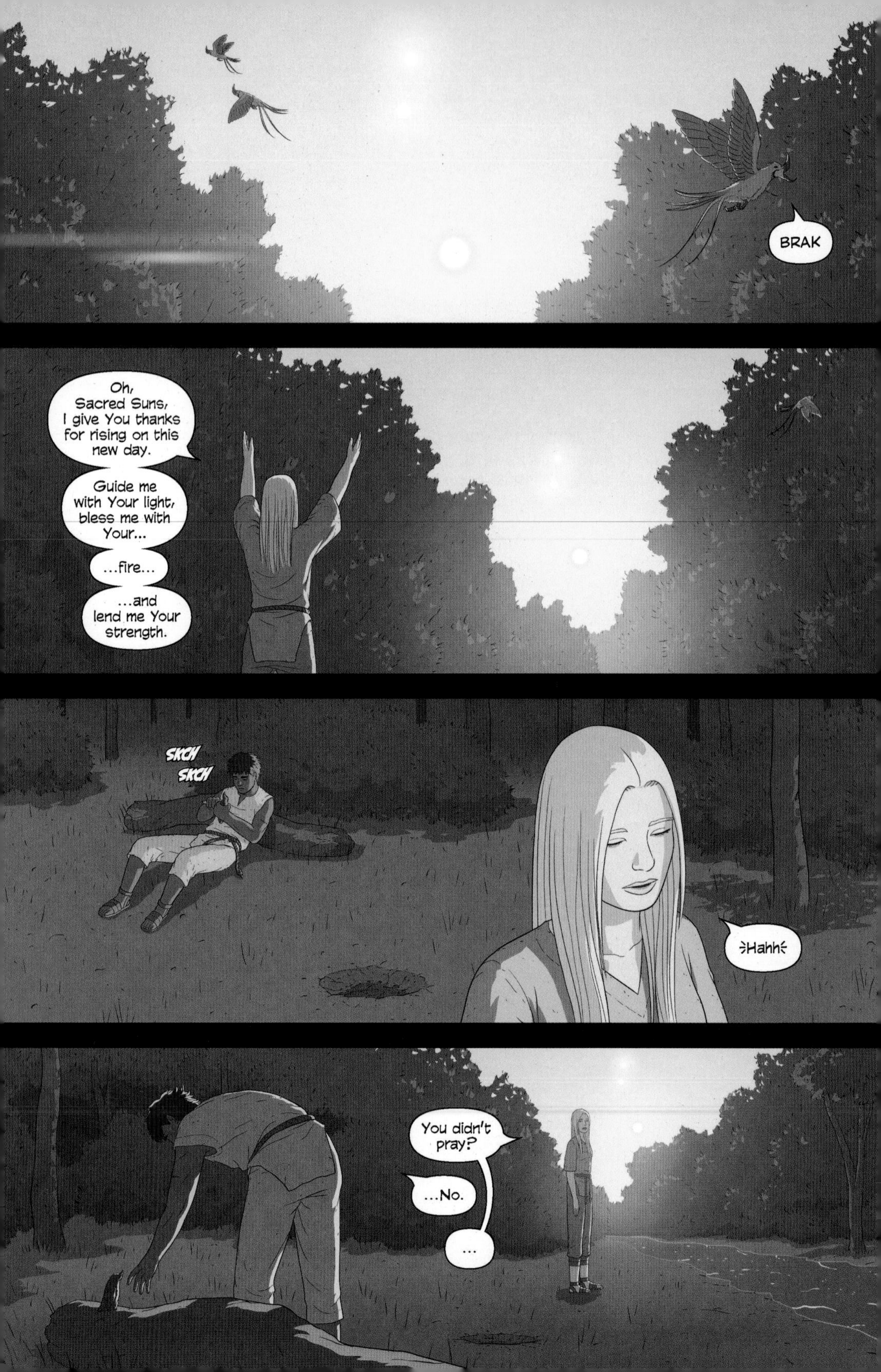
BRAK
Oh, Sacred Suns, I give You thanks for rising on this new day.
Guide me with Your light, bless me with Your...
...fire...
...and lend me Your strength.
SKCH
SKCH
Hahh
You didn't pray?
...No.
...

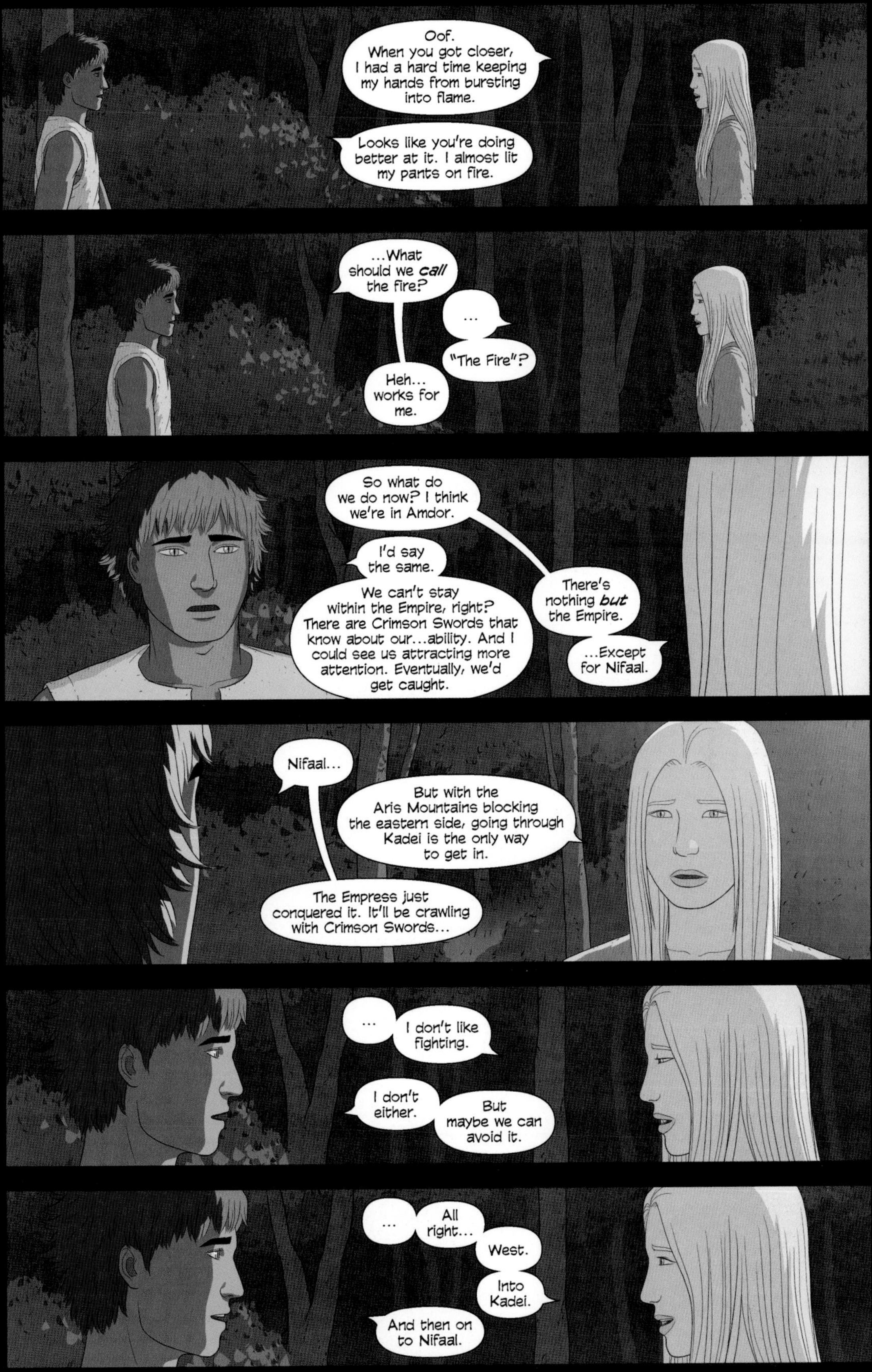

Oof.
When you got closer, I had a hard time keeping my hands from bursting into flame.
Looks like you're doing better at it. I almost lit my pants on fire.
...What should we *call* the fire?
...
"The Fire"?
Heh... works for me.
So what do we do now? I think we're in Amdor.
I'd say the same.
We can't stay within the Empire, right? There are Crimson Swords that know about our...ability. And I could see us attracting more attention. Eventually, we'd get caught.
There's nothing *but* the Empire.
...Except for Nifaal.
Nifaal...
But with the Aris Mountains blocking the eastern side, going through Kadei is the only way to get in.
The Empress just conquered it. It'll be crawling with Crimson Swords...
...
I don't like fighting.
I don't either.
But maybe we can avoid it.
...
All right...
West.
Into Kadei.
And then on to Nifaal.

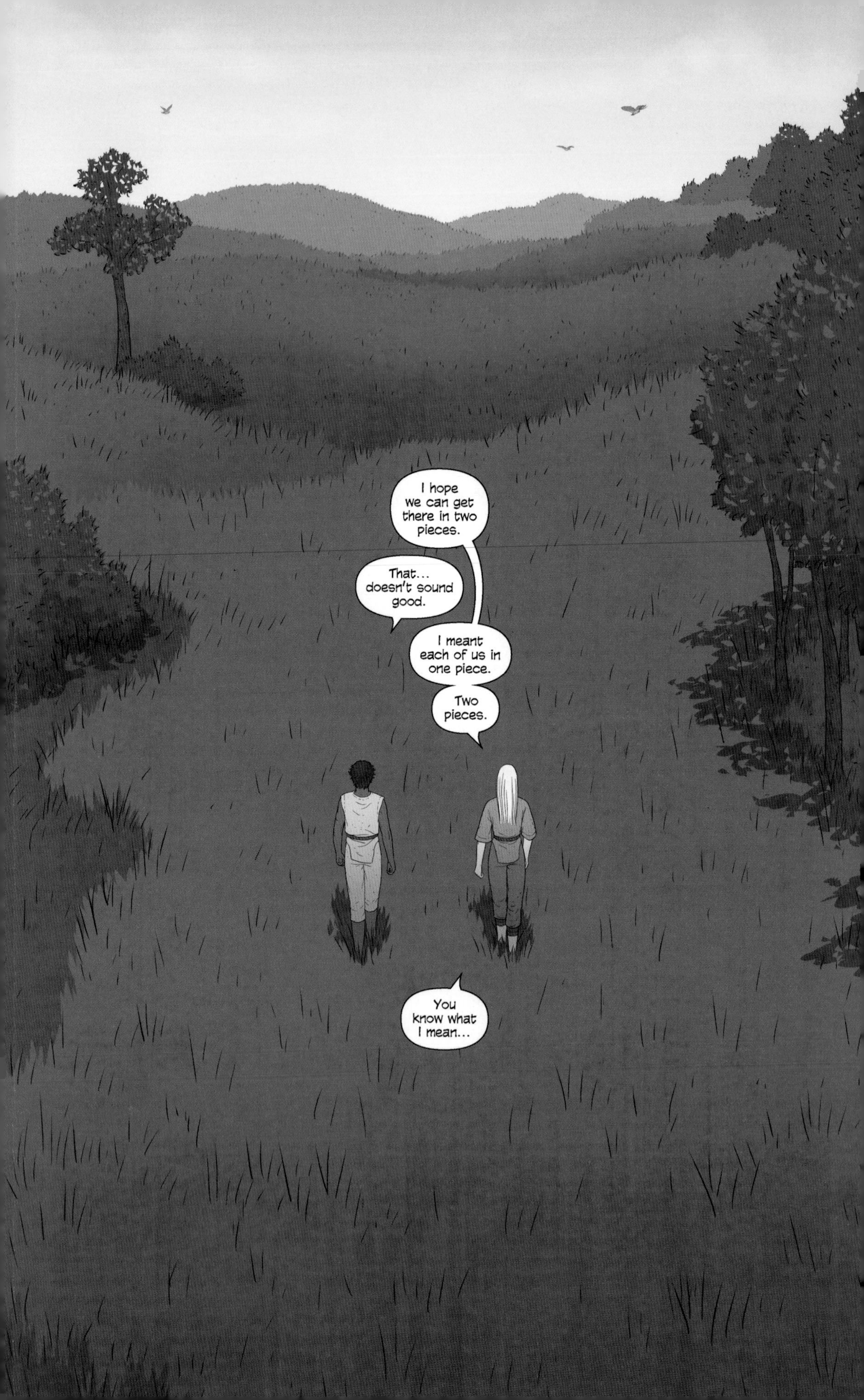
I hope we can get there in two pieces.
That... doesn't sound good.
I meant each of us in one piece.
Two pieces.
You know what I mean...

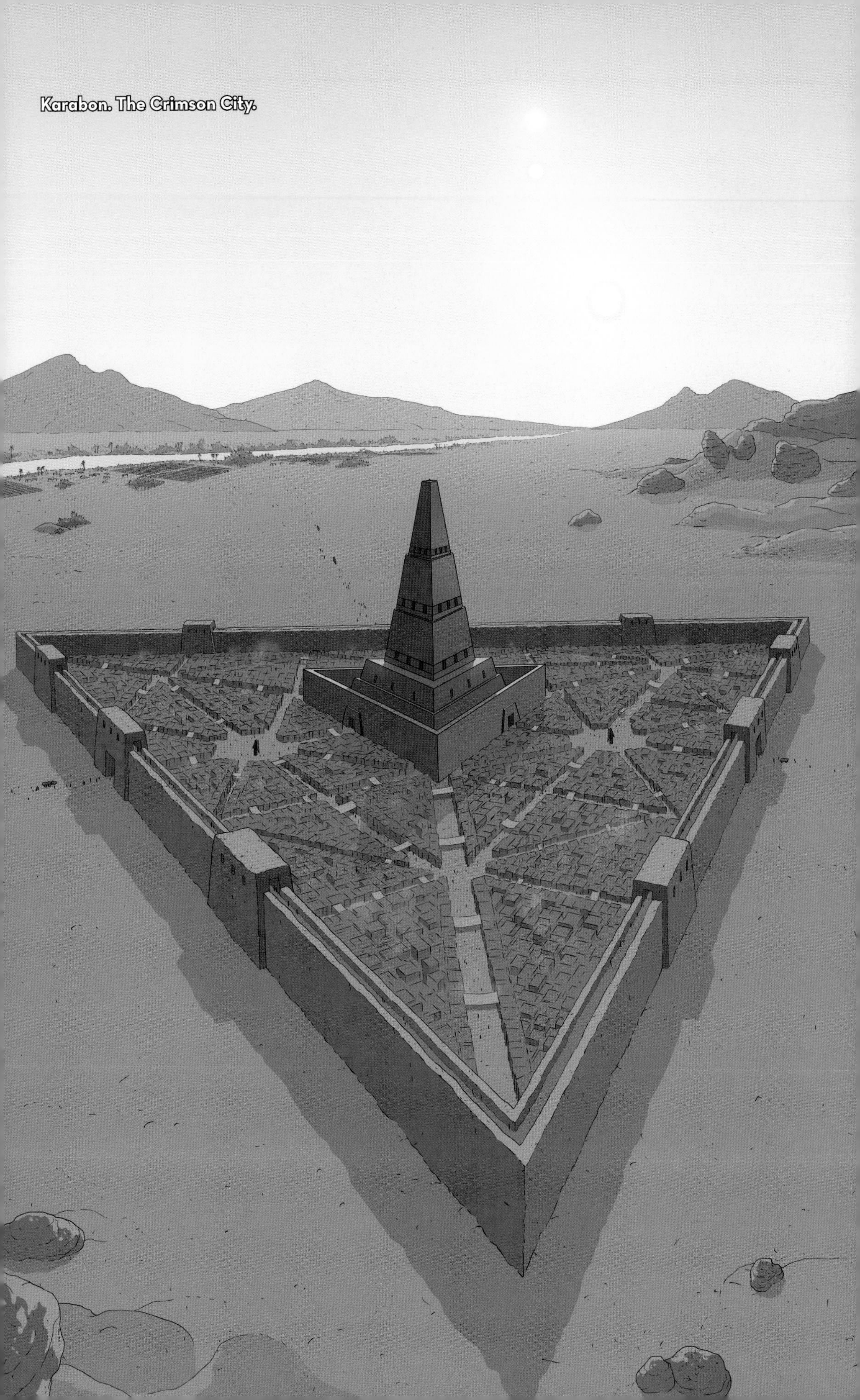
Karabon. The Crimson City.

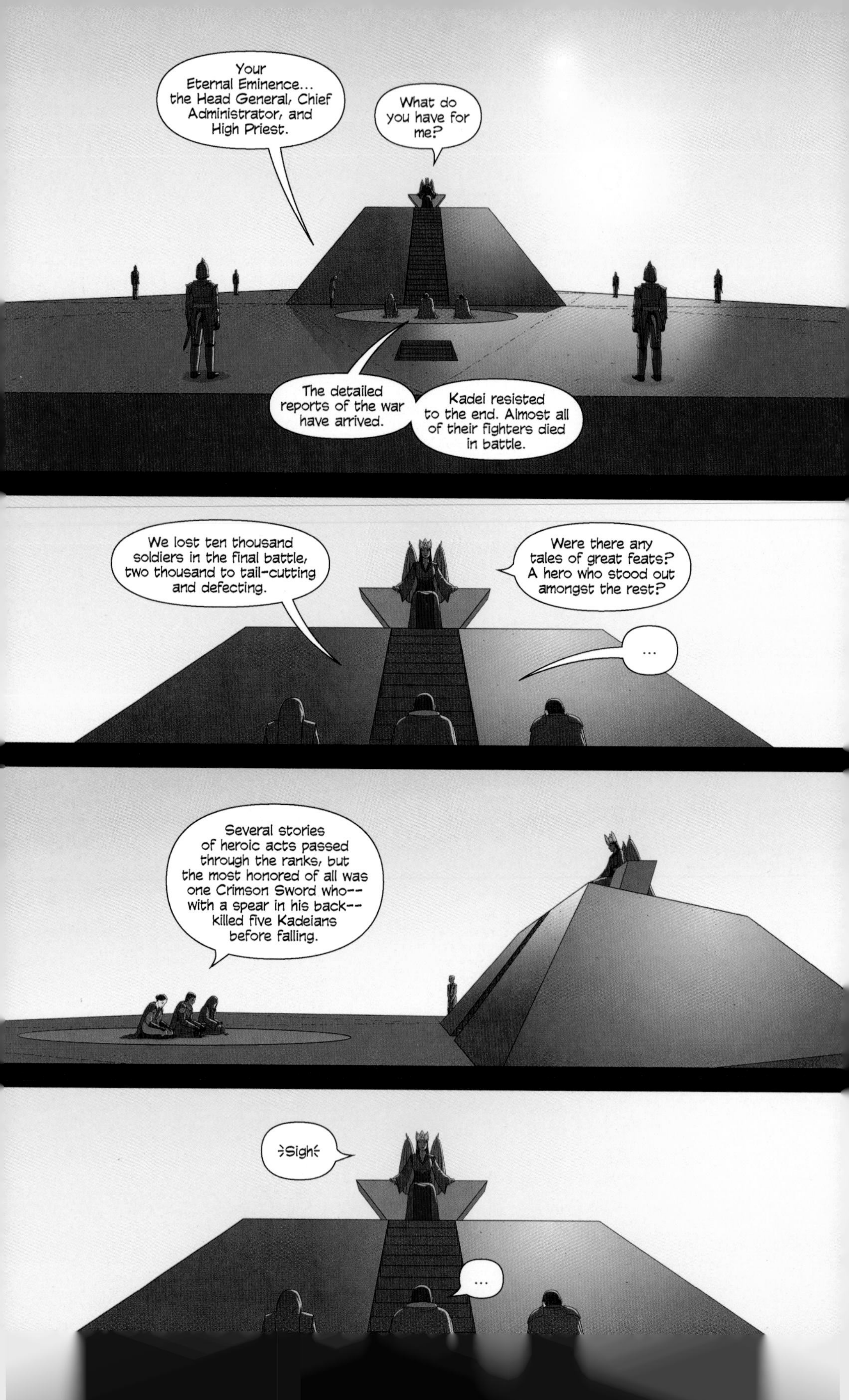
Your Eternal Eminence... the Head General, Chief Administrator, and High Priest.
What do you have for me?
The detailed reports of the war have arrived.
Kadei resisted to the end. Almost all of their fighters died in battle.
We lost ten thousand soldiers in the final battle, two thousand to tail-cutting and defecting.
Were there any tales of great feats? A hero who stood out amongst the rest?
...
Several stories of heroic acts passed through the ranks, but the most honored of all was one Crimson Sword who--with a spear in his back--killed five Kadeians before falling.
Sigh
...

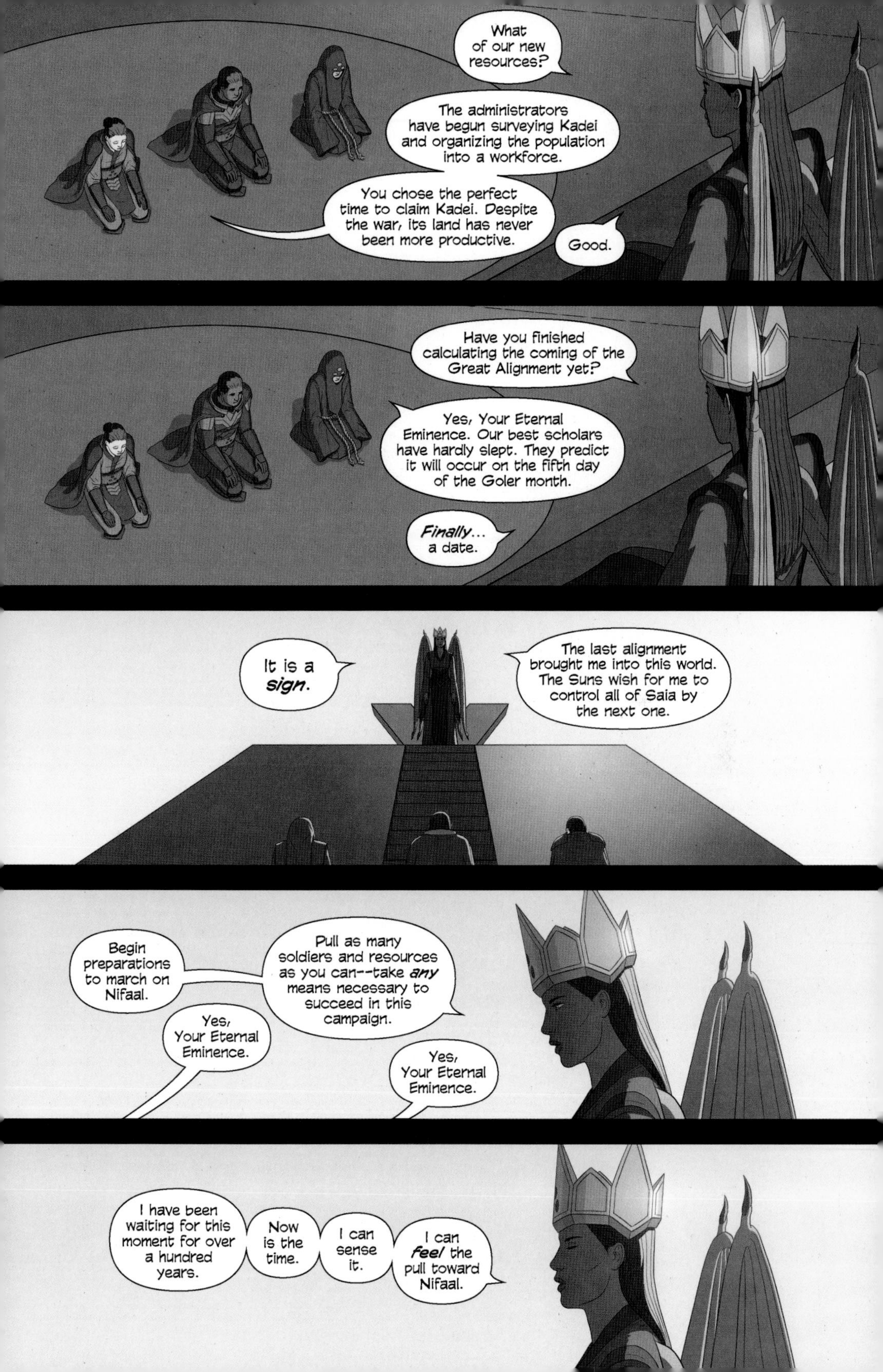
What of our new resources?
The administrators have begun surveying Kadei and organizing the population into a workforce.
You chose the perfect time to claim Kadei. Despite the war, its land has never been more productive.
Good.
Have you finished calculating the coming of the Great Alignment yet?
Yes, Your Eternal Eminence. Our best scholars have hardly slept. They predict it will occur on the fifth day of the Goler month.
Finally... a date.
It is a *sign*.
The last alignment brought me into this world. The Suns wish for me to control all of Saia by the next one.
Begin preparations to march on Nifaal.
Pull as many soldiers and resources as you can--take *any* means necessary to succeed in this campaign.
Yes, Your Eternal Eminence.
Yes, Your Eternal Eminence.
I have been waiting for this moment for over a hundred years.
Now is the time.
I can sense it.
I can *feel* the pull toward Nifaal.

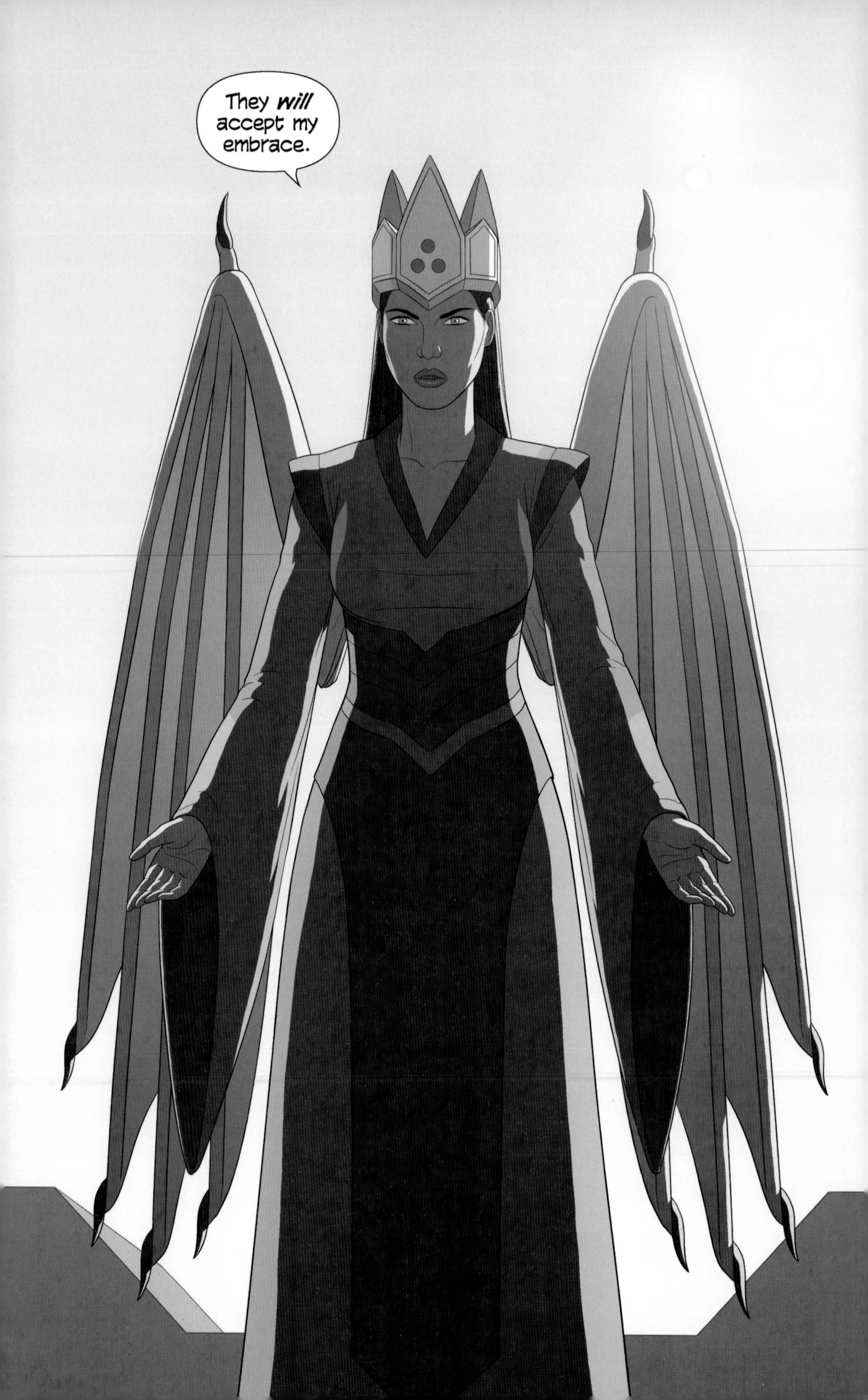
They *will* accept my embrace.

4

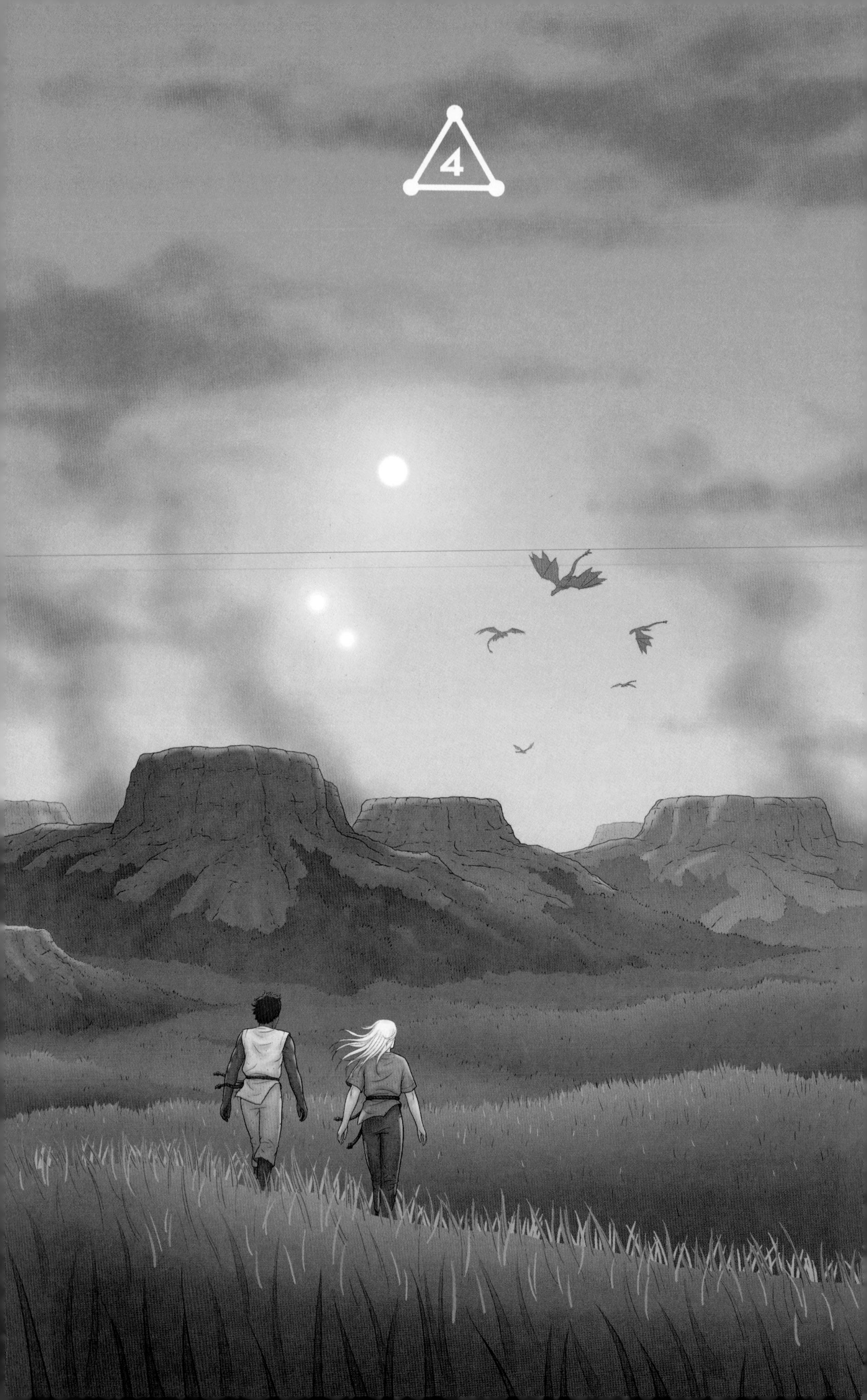

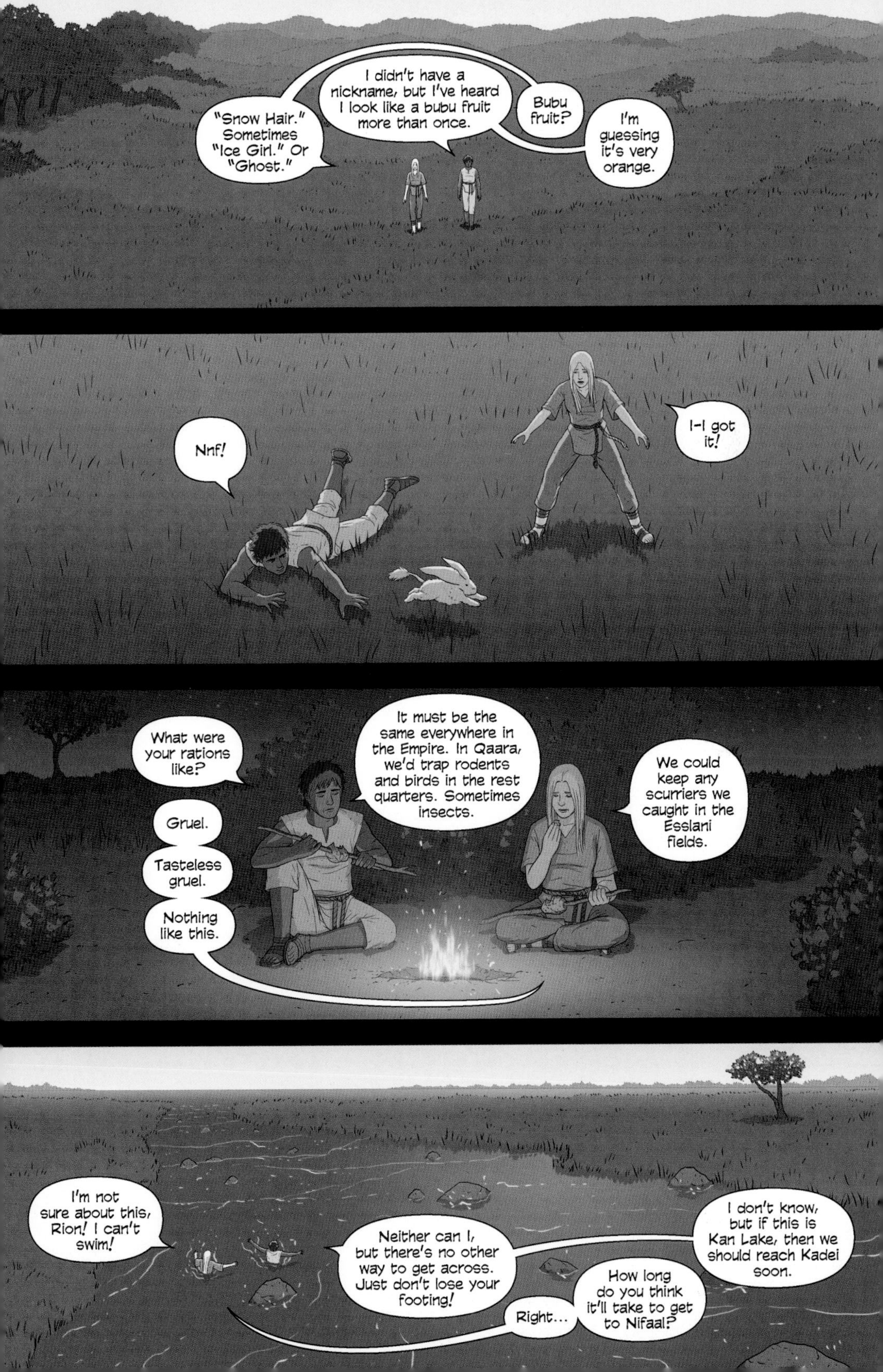
"Snow Hair." Sometimes "Ice Girl." Or "Ghost."
I didn't have a nickname, but I've heard I look like a bubu fruit more than once.
Bubu fruit?
I'm guessing it's very orange.
Nnf!
I-I got it!
What were your rations like?
It must be the same everywhere in the Empire. In Qaara, we'd trap rodents and birds in the rest quarters. Sometimes insects.
We could keep any scurriers we caught in the Esslani fields.
Gruel.
Tasteless gruel.
Nothing like this.
I'm not sure about this, Rion! I can't swim!
Neither can I, but there's no other way to get across. Just don't lose your footing!
Right...
How long do you think it'll take to get to Nifaal?
I don't know, but if this is Kan Lake, then we should reach Kadei soon.

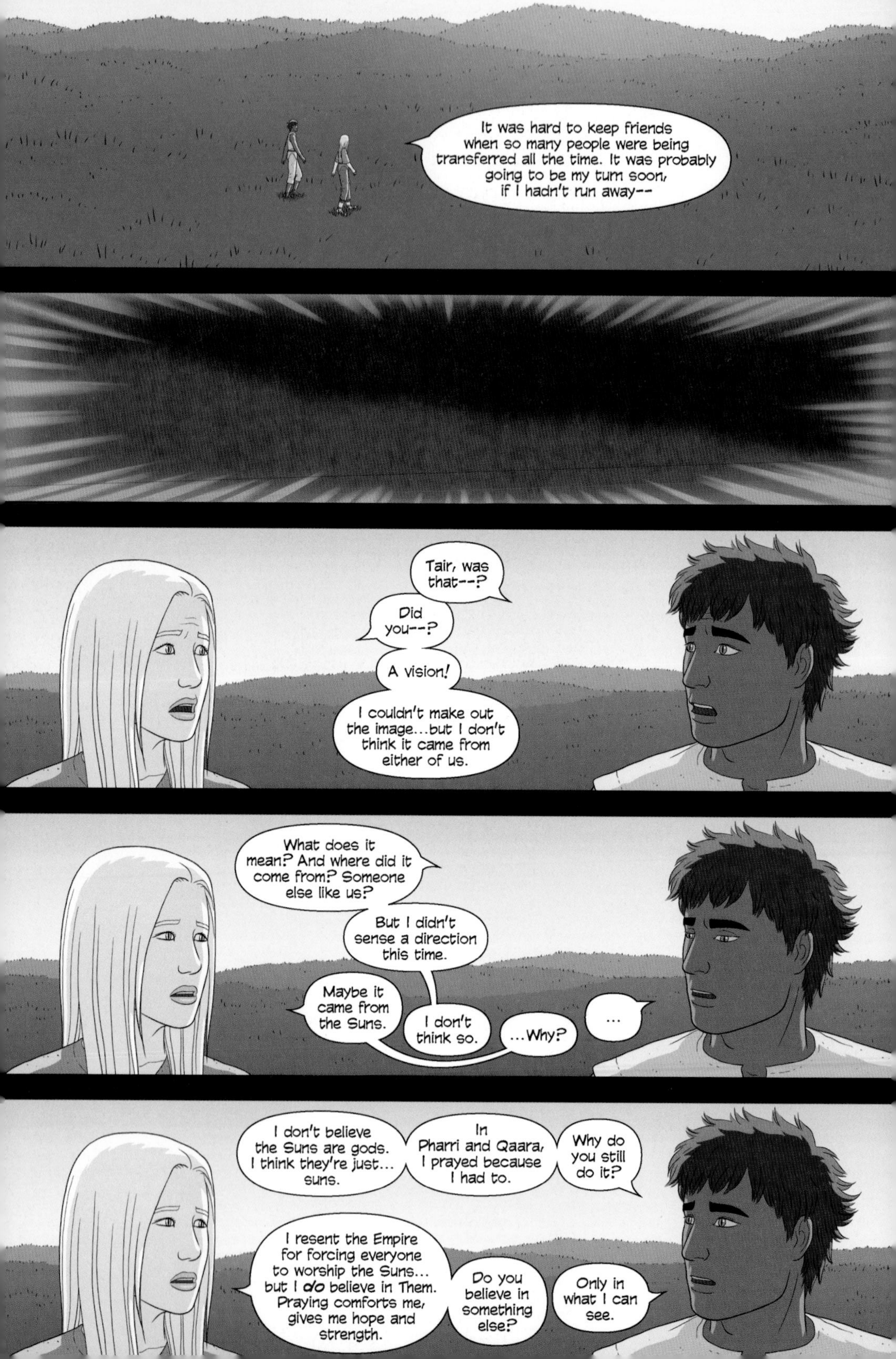
It was hard to keep friends when so many people were being transferred all the time. It was probably going to be my turn soon, if I hadn't run away--
Tair, was that--?
Did you--?
A vision!
I couldn't make out the image...but I don't think it came from either of us.
What does it mean? And where did it come from? Someone else like us?
But I didn't sense a direction this time.
Maybe it came from the Suns.
I don't think so.
...Why?
...
I don't believe the Suns are gods. I think they're just... suns.
In Pharri and Qaara, I prayed because I had to.
Why do you still do it?
I resent the Empire for forcing everyone to worship the Suns... but I *do* believe in Them. Praying comforts me, gives me hope and strength.
Do you believe in something else?
Only in what I can see.

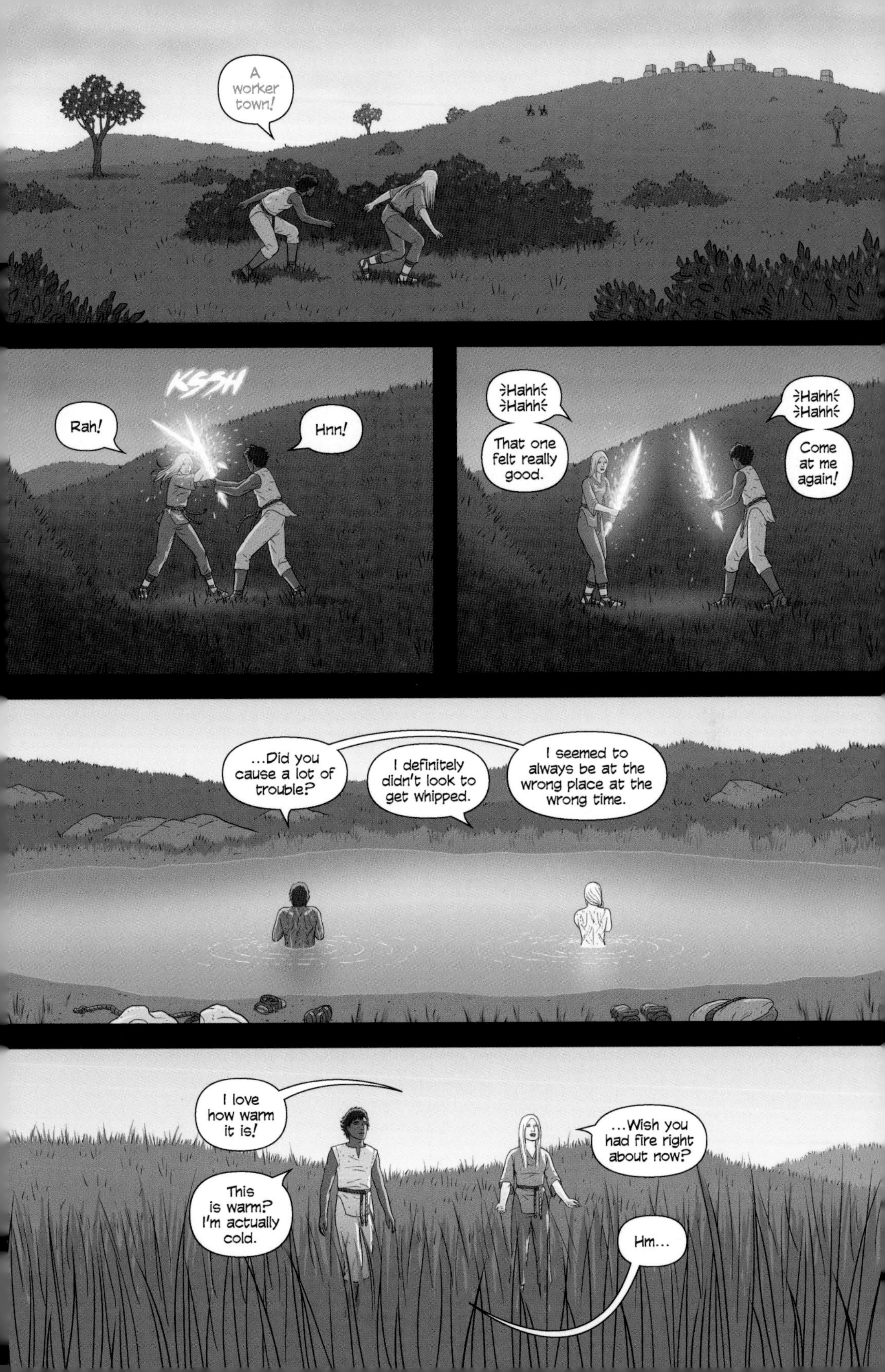
A worker town!
KSSH
Rah!
Hnn!
Hahh Hahh
That one felt really good.
Hahh Hahh
Come at me again!
...Did you cause a lot of trouble?
I definitely didn't look to get whipped.
I seemed to always be at the wrong place at the wrong time.
I love how warm it is!
This is warm? I'm actually cold.
...Wish you had fire right about now?
Hm...

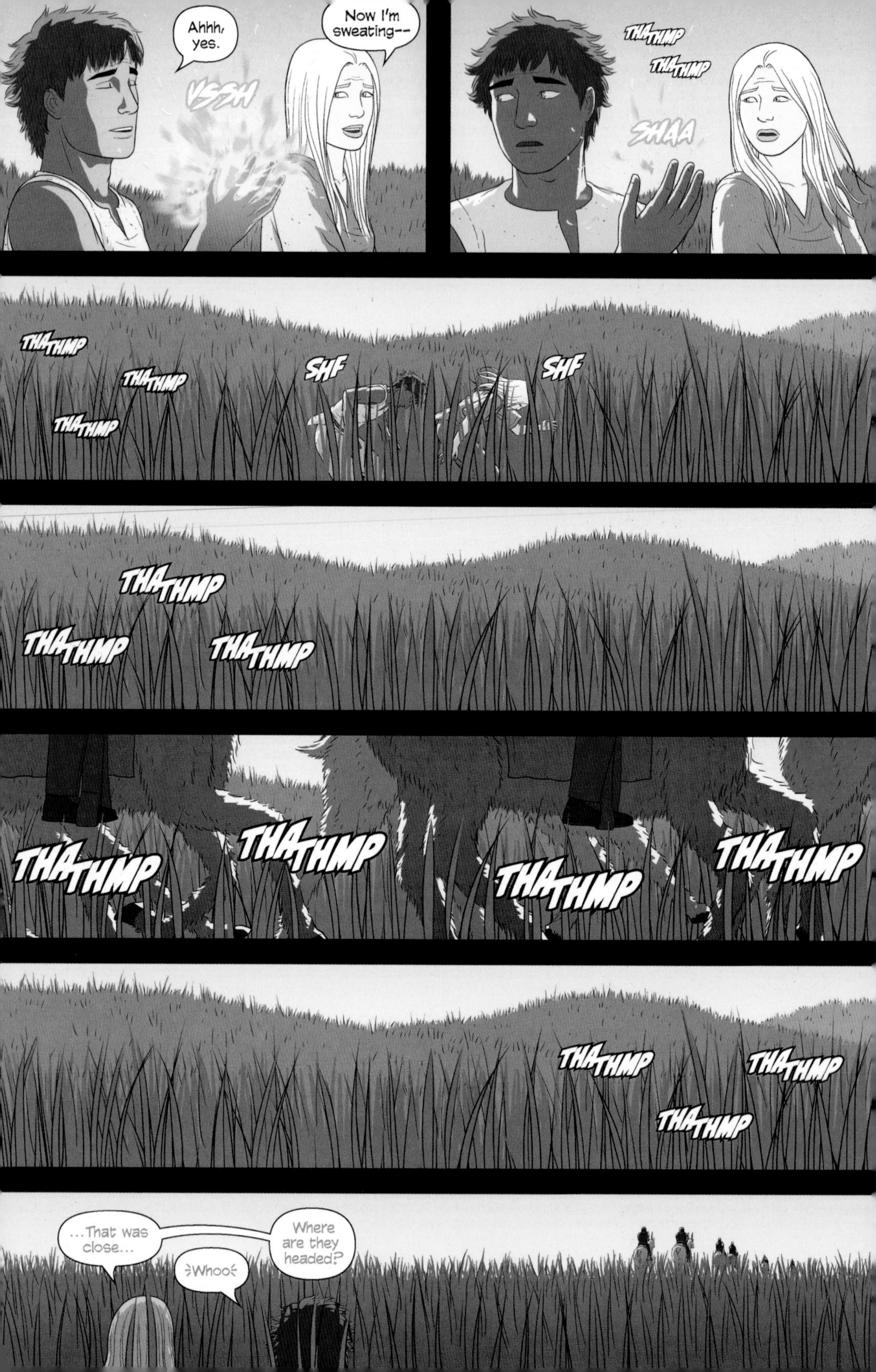
Ahhh, yes.
Now I'm sweating--
VSSH
THATHMP
THATHMP
SHAA
THATHMP
THATHMP
THATHMP
SHF
SHF
THATHMP
THATHMP
THATHMP
THATHMP
THATHMP
THATHMP
THATHMP
THATHMP
THATHMP
THATHMP
...That was close...
Where are they headed?
Whoo

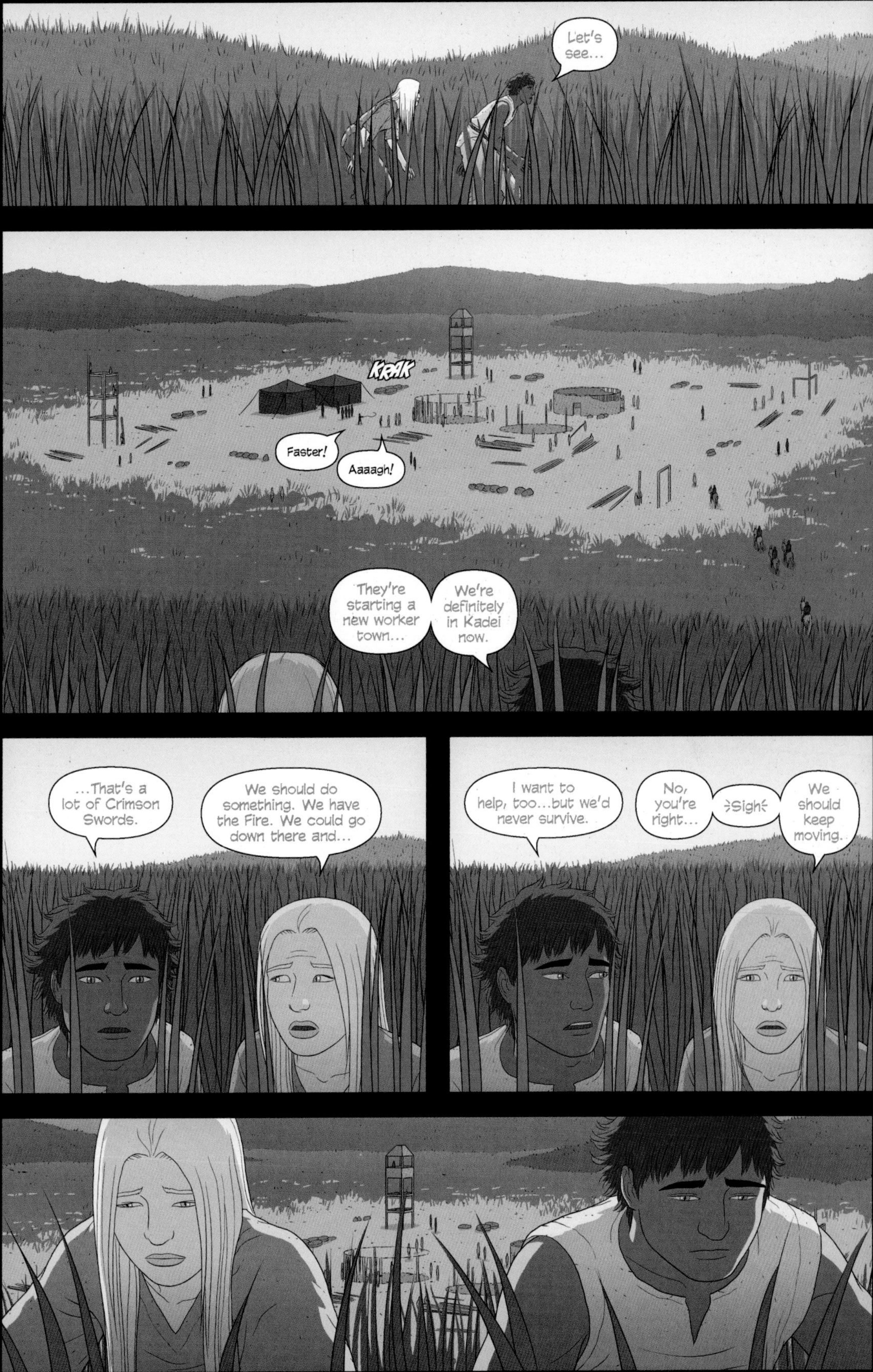
Let's see...
KRAK
Faster!
Aaaagh!
They're starting a new worker town...
We're definitely in Kadei now.
...That's a lot of Crimson Swords.
We should do something. We have the Fire. We could go down there and...
I want to help, too...but we'd never survive.
No, you're right...
Sigh
We should keep moving.

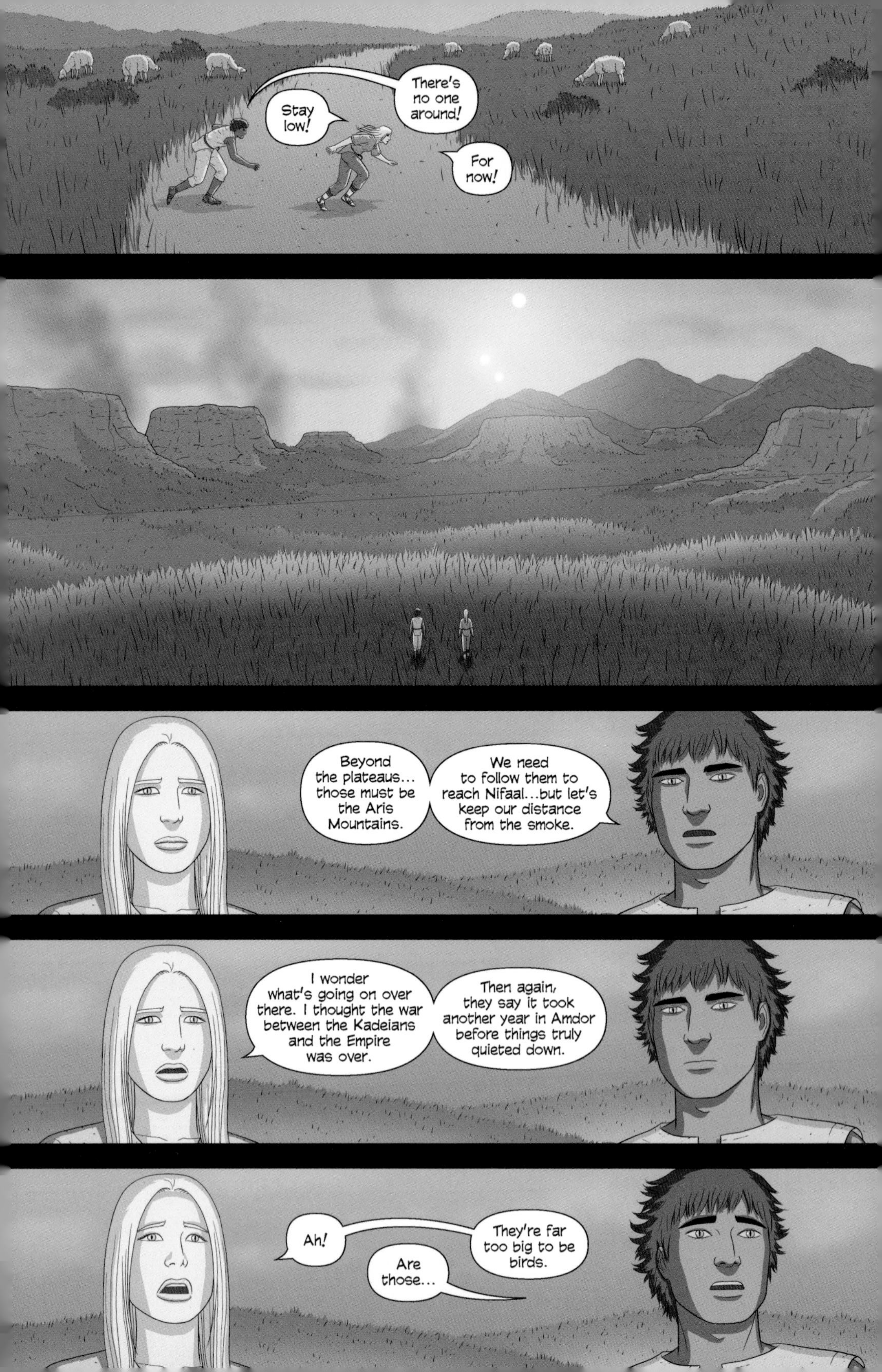
There's no one around!
Stay low!
For now!
Beyond the plateaus... those must be the Aris Mountains.
We need to follow them to reach Nifaal...but let's keep our distance from the smoke.
I wonder what's going on over there. I thought the war between the Kadeians and the Empire was over.
Then again, they say it took another year in Amdor before things truly quieted down.
Ah!
They're far too big to be birds.
Are those...

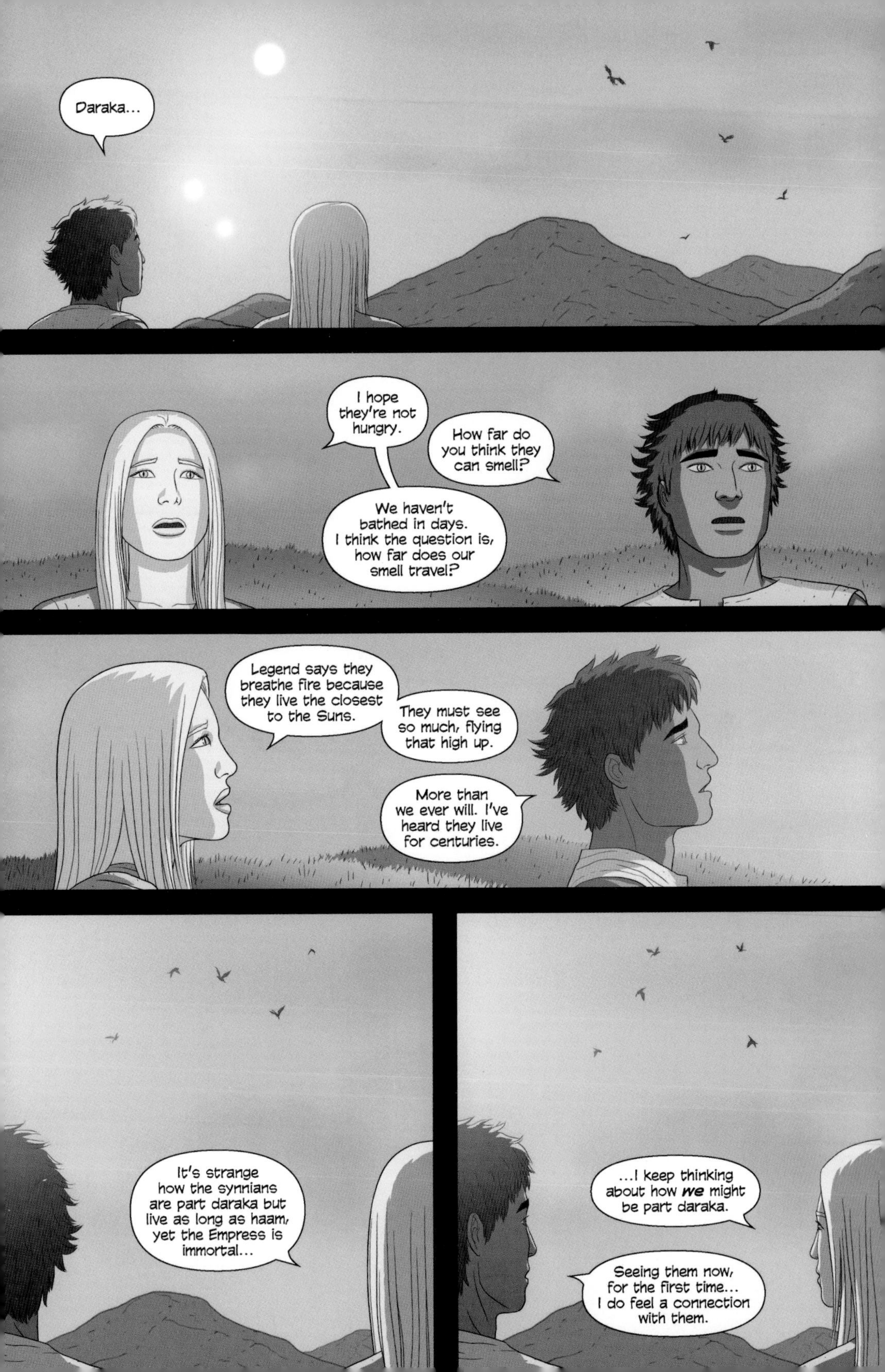

Daraka...
I hope they're not hungry.
How far do you think they can smell?
We haven't bathed in days. I think the question is, how far does our smell travel?
Legend says they breathe fire because they live the closest to the Suns.
They must see so much, flying that high up.
More than we ever will. I've heard they live for centuries.
It's strange how the synnians are part daraka but live as long as haam, yet the Empress is immortal...
...I keep thinking about how ***we*** might be part daraka.
Seeing them now, for the first time... I do feel a connection with them.

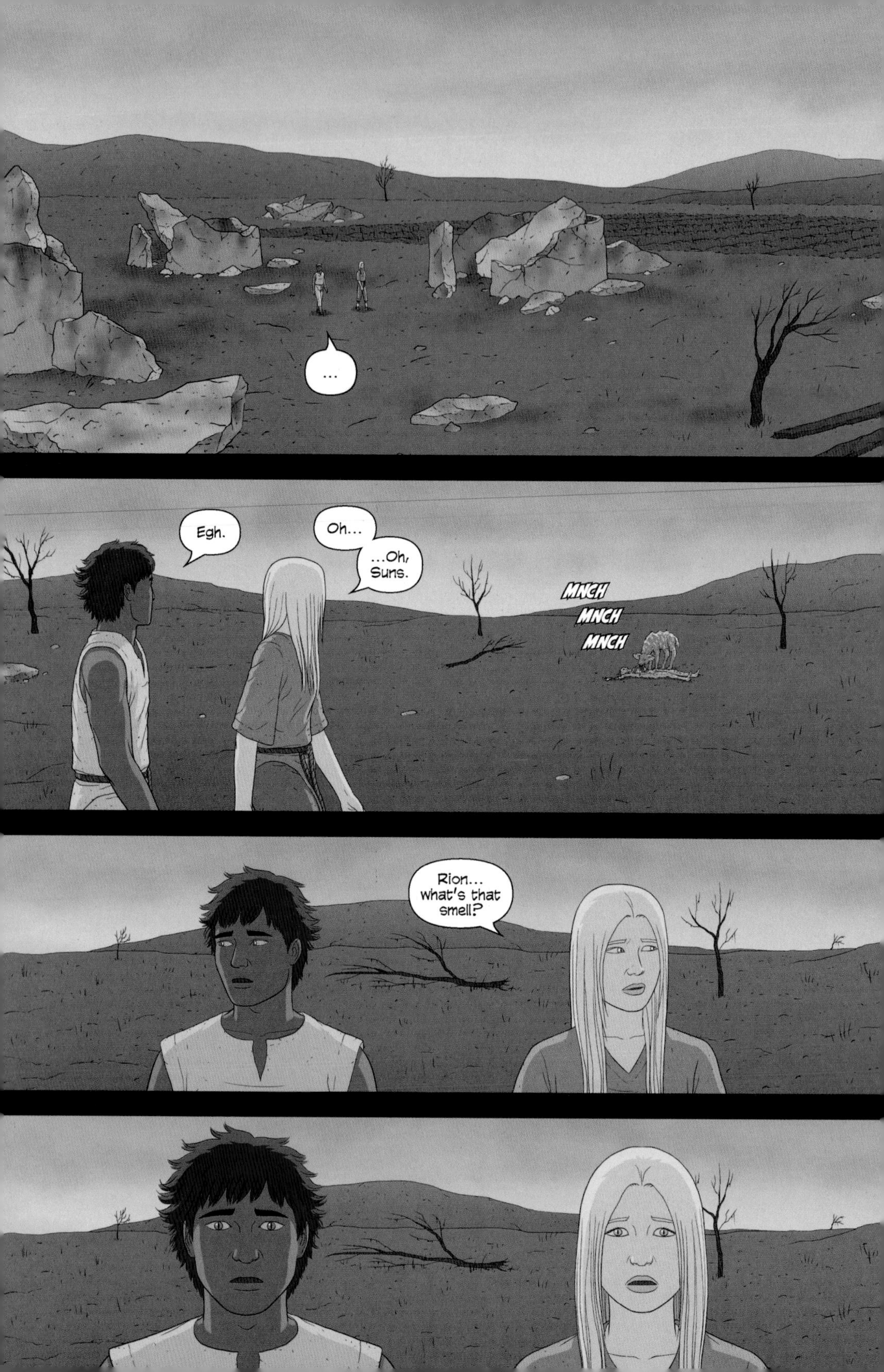
...
Egh.
Oh...
...Oh, Suns.
MNCH
MNCH
MNCH
Rion... what's that smell?

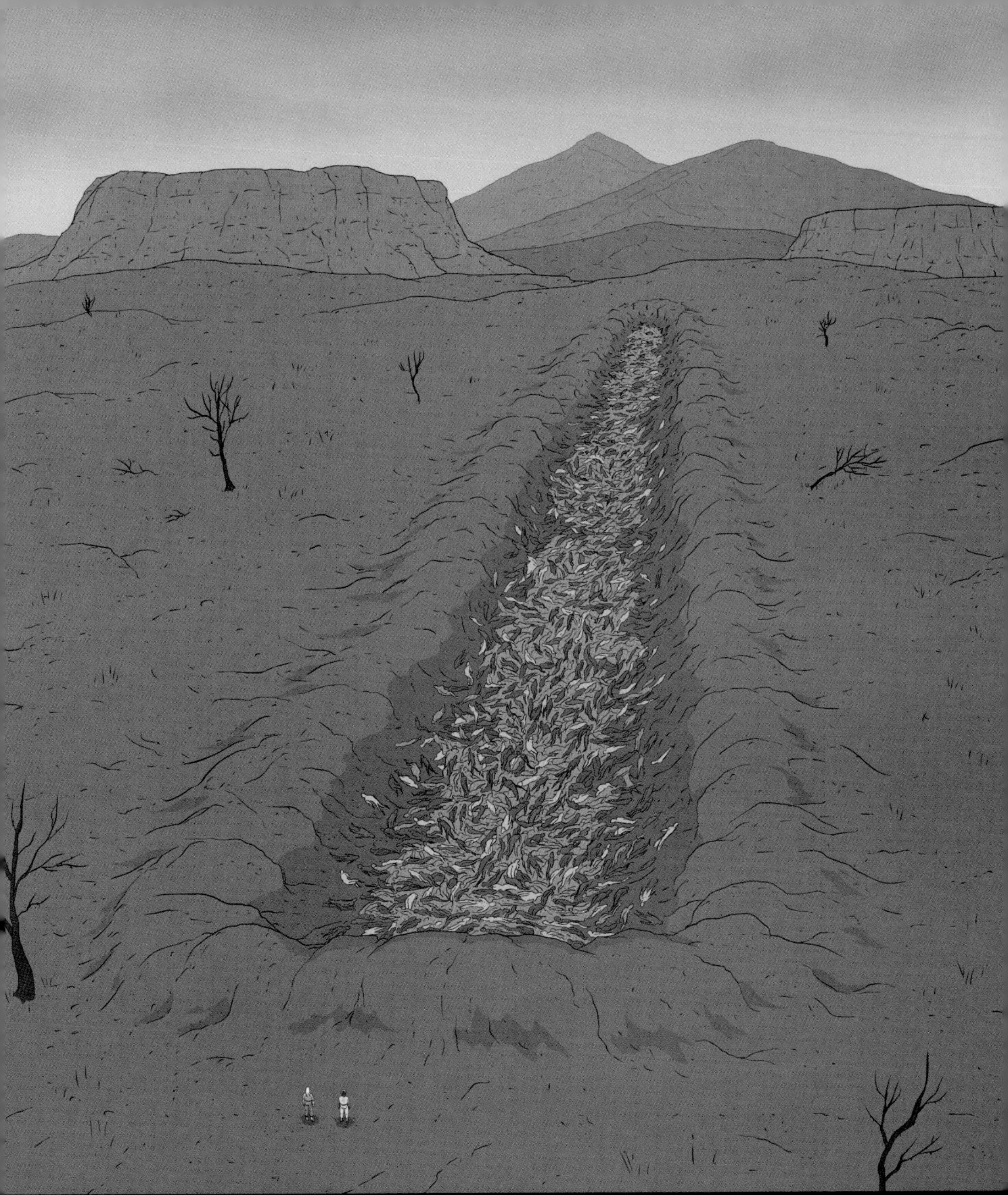

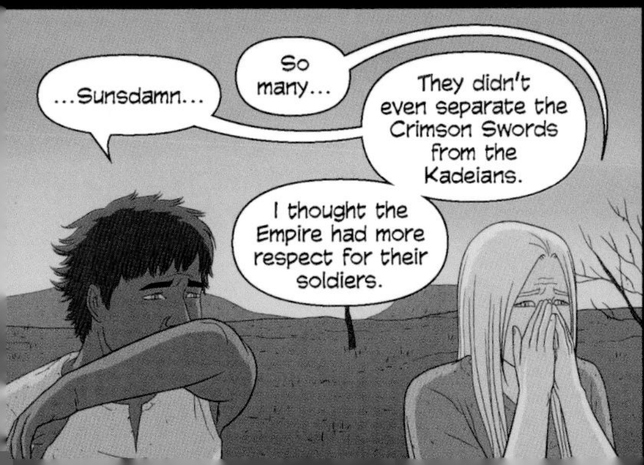

...Sunsdamn...
So many...
They didn't even separate the Crimson Swords from the Kadeians.
I thought the Empire had more respect for their soldiers.

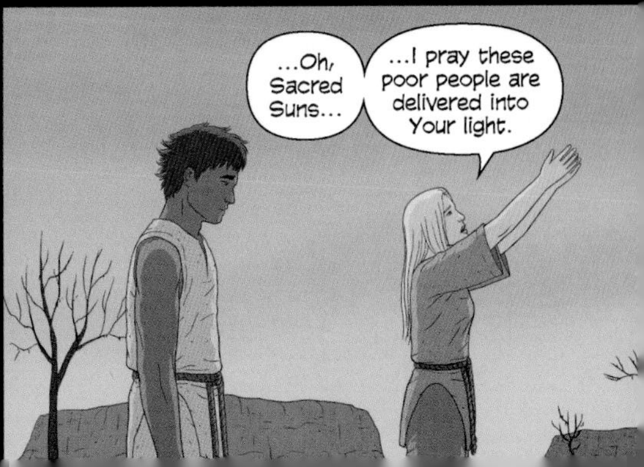

...Oh, Sacred Suns...
...I pray these poor people are delivered into Your light.

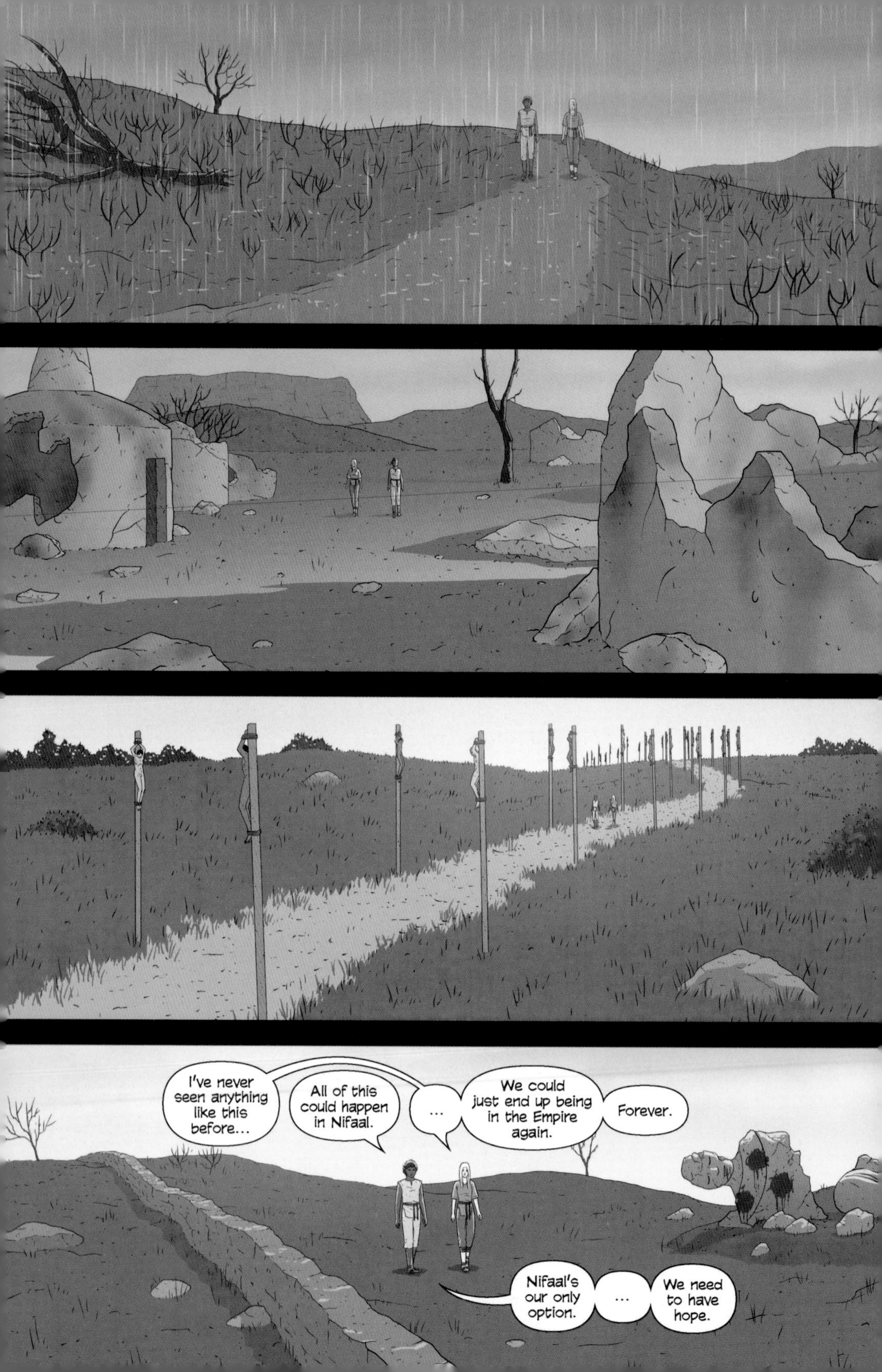
I've never seen anything like this before...
All of this could happen in Nifaal.
...
We could just end up being in the Empire again.
Forever.
Nifaal's our only option.
...
We need to have hope.

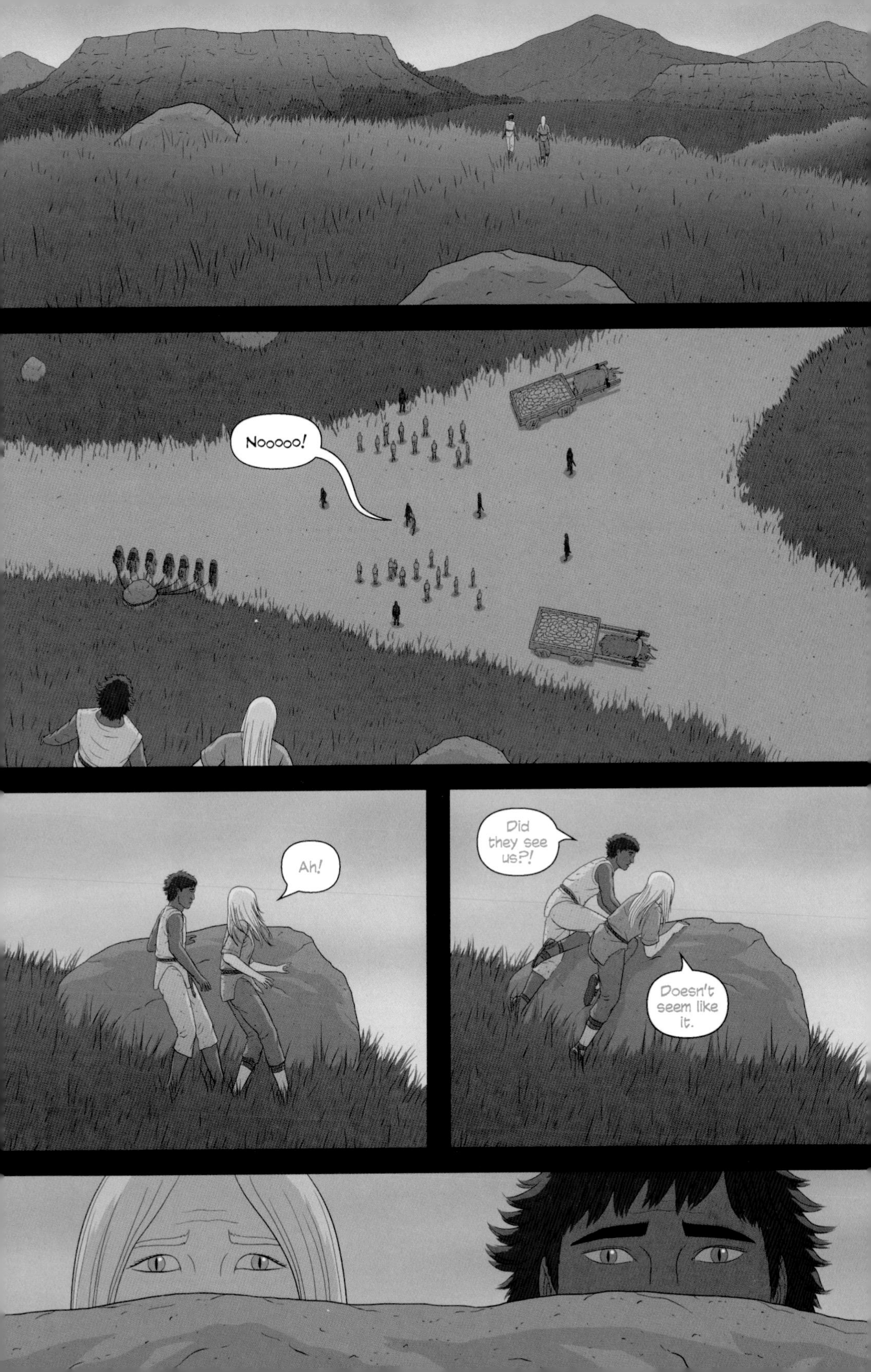
Nooooo!
Ah!
Did they see us?!
Doesn't seem like it.

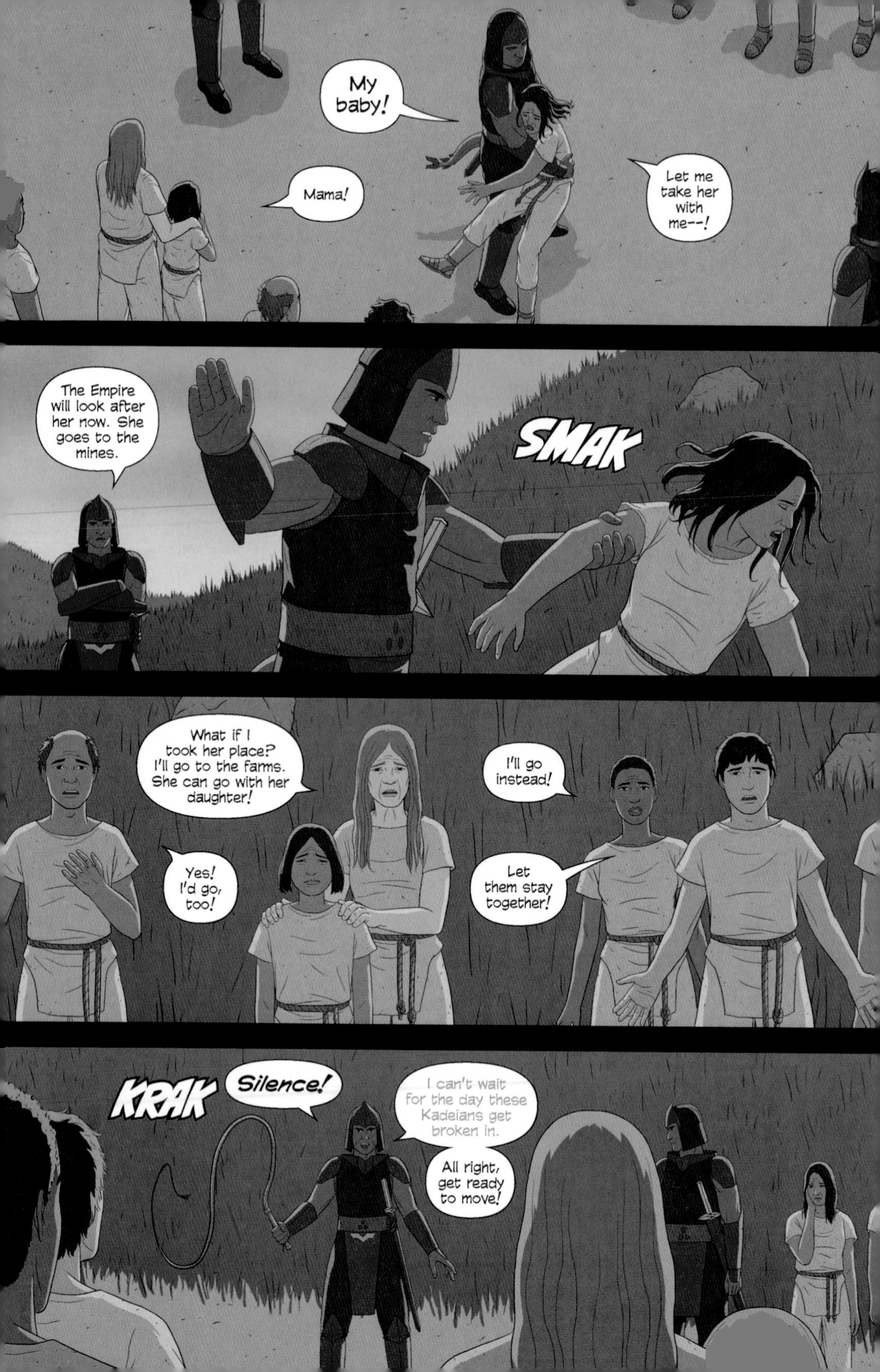
My baby!
Mama!
Let me take her with me--!
The Empire will look after her now. She goes to the mines.
SMAK
What if I took her place? I'll go to the farms. She can go with her daughter!
Yes! I'd go, too!
I'll go instead!
Let them stay together!
KRAK
Silence!
I can't wait for the day these Kadeians get broken in.
All right, get ready to move!

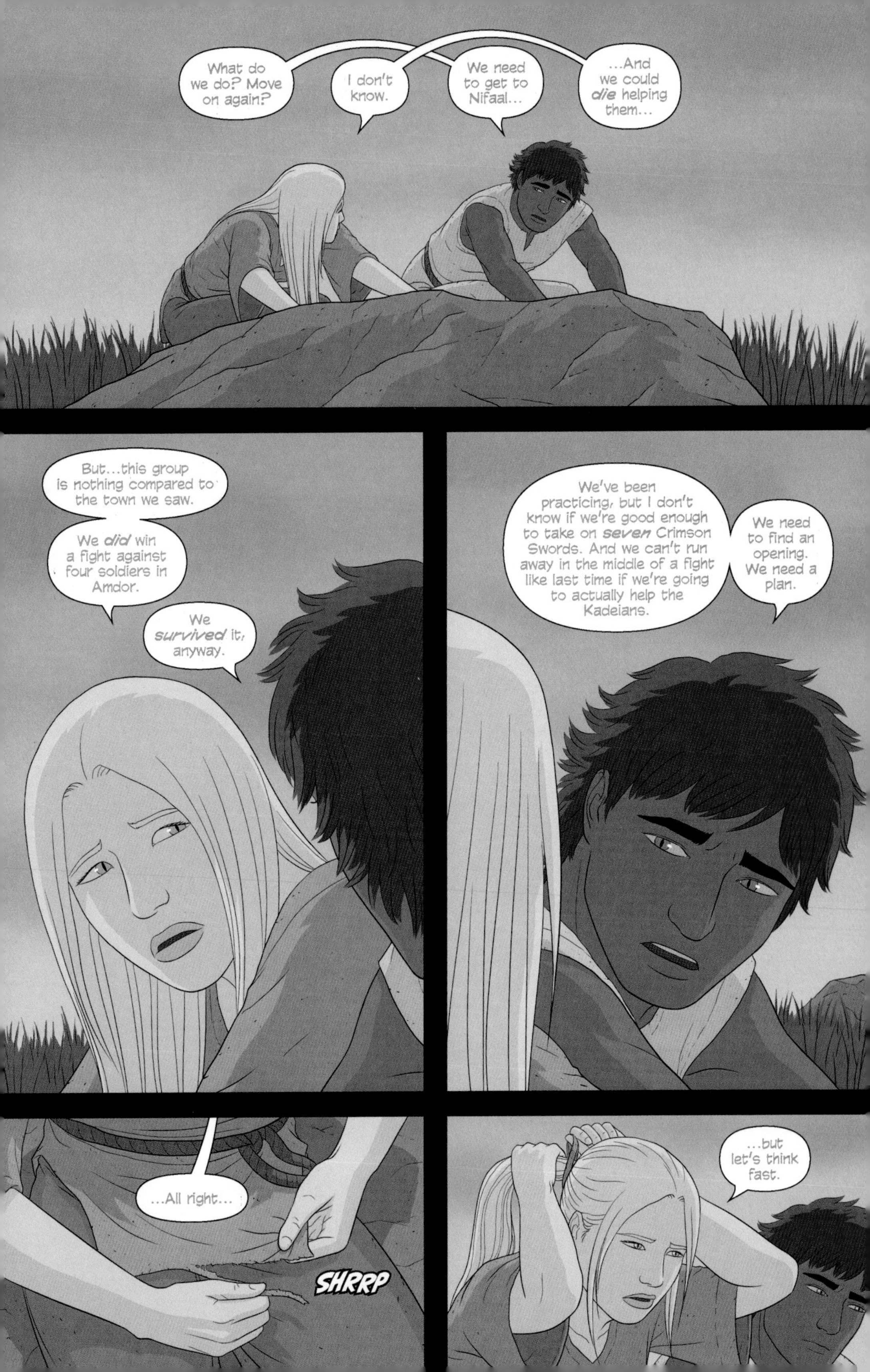
What do we do? Move on again?
I don't know.
We need to get to Nifaal...
...And we could *die* helping them...
But...this group is nothing compared to the town we saw.
We *did* win a fight against four soldiers in Amdor.
We *survived* it, anyway.
We've been practicing, but I don't know if we're good enough to take on *seven* Crimson Swords. And we can't run away in the middle of a fight like last time if we're going to actually help the Kadeians.
We need to find an opening. We need a plan.
...All right...
SHRRP
...but let's think fast.

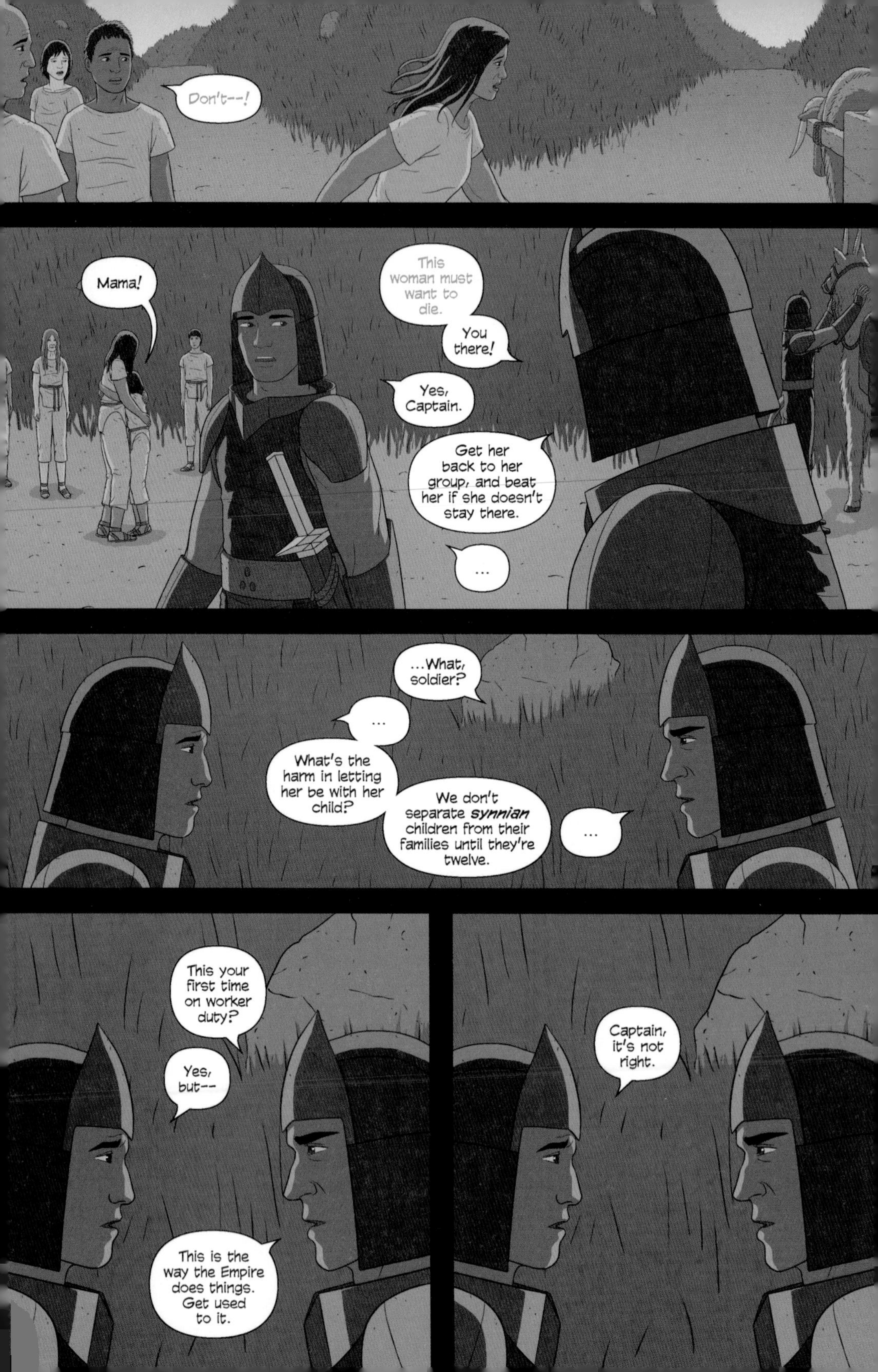

Don't--!
Mama!
This woman must want to die.
You there!
Yes, Captain.
Get her back to her group, and beat her if she doesn't stay there.
...
...What, soldier?
...
What's the harm in letting her be with her child?
We don't separate *synnian* children from their families until they're twelve.
...
This your first time on worker duty?
Yes, but--
This is the way the Empire does things. Get used to it.
Captain, it's not right.

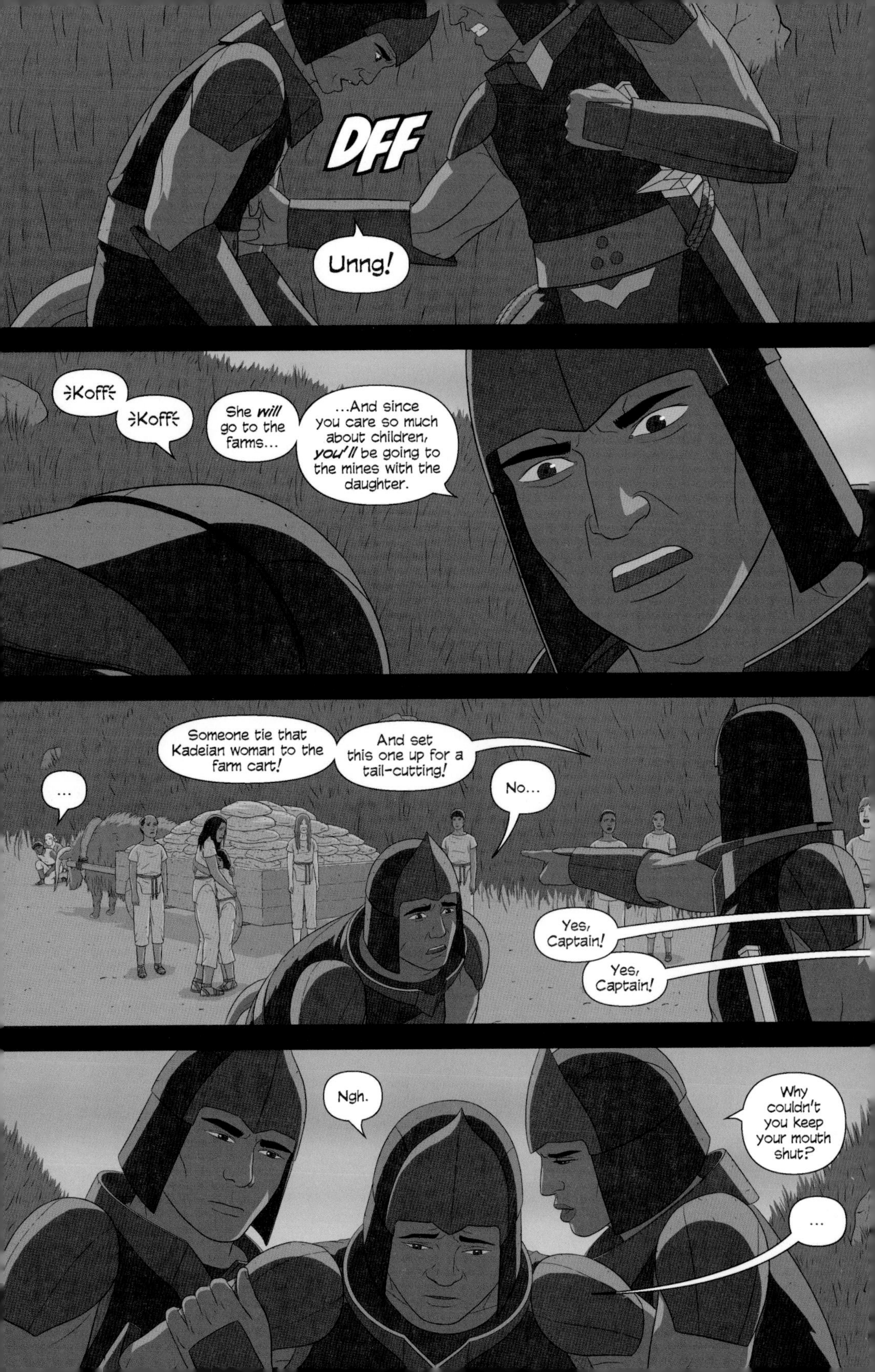
DFF
Unng!
Koff
Koff
She *will* go to the farms...
...And since you care so much about children, *you'll* be going to the mines with the daughter.
...
Someone tie that Kadeian woman to the farm cart!
And set this one up for a tail-cutting!
No...
Yes, Captain!
Yes, Captain!
Ngh.
Why couldn't you keep your mouth shut?
...

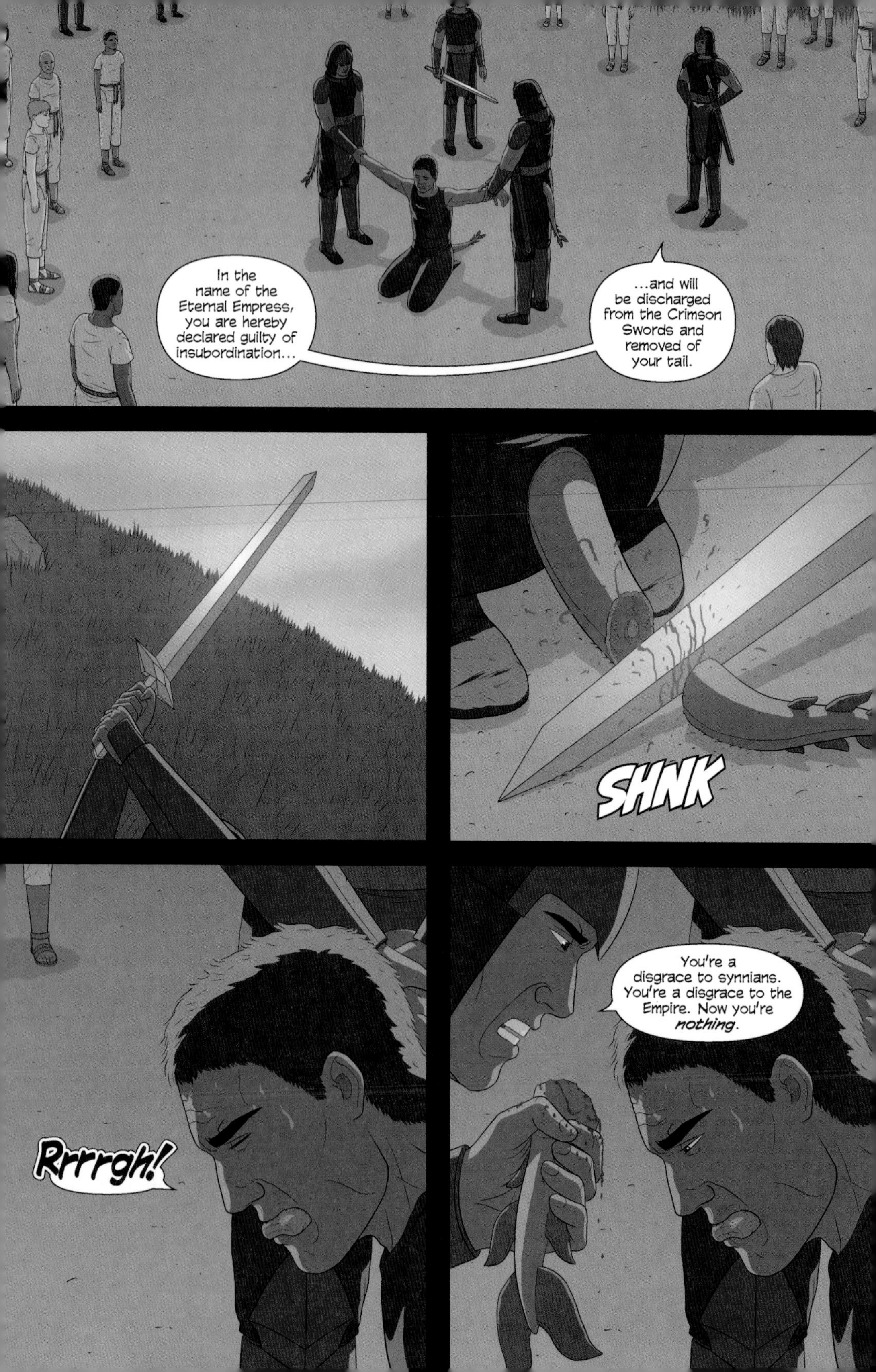
In the name of the Eternal Empress, you are hereby declared guilty of insubordination...
...and will be discharged from the Crimson Swords and removed of your tail.
SHNK
Rrrrgh!
You're a disgrace to synnians. You're a disgrace to the Empire. Now you're *nothing*.

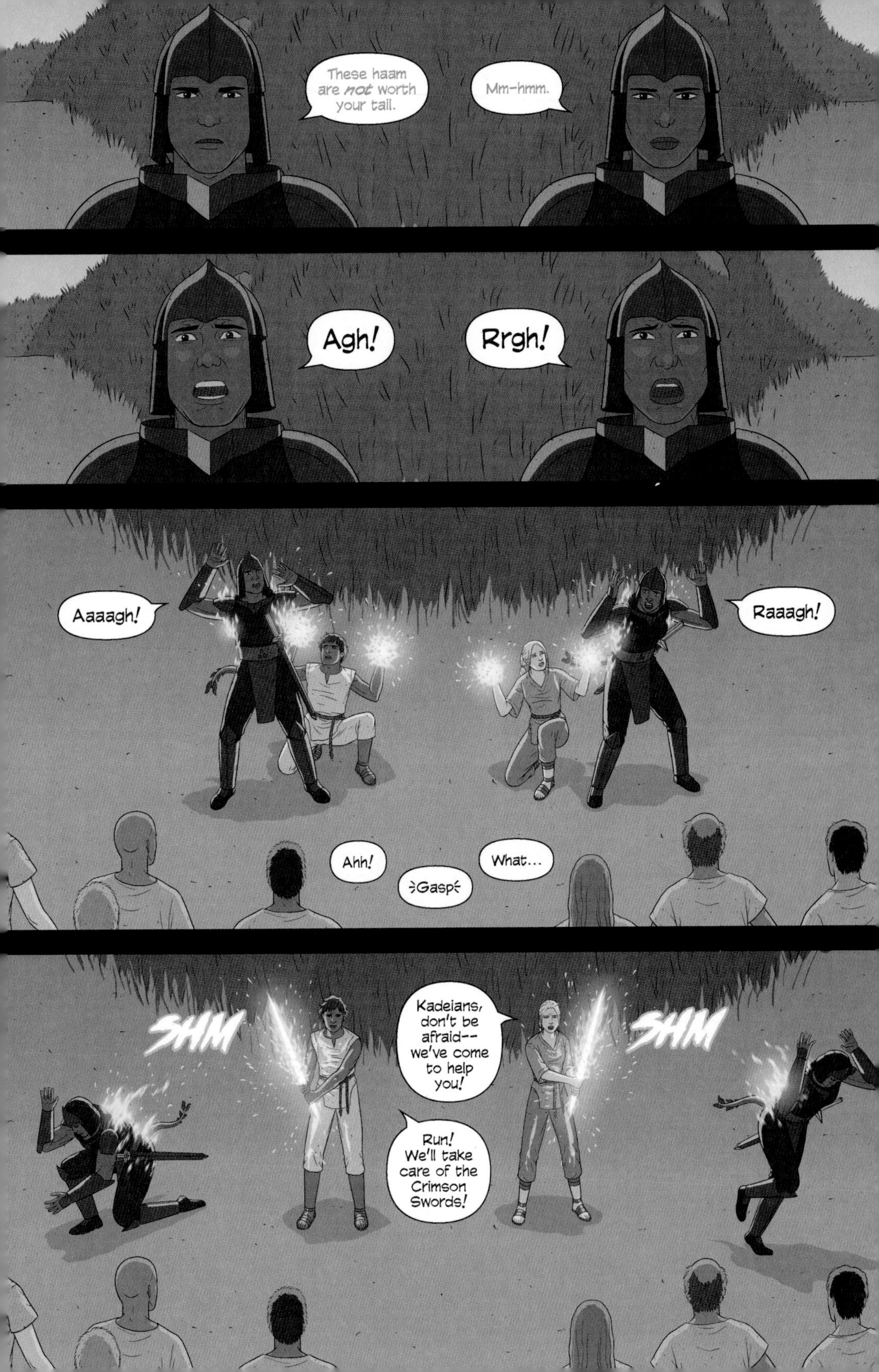
These haam are *not* worth your tail.
Mm-hmm.
Agh!
Rrgh!
Aaaagh!
Raaagh!
Ahh!
Gasp
What...
SHM
Kadeians, don't be afraid-- we've come to help you!
Run! We'll take care of the Crimson Swords!
SHM

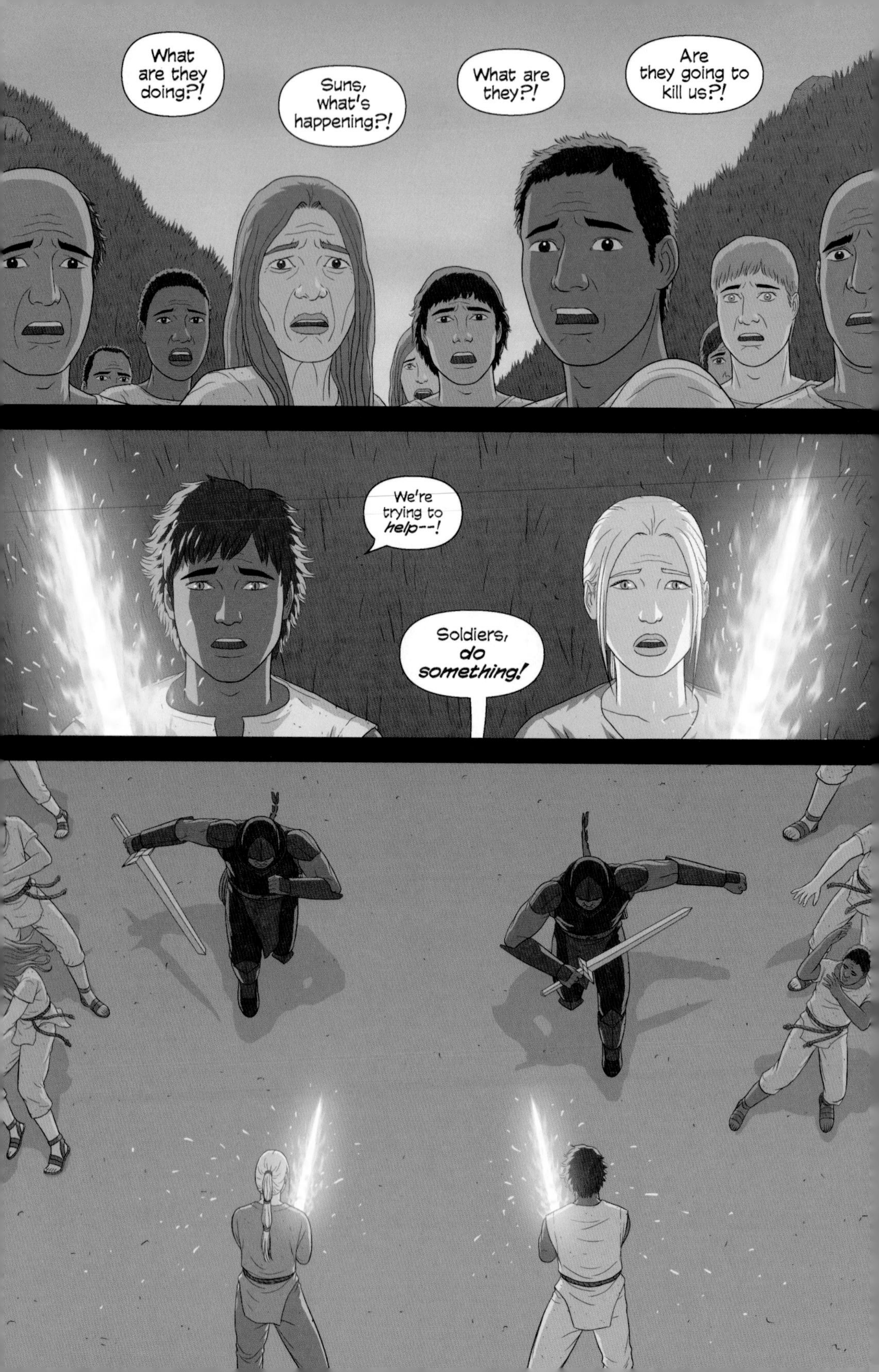
What are they doing?!
Suns, what's happening?!
What are they?!
Are they going to kill us?!
We're trying to help--!
Soldiers, do something!

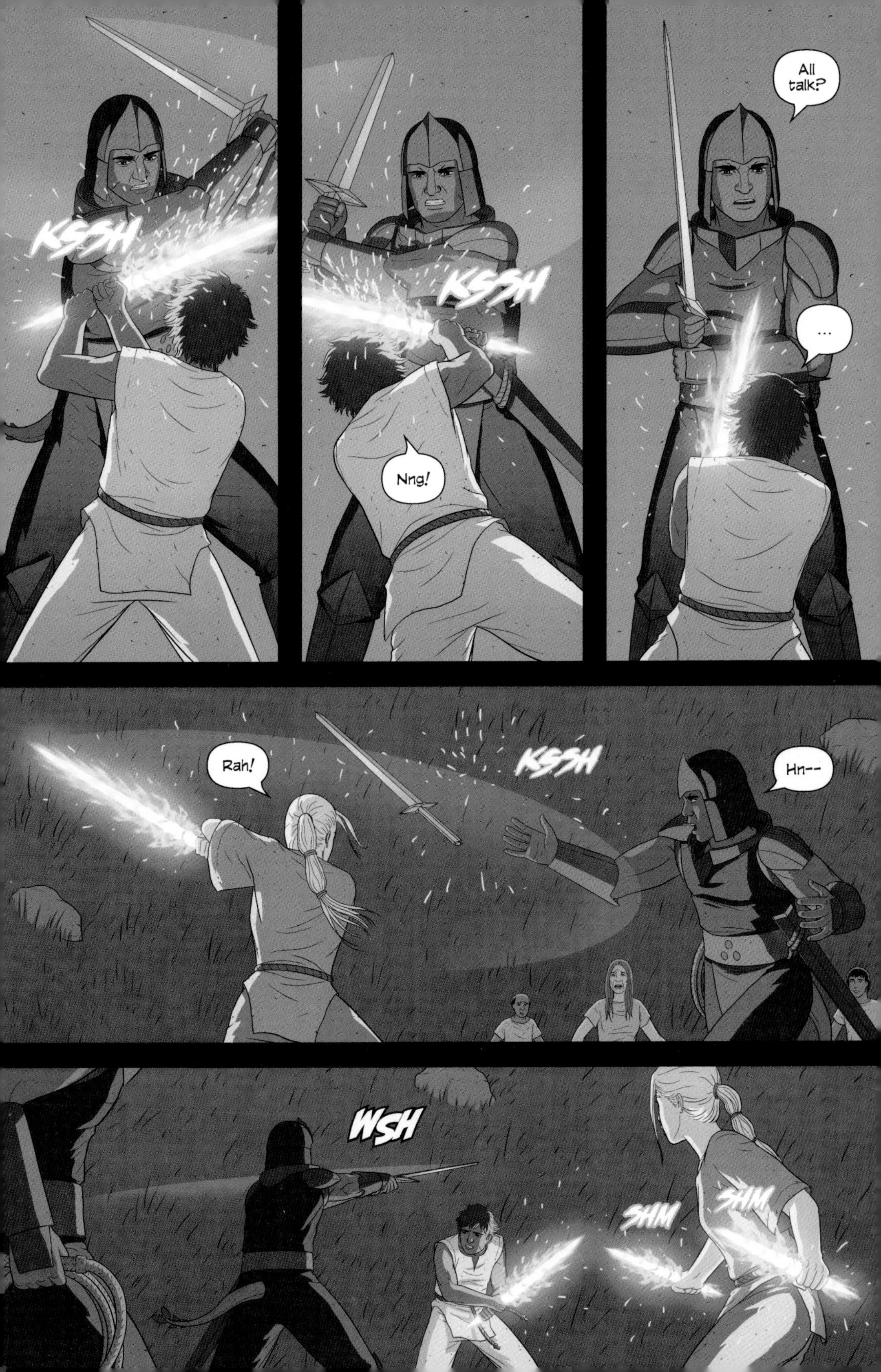
KSSH
KSSH
Nng!
All talk?
...
Rah!
KSSH
Hn--
WSH
SHM
SHM

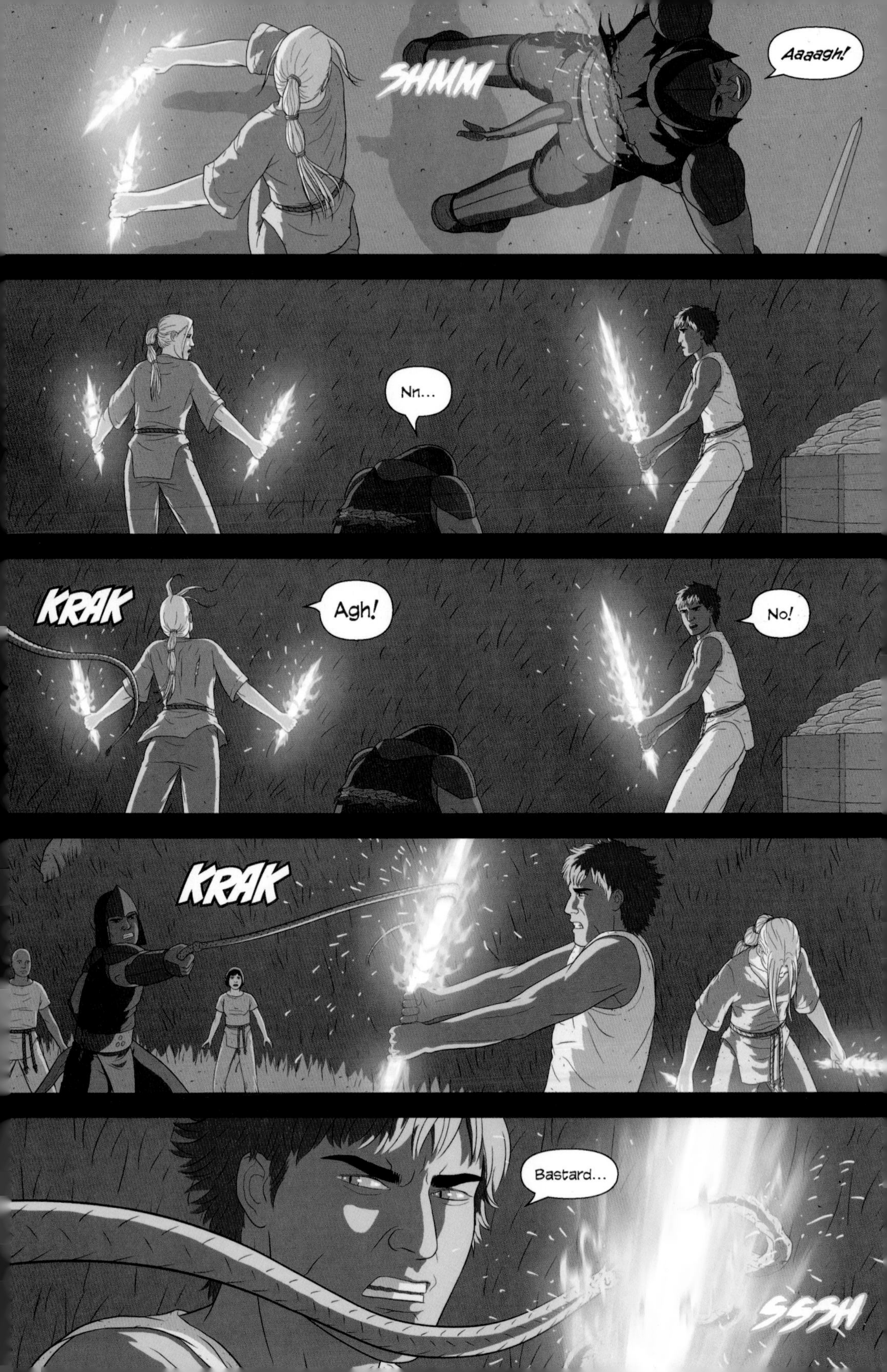
SHMM
Aaaagh!
Nn...
KRAK
Agh!
No!
KRAK
Bastard...
SSSH

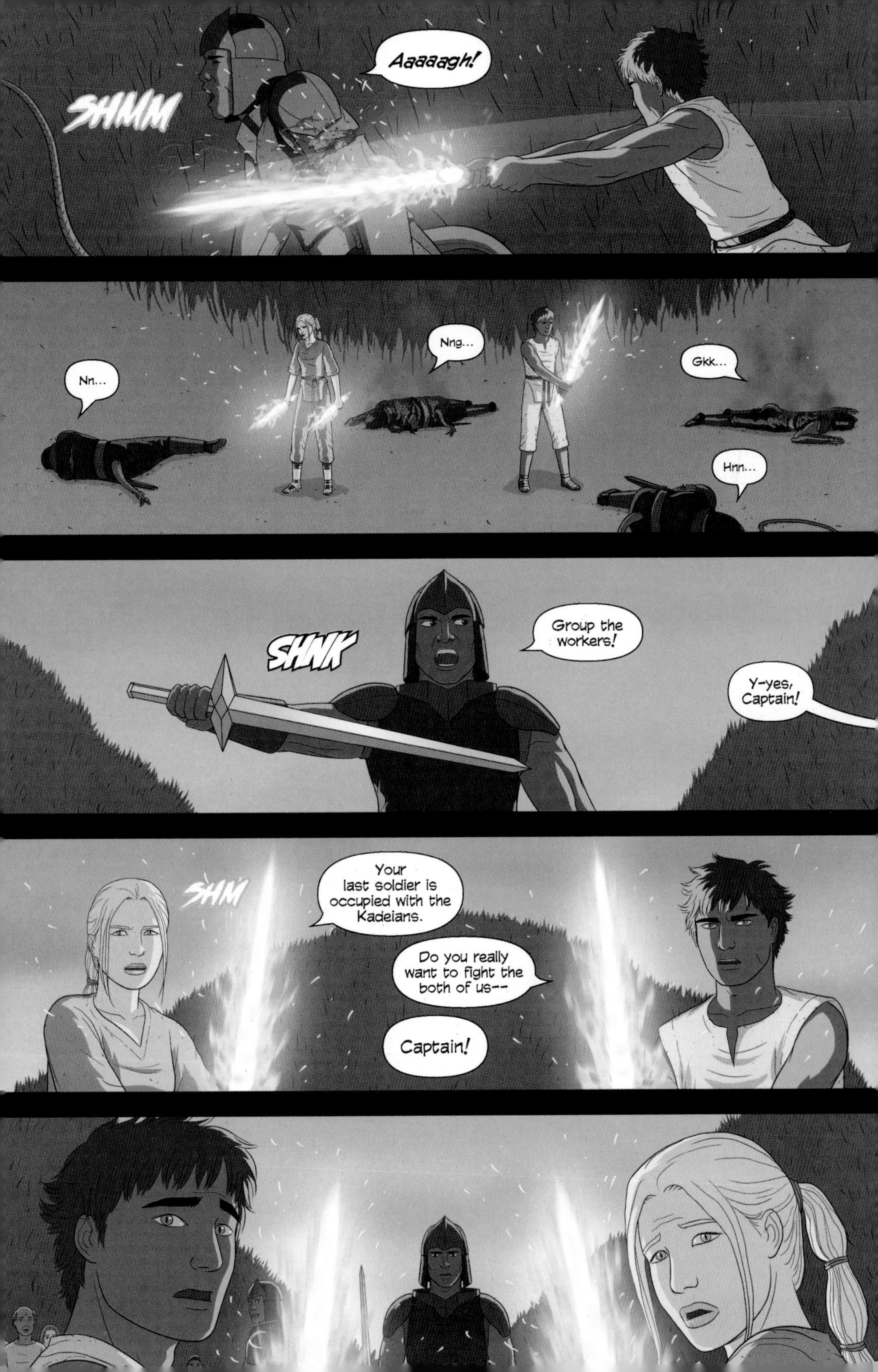
SHMM
Aaaaagh!
Nn...
Nng...
Gkk...
Hnn...
SHNK
Group the workers!
Y-yes, Captain!
SHM
Your last soldier is occupied with the Kadeians.
Do you really want to fight the both of us--
Captain!

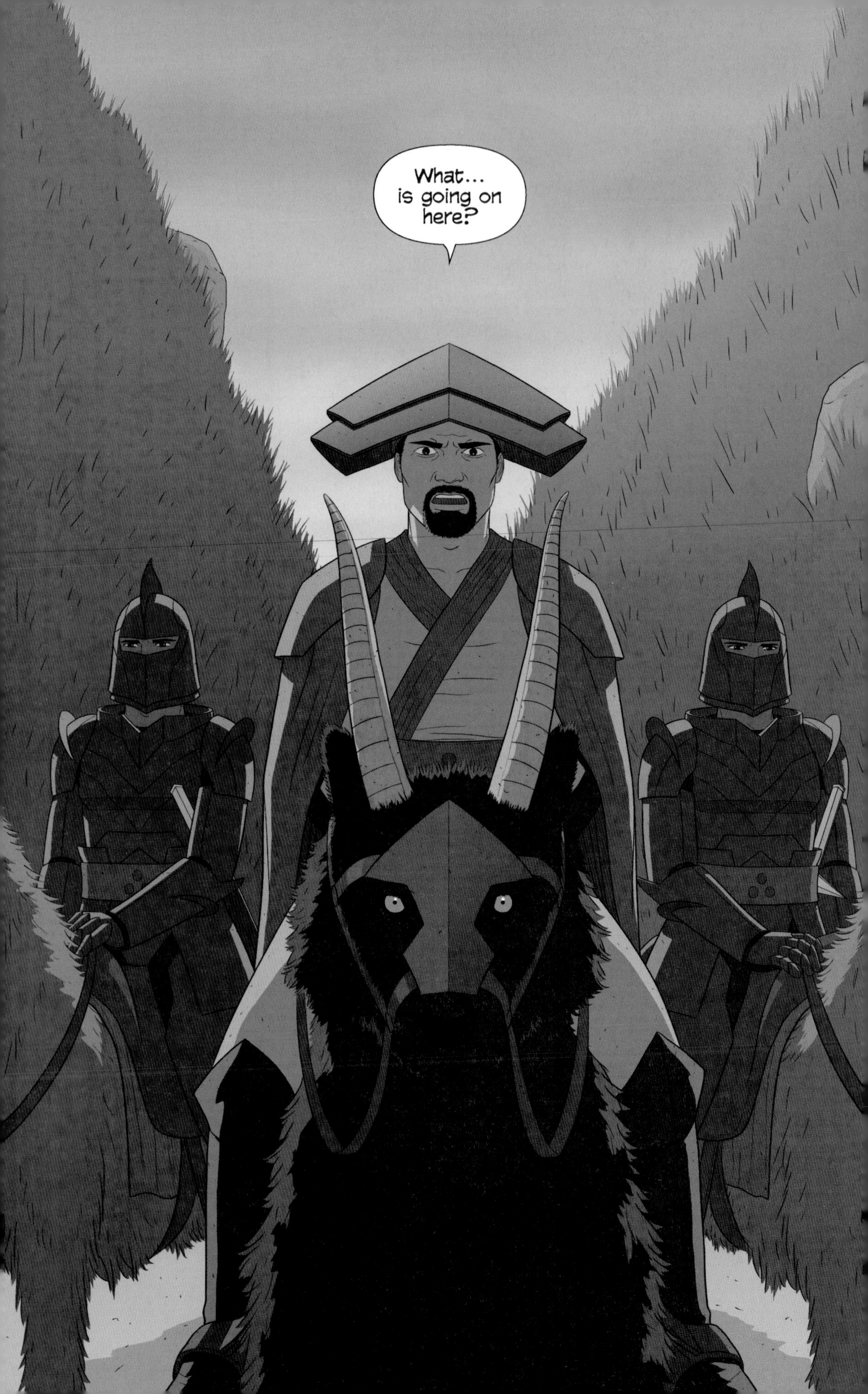
What... is going on here?

5

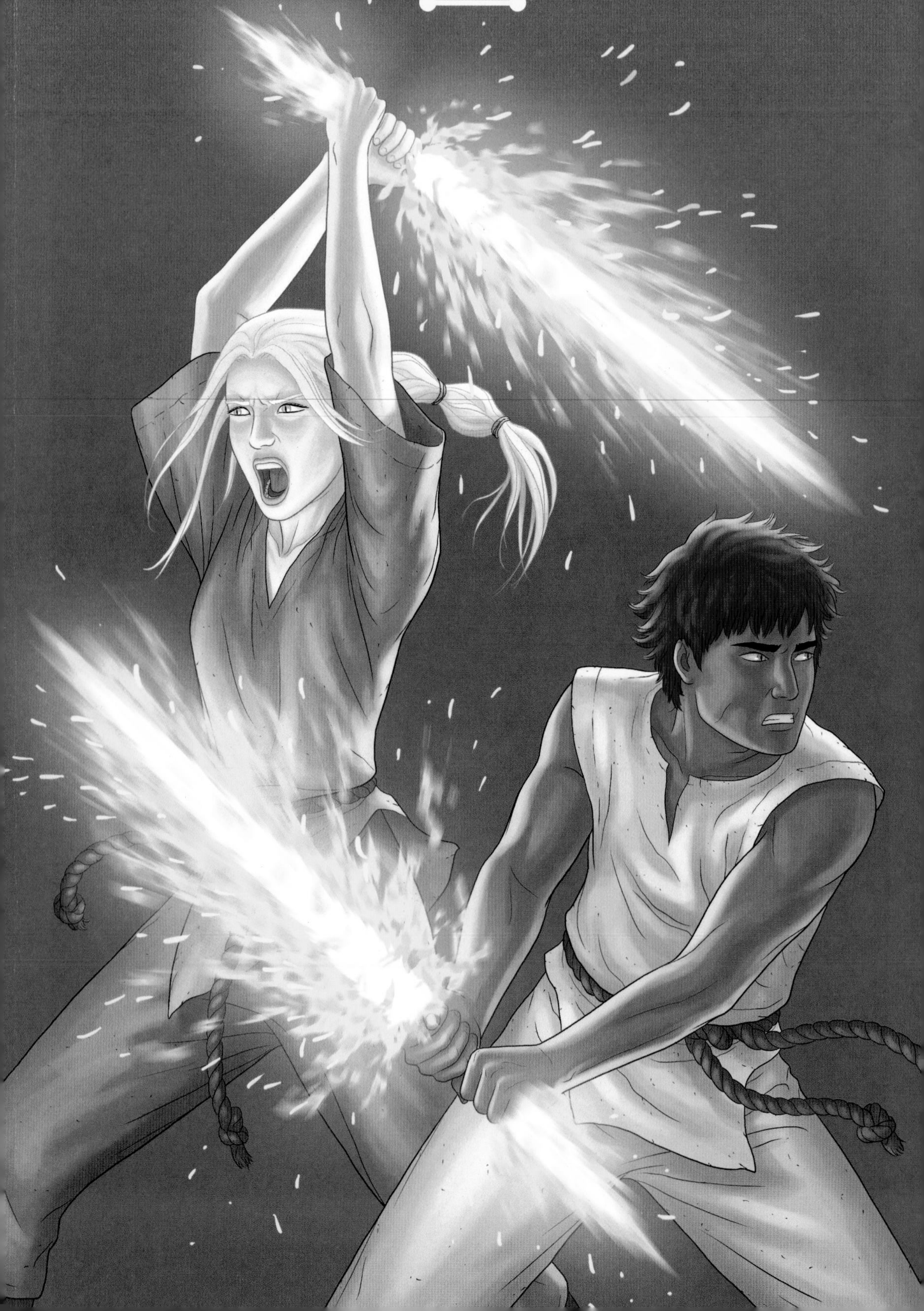

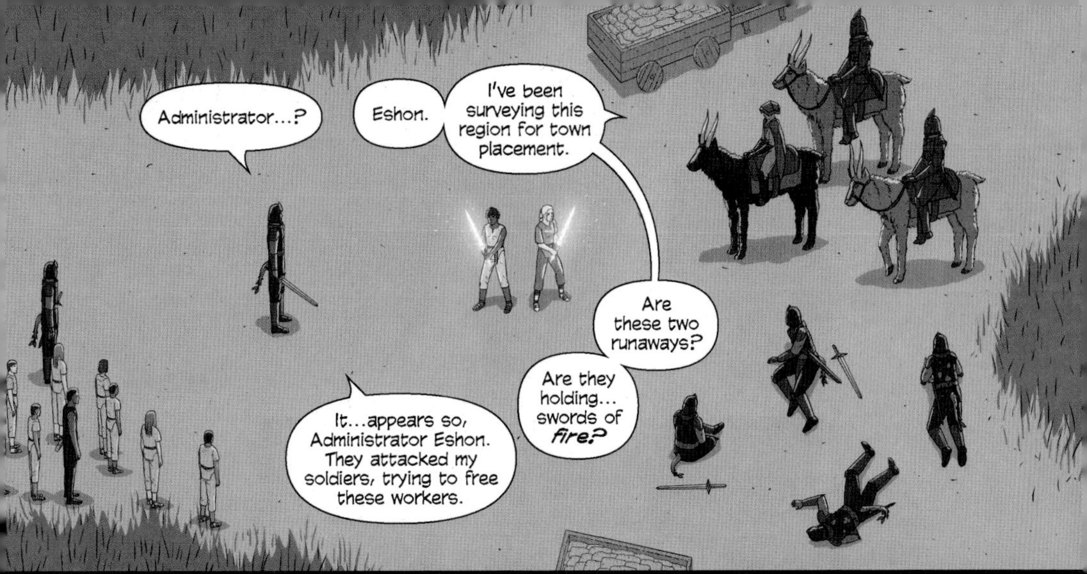
Administrator...?
Eshon.
I've been surveying this region for town placement.
Are these two runaways?
Are they holding... swords of *fire?*
It...appears so, Administrator Eshon. They attacked my soldiers, trying to free these workers.

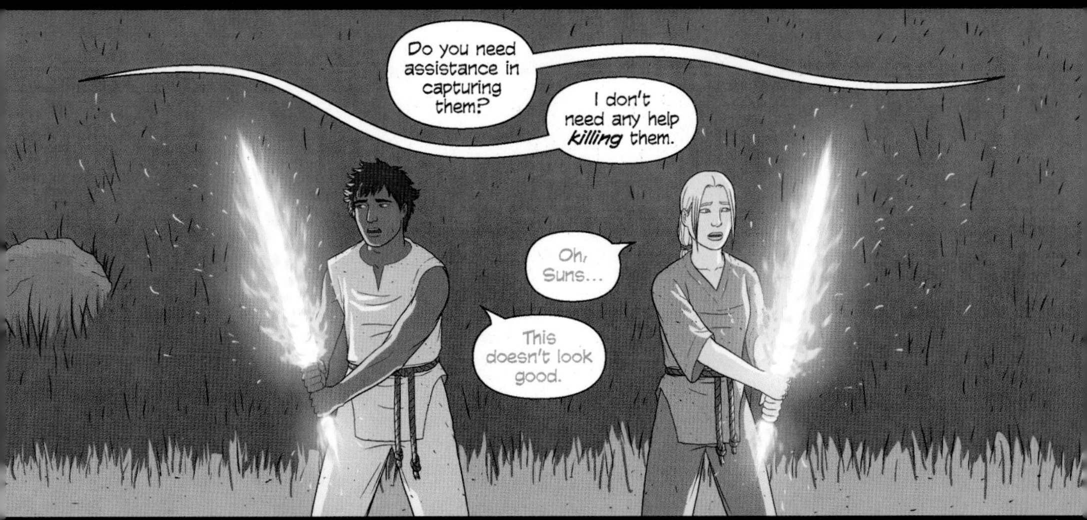
Do you need assistance in capturing them?
I don't need any help *killing* them.
Oh, Suns...
This doesn't look good.

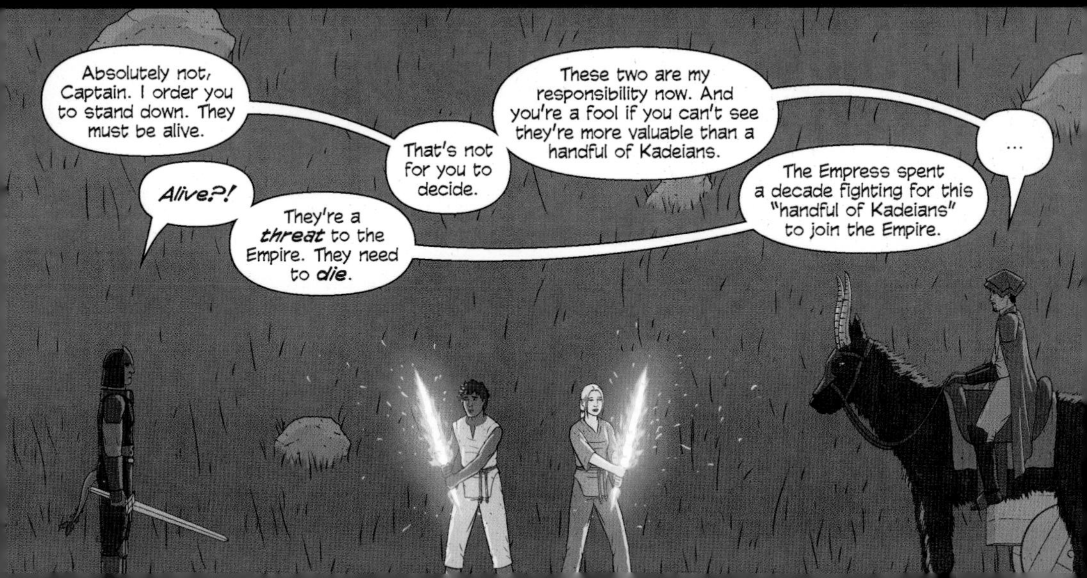
Absolutely not, Captain. I order you to stand down. They must be alive.
Alive?!
That's not for you to decide.
They're a *threat* to the Empire. They need to *die*.
These two are my responsibility now. And you're a fool if you can't see they're more valuable than a handful of Kadeians.
...
The Empress spent a decade fighting for this "handful of Kadeians" to join the Empire.

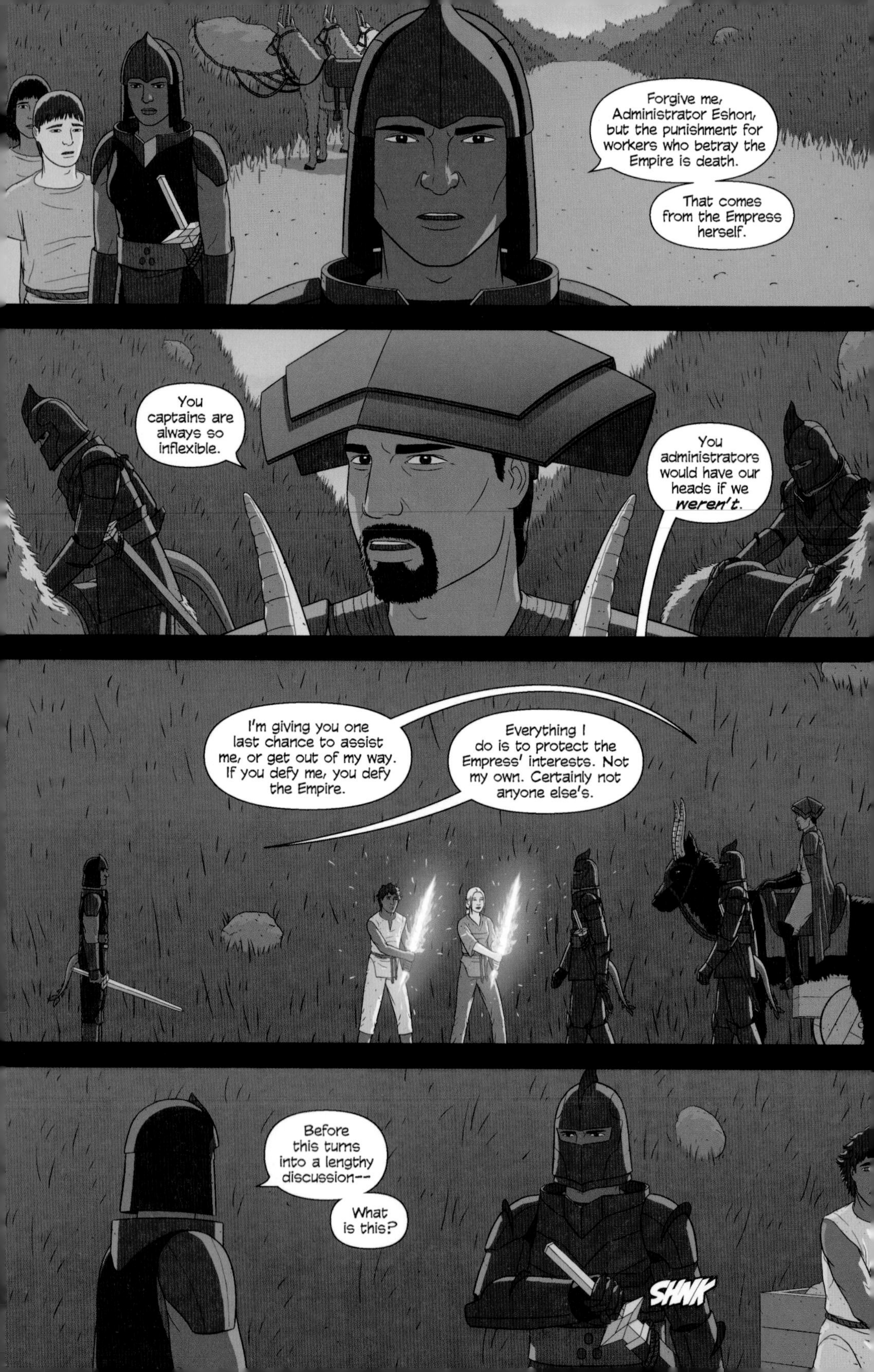
Forgive me, Administrator Eshon, but the punishment for workers who betray the Empire is death.
That comes from the Empress herself.
You captains are always so inflexible.
You administrators would have our heads if we *weren't*.
I'm giving you one last chance to assist me, or get out of my way. If you defy me, you defy the Empire.
Everything I do is to protect the Empress' interests. Not my own. Certainly not anyone else's.
Before this turns into a lengthy discussion--
What is this?
SHNK

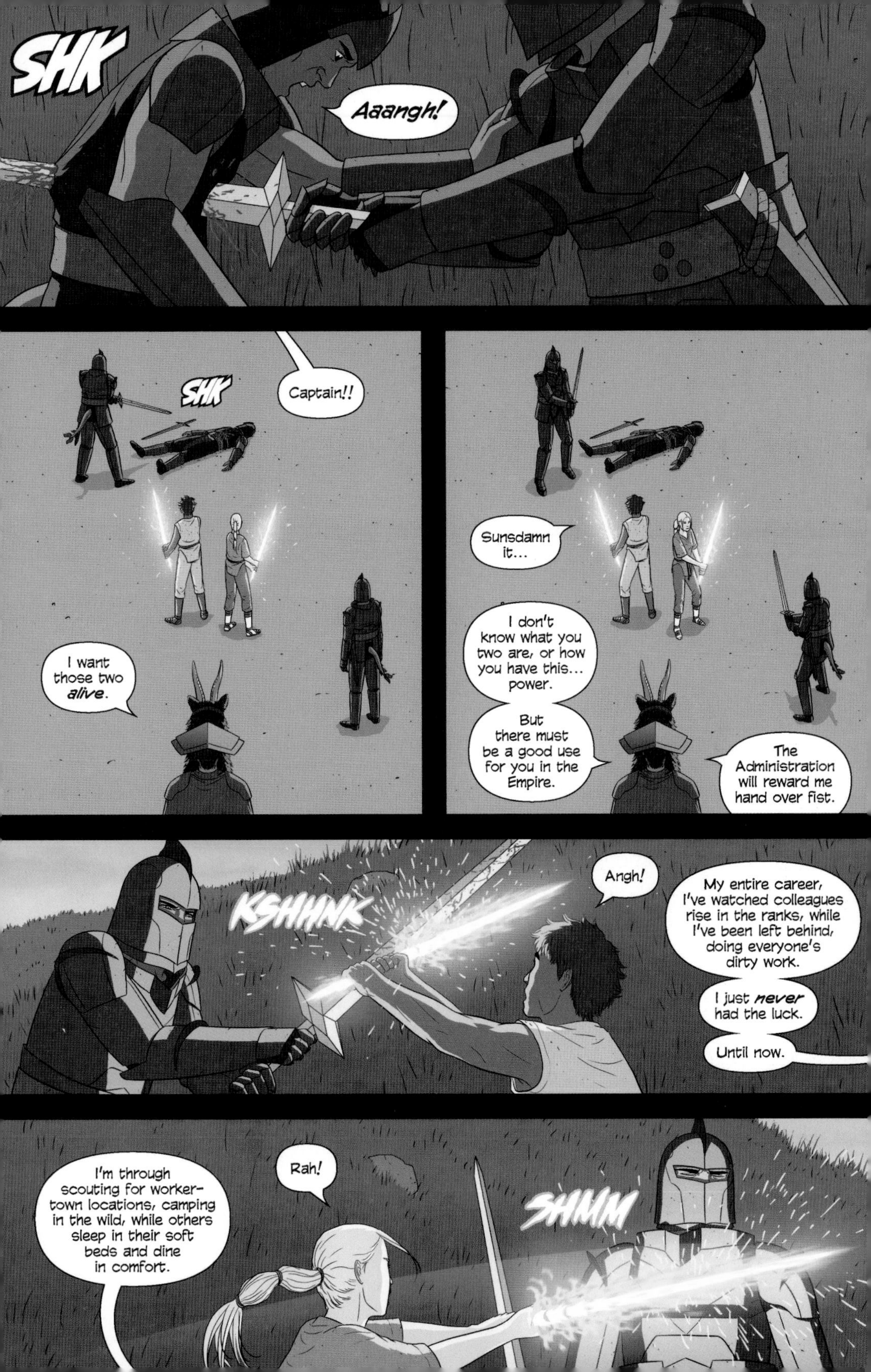
SHK
Aaangh!
SHK
Captain!!
I want those two *alive*.
Sunsdamn it...
I don't know what you two are, or how you have this... power.
But there must be a good use for you in the Empire.
The Administration will reward me hand over fist.
KSHHNK
Angh!
My entire career, I've watched colleagues rise in the ranks, while I've been left behind, doing everyone's dirty work.
I just *never* had the luck.
Until now.
I'm through scouting for worker-town locations, camping in the wild, while others sleep in their soft beds and dine in comfort.
Rah!
SHMM

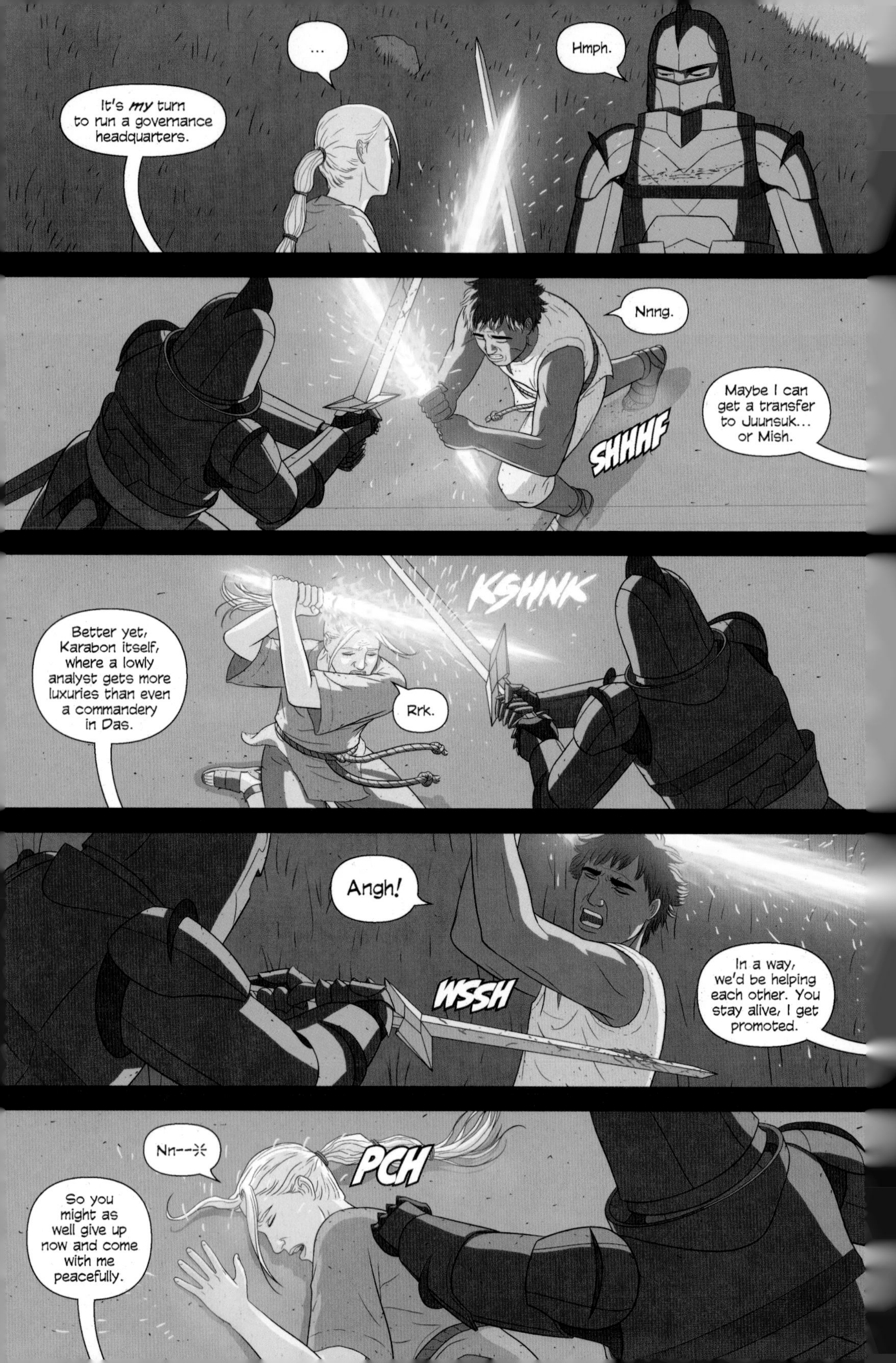
...
Hmph.
It's *my* turn to run a governance headquarters.
Nnng.
Maybe I can get a transfer to Juunsuk... or Mish.
SHHHF
KSHNK
Better yet, Karabon itself, where a lowly analyst gets more luxuries than even a commandery in Das.
Rrk.
Angh!
WSSH
In a way, we'd be helping each other. You stay alive, I get promoted.
Nn--
PCH
So you might as well give up now and come with me peacefully.

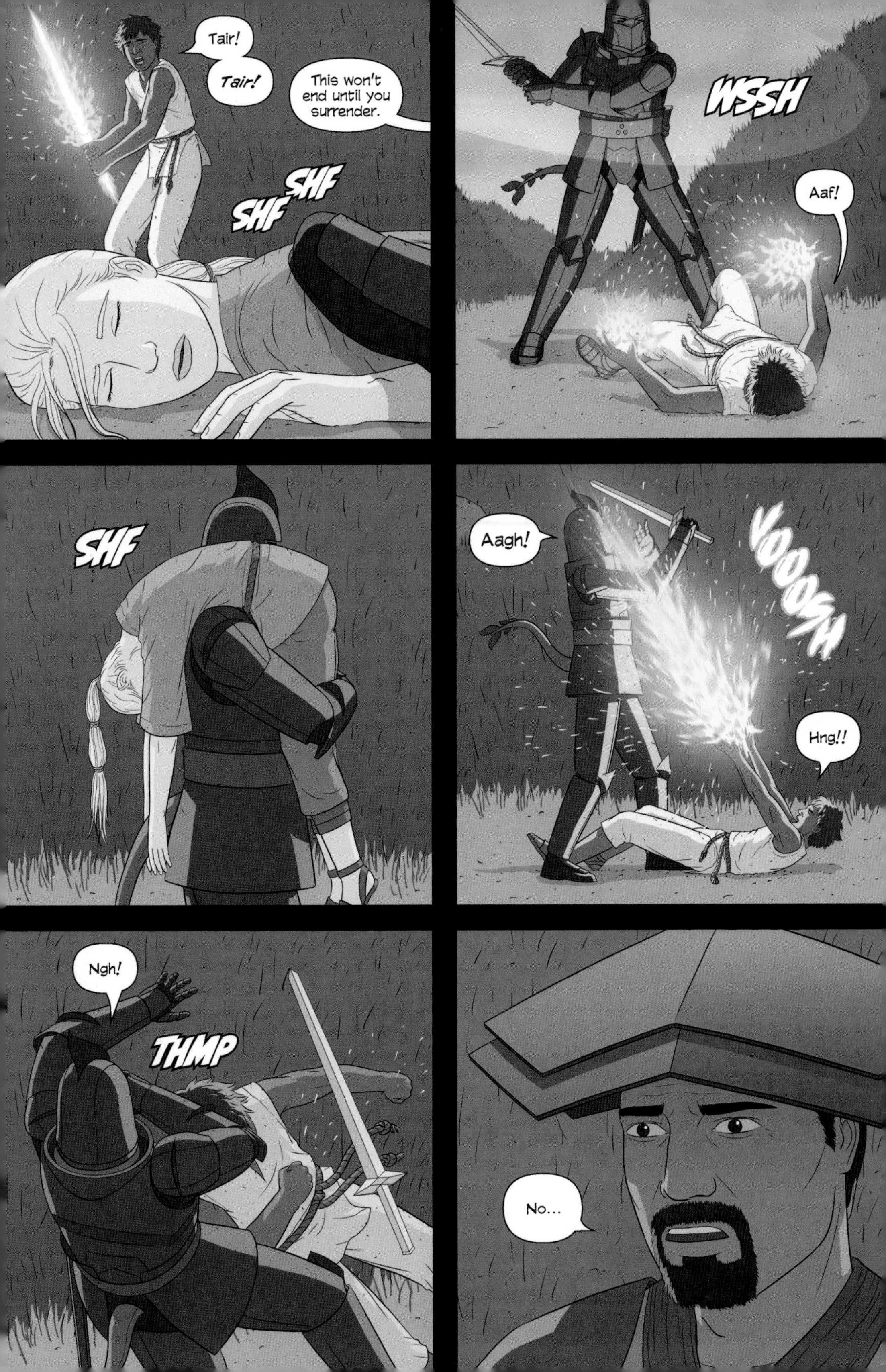
Tair!
Tair!
This won't end until you surrender.
SHF
SHF
WSSH
Aaf!
SHF
Aagh!
VOOOSH
Hng!!
Ngh!
THMP
No...

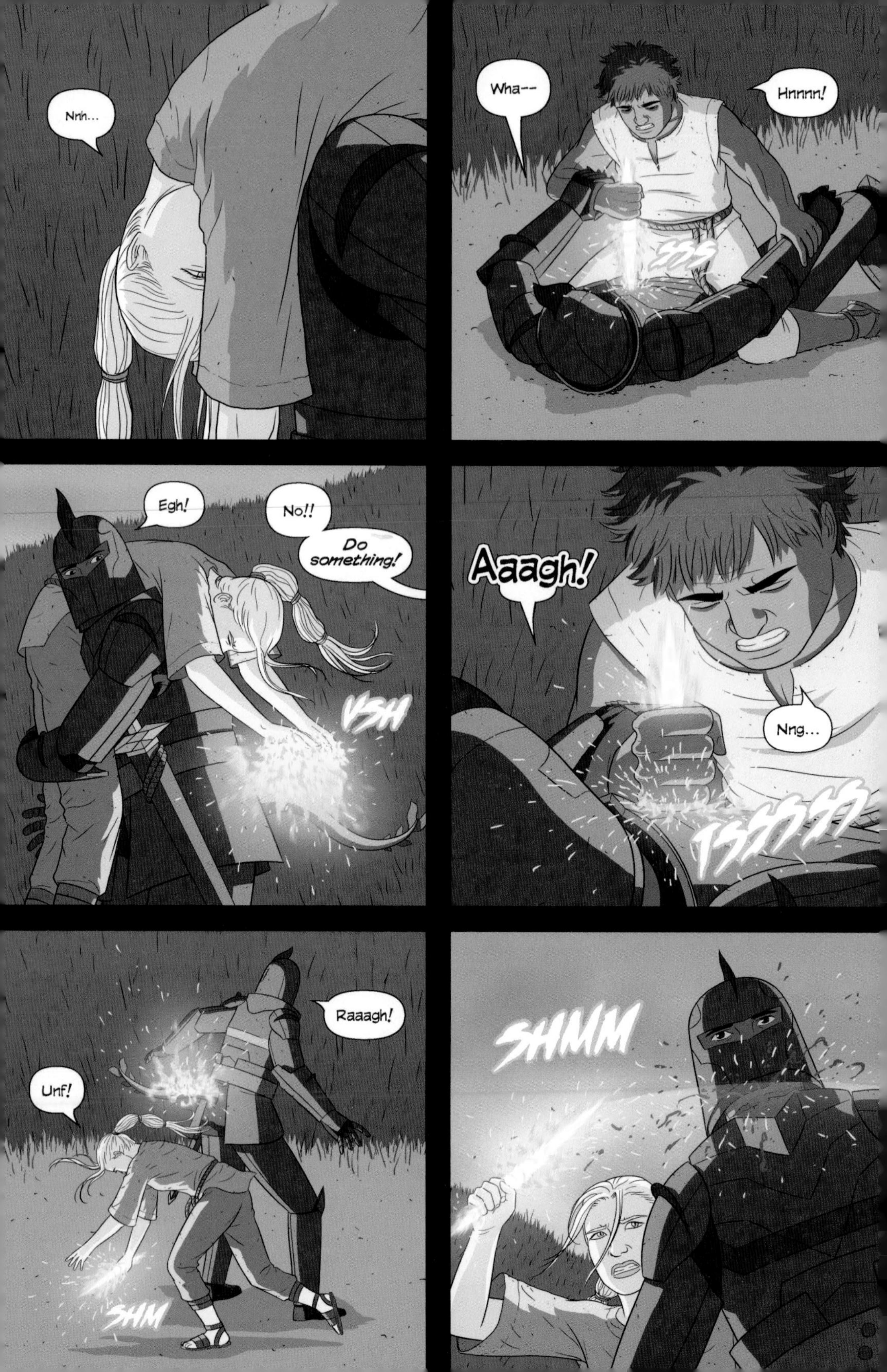
Nnh...
Wha--
Hnnnn!
SSS
Egh!
No!!
Do something!
VSH
Aaagh!
Nng...
TSSSSS
Raaagh!
Unf!
SHM
SHMM

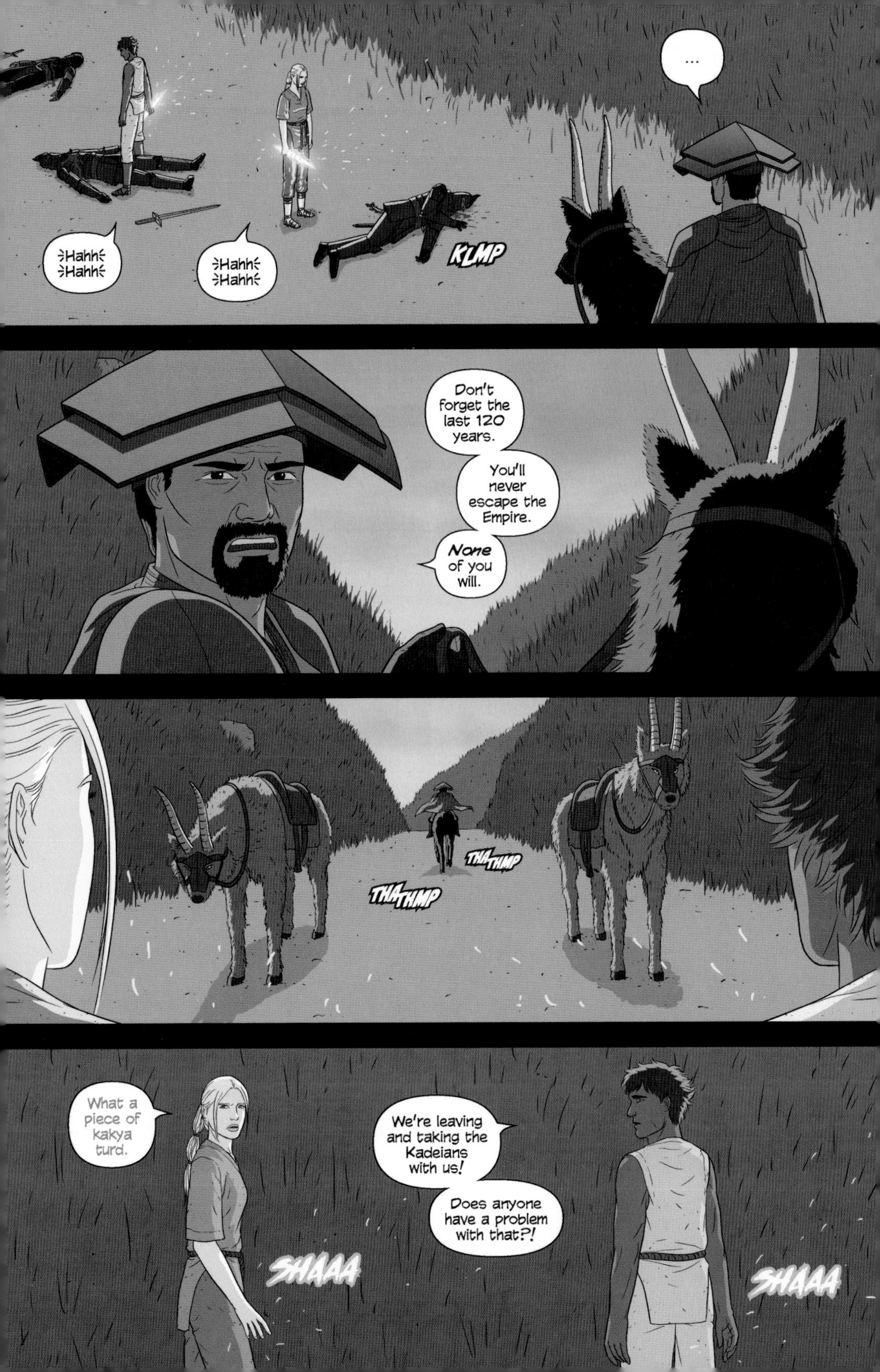
...
Hahh Hahh
Hahh Hahh
KLMP
Don't forget the last 120 years.
You'll never escape the Empire.
None of you will.
THATHMP
THATHMP
What a piece of kakya turd.
We're leaving and taking the Kadeians with us!
Does anyone have a problem with that?!
SHAAA
SHAAA

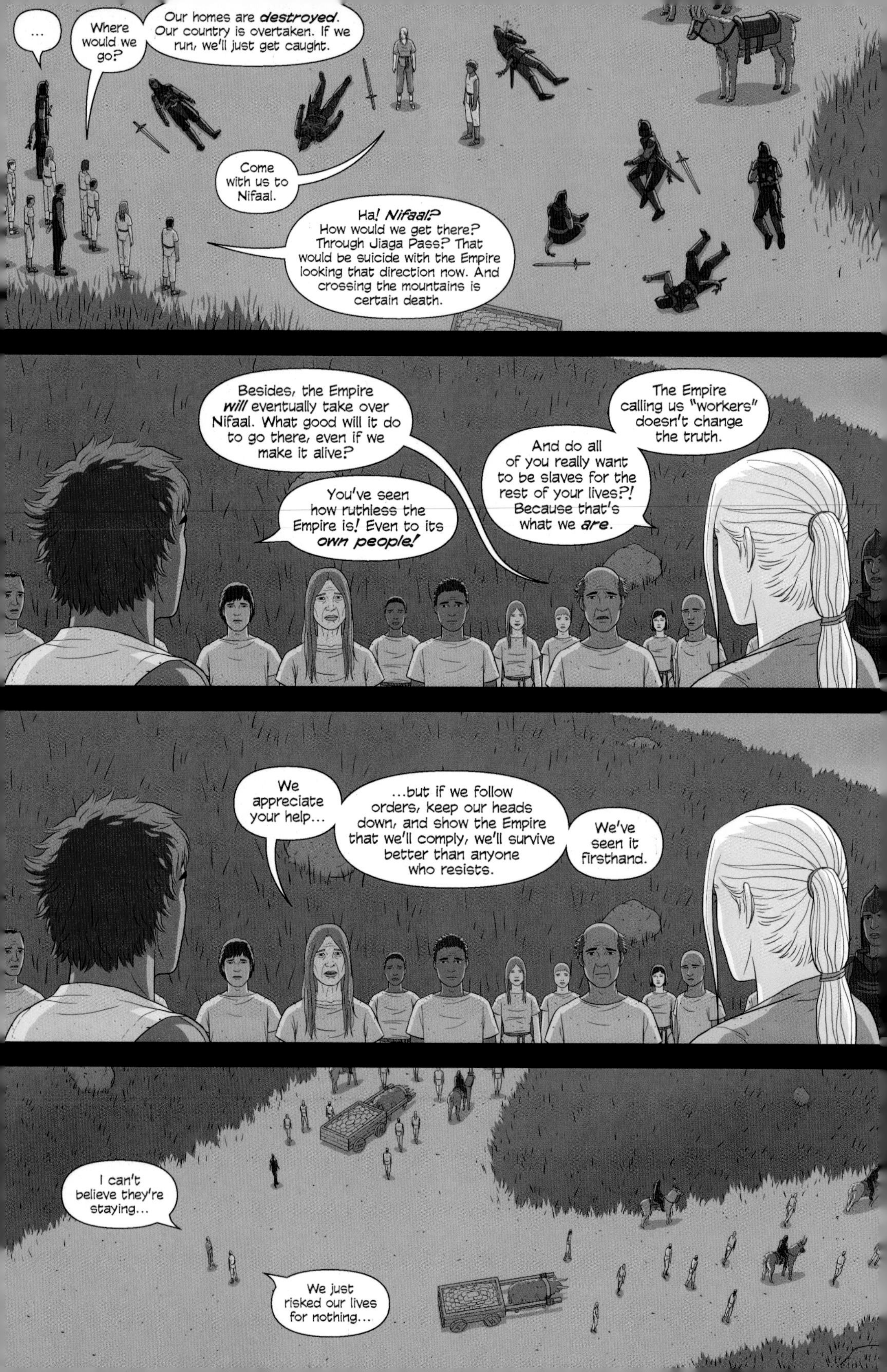
...
Where would we go?
Our homes are *destroyed*. Our country is overtaken. If we run, we'll just get caught.
Come with us to Nifaal.
Ha! *Nifaal?* How would we get there? Through Jiaga Pass? That would be suicide with the Empire looking that direction now. And crossing the mountains is certain death.
Besides, the Empire *will* eventually take over Nifaal. What good will it do to go there, even if we make it alive?
You've seen how ruthless the Empire is! Even to its *own people!*
The Empire calling us "workers" doesn't change the truth.
And do all of you really want to be slaves for the rest of your lives?! Because that's what we *are*.
We appreciate your help...
...but if we follow orders, keep our heads down, and show the Empire that we'll comply, we'll survive better than anyone who resists.
We've seen it firsthand.
I can't believe they're staying...
We just risked our lives for nothing...

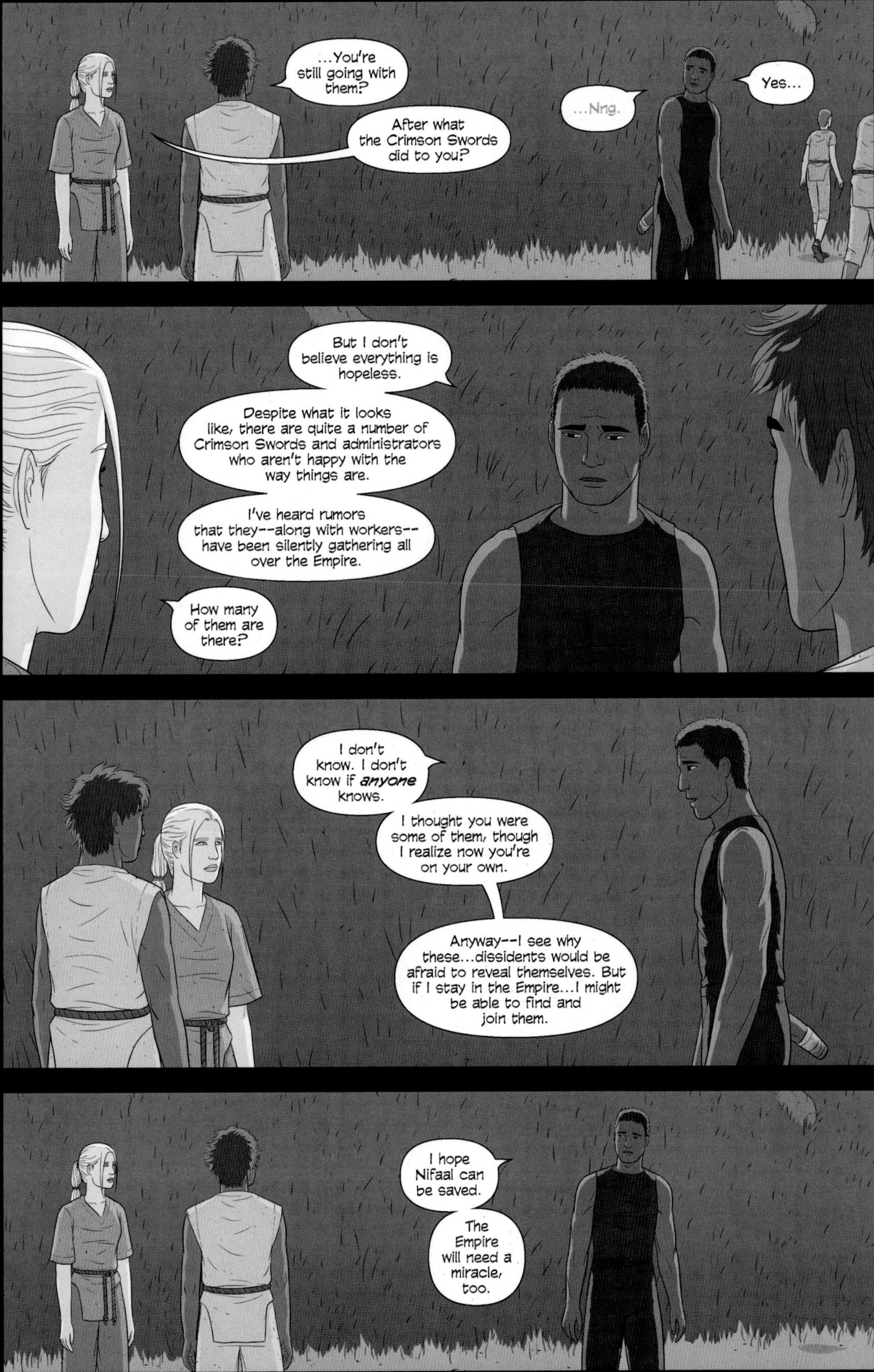
...You're still going with them?
After what the Crimson Swords did to you?
...Nng.
Yes...
But I don't believe everything is hopeless.
Despite what it looks like, there are quite a number of Crimson Swords and administrators who aren't happy with the way things are.
I've heard rumors that they--along with workers--have been silently gathering all over the Empire.
How many of them are there?
I don't know. I don't know if *anyone* knows.
I thought you were some of them, though I realize now you're on your own.
Anyway--I see why these...dissidents would be afraid to reveal themselves. But if I stay in the Empire...I might be able to find and join them.
I hope Nifaal can be saved.
The Empire will need a miracle, too.

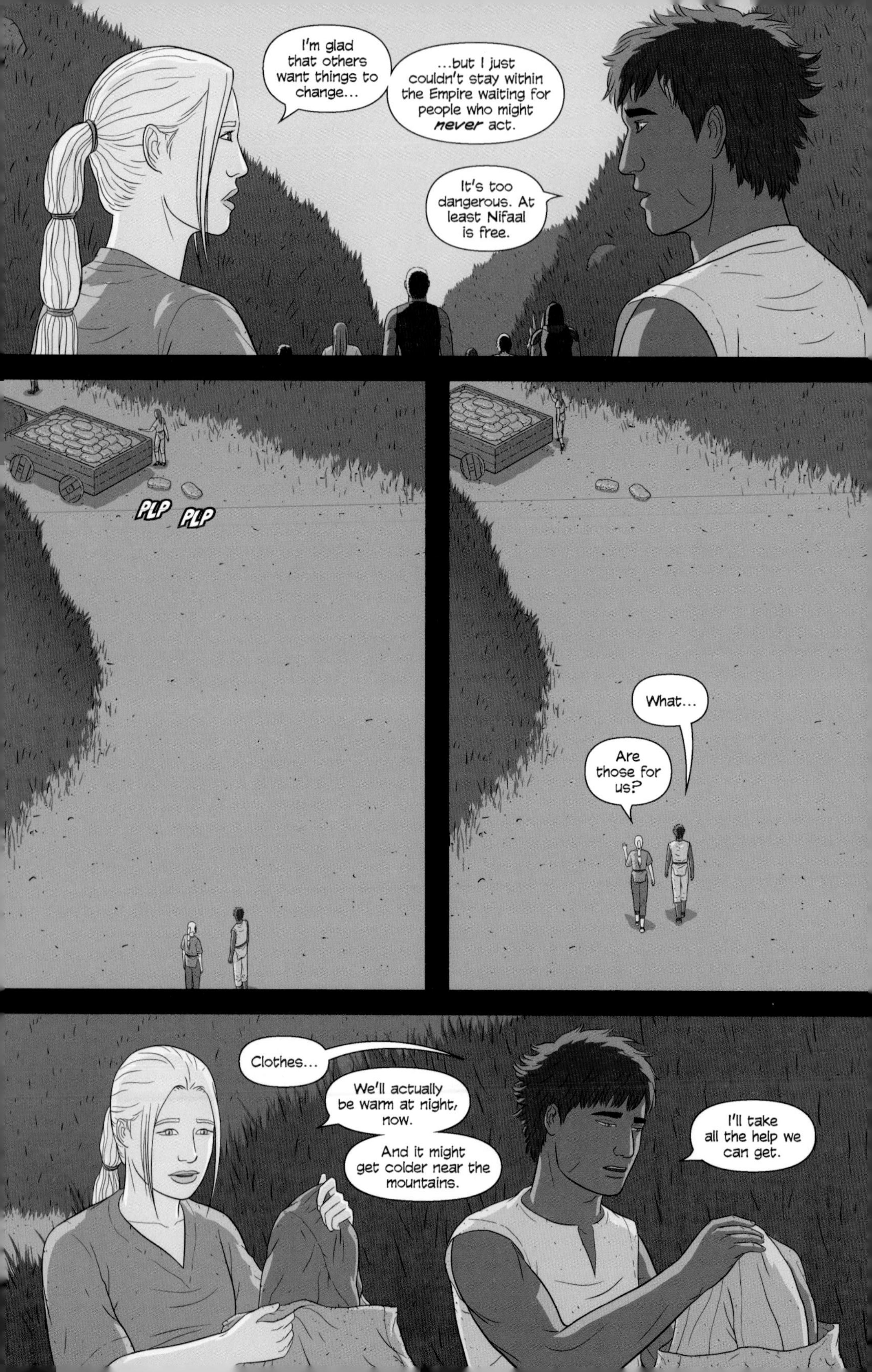
I'm glad that others want things to change...
...but I just couldn't stay within the Empire waiting for people who might *never* act.
It's too dangerous. At least Nifaal is free.
PLP PLP
What...
Are those for us?
Clothes...
We'll actually be warm at night, now.
And it might get colder near the mountains.
I'll take all the help we can get.

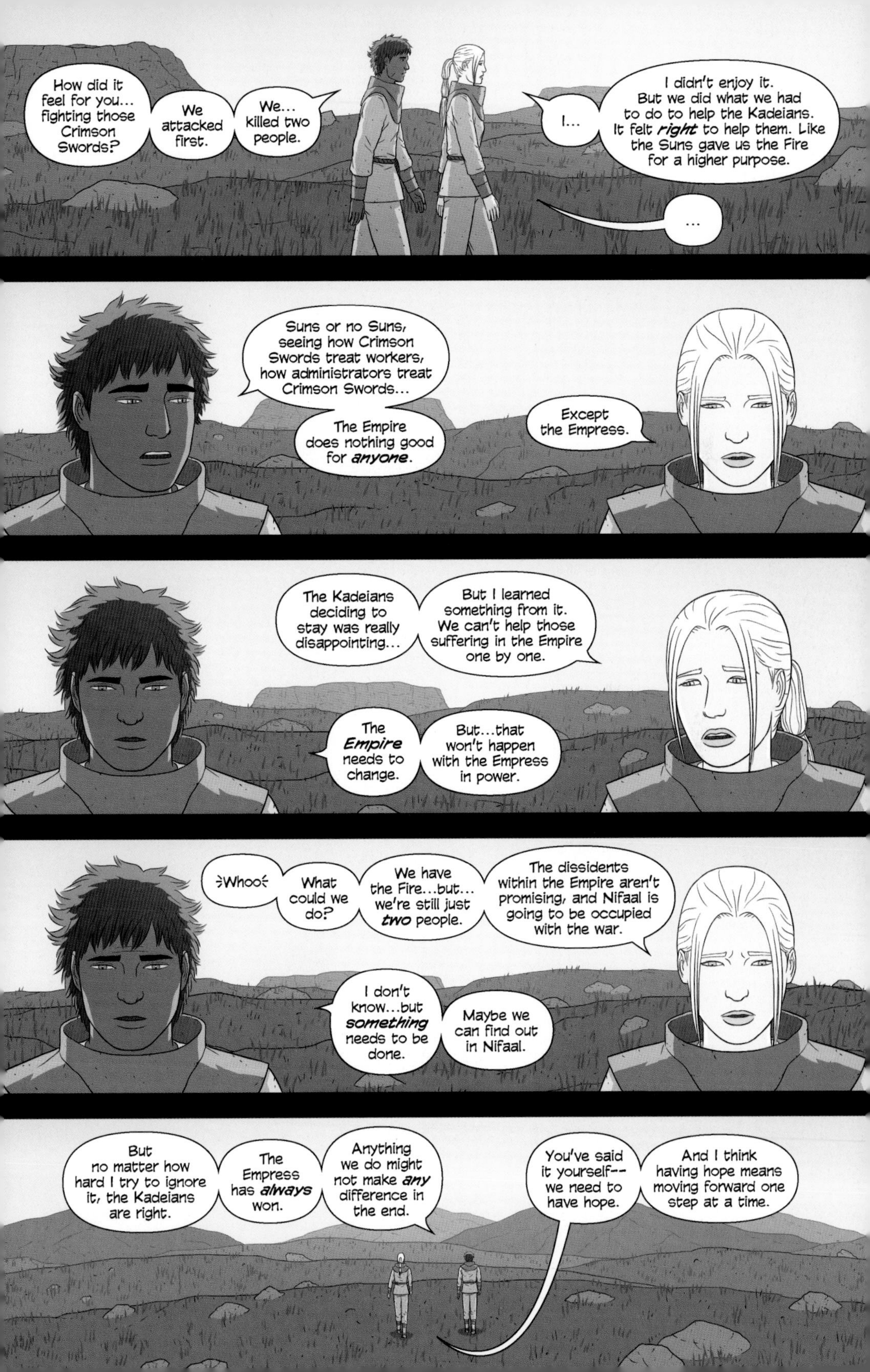
How did it feel for you... fighting those Crimson Swords?
We attacked first.
We... killed two people.
I...
I didn't enjoy it. But we did what we had to do to help the Kadeians. It felt *right* to help them. Like the Suns gave us the Fire for a higher purpose.
...
Suns or no Suns, seeing how Crimson Swords treat workers, how administrators treat Crimson Swords...
The Empire does nothing good for *anyone*.
Except the Empress.
The Kadeians deciding to stay was really disappointing...
But I learned something from it. We can't help those suffering in the Empire one by one.
The *Empire* needs to change.
But...that won't happen with the Empress in power.
Whoo
What could we do?
We have the Fire...but... we're still just *two* people.
The dissidents within the Empire aren't promising, and Nifaal is going to be occupied with the war.
I don't know...but *something* needs to be done.
Maybe we can find out in Nifaal.
But no matter how hard I try to ignore it, the Kadeians are right.
The Empress has *always* won.
Anything we do might not make *any* difference in the end.
You've said it yourself-- we need to have hope.
And I think having hope means moving forward one step at a time.

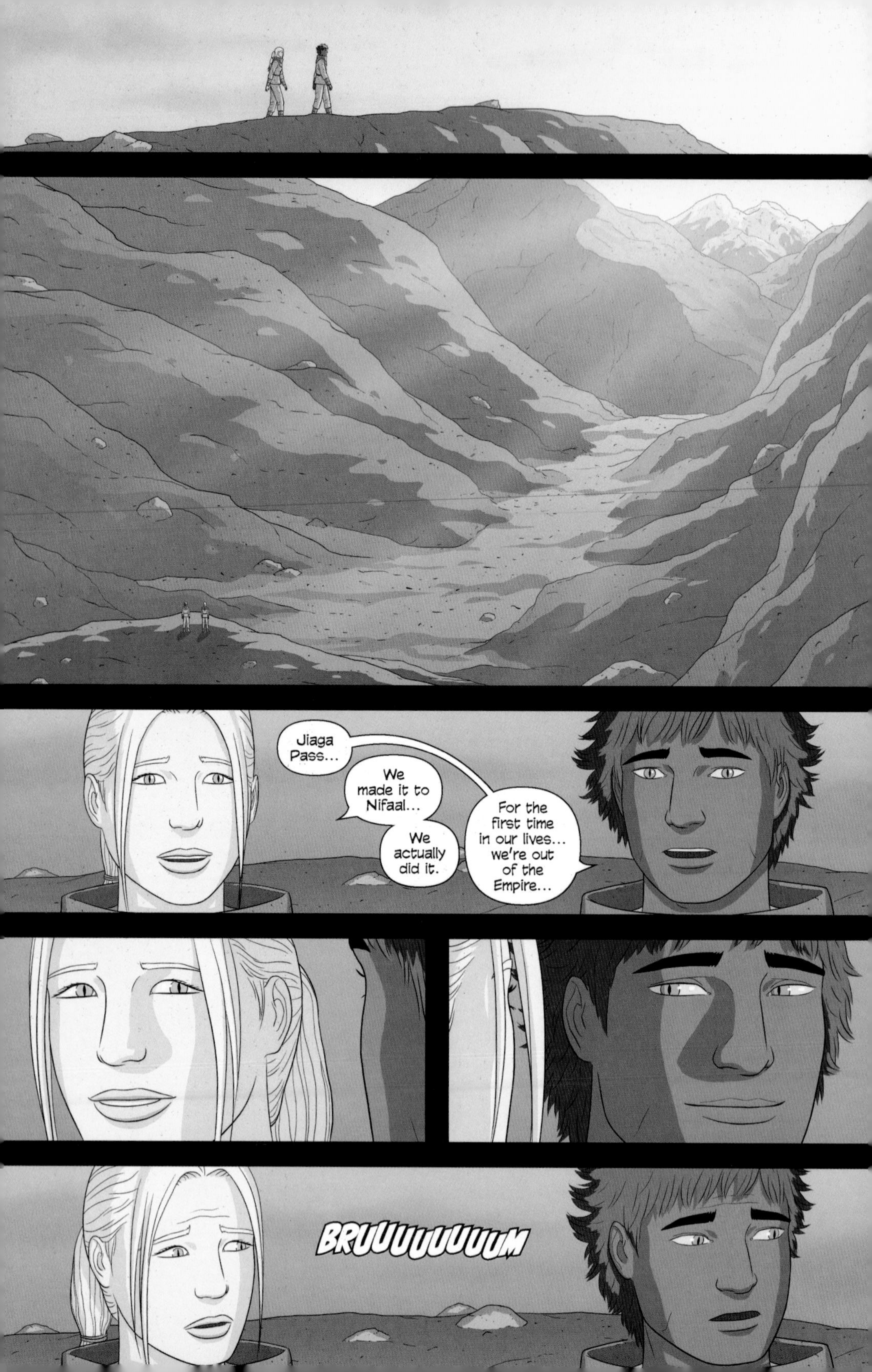
Jiaga Pass...
We made it to Nifaal...
For the first time in our lives... we're out of the Empire...
We actually did it.
BRUUUUUUUUUM

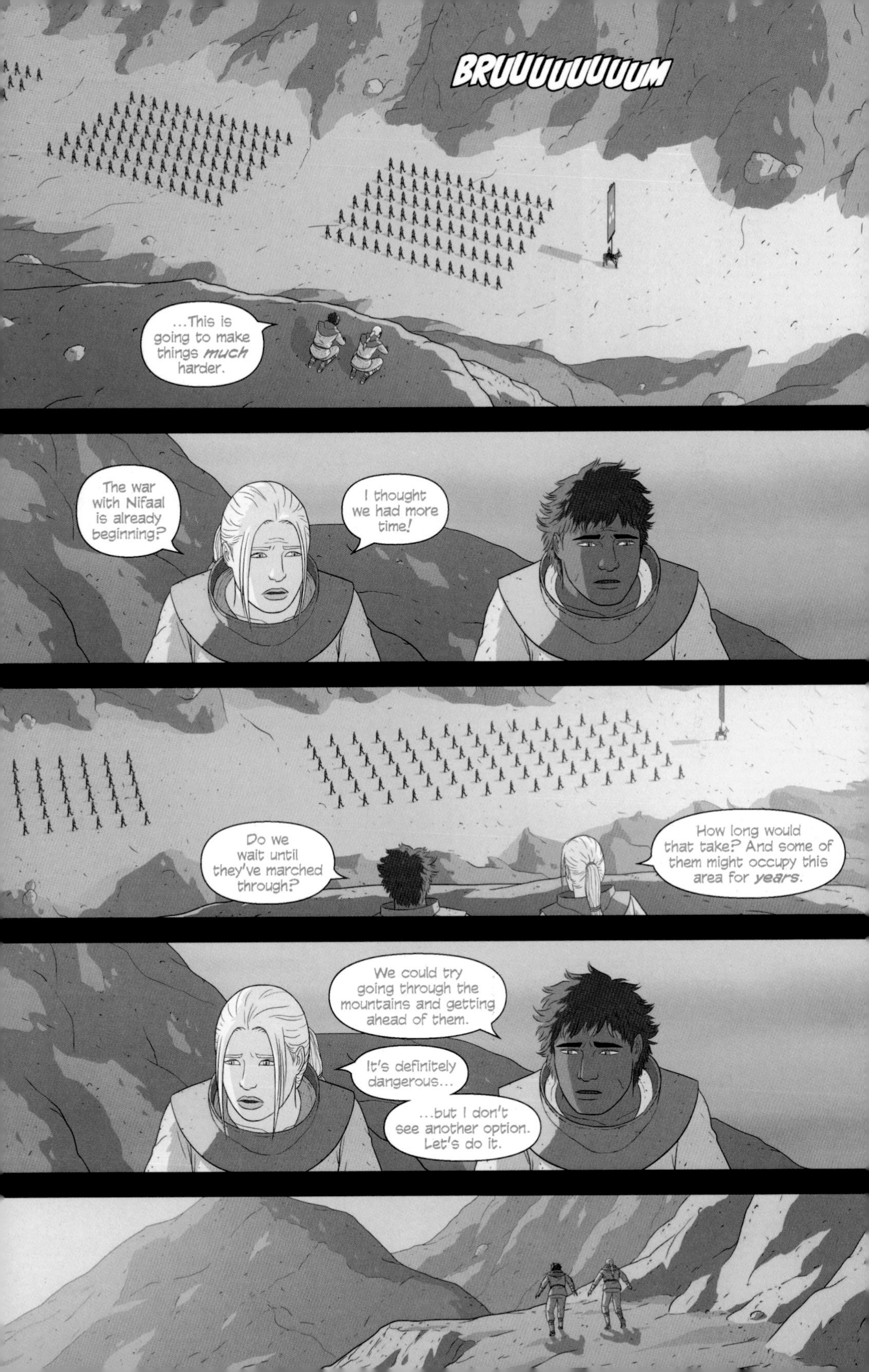
BRUUUUUUUUM
...This is going to make things *much* harder.
The war with Nifaal is already beginning?
I thought we had more time!
Do we wait until they've marched through?
How long would that take? And some of them might occupy this area for *years*.
We could try going through the mountains and getting ahead of them.
It's definitely dangerous...
...but I don't see another option. Let's do it.

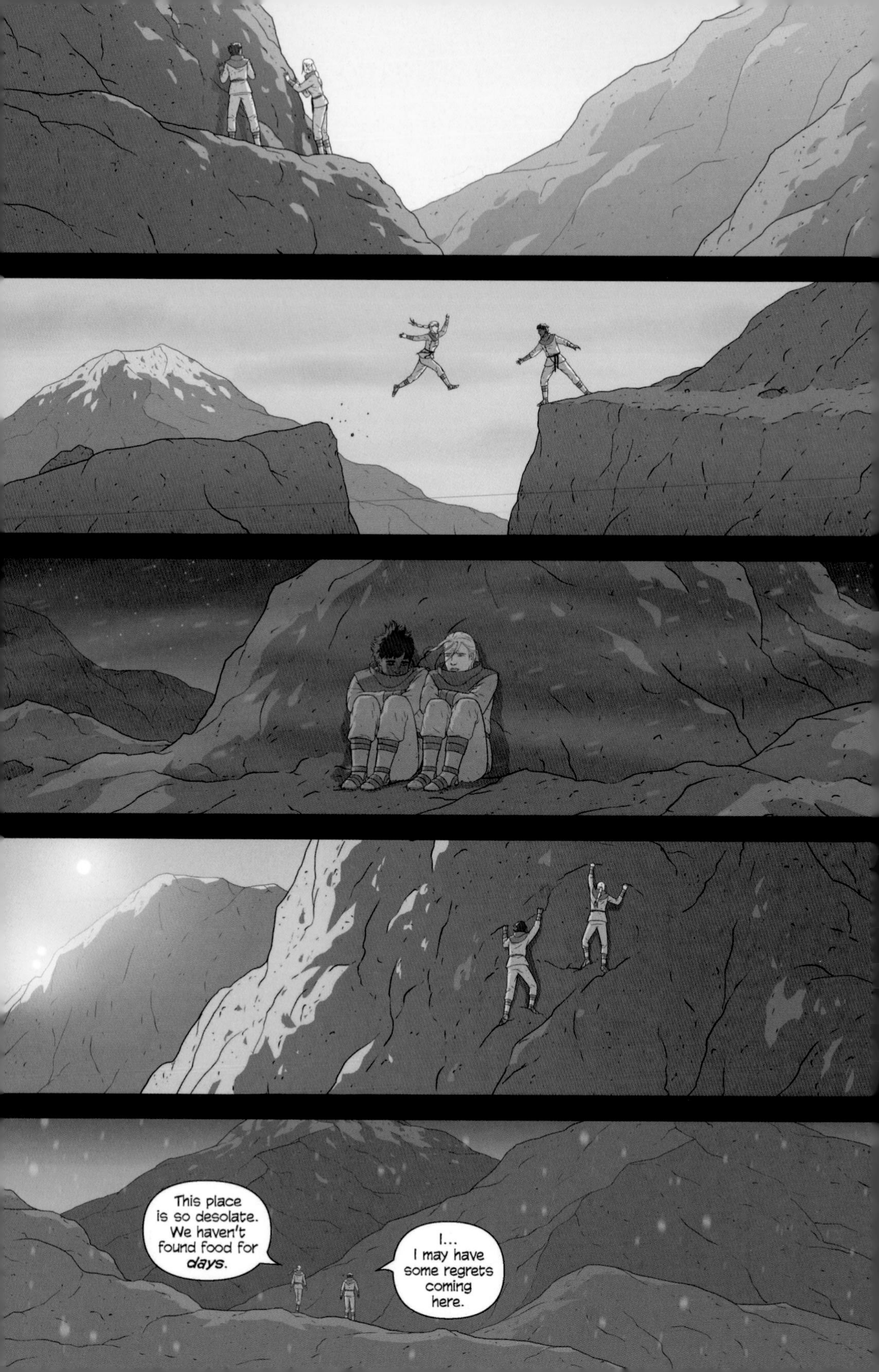
This place is so desolate. We haven't found food for *days*.
I... I may have some regrets coming here.

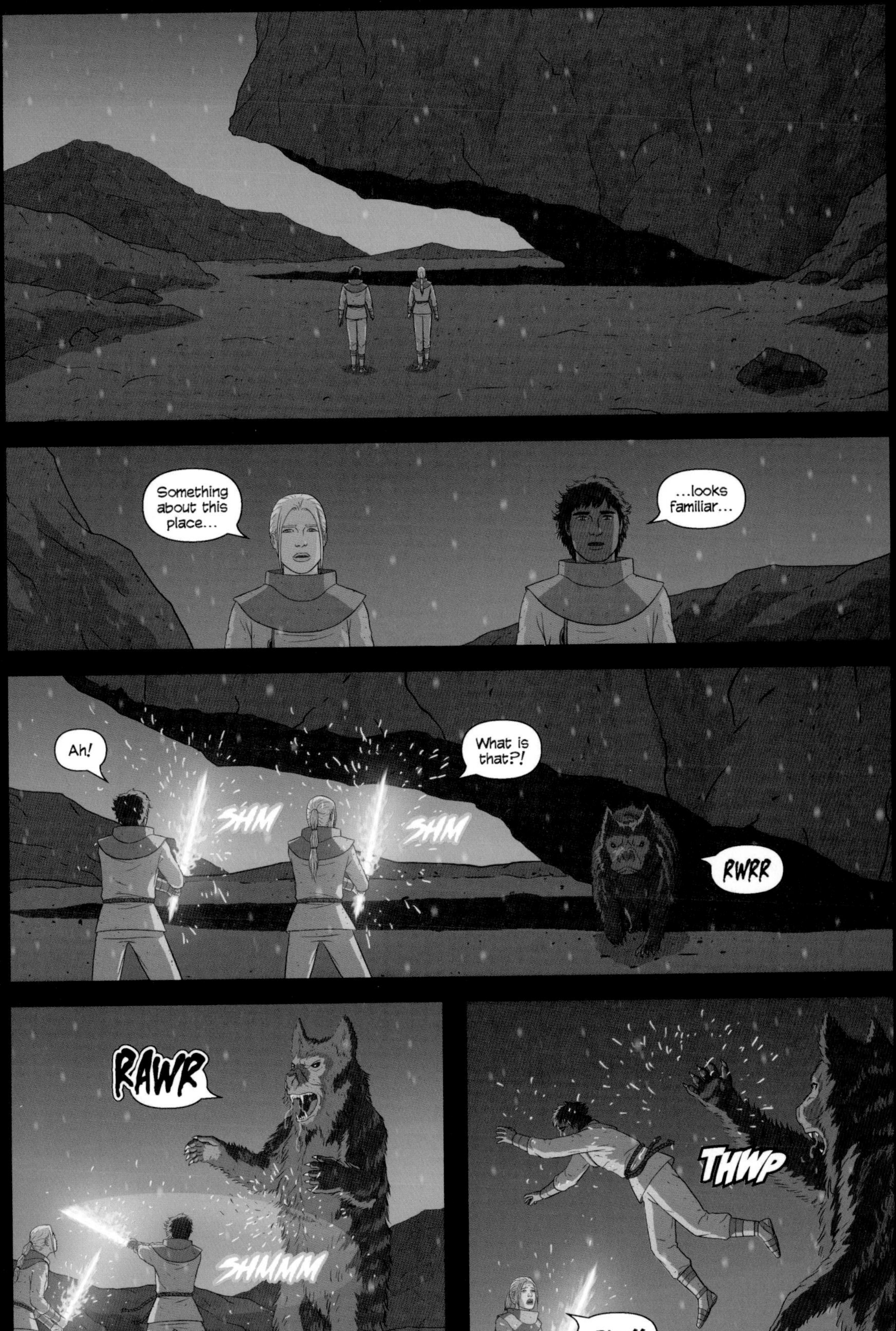
Something about this place...
...looks familiar...
Ah!
SHM
SHM
What is that?!
RWRR
RAWR
SHMMM
THWP
Rion!!

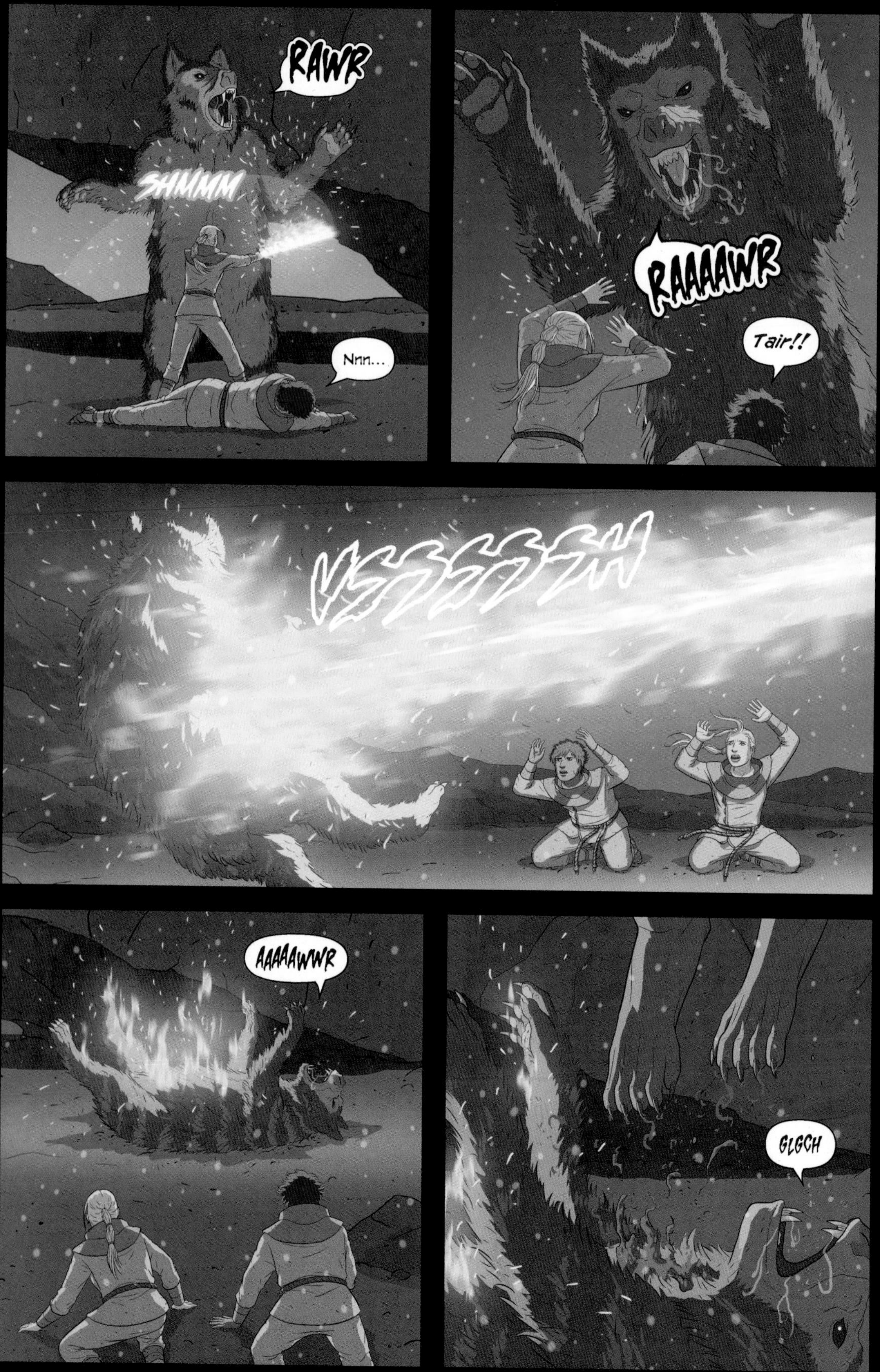
RAWR
SHMMM
Nnn...
RAAAAWR
Tair!!
VSSSSSH
AAAAAWWR
GLGCH

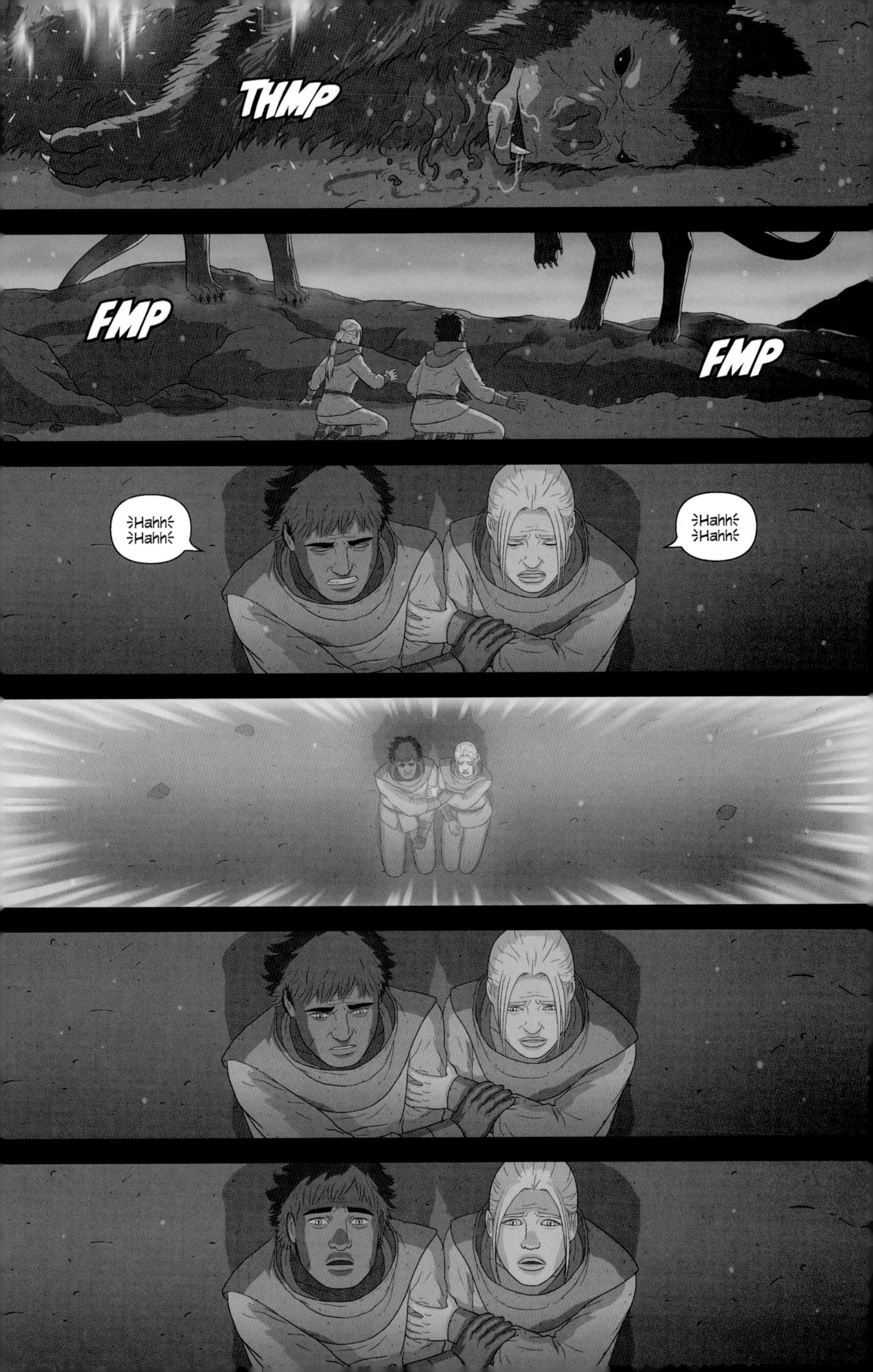
THMP
FMP
FMP
Hahh Hahh
Hahh Hahh

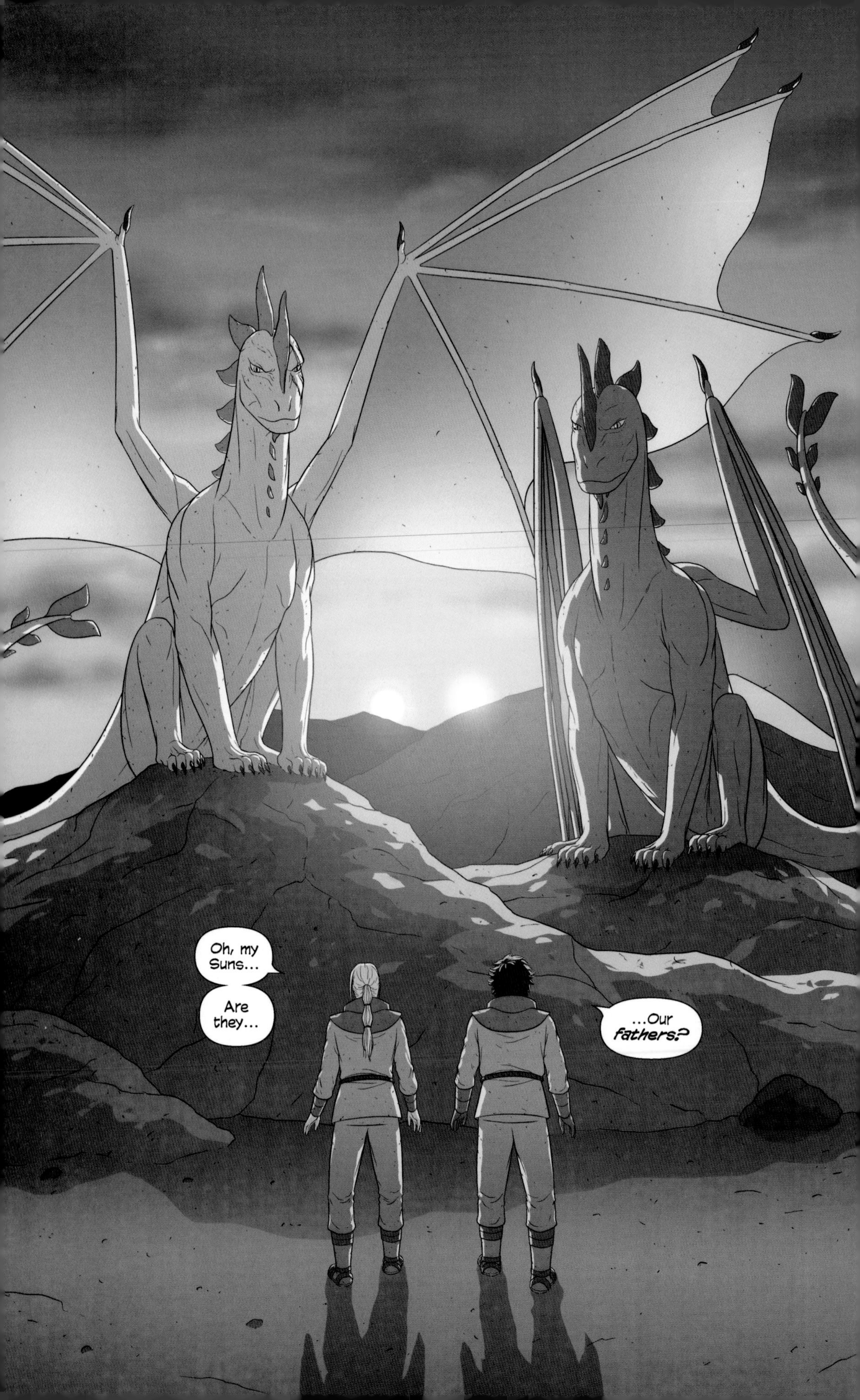
Oh, my Suns...
Are they...
...Our *fathers?*

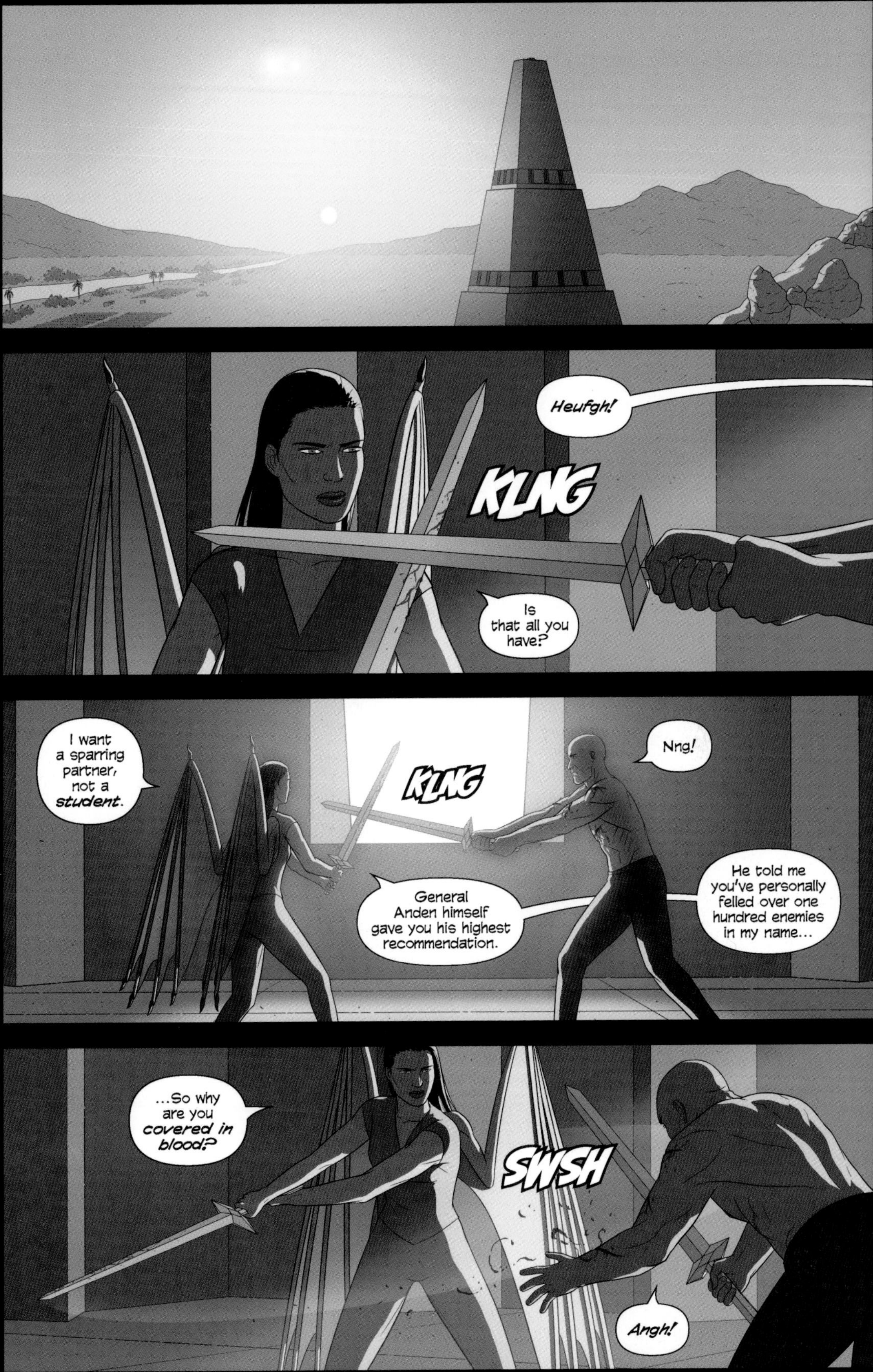
Heufgh!
KLNG
Is that all you have?
I want a sparring partner, not a *student*.
KLNG
Nng!
General Anden himself gave you his highest recommendation.
He told me you've personally felled over one hundred enemies in my name...
...So why are you *covered in blood?*
SWSH
Angh!

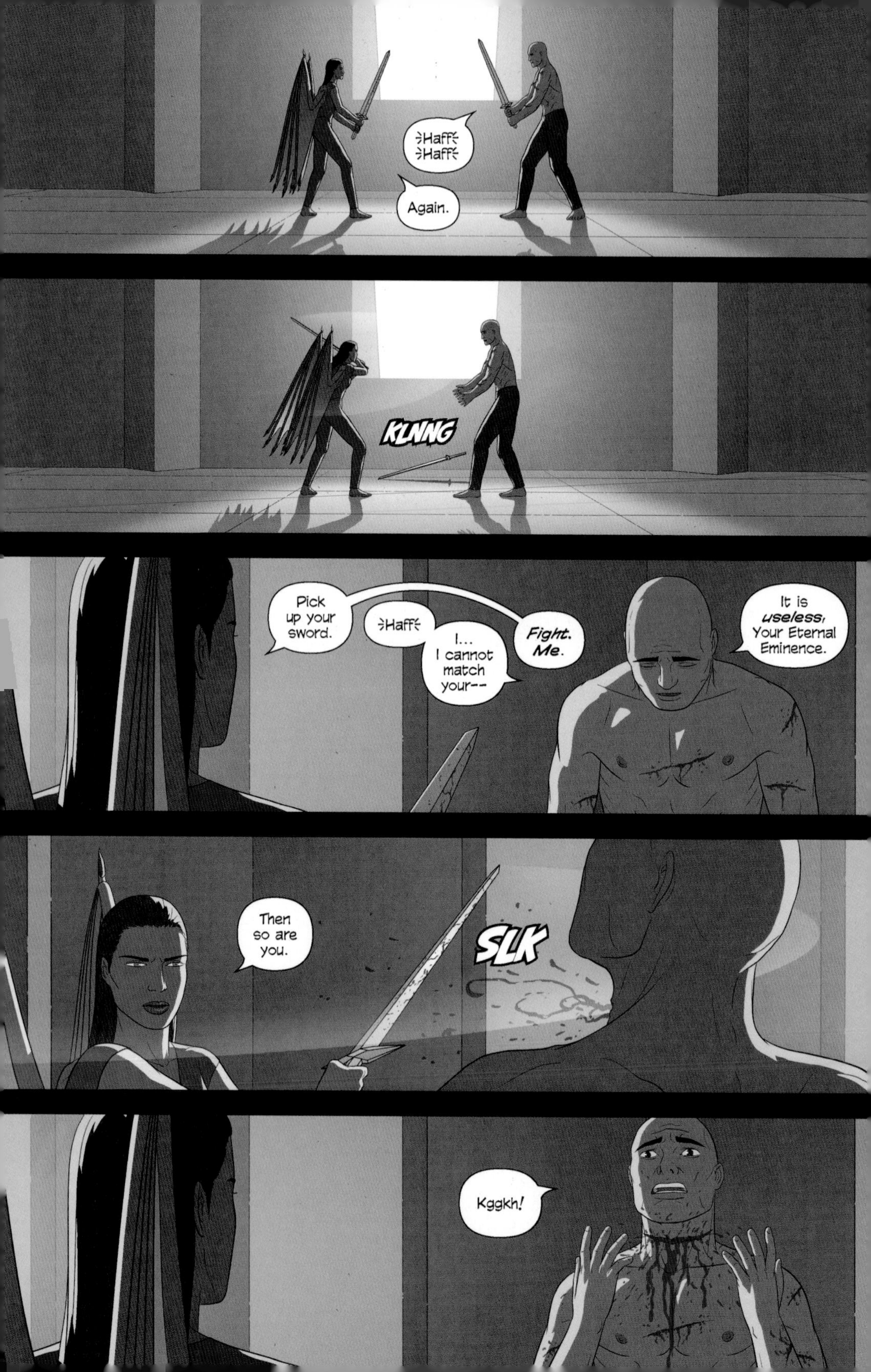

Haff Haff
Again.
KLNNG
Pick up your sword.
Haff
I... I cannot match your--
Fight. Me.
It is useless, Your Eternal Eminence.
Then so are you.
SLK
Kggkh!

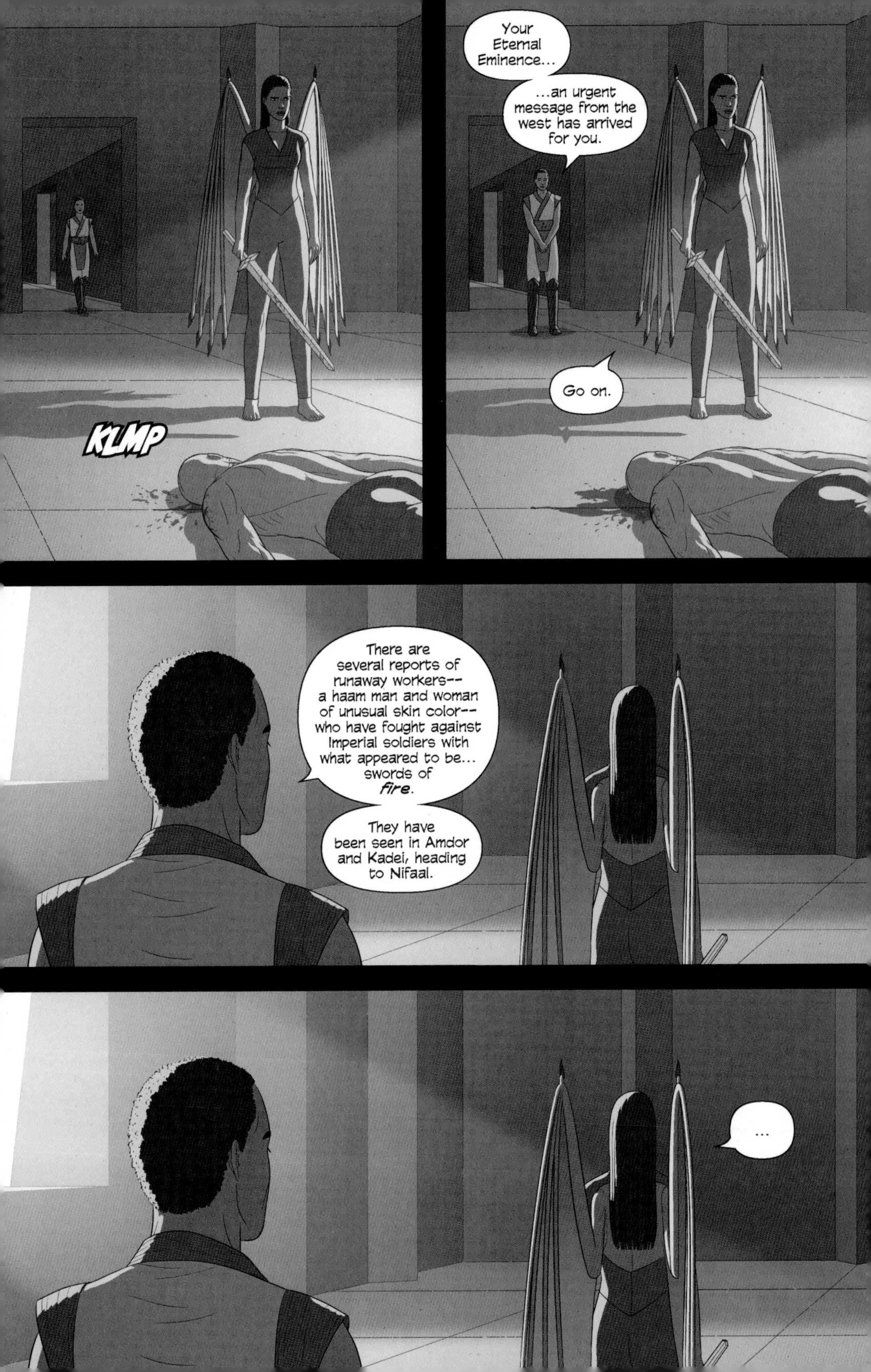
KLMP
Your Eternal Eminence...
...an urgent message from the west has arrived for you.
Go on.
There are several reports of runaway workers-- a haam man and woman of unusual skin color-- who have fought against Imperial soldiers with what appeared to be... swords of *fire*.
They have been seen in Amdor and Kadei, heading to Nifaal.
...

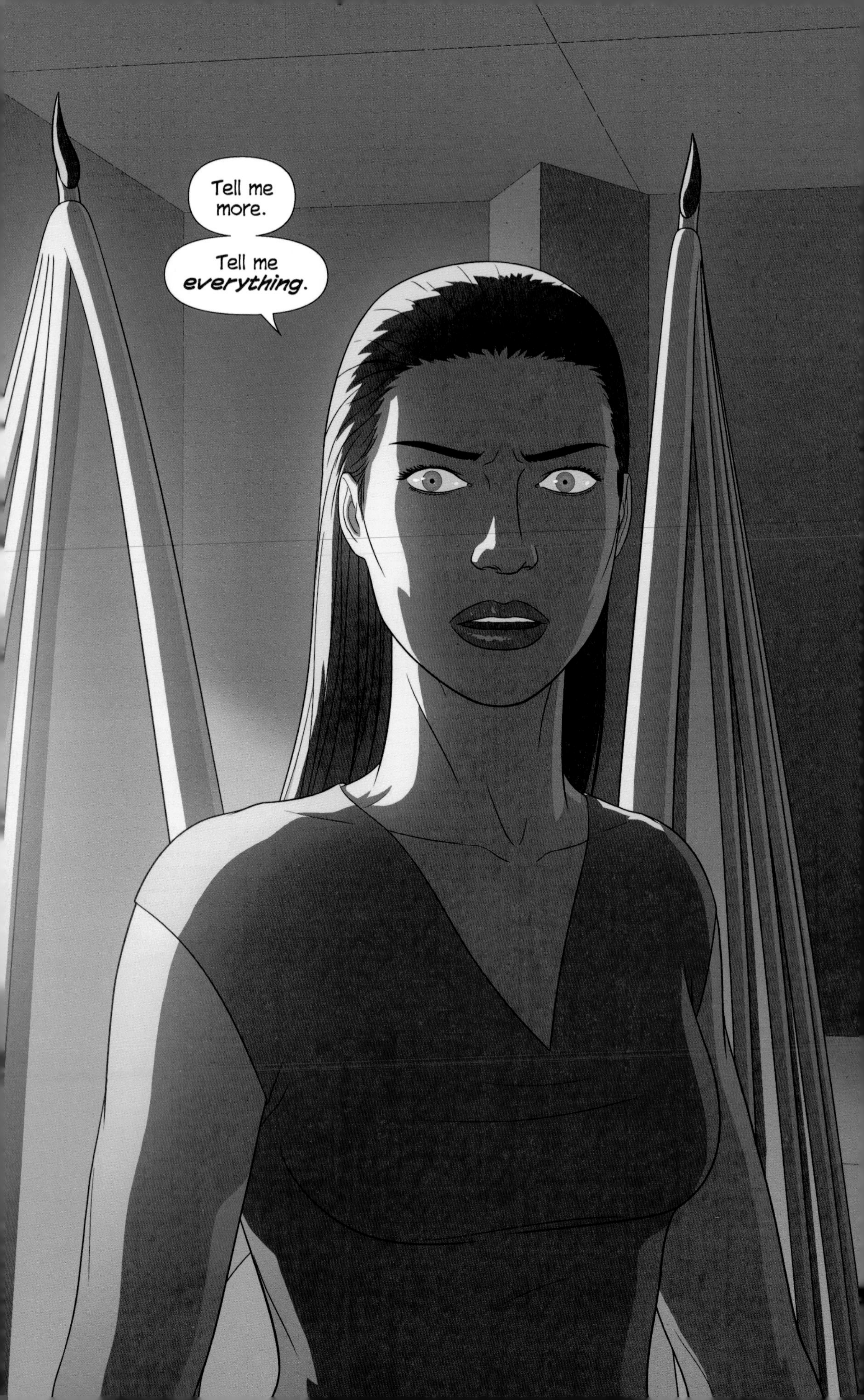
Tell me more.
Tell me *everything*.

Star Bright
AND THE Looking Glass

WRITTEN AND ILLUSTRATED BY

Jonathan
Luna

ON SALE NOW

ALEX + ADA
Jonathan Luna and Sarah Vaughn

ALEX+ADA
JONATHAN LUNA
SARAH VAUGHN
VOLUME 1

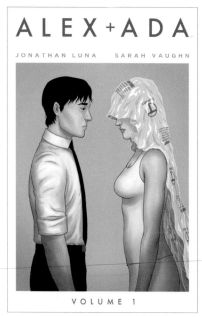

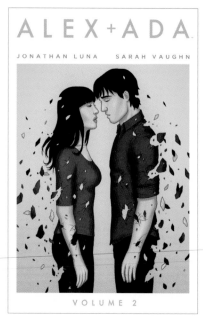

Volume 1
Trade Paperback
$12.99
ISBN: 978-1-63215-006-6
Collects #1-5
128 Pages

ALEX+ADA
JONATHAN LUNA
SARAH VAUGHN
VOLUME 2

Volume 2
Trade Paperback
$12.99
ISBN: 978-1-63215-195-7
Collects #6-10
128 Pages

ALEX+ADA
JONATHAN LUNA
SARAH VAUGHN
VOLUME 3

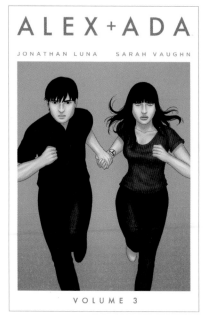

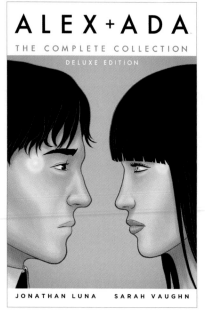

Volume 3
Trade Paperback
$12.99
ISBN: 978-1-63215-404-0
Collects #11-15
136 Pages

ALEX+ADA
THE COMPLETE COLLECTION
DELUXE EDITION
JONATHAN LUNA
SARAH VAUGHN

The Complete Collection
Deluxe Edition
Hardcover
$49.99
ISBN: 978-1-63215-869-7
Collects #1-15
376 Pages

To find your nearest comic book store, call: 1-888-COMIC-BOOK

A NOTE ABOUT THE SUNS

The changing configuration of the suns is an important element of ETERNAL EMPIRE. They may seem random, but every configuration is intentional. We wanted to display the suns (and moon's phases) in the most accurate way possible, so Jonathan and 3D-animation friends, Tim Ingle and Rommel Calderon, mapped out an extensive calendar of their movement.

There are numerous factors that go into the changing configuration of the suns:

1. The location of the viewpoint on the planet
2. The rotation of the planet
3. The tilt of the planet's axis
4. The revolution of the planet around the red sun
5. The revolution of the blue and yellow binary suns around the red sun

In ETERNAL EMPIRE, the suns' positions can appear to change drastically, even in one day. In this case, the rotation of the planet is the most contributing factor.

Because of the rotation of Earth, stars in the night sky can appear to spin as a whole. This "spin" also applies to the daytime with Earth's sun, and to the suns in ETERNAL EMPIRE. The "spin" of the suns in one day is not related to the revolution of the binary suns around the red sun--only to the rotation of the planet.

The diagram below gives an example of the "spinning" of the suns, showing three configurations at different times on the same day. At sunrise, the binaries are positioned at the top-left of the red sun. At midday, the binaries are at the center-left. At sunset, the binaries are at the bottom-left.

- Jonathan and Sarah

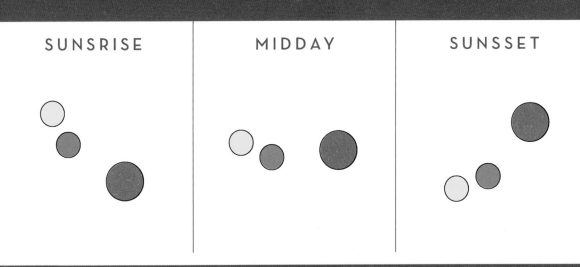

| SUNRISE | MIDDAY | SUNSSET |

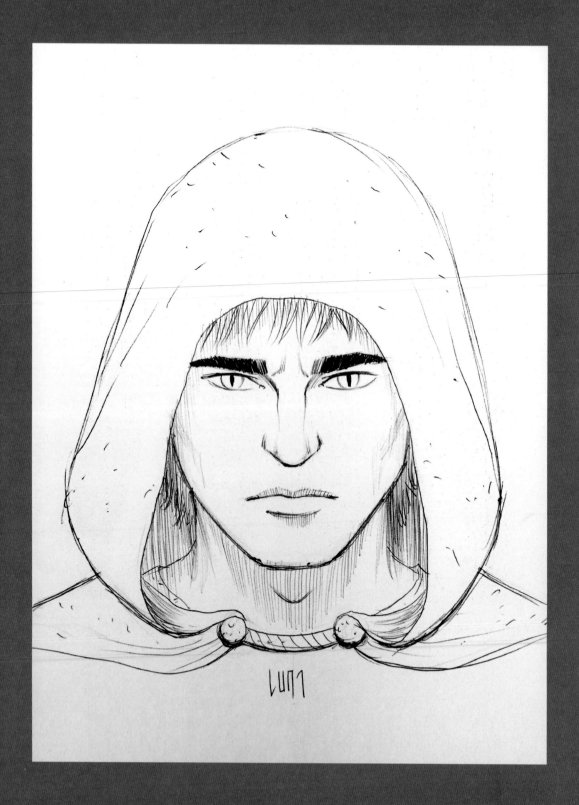

PROMOTIONAL SKETCH

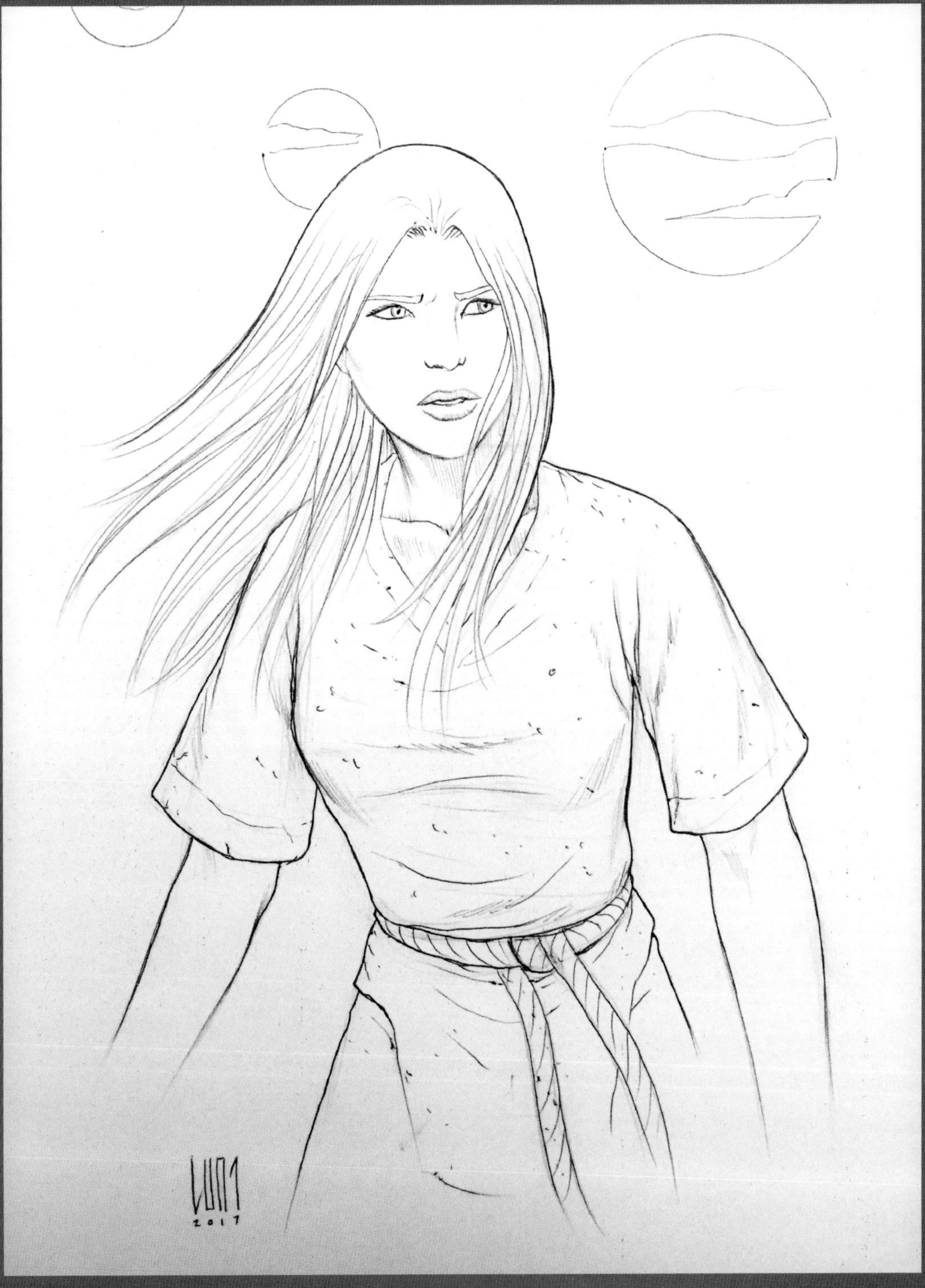

2017

PROMOTIONAL SKETCH

TO BE CONTINUED